THE WITCH'S TREE

ELENA COLLINS

B
Boldwood

First published in Great Britain in 2022 by Boldwood Books Ltd.

Copyright © Judy Leigh, 2022

Cover Design by Alice Moore Design

Cover Photography: Shutterstock

A CIP catalogue record for this book is available from the British Library.

Paperback ISBN 978-1-80280-018-0

Large Print ISBN 978-1-80280-014-2

Hardback ISBN 978-1-80280-013-5

Ebook ISBN 978-1-80280-011-1

Kindle ISBN 978-1-80280-012-8

Audio CD ISBN 978-1-80280-019-7

MP3 CD ISBN 978-1-80280-016-6

Digital audio download ISBN 978-1-80280-010-4

Boldwood Books Ltd
23 Bowerdean Street
London SW6 3TN
www.boldwoodbooks.com

To Irene, my mum.

PROLOGUE

Firefly sparks swirl up the chimney as logs hiss and smoulder in the grate, the blackened twigs twisted like charred bones. Smoke curls upwards, silent as a spell, as she holds out her palms and warms the span of her hands until they are too hot. Behind the window, a breeze blusters, seeping through the shutters. She smooths her skirt and stares into the hearth, watching flames leap, lick and slacken. There is no sound except the crackling fire. The blackthorn tree taps three times against the window, casting long shadows across the moon.

She moves outside on soundless feet to stand in the damp night garden. An owl sweeps its wings, hooting a single hollow cry; a hare leaps and is gone. She reaches slender fingers towards the sky as if to pluck something from it. Then the air becomes raw with cold as familiar voices echo from the old stone well. She knows the sound: it is as recognisable as her own heartbeat. She breathes out, murmuring softly in reply: it is her time now.

* * *

Over three hundred years have passed and the cottage stands solid through many changes. The old staircase has gone, the thatched roof has been tiled, the hearth is not quite as it was. The house hides so many memories, so many years of fingers touching the same walls, being warmed by the same fire.

She knows the house well: it is hers, she will not leave it. She peers through the windows, but her breath leaves no mist on the glass. The old stone well chatters and she whispers words that ripple in the deep water.

The blackthorn tree has remained in the ground for many times its natural lifespan, unbending in the dawns and dusks of each year: it belongs to her. Dark roots delve beneath the earth, deep as unspoken truths: its flowers blossom each May and sprout bitter fruits in October. It never rests and she too, can never rest.

Now two women stay beneath the same roof, sharing the same shelter. The walls keep out the cold, hold strangers beyond the door; it is a refuge where secrets and promises and love are precious treasures that have never been uttered for centuries.

Two women live in the house, embraced in its protective hold, watching, waiting. Two women, one then, one now.

1

MARCH, THE PRESENT DAY. MANCHESTER, ENGLAND

Selena had rehearsed what to say. She had imagined the perfect outcome, hoped for it with all her being: David would be delighted with the news, a baby, a new future for them both, away from Manchester, away from Veronica. She'd believed a new start was everything they had both wanted. She had been wrong. His eyes had darkened with anger; he'd shouted, she'd protested, he'd sulked, she'd cajoled, then he'd held her away from him and hissed, 'No, Selena. It can't happen. I didn't sign up for this. I'm sorry, but I can't do it. It's not what I want.' Then he had picked up his coat and left without another word, like a slap to the face.

Now, much later, as she gazed through the bedroom window at the night sky, at the busy road below, cars passing, people's lives continuing normally, Selena was numb. The harsh tone of David's voice still echoed in her ears. His mind had been made up in an instant, and she still couldn't believe the shock of it all.

Selena crawled into bed and stared into darkness, unable to sleep, unable to stop her mind racing. The conversation was playing over and over again, as if it was still happening, although David had left hours ago. She had watched him turn away, noticing the stubborn set of his shoulders as he closed the door. How had it gone so badly when she had imagined he'd take her in his arms and promise to look after her? She'd hoped this would be the reason he would finally leave his wife.

Selena rolled over, her hands cradling her abdomen; the baby was not showing yet at seven weeks. She asked herself how she felt, and immediately three powerful emotions charged back at her. She was hurt: David had broken her heart, along with all her hopes and dreams. She felt foolish: she should have seen the signs. Claire had warned her: once she'd discovered that David was married, she knew that it was wrong to love him. Then she felt a happiness, a lightness: she was expecting a baby, a new life, and it filled her with joy. The three emotions battled for supremacy. Of course, the baby won hands down, but Selena felt deeply hurt and embarrassingly foolish.

She heard the door to the apartment click: Claire, her flatmate, was keeping late hours: she had been to a party. Selena's first thought was to slip out of bed, reach for her dressing gown, run to Claire, hug her and burst into tears. Claire would fling her arms around her, give her a shoulder to cry on; she would say 'I told you so.' And it was true, Claire had repeated it, many times: a relationship with a married man was bound to end in tears, especially one like David, often self-absorbed, uncommitted and capable of manipulation. But Selena had not meant to fall in love with a married man. David had not mentioned his wife for the first six months, then, out of the blue, he had held her hand tenderly, gazed into her eyes and told her he had something he desperately needed to tell her. He promised that he truly loved her, that he and Veronica were long over, that his wife was vulnerable, brittle, and he was waiting for the right moment to leave. They no longer shared anything together, not their lives, not their bed: the marital home was an empty, loveless shell. Selena had believed him eagerly, loved him passionately, she had trusted him completely. Then, a month later, she'd discovered that she was pregnant.

Selena heard a soft thump, a muffled expletive. Claire had probably stubbed a toe: no doubt she had drunk a few glasses of wine. Tonight was not the best time to ask for sympathy. Selena would talk to her tomorrow.

She rolled over in bed because her phone was buzzing: David! She had texted him earlier, twice, begging him to reconsider, and now he had answered. She grabbed her phone from the bedside table, imagining a frantic apology, promises of love: he would tell her he had reacted stupidly; he'd changed his mind – everything would be all right. But the number wasn't one she recognised.

She held the phone to her ear and mumbled 'Hello.' There was no reply, just silence, the strange sound of someone listening, then the line crackled, dead. Selena groaned, wondering who would call a wrong number at almost two o'clock in the morning. She cradled her belly and squeezed her eyes shut. Sleep was the best option, but it would not come easily.

* * *

The following day, Selena's sleepless night showed in her bleary eyes as she hunched over the breakfast table in her dressing gown clutching a cup of peppermint tea, her red hair held back in a ponytail, her brow smudged with tiredness.

Claire, in contrast, was bright-eyed and fully dressed. Her spiky blonde crop was damp from the shower as she stood by the worktop pouring black coffee. She told Selena what she already knew. 'You look like death. I assume it went badly with David.'

'Worse than badly.' Selena's eyes filled with tears again. 'I've been so stupid, haven't I?'

'You know you have,' Claire said kindly, sitting across the table, reaching over and taking her hand. 'What did he say?'

'Basically...' Selena shook her head. 'He doesn't want to have a child with me; it was unplanned, and he said – what was his phrase? – "I didn't sign up for this." Then he suggested I was trying to trap him. Do you know...' her eyes widened, '... he even said that his wife would be devastated if she knew he had a pregnant girlfriend because she can't have children. In all of this, he put Veronica first, and that tells me what I already suspected, that he has no intention of leaving her.'

Claire wrinkled her nose. 'Do you think she knows about the two of you?'

'She doesn't. He's been promising for the last month to tell her when the time was right. There was always something – her mother was ill, then she was too fragile. And, of course, I trusted him. But now...' A tear slipped down her cheek.

'Now what?' Claire sipped her coffee, her expression quizzical. 'What are your plans?'

'I've learned a hard lesson.' Selena wiped the tear away with the back of her hand. Another tear followed quickly. 'But I'll bring up my baby alone. I can manage – oh, my goodness, Claire – I never thought – this is your flat. I'll find somewhere else...'

'Don't even think about it.' Claire's tone was firm. 'You'll stay here. You can look after the baby and keep painting. We have the gallery together. You are in a strong position financially. Look at everything as a positive, Selena.' She squeezed her hand. 'It's a baby, a new life. That's so exciting.'

'I wanted to share it with David. I hoped we'd find our own place together; I hoped...' Selena took a deep breath. 'Oh, I've been so stupid. I should have left him as soon as I found out that he was married.'

'Okay. Positive thinking.' The toaster ejected bread and Claire was on her feet, knife poised, spreading butter. 'We'll go down to the gallery together and sell some paintings. The latest ones you've done are attracting so much interest, the landscapes, Pendle, North Yorkshire.'

Selena sighed. 'All painted from photos I took when I was with David.'

'David's let you down. He promised so much, but he just never came up with the goods, did he?'

Selena shook her head miserably. 'I truly believed that he wanted a new start with me. He swept me off my feet. How could I have been so naïve?'

'He's unreliable. And selfish. Seriously, there are better people out there, trustworthy men, nice ones – or no man at all. That's a choice too.'

Selena nodded weakly. 'David was a terrible choice – you always said that.'

'Even before he told you he was married – and how long into your relationship did you discover that nugget of information? Six months?'

'Yes – he always had to be somewhere else, and I just believed what he told me, that he was travelling for work, staying in hotels, photographing different locations. I can't believe how deluded and pathetic I've been,' Selena said. 'And when I found out he had a wife, it was too late. I was in love with him. And he told me not to worry, he was going to leave her...'

Claire sighed. 'I have to say, I always knew he was a liar, with his flowers and flattery and that soft wheedling voice he has.'

'You told me often enough,' Selena admitted. 'We don't have much luck in love, do we, Claire?'

'Let's not go there, regretting things, feeling sorry for ourselves. Our luck is fine. We're single, independent, solvent.' Claire hooted a laugh, the wave of her hands dismissive, carefree. 'I'm over a bad marriage. I have this flat; we share a business that's doing really well, our paintings sell like hot cakes. You have a baby on the way. It all looks good from where I'm standing.'

'Do you really think so?' Selena wasn't sure. 'We both left uni – what – fifteen years ago? This isn't how I thought things would be by the time I was thirty-eight. A single mum-to-be, painting my pictures in your flat...'

'We're fine.' Claire's mouth was full of toast. 'Come on – get dressed and we'll go down to the gallery, open up, make some money, chat to some clients.'

'That's where I met David. He was so interested in my paintings, in me, so charming and attentive.'

'The D-word is banned.'

'But what if he comes in to see me? What if he apologises, says he's sorry and he's changed his mind?' Selena was surprised to hear the hopefulness in her voice. She was annoyed with herself, with her weakness where David was concerned.

Claire laughed again. 'So what if he does? You tell him where to go. He's let you down. He's spineless.'

'You're right. But I feel so – dreadful.' The tears still shone in Selena's eyes. She took a breath, now determined. 'Yes, okay, just give me twenty minutes to get my act together. I can do this. Life goes on.' Her phone buzzed and Selena picked it up, murmuring a hello, listening for a moment, then she put it back on the table. 'Nothing. Just silence. How odd.'

'Wrong number,' Claire said. 'Come on – let's get Saturday underway. We have a living to make – three mouths to feed.'

Claire winked and Selena eased herself up into a standing position. Her back was aching and she felt lethargy creep into her muscles and settle there, but she would put her best foot forward. Claire was right. She'd give herself a month to get over the heartache, then she'd be fine.

* * *

An hour later, Selena and Claire had opened the doors to Ariel Art, their gallery in a lively bohemian street close to the centre of Manchester. Claire had filled the coffee machine, which was bubbling away at the back of the gallery, the aroma of Arabica beans filling the shop. A few customers had arrived, perusing the paintings on the wall. Several pictures were Claire's, bold images in the Social Realism style: gaunt families, distorted faces, splashes of bright colour. There were many other artists' work, Cubist, Abstract, African art, but it was usually Selena's paintings that took people's breath away as they stared at stark landscapes, dark moody hills, low-hanging skies, turbulent storms.

She was seated on a stool, watching an older couple gaze at her interpretation of Pendle Hill, murmuring in low voices. Claire strode across to talk to them confidently, all crimson smile, tight jeans and shining blonde crop. Selena was feeling cold; she rubbed her hands together briskly. It was a blowy March morning outside, a few leaves and a stray piece of litter whirled up in the wind; she shivered. Despite being wrapped in a shawl, a long dress and thick boots, her bones ached. As she watched Claire chattering animatedly to the couple who were praising Selena's painting, she suddenly felt weary.

Selena gazed around the little gallery, once a second-hand clothes shop which she and Claire had chosen for its perfect location and wide, double-fronted windows. They had painted the whole place sail-white, installed gold lighting and marvelled at how popular their project had quickly become. That had been ten years ago: Claire had been married to a musician called Ross and Selena had been living with Flynn, who had been her boyfriend since university.

So much had changed since then: her life had been a steady merry-go-round of unsuccessful partners, every relationship beginning with new hope and inevitably ending badly. The gallery and Claire were the only constants in her life.

Claire was talking to the cheerful couple; a bearded middle-aged man was loitering near the coffee machine. A professional-looking woman with huge round glasses was gazing at Selena's painting of the Yorkshire Moors, Robin Hood's Bay, another place she'd visited with David. A woman swathed in a black coat had just entered the gallery, her dark hair and sunglasses making her look a little like a sixties film star, like Jackie O.

Selena caught Claire's eye, noticing the small wiggle of her finger as she called her over. 'Perhaps you'd like the artist to tell you a little about the painting?'

Selena moved across to the couple, the slim woman in a smart suit, the man in a heavy overcoat with a neat goatee beard.

The woman's eyes shone. 'Oh, I know exactly where this view is. Pendle Hill is such an incredibly atmospheric place. I love the way you've captured the mystery and the magic of the place.'

The man agreed. 'I was born near there, in Blackburn. Daphne and I know the area well. It's a fabulous painting, so bleak and beautiful. When did you paint it?'

'Last winter. I went there with my b— with my brushes and paints,'

Selena said. 'Yes, Pendle Hill is such a great place to paint. The scenery somehow pulls you in.'

'Oh, it does – once you're there, you feel so swept up in the history of it all.' The woman smiled at her husband. 'We should buy it, Bob – it would be lovely in the hall.'

'We saw it on your website,' the man added. 'We both thought then that we'd have it.' He gave a light laugh. 'We'll spend the inheritance before the grandchildren get it.'

'Great idea,' Claire enthused. 'Selena's landscapes don't hang around in the gallery for long.'

There was a pause, then a strained voice came from behind them. 'Selena Cain?'

Selena whirled round. The woman wearing the black coat spoke her name as she whipped off the sunglasses.

'Yes, I'm Selena...'

'I'm Veronica Marsh. David's wife.'

Selena stood completely still. 'Oh...'

'I saw something on his phone last night – two texts from you, begging him to visit you. So, I asked him straight out and David told me everything – about how you've been throwing yourself at him for months, how he's told you to leave him alone. Now I'm here to tell you to stay away.'

Selena's legs weakened and she felt Claire move to stand next to her, placing a warm hand on her shoulder. The cheerful couple shifted closer, looking at Selena with sympathy.

Veronica stared around the gallery and back to Selena. 'You won't take him from me, no matter how hard you try, how often you follow him round and send him texts.'

'What...?' Selena's words were suddenly sucked from her mouth.

Veronica jabbed a shaking finger in the direction of the bearded middle-aged man by the coffee machine. 'I wouldn't stay here – I have it on good authority that she chases everything in trousers.' She turned her anger on Selena. 'David has told me everything.' Veronica whirled towards the older couple who had moved away from the painting and were staring. 'Don't buy anything from this woman. She's been chasing my husband since Christmas. She rings him constantly, texts him and she stalks him non-stop. She's fixated.'

'That's really... not true,' Selena stammered.

'You should ask David for the facts,' Claire began, but Selena's eyes were tearful, begging her to say no more.

'I have, and he's told me the truth,' Veronica said, her voice quivering. 'You're nothing but a homewrecker, a man-eater, a sly scheming witch.' She seemed to lose strength; her body sagged weakly beneath the coat and for a moment she looked close to tears. With a quick movement, she replaced her sunglasses and moved towards the door. Her voice was strained. 'I'm going home now to be with my husband. I hope you can sleep at night after what you've done.'

The door slammed, a light chime of the bell, and Claire helped Selena back to her stool, sitting her down with a gentle pat on the shoulder, then she turned to the customers and flashed a smile. 'Local theatre group, practising their latest amateur dramatics.' She whispered, 'Sit tight, Selena. I'll get you a peppermint tea in a minute. She's said her piece. She won't be back.' Claire offered the older couple a charming smile. 'So, do you want to buy the Pendle painting? I'm so sorry about the interruption by the fishwife.'

Selena watched, in a daze, as the couple spoke softly to Claire, approaching the till, taking out a credit card. She put a hand to her brow; the room was spinning in front of her like a fairground carousel and she felt light-headed. She could hear the echo of voices as people mumbled, Claire's light chatter, the woman's sympathetic tutting as she gazed across at Selena. Then she felt something move deep in her abdomen, a tightening cramp, a gripping and a sudden letting go. Then she felt the trickle of blood.

2

MARCH 1682. ASHCOMB, SOMERSET

The young woman wearing the well-patched grey dress, a scarf covering pale red hair, delved deep into the damp soil. She felt a sharp gust of wind blow through the thin material, but she was used to being cold. She had planted the parsnips months earlier in the garden of Slaugh Cottage and her deft fingers scrabbled in the dirt, pulling out three fine vegetables.

She wiped her grimy hands on her apron and stood up, closing her eyes for a moment. She was small and slight, her frame slender beneath the long frock that trailed in the mud. The harsh wind blew again, tugging strands of hair from the scarf and lifting them across her face. She smiled, welcoming the buffeting breeze as an old friend. Then she bunched the parsnips in her apron and rushed back to the cottage, through the narrow stone hall into the warmth of the downstairs room, where a fire burned in the hearth and a single tallow candle was burning on the table.

A man's voice murmured, 'Is that you, Grace?'

'Who else would it be, Father, the King of England?' She paused for a moment, gazing at him slumped in the wooden chair, his cheeks flushed from the blaze. 'Just give me a moment. I have some parsnips here for the pottage. Tonight, we'll eat as well as King Charles and his Portuguese Queen Catherine.'

Will Cotter turned his eyes back to the fire and watched the flames flicker. His daughter was fond of making light-hearted quips, but he liked her gentle prattle; she kept the home alive with her bubbly chatter and he would seldom ask her to hold her tongue. His eyes were heavy and for a moment he felt warm and soothed in the firelight, then sleep took him.

Grace gave her father one last look, checking he was comfortable, then she moved on light feet to pick up the bucket she had set down in the corner. She had drawn water from the well earlier, and now she cleaned and sliced the parsnips carefully, adding them to the beef bones, potatoes, onions and grains already in the pot. She returned to the fireplace, sidling past her father, easing the blackened cook pot onto its hook over the flames.

'The bread's baked now, I hope.' She picked up a cloth and slid her hands into the bread oven built in to the wall on the side of the fire, pulling out the brown-topped loaf, setting it down quickly on the wooden table and waving her hands to cool them. 'Yes, we will eat well tonight.'

Will's eyelids flickered open and he said, 'You're a good girl.'

Grace studied her father carefully. Forty-two years old and ravaged by a lifetime of farm work, he was thinner now; his long legs stretched towards the hearth, ending in boots that hissed and steamed in the heat. Worry had furrowed his brow and faded his red hair. She watched the troubled rise and fall of his chest beneath the linen shirt and frowned. He was one of the oldest of the men who laboured on the farm, and Grace worried about his health constantly. Suddenly an idea came to her. 'Will you take a mug of mulled ale, now, Father? That would set you aright before we eat.'

Will nodded as if speaking might require too much effort.

Grace bent down and lifted the pitcher from the hearth, feeling the heat of the blaze briefly scorch her skin. She poured the drink into the tankard and set it in his hands.

He gripped it, his large labourer's palms shaking with weariness as he brought the ale to his lips. He supped once and sighed. 'Ah, this is good. Then after we have eaten, I am for my bed.'

'I will wait up awhile,' she replied. 'Next Tuesday is Lady Day, the twenty-fifth, the day Our Lady was spoken to by the Angel, so I want to have everything made clean and tidy. It gives me but three days – tomorrow is Sunday and we must go to church. There are things I want to do, to make ready. I want to tidy the house; I want to collect a pail of milk and some cheese from the farm. I have my herbs to tend...'

Will was watching her, the flames reflecting warm light in his eyes. 'You remind me of your mother, Grace. Always busy, always something to tend, something to mend.'

Grace nodded, her expression soft. 'I miss her too.'

'I think of her each day that passes. You were just twelve years old when we lost her. It was ten years ago now, on Michaelmas, when she was taken in her bed, carried off by the fever.' His hands clutched the tankard. 'You've never complained since – the cooking, the mending, the weeding on the farm. You're just like she was, strong, kindly-natured, patient.'

'I learned from her,' Grace said quickly. 'And I learn from Grand-mother Bett in the village, how to sew and use the spindle, to work with simples* and plants to heal, and I am grateful she showed me how to bake bread and cook. I will go to see my grandmother before church, take her a few bits for her pot.'

'She's a good age now, Bett. Sixty years and still hale and hearty. It's a pity your mother wasn't blessed with the same healthy disposition.' Will began to wheeze, then he coughed, air caught in his throat, struggling to breathe. He leaned forward and sipped his ale slowly. 'Ah, I miss her, my Anne. Taken too soon.'

Grace took the tankard from his fingers and set it down by his feet. 'I will slice the bread now, Father, and fetch the last of the butter. Then we can eat.'

Will closed his eyes, relishing the sound of his daughter bustling round, her footsteps fading as she moved to the adjoining room at the back of the cottage where the butter and cheese were kept inside the small pantry and the dried goods were stored.

For a moment, Grace paused, fingering the bunches of dried roots that hung from the rafters, touching the thyme tied with string, checking a few sweet stalks of lavender, bowls of berries and herbs. Then she was back at the table, busying herself and humming a tune.

Her presence soothed him, somehow making him feel secure, the master of his own home, where he was respected: there was precious little esteem in the life of a farm labourer living in a tied cottage, but Grace brought a homely peace to the house. His wife, Anne, had the same gift of creating calmness around her, and her mother too, Bett White. After a long day on the farm, tending cattle, ploughing fields, Will seldom had much energy left for conversation, but it was reassuring to listen to Grace chatter. All he wanted to do each evening was to sit in his chair staring into the fire, remembering, watching the pictures form in the dancing light, resting his aching limbs. But Grace, who stood behind him slicing crusts from the loaf, had other ideas. At the end of the day, when her father retired to his bed, that was the moment she longed for most.

*Herbs

* * *

Several hours later, Grace stepped outside into the moonlit garden, breathing in the fragrance of damp grass. Her father was already slumbering in his pallet bed and he wouldn't wake until after seven tomorrow, it being Sunday; the extra hour's sleep would be beneficial. And now the night garden was her own domain.

Grace removed the headscarf and shook her pale red hair free, then she tugged the kerchief from her neck, instantly feeling the wind's bite on her skin. She lifted her arms, allowing the breeze to encompass her, to ruffle her gown and blow against her neck like the cold breath of a lover. She closed her eyes with the pleasure of it.

When she opened them, the moon shifted from behind a cloud,

gliding across the indigo sky, round as a beaten-metal coin. In the distance, an owl hooted. Grace cupped her hands to her mouth and returned the same low sound. The owl replied, and Grace smiled.

She wandered through the garden, trailing her fingers in crop of lavender stalks, lifting them to her nostrils, inhaling the faint scent. Soon the flowers would bloom again and she could dry them, use them to make a poultice to ease inflammations and swellings. She knew that a few cabbage leaves, heated and pressed flat, would heal a bruise or a swollen ankle. Calendula and yarrow made to a paste with hot water and tied in muslin would soothe most agues. Her mother and her grandmother, Bett, had shown her the ways of using herbs and plants since her childhood, and she kept her garden full of everything she needed. Grace would dry herbs and make teas to calm and soothe, to help sleep come. Parsley, watercress, mustard, burdock, meadowsweet and celery grew in her garden so that she could make infusions. Her father's joints were often swollen and sore; a poultice of ragwort leaf, cabbage, turnip and coltsfoot boiled in milk with oats and butter would ease his pains.

The moon slid behind a cloud and Grace turned back to the house. The blackthorn tree that grew outside was almost in full flower, and she moved towards it, her fingers lightly touching the spikes on the branches. It was her favourite tree. She whispered, 'May I pluck a bloom or two for myself?' She lifted two tiny white flowers and folded them behind a strand of hair, close to her ear. 'Thanks be to you.' Grace touched the dark wood again with a careful finger, tracing the edges of the delicate petals: she loved the blackthorn for its slender trunk and dark green leaves, its black bark and spiny branches. She loved the way the fragile blooms could be woven into a bridal head-dress for a spring wedding, but it would be bad luck to bring the flowers indoors.

Each October, Grace used the dark berries to make sweet sloe gin and they were useful in the cook pot to impart flavour. But, most of all, she remembered that a scratch to the flesh from the spikes could be deadly; a piece of blackthorn burying itself under the skin might cause severe infection, swelling and pain. A thorn in the hand might make the joints stiffen and poison the blood.

Grace walked in the thick darkness towards the old well as the wind lifted her hair. She paused next to the old stone well that was sunken into the earth, gazing into the black depths. As she stared, she could see the inky water ripple, exploding the reflection of the silver moonlight above. She gave a soft laugh and the echo returned it to her from deep in the ground. She asked, 'How are you this night?' and the well replied with the same question, the hushed chorus of many voices. She smiled. 'I am most hearty,' enjoying her own chattering well where she could unlock the treasures of her heart, and her words would come back to her in a breathless spell. She whispered a name once, 'Nathaniel Harper,' and the echo returned the secret sound, tender as a lover's voice. She stared into the swirling water at the bottom of the well and the moon slithered away, leaving the depths dark as pitch. She whispered again, 'Nathaniel Harper and Grace Anne Cotter,' and her words bubbled back softly in answer.

Grace pressed a hand against the stone top of the well, a promise to return the next evening. In the bright light of morning, she would draw the day's water in the wooden bucket, but under night's dark cloak, the well shared her secrets and kept them safely locked in its depths.

She wandered through the garden towards the wooden gate, resting dreamily awhile, leaning her head against her arms. The wind had died down and, despite the cold night air, Grace felt warm, skittish. She blinked and turned her gaze towards the big farmhouse at the top of the hill where the Harper family lived, where her father toiled most days, where she too went to weed crops and sometimes to milk cows. She liked the farmer, Joseph Harper, who was a solid, quiet man, although his wife, Harriet, could be sharp of tongue and stern to the girls who worked for her. But her son, Nathaniel, was the apple of his mother's eye; he was the reason Harriet was so quick-tempered with any young woman who offered him a smile or a furtive glance.

Nathaniel, at twenty-four, was tall, broad and handsome, with dark hair and deep-set blue eyes. He sported the best leather boots; a sheepskin cloak; a woollen hat and mittens kept him warm throughout the long winter. But now spring was here, Nathaniel wore an open-necked white shirt and breeches that fitted him snugly. Grace couldn't help the way her breathing quickened when he smiled in her direction, or when he doffed his hat on Sundays after church, standing at the lychgate a distance from his mother's glance so that he could extend a polite bow and murmur, 'Good day, Mistress Grace.'

The owl fluttered low over Grace's head, hooting softly, and Grace looked up. 'Oh, it is later than I thought. There are but wo days until Lady Day and there is much to do in the house and the garden. I will need to get up early and before church I must go to see Grandmother Bett.' She glanced up at a tall tree, where the owl was roosting, and waved a hand, then she wrapped her kerchief around her neck, pulling the scarf over her tousled hair, and scurried back towards the house.

She opened the door, rushed through the hall and stepped into the warmth of the downstairs room where the fire still glowed. The tallow candle was flickering, almost spent. Her father's chair was empty, but his tankard and the pitcher were on the hearth. Grace lifted the tankard to her nose, inhaling the sweetness of the dregs, now cold, and sighed. 'I am for my bed – this will wait until tomorrow to be washed clean.' She placed it on the table, then she trod on soft feet up the wooden staircase towards her bedroom, the smallest room in the cottage, nestling beneath the thatched roof, with the small pallet bed covered in a patchwork quilt painstakingly made by her mother some twelve years ago.

The room was in darkness, except for the smouldering embers. Outside the window, a breeze buffeted the thin wooden shutter, and a branch of the blackthorn tree tapped three times and was still.

3

Selena knew, as Claire drove her to the hospital, that there was no hope. She had known from the first moment in the gallery as the pain gripped her abdomen and held that she had miscarried, although the nurse told her the certain truth in a soft Scottish brogue as she perched on the end of the hospital bed.

'It was early days. Lots of babies miscarry before twelve weeks. And there wouldn't have been anything you could have done to make the outcome different – you mustn't keep saying that it was your fault.'

'It was because of the anxiety I've been through recently.' Selena wiped her eyes with the tissue she balled in her fist. 'I've been under a lot of stress.'

The nurse shook her head. She was young, in her twenties, freckles on her nose. 'Do you have someone who will support you? The baby's father? A relative or friend?'

'My flatmate has been lovely.' Selena took a huge breath. 'I've just split up with my partner. He didn't want children.'

'You have plenty of time to decide about starting a family.'

'I'm thirty-eight,' Selena blurted.

The nurse's voice was soft with sympathy. 'Lots of women give birth in their late thirties, early forties. Royalty, Madonna, David Bowie's wife.' She touched Selena's arm. 'You take your time and heal first, both physically and emotionally.'

Selena nodded. Claire would be waiting outside to take her back to the flat. This time, she was returning without a baby; she was empty, alone. As the tears began again, she realised that she had no idea what she would do next.

* * *

Later on, around six o'clock, Selena installed herself on the sofa, her legs raised on cushions, a cup of tea in her hands; she intended to spend the whole evening watching television, although she doubted that she would take much in.

Claire moved to sit next to her, wrapping an affectionate arm around her shoulders, her voice filled with sympathy. 'How are you feeling?'

'I'll be fine.' Selena forced a smile. 'Are you off out tonight? Wine bar? The usual crowd?'

'Do you want to come?' Claire asked gently.

'Oh, no, I couldn't.'

'Then we'll have a night in together, shall we?' Claire snuggled closer. 'Are you up to a takeaway, pizza, a bottle of wine?'

'I wasn't drinking any alcohol because of the baby...' Selena's eyes filled with tears and she was immediately cross with herself. 'It doesn't seem right, not yet.'

'Of course,' Claire said. 'You've been through an awful lot...'

'I feel like – my life's a crumbling house, everything falling to pieces, every room filled with rubbish. There's nothing at all to hope for. Everything I thought I had – the baby, David, a future – it's all suddenly gone. And I'm cross with myself – I was too eager to believe David when he promised the earth, but I'd seen the signs. I should have known – and now I just feel stupid and embarrassed and sad.'

'I'm sure you do – but everyone makes mistakes and you'll move on in time.' Claire sighed. 'It will take a while. The hypothetical house might seem a mess right now, but we'll clear all the rooms one by one, you'll see.'

'I thought about going to my parents' place in Buxton, maybe staying there for a few days,' Selena said quietly. 'But I'm too old to go running back to Mum and Dad with my problems.'

'Whatever feels right – you know best.'

Selena gasped; a sudden thought had come to her. 'Claire, do you think I should tell David? I mean, should I phone him and say that the baby is...?'

'And what would he do?' Claire flushed with sudden anger. 'It doesn't concern him. He left you. He has no right to know anything now...'

'What if I bump into him? He's a photographer, he goes to all the big exhibitions, our paths are bound to cross.'

'In your place, I'd just ignore him – I don't respect him for what he did to his wife or to you, but you know what I think about it all. He's a smooth operator. I could see that he was untrustworthy from the get-go, and it was awful to watch you fall for his lies.' Claire's hands became small fists. 'He let you down. He should have stayed with Veronica in the first place. He's deceived you both.'

Selena nodded. 'You're right. He must have denied that we were ever together; he told her that I was chasing him. Oh, what a mess.'

'You're better off without him. He's a cheat – no doubt he'll do it again and again,' Claire snorted. Then she made her voice light. 'Now, I'm going to get us some nibbles and we'll watch a whole box set of something really good.'

'Nothing weepy, nothing romantic, please,' Selena begged. 'I don't want to blub all night.'

'*Peaky Blinders* it is, then.' Claire said. 'Or *Breaking Bad*.' She leaped up from the sofa and rushed into the kitchen. Selena could hear her bustling around, opening cupboard doors.

She closed her eyes for a moment. Her mind was blank. Then she thought about the baby, the child she would never meet. Would it have been a boy or a girl? Would it have had her red hair and brown eyes, or David's dark curls and his blue gaze? She would never know.

Her phone buzzed and Selena reached out, almost in a daze, picking it up without thinking, holding it to her ear. 'Hello?'

'Selena, you and I need to talk.'

'Veronica?' Selena froze.

'I'm just so confused.' The voice rose with anxiety. 'Why did you make a play for my husband? I need to know what happened – it doesn't make any sense. David has told me that it was embarrassing, how you followed him around – he felt sorry for you. So, when did it all start?'

Selena caught her breath. She didn't know how to respond. She couldn't mention the baby: there was nothing that she could say that would give Veronica peace of mind. It was better to say nothing at all.

Veronica continued, her voice strained. 'I just don't understand how you came to have his phone number. David tells me he didn't encourage you. Explain to me what went on between you, why you kept pestering him. All he told me was that you wouldn't keep away. When did you meet him?'

'I'm sorry... I can't talk about it...' Selena pressed the button, cutting her off, and quickly placed the phone on the arm of the sofa at a distance from her, as if it had just burned her fingers.

Claire arrived behind her, holding out a bowl of guacamole and tortilla chips. 'Was that his wife on the phone? I heard you say the name Veronica...'

'She's very upset,' Selena said. 'She wants to know all the details and I can't tell her, can I? She doesn't know the whole story, which is awful because if I could tell her the truth, she might understand. Or it might break her heart.'

'Poor Veronica is a victim too.' Claire sat down. 'She thinks that you've tried to take away the man she loves. At least you're rid of David now. She still trusts him.'

'But what if she rings me again? What if she comes back to the gallery when I'm there?'

Claire shrugged. 'She'll need space if she's going to get her marriage back on track, although I'm sure it's only a matter of time until David does the dirty on her again. Perhaps you should go to your parents' place for a week or so after all, until it all blows over.'

Selena leaned her head back against the soft comfort of cushions. 'I do understand that she's hurt and insecure, but at the moment I need some time alone. I don't need this, not after the last twenty-four hours.'

'Let's forget about Veronica. And let's forget about pathetic David too. If she calls, don't answer. I'll look after things at the gallery – if she comes in, I'll tell her you're not available – or I might even tell her what a cheat David really is.' Claire reached for the bowl of tortillas and pressed a button on the remote. 'Let's lose ourselves for a few hours and watch Cillian Murphy. I've seen the whole series twice. You'll love it – it'll certainly take your mind off other things.' She patted Selena's arm as the television screen burst into life. 'I know this is tough for you. I'm here for you all the way. But you're strong – you'll come through. Time is what you need now. Time and space.'

Selena nodded, concentrating on the flickering screen. She wasn't taking in the storyline as the images washed over her: a man wearing a coat and a flat cap was riding a horse through a cobbled street; it was probably the nineteen twenties or thirties, possibly somewhere in the Midlands; there was a family, men arguing. Selena was thinking about the baby, her hand on her belly, massaging the emptiness as if her round palm might heal the aching. Her thoughts drifted to David, who was most likely somewhere not many miles away, with Veronica. She imagined them out for a meal together, Veronica's expression troubled, asking how he had met Selena, and David smiling and squeezing her hand gently as he fabricated lies in a smooth tone. Veronica would hang hopefully on every word, wanting to believe him. Selena knew only too well how convincing he could be. Claire was right: David had hurt both women. He was the villain in this melodrama, and Selena felt a surprising rush of sympathy for Veronica, who was trying to save her marriage.

On the screen, two brothers were arguing; a man was smoking a cigarette, his blue eyes hard and determined. Selena thought about the baby again. She had imagined a little girl, a soft bundle of warmth, little fists, tufts of light hair, that sweet smell. Selena swallowed hard. Tears had started to prick her eyes. On the screen, the man in the flat cap had left the town and he was in the countryside now, in a large field with several other men. They were identically dressed in flat caps, smart jackets, and they each carried a shotgun over their shoulders as they walked purposefully through pale tufty grass. The man at the front still had a cigarette in his mouth; he wore leather gloves and a smart watch and fob chain across his waistcoat. Then Selena noticed the tree in the background, a broad oak, its wide branches stretching towards a pale sky heavy with clouds. She was suddenly lifted by the urge to create the picture – not the men, but the peacefulness of the open field, the strength of the oak tree, the breadth of the sky. She knew exactly how the painting would be, once finished, the hues of gold and pale green, the silver greys and ochres. Then it came to her. She needed to paint in the countryside, surrounded by nature, its calm, its peace.

She could leave Manchester for a month or two, longer even. Why not? The gallery would take care of itself and she would take care of her own healing. Claire had said it: she needed time and space, and that was exactly what a stay in the countryside would bring. She would paint lots of pictures, she'd experience the daily stillness and solitude; she'd focus on herself and complete many pieces of art, creating something fresh in an entirely new setting. And she'd be away from Manchester, from David, and, by the time Selena was ready to return, her affair with David would be a thing of the past. She'd start again, she and Claire: the gallery would go from strength to strength; she'd be ready for the city, for friends, for a social life. And she'd take it from there.

Selena reached for her phone, thinking. She'd go somewhere a long way from Manchester, somewhere rural. Cornwall and Devon were just a little too far away, so her fingers typed the words *Somerset* and *cottages to rent* into the search bar and instantly hundreds of homes appeared on the screen: expensive, extravagant houses. Selena refined the search, moving her thumb: *two bedrooms, garden, village location, rural*. This time just three houses appeared. One was a chocolate-box thatched cottage in the middle of a village, not far from the local pub. The second was a bright yellow house, very charming, with a swing in the garden and a trampoline, clearly suitable for a small family: the rent was high. The third cottage stood behind a wooden gate; there were plants, bushes and several trees in the garden and an old stone well. It was a seventeenth-century building, with a porched door, cob walls partially limewashed in white, that had been modernised and updated over the years. It had an oil-fired Aga and a newly refurbished kitchen. Selena stared at the rent: she couldn't believe that was the monthly rate: it was so cheap, it must be a misprint, surely.

She scanned the website, gazing at the interior: two bedrooms, beautifully furnished, an extended kitchen, an oak-framed conservatory at the back that would make a wonderful room in which to paint. Her eyes were drawn to the whitewashed living room. There was a huge fireplace with a new wood burner, a wide window, a comfortable sofa. She imagined herself there, quiet, at peace, surrounded by her paintings. She would begin by painting the garden, the new March blooms, the April buds.

Selena pressed a button on her phone. The owner was a Mrs Lesley Russell and Sloe Cottage was immediately available to let. There was no harm in giving her a call.

4

On Sunday the twenty third of March in 1682, Grace Cotter rose at daybreak and rushed outside into the garden, wearing only her shift, to draw water from the well. The garden was silent, except for the early flurry of insects, and the air was cool as she splashed her face and hands with fresh water. She quickly rubbed the rest of her body, rinsing her hair with clean water from a pitcher, massaging her scalp with deft fingers, drying herself on a thick linen cloth. Then she set about washing clothes, drawing more water in the bucket and filling the tub, carefully adding the mixture of wood ash and a little urine from her chamber pot and scrubbing the shift and the grey dress she had worn yesterday. She paid particular attention to the muddy hems, rubbing hard with her knuckles, then paddling the linen with a wooden bat. Then she dragged out the heavy clothes, squeezing the water from them, and hung them to dry on the bushes. She set to washing her father's work clothes, which was always a hard job as his daily toil on the farm left them heavy with soil and sweat, but the air was fresh and would render them clean, and her own patched dress would dry well.

Grace returned to Slaugh Cottage massaging her chafed hands; her knuckles were sore and rough. Her hair was still wet and her skin was chilled beneath the thin shift, but she moved quickly into the living room to warm herself, blowing on the embers of the fire in the grate and fanning them until they glowed, adding twigs and then logs, filling the black kettle and hanging it over the fire on the hook. She cut bread and placed it on her father's platter on the table, with cheese and a slice of cold mutton, then she filled his tankard with fresh milk from the pitcher. He would rise soon, wash and break his fast later than usual, as was customary on Sundays.

Grace hurried to her room and opened the clothes box by her bed, taking out her Sunday dress, a cream linen garment she kept for best. She pulled it on, smoothing the skirts, wrapping a clean kerchief around her neck, arranging her damp hair and covering it with a cream bonnet. She scurried downstairs again into the small back room, selecting items from the pantry: she had made a seed cake for her grandmother, which she placed carefully in a basket with a pot of blackberry jam. She had made several batches of jam last autumn: the weather had been warm and the plentiful berries had lasted until mid-October. Grandmother Bett had a sweet tooth and would be grateful for some sugary preserves to go with her bread. Grace added a pot of pickled cucumbers.

She was about to leave the pantry when a book on the shelf caught her eye. It was her mother's seldom-used copy of *The English Hus-wife* by Gervase Markham, containing recipes, remedies and instruction. Grace held it in her hand, turning it over, her fingers pressing the creamy pages that her mother had once touched. She did not know many of her letters; she had been taught at her mother's knee to write her name, but she could not read. In truth, her mother could not read or write well either: the book had been given to her, a treasure, and she had kept it as such without being able to decipher much of the contents.

Grace opened the first page and ran her finger lightly over the first few words, although she had no sense of what the writing meant. *Thou mayst say (gentle Reader) what hath this man to doe with Hus-wifery, he is now out of his element.*

Grace smiled. There was one particular recipe her mother used to make, a rich spicy gingerbread. Grace would bake some tomorrow, in time for Lady Day on Tuesday, so that they could share it in the evening. She imagined her father's expression as he'd nibble the sweet cake and taste the warm sharp bite of ginger, bringing back fond memories of when they were a family of three, sitting together around the fire. Those were the times when he had been most happy.

Grace heard her father moving upstairs, his slow footfall heavy on the wooden steps, then he was in the living room, his clothes dishevelled, his face tired. She offered him a smile. 'So, good day to you, Father. I have prepared you a feast – bread and cheese and mutton, and the creamy top from the milk. It is all laid on the table.' She gave a little skip, the basket in her hand. 'I am now on my way to see my Grandmother Bett. I will meet you at church.'

He was staring at her, his eyes shining. 'You are a comely young woman, Grace, and full of goodness. You remind me so much of Anne.'

'But my hair is as yours, Father, too much like the colour of strawberries. Mother's locks were dark, and they would curl in ringlets. Mine will not hold a curl at all, even if I wrap it in rags and sleep in them all night.'

'You have her sweet nature.'

Grace bobbed a half-curtsey, flushed with happiness. 'I am glad I remind you of her, and that it gives you good cheer. Your Sunday clothes are freshly clean. I put them back upstairs on Friday. So, I will see you later, smartly dressed and in church.'

Will Cotter flopped in his chair, stretching out long legs. 'It would be a better day if I could stay here and rest. Reverend Walters vexes me. His sermons are too lengthy.'

'Father!' Grace pretended to be surprised, but her eyes twinkled with mischief. 'You know that we can be fined for not attending church, and we cannot afford it. You told me yourself, a fine for not attending church can be more than we earn in a year. So, to church you must go.' She waved her basket, making her skirts rustle. 'I will see you at St Bartholomew's, dear father. And be warned, sitting by the hearthside will make you fall asleep, and if you doze the morning away, you will be tardy to church.'

* * *

Grace walked the half-mile into Ashcomb village, past rows of low-thatched cottages and the village inn, The Royal Oak, renamed over twenty years ago in the King's honour after the restoration of Charles II in 1660. Grace had learned the story of the King hiding in the branches of an oak tree from her grandmother, who seemed to be a source of any gossip or news that was happening inside and outside the village.

A young man passed her by in the street, Ned Shears, one of the farm labourers who worked with her father, and he doffed his cap, mumbling, 'Good morning to ye, Mistress Grace,' and she wished him a good day quietly, her eyes cast down modestly.

She arrived at her grandmother's cottage, a small thatched house with white cob walls. Her grandmother was standing by the doorpost, smiling through her few remaining teeth. She wore a white cap and a clean apron and she waved as Grace approached, before rushing forward and kissing her cheek. 'I knew you'd come by to see me before church today.' Her voice was soft as rustling leaves. 'Come inside, come inside.'

She led the way into the house; there was one dark room downstairs where a fire was burning in the hearth, a blackened kettle hanging from a hook, and an old spinning wheel stood in the corner, a stool next to it.

Bett White patted Grace's arm affectionately, then she took her hands in hers, turning them over and frowning. 'Look at your hands, Gracie Cotter. They are chapped and raw. Have you been washing clothes and not drying them properly?' Before Grace could answer, she tugged her towards the hearth and urged her to sit down. 'I will have to make amends. I'll put some oatmeal paste on them. They'll be as soft as a lady's silk kerchief when I've finished. So, tell me, what are the ingredients of a good oatmeal paste for the hands?'

Grace answered dutifully. 'Four ounces of lard, six ounces of honey, eight ounces of oatmeal, three egg yolks, all mixed together.'

'All the village women swear by my oatmeal paste.' Bett had moved to a shelf in the corner and was returning with a pot. 'They say it makes the skin exceeding soft and supple. It is good for the skin after birthing too.' She took Grace's small hands in hers and began to massage the salve into her skin. 'So, my girl, how are you? How is Will?'

Grace closed her eyes, enjoying the steady rhythm of her grandmother's strong fingers against her palms. 'My father is well. And I am well too.' She smiled. 'All is well, thanks be to God.'

'Your father is a good man. You are lucky, child, to have a father who treats you with such kindness. A tolerant father is a rare thing, especially as you are a young girl of marriageable age. But I fear he gives you far too much freedom.'

'He sleeps early most evenings and leaves me to tend my herbs in the garden. And I care for him as much as I can. He is old now and tired from his daily toil. I must make time later to collect some nettle leaves, to bruise and mix with wallwort to comfort his aching joints. I do my best to ease his pains.'

'Let me ease ours, I have warmed some cider for us,' Bett said softly, pouring from a fireside pitcher, filling two pewter tankards. 'Already today I have drunk two mugs of it.' She noticed Grace's admonishing expression. 'Do not think me a swill-belly. It is purely to keep me warm.'

'Then why do you drink so much of it in the summertime?' Grace teased.

'Then, it keeps me cool,' Bett retorted playfully. 'Come, Gracie, and see. I have been mending. I am making that linen dress of yours into a gown fit for a lady.' She tugged Grace's sleeve over to the corner, pulling a cream dress from her large sewing basket. 'It will be perfect for May Day. I'm going to embroider it with little white flowers, like the ones on the blackthorn, and you can wear it at the May dancing. You will be a beautiful May Queen.'

Grace held up the gown and gave a small twirl.

Bett clapped her hands gleefully. 'Oh, you will make such a wonderful bride one of these days.'

Grace moved towards the fireplace, picking up her mug of mulled cider, sipping slowly. Her eyes were thoughtful. 'I think not.'

Bett, her tankard clutched in the other hand, patted Grace's knee. 'And why not?' She leaned forward. 'I think perhaps some young gentleman has already caught your eye?' She noticed Grace's cheeks flush pink. 'Indeed, I can see I'm right. Tell me, Gracie, for I know of all the eligible young bachelors in this parish.'

Grace shook her head. 'I do not think of marriage, Grandmother. My father needs me at home. And I am content to stay there, to care for him.'

Bett raised an eyebrow. For a moment she was deep in thought, examining Grace's expression, the downcast of her eyes, the pressing together of her lips. 'Ah, you are a good girl, I am certain of it. But you cannot deny what is in your heart. Your mother had married your father at your age. I was married by the time I was twenty, and those were precious years with my John, God rest his soul. Young women of your age have children, and many of them too. Love is the way of the world, and it is natural to seek it.'

Grace shook her head. 'I have no such fancy...'

'But you do.' Bett took another long draught from her cup and her eyes sparkled. 'I can see it. And it is a young man of the parish.'

'In truth, there is one goodly man, Grandmother, but we have rarely spoken, except in polite greeting. He knows who I am, where I live. But he will not choose me.'

'Why not? You are pretty, you are modest, skilful; you are not afraid of hard work.'

Grace whispered, 'He is the son of Joseph Harper, the farmer who pays my father's wages, who owns the house I live in. He will not have eyes for one such as me.' Her gaze stayed on her hands that held the cup on her lap.

'Then I will charm him to come to you. I can make a love potion by mixing the pretty little periwinkle flowers with leeks and earthworms.

And I can assure you that it will work.' Bett's eyes gleamed. 'How else do you think such a one as John White, who could have had his pick of all the girls in the parish, came to choose me?'

Grace sat up straight, her voice indignant. 'I can make such a potion myself, if I need so to do, Grandmother.'

Bett laughed. 'Of course you could. I taught your mother and she taught you well.'

'If Nathaniel Harper likes me, then I wish him to like me because he does, not because I have charmed him to do so.'

'And that is very wise. But, just in case he should need a helping hand, so that he can find the path to Slaugh Cottage to court you in the evenings, perhaps I'll make something I can leave on his doorstep at the farm, or slip into his hand at church, to speed his ardour.'

'Grandmother...' Grace saw the mischief in Bett's eyes.

'Come, let me look at the fine things you have brought in your basket. I can see cake, and my favourite jam. Pickles too.' Bett changed the subject with a quick smile. 'Then we must break some bread, have a bite of cheese. I have eaten nothing all day and I am quite gut-foundered.'

Grace rose from the seat. 'Oh, do let me prepare a platter for you.'

'No, we have much to talk about, so let us get the food together. I want to tell you about Kitty Stokes, who lives near the church with her husband. She is with child and just a few weeks from lying-in. I will deliver the child, but you must come with me to help, Gracie, because I fear it will not be an easy first birth. You know Kitty, she that was Kitty Watt?'

'I think so, Grandmother. She is the same age as I, a year younger.'

'Her grandfather was George Watt: he was killed at Dunster castle when I was a young mother, and Anne was at my knee. The Somerset menfolk defended the castle with Robert Blake against the Parliamentarians. That castle changed hands more times than the weather changes in April. Things were hard for us when I was younger– first the Lord Protector was in charge, then the Puritans. And the Puritans wouldn't even let us celebrate May Day, not in those days – they called dancing a heathenish vanity. A year ago last February, Kitty Watt married Edmund Stokes, the grandson of Harry Stokes who was a great friend to my John back in the day.'

Grace nodded slowly. 'Of course. I am glad to help you if I can.'

'So, let us eat and you can tell me all about your young man, Master Nathaniel Harper.'

'Oh, he is not mine, and there is little to say. He is an ordinary man – he has two arms, two legs, one nose.' Grace smiled to herself. 'He is just a man like any other.'

'No man is like any other, and that is God's truth,' Bett said with a smile, then she bustled towards the corner of the room and began to slice bread and cheese.

Grace watched her grandmother for a moment, about to join her, when she gazed into the depths of her cider mug. The liquid was murky, ink-dark, like the bottom of her well, but for a moment she thought she glimpsed a shadow in the sediment, a figure that cleared and became a shape she was familiar with. It was exactly as she remembered him, wearing fine leather shoes, an open-necked white shirt and breeches that fitted snugly. He was standing by the lychgate outside the church, staring in her direction. Grace caught her breath as the image of Nathaniel Harper swirled away and disappeared, leaving her heart beating quickly and the dark dregs of the drink sinking to the bottom of the tankard.

5

Lady Day, the twenty-fifth, came and went, and the cottage was freshly brushed and tidied. Grace and Will ate gingerbread in front of the hearth; it was well-spiced and delicious, exactly as Anne would have baked herself. Then, on the following Sunday, Grace watched Nathaniel Harper throughout the service in St Bartholomew's church, smart in his Sunday clothes, standing in a front pew between his mother and father. He did not seem to notice her, but Grace marvelled at his lusty voice rising above all the others as he sang the hymns, and she examined the slope of his shoulders as he sat motionless, his hands clasped, while the rector spoke his long sermon and her father dozed next to her. On Grace's other side, Bett was silent as she observed her granddaughter through the corner of her eyes, the slight movement of Grace's mouth as she gazed around the church, as her eyes flickered and rested on the farmer's young son.

The month of April arrived, with brighter days, the sun tentative and warming. The tiny white blossom on the blackthorn tree outside Slaugh Cottage held firm in the breeze, pretty as a cluster of pearls. Grace worked hard each day: there was plenty of weeding to be done in the fields. Then, after work, she prepared her father's meals and washed his clothes; the ploughing often continued on until late in the evening and Will was weary most nights. He would take himself off to his bed early and Grace would slip outside to listen to the deep gurgle of the water in the echoing well, and she would whisper the secrets of her heart.

Then, one Friday at the end of April, Grace was called from her weeding to help the milkmaids in the strawed-down barn, and she scurried across the field, looking forward to the chance to rest her aching back. When she arrived, she was greeted by Alice and Nancy Bryant, two sisters who were around her age, already busy milking two docile cows. Nancy glanced across the barn as she heard Grace's footfall. 'It's good you're here, Grace. Mistress Harriet wants the curds for buttering and the whey to drink, and we cannot work quickly enough. She's in a bad humour today.'

Grace took a wooden stool and sat quietly, placing a pail beneath a brown and white heifer. She rested a reassuring palm on the cow's flank and spoke in a gentle voice. 'So, it's plenty of warm milk I need from you today, Mistress Cow, if you'd oblige.' She rubbed her hands hard, warming them, wiping them on her apron, and then wrapped her fingers around the teats. 'Let down your milk for me, please,' she murmured, and quickly there was the sound of liquid squirting into the pail. Grace rested her cheek against the cow's side, closed her eyes and breathed softly as the cow gave a low sound of contentment.

Alice Bryant, round-faced, rosy and dimpled, sat upright. 'How do you do it, Grace? The cows yield their milk readily for you.'

Grace smiled: the sisters usually chattered non-stop and the cows were too often ignored and handled roughly with cold hands.

Nancy, her face lean, her chin sharp, with an intensely blue stare, agreed. 'Grace has a special way with the animals. She talks to them so soft, and they do her bidding.'

'And is it the same with menfolk, Grace?' Alice asked.

Grace said nothing, bowing her head as the creamy milk splashed into the pail.

Alice smiled. 'I wish I could charm the man of my dreams. I can't even coax this cow to please me. I've laboured all day with one bad-tempered beast after another and my pails fill too slowly. Mistress Harriet is already angry with me.'

'Old Mother Harper is a triptaker – she finds fault where there is none,' Nancy said bitterly.

Alice agreed. 'And she hates us milkmaids – she is afraid that one of us will smile too sweetly at her son and he will smile back. He is very cheerful with the village maids – I am sure he is looking to choose a wife.'

'And there are few who would refuse him,' Nancy said. 'Nathaniel Harper is a good catch for any woman.'

Grace was not listening. As she was milking, her cheek touched the warm hide, breathing the cow's thick smell, encouraging her to relax too.

Alice smiled. 'So, Grace, can you charm the men as you do the animals?'

Nancy laughed. 'Grace, you must teach us your ways. There's many a young man in the parish who might take heed of a—'

'Why is there so much talking here?' An angry voice preceded the lean woman who marched into the barn, clad in a linen dress, kerchief and tidy bonnet. 'I pay you to milk the cows, not to loiter, Nancy Bryant. If you're going to chitter-chatter all day, then it's best you get yourself off home. And you too, Alice.'

Alice's creamy skin flushed pink with embarrassment. 'Oh, please forgive me, Mistress Harriet...'

'We were trying to coax the cows to give more milk, as Grace does – we weren't chattering...'

'Hush your mouth, Nancy.' Harriet Harper walked around, inspecting the pails. 'Grace, your pail is already full. Now leave this cow be, and bring in another.'

'I will turn her out into the field,' Grace said, but her fingers were stroking the cow's flanks. She whispered thanks to the cow and began to untie her.

Harriet was flushed and angry. 'She fills a pail in the time that you two take to fill half. Now make yourselves busy, both of you.'

'Yes, Mistress,' Nancy mumbled and Alice put her head down as if she was already working harder, both milkmaids gritting their teeth and pulling hard on the teats to prove that they were engrossed in filling their pails.

Grace moved her pail to one side and led the cow away towards the field. As she walked away, her boots soft in the mud, she heard Nancy Bryant grumbling about how the mistress would expect them to collect a lot more milk now Grace was working her magic with the cows. Grace's eyes flickered closed and she sighed. It was not her fault that she understood animals so readily: they recognised in an instant that she would be calm and patient with them.

When she reached the field, she glanced towards the hedgerow and noticed a cluster of pennywort, the pretty round leaves growing low to the ground. She would return later and pick an apron full: it was a beneficial herb for her father, with his stiffening joints, and it had many other uses: it was good for the heart, for the passing of water and it worked against melancholy. Besides, it tasted sweet raw and flavoursome in a stew pot.

Grace patted the cow, releasing her with a soft word and stared back towards the milking barn. She would work a little longer today, perhaps milk a dozen more cows, then it would be time for her to return to Slaugh Cottage. She had some mutton put by in the larder for a stew tonight and her father would be pleased to come home from ploughing to a fire roaring in the hearth.

She glanced across the field to where their cottage was nestled: from the vantage point of the farm, she could see the blackthorn tree against the side of the house, the taller trees a distance away, by the wooden gate. The well was visible in the corner and, opposite, her little plot of vegetables, herbs and flowers.

Grace turned towards the edge of the field, where a cow was moving towards her already, udders swinging heavily. Grace smiled and held out a hand.

* * *

Selena gazed briefly towards a field of cows and smiled as she drove the Škoda Fabia through twisting roads across the Blackdown Hills towards the village of Ashcombe, the satnav suggesting that she was less than a mile away. The roads narrowed, slicing through farmland and she hoped she wouldn't meet a piece of farm machinery coming towards her as she would have to reverse. There were fields either side full of pigs, sheep; a herd of cows stared out as she passed a barred gate, then she drove up a hill, took a left turn at a crossroads and the road became a lane with grass growing up the middle.

The satnav told her she had arrived and she gazed to the right, where a large white farmhouse gleamed from the top of a hill, then she saw, to the left, a pretty cottage nestled back from the road in its own garden. Selena recognised the front of Sloe Cottage from the photos on the website. She pulled in to a gravel drive and switched off the engine, leaning back in her seat, gazing at the white and stone-fronted cottage that would be her home for the next few months. The front garden was neat; primroses and bluebells were in bloom and an apple tree was about to flower. To the left was a quaint stone well and a spindly tree was in blossom outside the window.

Selena picked up her phone and checked the numbers of two missed calls: she was sure one was from Veronica, and she was determined that she wouldn't answer her again. She reminded herself to block the number. The second call had been from Claire, so Selena pressed a button to call her back.

'I've arrived,' Selena made her voice sound cheery; she had promised Claire that her time in rural Somerset would be about moving forwards, about recuperation and painting, not about being isolated and spending time regretting her relationship with David.

Claire sounded equally happy. 'I'm in the gallery and I've just sold another of your paintings, the one of the Horseshoe Pass. So, you'd better get cracking on some more – they are shifting like hot cakes.'

'I'll see what I can do,' Selena said. 'It seems really peaceful and calm here. There are plenty of gorgeous views.'

'What's the cottage like?' Claire asked, full of interest. 'I need to know what my bedroom is like – I'll be down in a few weeks for the weekend and you can take me to the local village pub. Oh, a rural retreat – I'm so excited.'

'I haven't been inside yet,' Selena replied. 'But I'll let you know.'

'Was it an easy drive down?'

'It took me four and a half hours, driving slowly, so you'd get down here in less than four.' Selena noticed the front door open and a woman appeared, waving an arm in her direction. 'Claire, I think that's Mrs Russell now – she's just come out of the cottage.'

'I expect she's been giving the place a quick once-over,' Claire said.

'I'll text you later – and send some photos.' Selena gesticulated towards the woman in the doorway, a light movement of her fingers. 'I'd better go.'

'I'm so excited – good luck,' Claire replied, then there was a click and she had gone.

Selena slid out of the car and moved towards the small, pleasant-faced woman who appeared to be in her sixties, wearing jeans and a light jacket, who was waiting for her.

'You must be Selena – I'm Lesley.' The woman held out a hand. Her hair was dark, streaked with grey, and she had a warm smile and cool fingers. 'You're a bit early.'

'The roads weren't too busy,' Selena said by way of apology. 'But I'm so excited to be here now.'

'Come on in – and welcome. I'll show you around Sloe Cottage.' Lesley Russell stood in the porch and held the door open. 'And we're just across the road in the farmhouse, if you need anything.' She pointed to the white house at the top of the hill. 'It will be nice to have a neighbour. Did you say you were an artist?'

'Yes.' Selena followed her into the hall. The air had suddenly become chilly and there was very little light. The floor was uneven and the walls were a mixture of grey stones and dark wood. She looked around. 'This hall must be very old.'

'The front part of the cottage is original, seventeenth century.'

Lesley waved a hand to propel them both forwards. 'Come on into the living room.'

Lesley led Selena into a square room with white walls and a large bay window, an alcove set into the corner. A fire was burning behind the glass doors of a wood-burning stove and a warm amber glow filled the hearth.

'I lit a fire for you.' Lesley indicated a pile of logs in a basket. 'You'll probably need the heating on throughout the summer. This room never seems to get very warm, especially since the windows aren't double glazed in here, but the wood burner gives it a lovely homely feel.'

'What can I smell?' Selena sniffed the air. 'Is that lavender?'

Lesley shook her head. 'It's too early for lavender, although there's some in the garden. Maybe the last tenant had a scented candle?'

Selena shivered. Her fingers were cold; despite the bright spring sunlight outside, the air held a stubborn chill. She stood closer to the stove and rubbed her palms together. 'This feels very homely and comfortable.'

'There is an original bread oven at the back too,' Lesley told her. 'Although it's not a working oven now. And over there in the corner, where there's an alcove in the wall, that used to be a stairway to the upstairs bedrooms. Of course, that's been gone a long time.'

'It all looks wonderful,' Selena gazed at the soft mustard-coloured sofa in front of the fire, the light wooden dining table in the corner. 'I'll enjoy spending time in here.'

Lesley met her eyes. 'Most people who stay here seem to prefer to be in the extension – it's warmer and more modern. Come and see the kitchen and then we'll go upstairs. I suggest you sleep in the master bedroom – that area of the house was added much later, in the nineteenth century. This old part is quite dark, but you'll love the bright extended kitchen – it's the heart of the home – and the oak conservatory was added recently. It'll be a perfect place for your painting.'

'It will,' Selena agreed, but Lesley had already left the room and was on her way towards the kitchen, chattering about the lobby that led there, how there was a useful pantry for dried goods and cans, how it had been a small back room for storage many years ago.

Selena turned to follow, but her eyes were held by a movement outside the window. The blackthorn branch twitched, rattling the windowpane, a movement on the wind, pressing creamy blossom against the glass. Selena pulled herself away and followed Lesley through the lobby into the kitchen.

6

_____

Lesley showed Selena around the house through the spacious kitchen and up the narrow staircase, along the landing with two bedrooms and a family bathroom, insisting that she'd be most comfortable in the master suite. Selena agreed: it was a bright room with a new en-suite shower room above the kitchen that overlooked the back garden, and the pretty white wallpaper with tiny daisies was much more uplifting than the cold, gloomy second bedroom. Lesley explained that the spare bedroom had been two small rooms in the seventeenth century, but now it was one long room which seemed to be in perpetual shadow despite the bright curtains and duvet, because it was situated over the chilly lounge. Keeping the fire on downstairs would soon warm the space for any visitors Selena might have, Lesley reassured her.

They came back downstairs and Lesley made herself and Selena a cup of tea while showing her where everything was in the kitchen. She had already stocked the fridge with basics and had bought two bottles of wine, one red, one white, as a welcome present. A bunch of daffodils had been placed in a clear vase on the window ledge and there were fresh vegetables in a wooden rack. Selena cradled her mug in her hands, feeling the heat warm her fingers. The kitchen was cosy; a bright red oil-fired Aga belted out heat as they sat at the wooden table, an opened packet of biscuits between them.

'So,' Lesley said. 'What do you think of the oak conservatory?'

Selena smiled. 'It's perfect. I can't wait to move my art materials in there. It's going to be a really good space to work in.'

'And there's a sofa and a small TV in there too, so you could make it your main living space, with it being so warm and so bright.'

'I might.' Selena sipped her tea. 'So, do you own the land around here, Lesley?'

'My great-grandfather owned all of it, as far as you could see, years ago – but over time, a lot of the land was sold off to local farmers. Sloe Cottage was built for farm workers, but my husband and I run it as a holiday cottage now.'

'It's a lovely home,' Selena said. 'When was it last occupied?'

'A family rented it over the Christmas period.' Lesley frowned. 'It's been used more as a short-term stay, Airbnb. You're the first person who has stayed longer than a fortnight in years.' She offered a cheery smile. 'So, anything you need, just pop over. We'll keep you supplied with eggs – we have dozens of chickens.'

'Oh, that's so kind of you.'

'Hilltop Farm used to be much bigger, but we keep a cottage garden and a couple of horses in the paddock now Ian and I are retired. One of the fields beyond this cottage is ours too – usually we let other farmers keep their sheep and cows there, but you're welcome to use it if you need to paint. There's lots of wildlife around here – rabbits, squirrels, foxes. You might even see deer.'

'Oh, lovely.' Selena was already imagining photographing animals, sketching and painting them. 'And what about the village? There's a pub and a shop, isn't there?'

'Yes, The Royal Oak and a mini supermarket in the Post Office. Ashcombe's a very friendly place and just a short walk from Chitterwell.'

'Chitterwell?'

'Oh, yes, this area around here, these two cottages with the farm-land, is called Chitterwell – the village itself is Ashcombe.'

'Okay.' Selena gazed around the kitchen. 'Well, I'm looking forward to cooking my first supper here tonight.'

Lesley scraped back her chair. 'Then I'll leave you in peace. Don't forget – Ian and I are just across the road if you need anything.'

'Thanks,' Selena said. 'I think I'll use the rest of the afternoon to unpack my things.'

'Right-ho. Now...' Lesley counted on her fingers 'Today's the second of April, so you're all paid up until the end of June, with the option of staying on longer if you want to. And, of course, do feel free to have visitors.'

'My friend, Claire, will come down – she's my business partner in Manchester.'

'It will be nice for you to have some company – the village is fairly quiet, although Taunton's busy, and only twenty minutes away if you need a bit of life...'

Selena wondered if Lesley was about to ask if she had a partner, but her expression clouded over and for a moment, she was lost in thought, then she smiled again.

'Well, I wish you a wonderful stay, Selena.'

'Thanks.' Selena held out a hand. 'It's great to be here. I'm going to enjoy it so much.'

* * *

Several hours later, Selena had moved her belongings into the cottage. Her art materials had been set up in the conservatory and her clothes had been put away neatly in the main bedroom. Her photographic bag was on the table, containing a digital SLR that took sharp pictures of her paintings for the website. She glanced at the two bottles of wine Lesley had left on the table, but she wasn't ready to drink alcohol yet. She'd save them for another time, perhaps when Claire came down to visit.

Selena glanced at the kitchen clock; it was past six and she had a slight gnawing sensation in her stomach. She hadn't eaten since breakfast. She sighed; a sandwich would do, maybe she'd make something small later. She rubbed her fingertips against her temples, chiding herself; she intended to build up her strength again, both physically and emotionally, and that meant regular meals, immersing herself in the rhythm of work and taking long walks in the spring sunshine. She needed this time alone to get over the feeling of loss that still rested on her shoulders like heavy hands. Thoughts of David made her feel foolish now; she had ignored the warning signs that he'd never leave Veronica. And the memory of losing the baby made her eyes fill with tears. The miscarriage had left her feeling lonely, empty and fragile. But she would build up her strength here in Sloe Cottage.

Selena picked up her phone. The camera was a good one, bought specifically for taking landscape pictures that would support her painting. She took a photo of the kitchen, the red Aga, the daffodils in the window, and sent it to Claire with the message:

With greetings from Sloe Cottage.

She received an immediate reply:

It all looks lovely. I'm off to the wine bar soon – but I can't wait to slum it in the countryside.

Selena rested her head in her hands; Claire would be out until the early hours, drinking and laughing. Selena had lived the same lifestyle once, meeting friends, enjoying late-night parties, not long before she'd met David; she wasn't sure that lifestyle would suit her now, probably not ever again.

A missed call on her phone caught her eye; it was Veronica again. Selena had done the right thing in coming to stay in Somerset. She didn't want to wallow in the memories of betrayal and she wasn't ready to answer Veronica's many questions. She wasn't running away; she was allowing herself time and space to heal. With that thought uppermost in her mind, she blocked Veronica's number then she burst into tears. Thoughts of the baby she had already begun to love filled her with an almost unbearable sense of loss.

Selena took a deep breath. She would explore the cottage; she gazed towards the door that led to the bright oak-framed conservatory beyond the kitchen, where her art materials were laid out. But, instead, she went in the other direction, through the lobby, past the pantry and into the living room. The light outside was grey, but inside the room glowed orange with the warmth from the wood fire and one small table lamp. Selena moved to the mustard-coloured sofa and sank into its depths, then she stretched out her palms towards the wood-burning stove, warming them, and opened the doors, picking up a log, throwing it onto the fire. The log crackled and flames licked.

* * *

Grace stretched out her palms, warming them, and picked up a log, throwing it onto the open fire. The log caught, sparks flying up the chimney. Her father was dozing in his chair after a long day at work so she smoothed a lock of hair from his eyes. A tired sigh shuddered from his lips as she wandered quietly away.

It was cool outside in the garden, the skies starless, the moon a thin crescent that hung low. Grace inhaled the fragrance of damp grass and something else, a sharp scent – a vixen was nearby, probably with her cubs born in March. She stood by the blackthorn tree, fingering the sharp spikes, then she went to the well, staring into the darkness. She whispered to herself, 'Rose petals and honey, I could make a love potion from them, that would bring him to me. But perhaps if I just say his name and ask for him to appear...'

Grace mouthed one word like a charm, the moon slipped overhead and, for a second, she saw traces of silver reflected at the bottom of the well. She gathered her apron and strolled towards a clump of nettles at the edge of the garden. The tips would be new and fresh. With strong fingers, she pinched the leaves, dropping the nettle tops into her bunched apron. Above her, an owl fluttered its wings as it flew towards a tree beyond the gate, settling on a branch in a rustle of leaves.

Then she was alerted to a noise down the road, heavy rhythmic footfall: she saw the shape, a man walking down the lane towards the gate. She recognised the swagger; even though it was dark, she knew the silhouette, the tight breeches, the bright white of his shirt. Grace held her breath as Nathaniel Harper passed: he was on his way home and he was merry. He must have spent the evening in The Royal Oak.

He paused by the gate and she heard him call, 'Good evening to ye, Mistress Grace.'

Grace replied quietly, 'Master Nathaniel.' She was not sure if he had been mocking her with his courteous address, the tone of his voice too familiar, but he was still there, leaning against the gate, watching her.

'Next week is the May Day revelry on the village green. I hope you will not refuse a dance with me.'

Grace waited, unsure what to say, then she murmured, 'Good night to you, Master Nathaniel.'

He laughed, a soft sound of contentment, and walked away. 'Good night, Mistress Grace,' came back on the night air and she realised her heart was beating fast.

Grace brought the ends of her apron tightly together, the nettles enclosed in the folds, and dashed back towards the house. She rushed inside, shutting the door, into the warmth of the room. Her father was still asleep in front of the grate, one side of his face burnished red in the warm glow. A single light from a candle flickered.

She slipped quietly into the back room, dropping the new leaves into water from the jug, then into the vessel to be crushed with a pestle. She brought her work to the table, pounding and grinding the nettle leaves while her father snored quietly. As Grace crushed the leaves to a pulp, her mind was not on her task. She was thinking about May Day, about wearing the cream dress her grandmother had embroidered with little blackthorn flowers; she was imagining herself dancing in the warm embrace of the handsome farmer's son. She saw herself smiling up at him, wearing a garland of flowers, the music of the pipe and tabor resounding in her ears.

* * *

Selena opened her eyes and blinked into the firelight, suddenly awake. The logs in the wood-burning stove blazed as she placed several more inside and closed the doors, hoping there would still be embers to coax to life in the morning. The room was dark, shadows lurking, one small lamp glimmering in the corner. It was late, past eleven; Selena had dozed for several hours. She would get up tomorrow, eat breakfast and start painting.

She stretched out her arms and sighed, easing herself from the sofa, switching off the lamp. The room was suddenly pitch black and Selena felt her way to the door, leaving it ajar as she padded on soft feet into the lobby. The air was icy as she wandered towards the light that came from the kitchen. Selena climbed the stairs to the landing; she was tired but full of optimism. From nowhere, a little folk tune was buzzing in her mind, the joyful sound of pipes, the beat of a drum. She began to sing in a whisper:

> *'I have been wandering all this night,*
> *And some time of this day,*
> *And now returning home again,*
> *I've brought you a branch of May.'*

Selena passed the second bedroom, pushing open the door into the master, and gazed at the pretty white flowers on the wallpaper, her pyjamas already laid out on the bed, her toiletries arranged in the ensuite. She placed her phone on the bedside table and picked up her toothbrush. Downstairs, she heard the door to the lobby close with a soft clunk.

7

Selena stood back in the bright oak-framed conservatory to study her painting: the garden was corn-yellow, basking in a shaft of sunlight. Bluebells, tulips and daffodils crowded together in a mass of colour, tall trees behind, then the field stretching away into the distance. It was not finished yet, but it exuded rural tranquility. She had worked on it and its companion – the field of cows leading to Hilltop Farm – on and off for just over two weeks and she was pleased with her work. Claire would be delighted; the paintings would be popular in the gallery, celebrating exactly the sort of scenery that many people wanted to display in their own homes. She took several photos and sent them to Claire for their website with a brief affectionate message. She was in a hurry to start on her next picture; the spring weather was here and she wanted to be outside, to paint the front garden, the trees and the view of the farm opposite.

The last two weeks had been perfectly quiet, just as Selena had hoped; she had the luxury of time for herself, to paint and reflect and heal. Lesley had called round twice with eggs and stayed to chat for half an hour or so, but otherwise Selena had enjoyed the solitude.

She picked up her paintbrush, making a small adjustment, then her phone buzzed and she assumed that it was Claire commenting on the photos. She held it to her ear. 'Hello?'

A low voice filled her ear. 'Selena, I need to talk to you, please.'

'Veronica...' Selena caught her breath. She had blocked the number: it must be a different phone.

Veronica's tone was flat. 'I came to see you in the gallery, but you weren't there. There are so many things I need to know and David won't talk to me about it.'

'Please, let's just move on, if we can,' Selena said.

'The point is, he says that you tried to break up our marriage, but I'm so confused. It's not making sense – what was his part in it all?' Veronica's voice shook. 'There's so much I don't understand. How long have you known him? How did you meet?'

'I can't really talk about it. I'm so sorry – I just want some peace and quiet...' Selena trailed off. Veronica had already started to ask more questions and Selena knew she couldn't mention the baby. Her throat was suddenly swollen and her eyes filled with tears. She muttered, 'I hope you can find some peace...' and cut off the call, moving her fingers swiftly to block the new number, a landline.

Claire would be in the gallery, on her own and probably busy, so Selena wiped her eyes and texted her friend quickly to explain that Veronica was pushing for answers again. Claire's response was immediate and soothing: Selena must simply stop taking Veronica's calls and take time to focus on her own healing.

She put down her brushes and placed a cool palm against her forehead; in truth, she felt sorry for Veronica, who was frantically seeking answers to the questions that David clearly was avoiding. He had betrayed them both and Selena wished that she could say that. But Veronica was desperate to believe that her husband was the innocent party.

Selena needed a break; she'd make a cup of tea; it was almost lunchtime. She'd go for a walk in the afternoon and take her sketch pad. She wanted to make another rough drawing of the blackthorn tree, but this time in close detail: a thorny branch, a single blossom.

There was a loud rap at the front door; someone was banging the heavy brass knocker: it wasn't Lesley's usual soft tap-tap. Selena pushed her phone into a pocket and wandered through the living room, momentarily checking that the fire was still glowing through the glass doors of the wood burner, and into the hall. She opened the door to see a fresh-faced woman wearing round glasses, her shoulder-length hair a pretty pale lilac colour.

The woman leaned forward and offered a cheery smile. 'Hello. You've just moved in recently, haven't you? I called round to see how you were settling in.'

Selena was a little dumbfounded. 'Yes, fine thanks...'

The woman thrust out a hand. 'I'm Laura Fletcher. I live in Ashcombe. I heard an artist had moved in here, so I thought I'd pay you a visit.'

'Ah, I'm...' Selena was conscious that she probably had paint on her face. 'Yes, I've come here to paint.'

The woman smiled broadly. 'That's wonderful. I'm so glad there's a new face in the village. I hope it's okay to pop in and give you a quick heads-up on the place – it's not as if I don't have plenty of free time. I'm not interrupting you mid-brushstroke, am I?'

'Oh – not at all, er – would you like to come in for a cup of tea? I'm Selena Cain, by the way.' Selena stepped backwards, not sure that she wanted a visitor, not yet. The cottage was her place of solitude, still filled with thoughts of her baby. But she knew she ought to make an effort to be sociable.

Laura was already inside the door, gazing around the hall. 'I'd love a cuppa, thanks, Selena – just ordinary tea, builder's, two sugars and milk. Isn't this a beautiful old cottage?' She glanced at the stonework for a moment, taking in the dark wood, then she rushed forwards, impatient to see the rest of the house. 'The hall is so original... and look at this lovely sitting room. And it's so cosy with the fire on. Mind you, you need it in here, all these thick stone walls.' Selena led the way to the kitchen and Laura added, 'Our old cottage has been renovated over the years too, but, oh, look at this lovely kitchen, and the conservatory. I live with my dad. He's been widowed for a year and he's been finding it a bit tough. Our place is poky by comparison.' She settled herself in a chair at the table and watched Selena fill the kettle. 'So, are you here by yourself or with family?'

Selena shook her head, a little overwhelmed. She was unsure how to explain the real reason why she had fled to Somerset so she said, 'By myself – it's a painting retreat.'

'Oh, how glorious,' Laura said. 'Please promise me I'm not interrupting your work...?'

'I was about to stop for a break.' Selena tried a welcoming smile as she poured hot water onto teabags. 'It's perfect timing.'

'I hope you don't mind me calling in on the off-chance,' Laura raised her eyebrows. Selena placed a mug in front of her and a packet of chocolate biscuits. Laura ripped the packet open and took one. 'My favourites – make sure I don't have more than two.'

'Not at all.' Selena sat down at the table. 'So, tell me about the village? How long have you lived here?'

Laura waved a hand. 'I came here just before Christmas – I'm a comparative newcomer. My dad retired to Ashcombe after being a history teacher in Minehead. He has lived here for over ten years, a year by himself, bless him.' She paused for a moment, her expression filled with sadness, then she reached for another biscuit. 'Before I came to Ashcombe, I lived in Bristol and I taught at a primary school. I loved it. But then my contract came to an end – it was a temporary post, covering for someone on maternity leave. And my mum had passed, and my dad was so lonely. He's always forgetting to take his blood pressure tablets; he's a bit self-absorbed and doesn't get out enough, and I was jobless, so – here I am, back in the family nest.' She rubbed her hands together. 'I'm just itching for a project, though. I help out here at the local primary whenever I can, which is one reason for me visiting you, actually. There are no art teachers there... Do you think you could find time to pop into the school, maybe do a workshop with years five and six?' Laura raised dog paws, begging. 'The pupils would be so grateful. And you're going to love it here. Ashcombe's lovely.'

'Well, I've come here to paint,' Selena explained again. 'I share a little gallery in Manchester with a friend – she's my flat mate – and I'm hoping I'll have lots of paintings finished by the end of June. But I don't see why not. I'm staying for a few months and I might be able to spare the time...' Selena examined the paint on her hands, imagining herself standing in front of a classroom full of lively youngsters. She wasn't sure that she was ready for that, not yet, but here she was again, agreeing to please others.

They sat quietly for a few moments drinking tea. Selena watched Laura gaze around the room, her eyes busily taking in every detail. Then she helped herself to biscuits, chattering about the weather, the friendly people in the village, how Selena would soon become part of the community. Selena nodded, trying to listen, but her thoughts kept sliding back to her life in Manchester, to the future she'd hoped for, the precious life she had lost. It felt strange, the idea of becoming sociable again, making new friends, and the possibility of visiting a school made her skin prickle with apprehension. But Selena reminded herself that she'd intended to try harder, and the arrival of this bubbly visitor gave her the perfect opportunity.

Then Laura drank the last mouthful of tea and her eyes widened with sudden interest. 'Can I see some of your pictures?'

'Come through to the conservatory,' Selena scraped her chair back, smiling warmly. 'I've completed two, more or less, and a pad load of sketches. Come and see.'

Selena led the way into the bright room where two easels stood holding canvases. Laura gasped. 'Oh, these are lovely – you're so talented.'

'I'm glad you like them.'

'You'll have to come up to the cottage and have tea...' Laura was full of enthusiasm. 'It's been great meeting you, and I do hope I can organise a date for you to pop into the primary school. I'll talk to the class teacher, Scott, and we'll catch up again soon.'

'Yes, I'd like that.' Selena gazed at the woman in gold-framed glasses with lilac hair, who was wearing patched jeans and a casual jacket. She was warming to her. A local friend would be nice.

'Do you drink?' Laura asked and noticed Selena's anxious expression. 'I don't mean like a fish, I mean the odd drink at a pub. Only, we could meet at The Royal Oak for a glass of something. Maybe this Saturday – what's that? The twenty-third. At half seven, how would that be?'

'That would be lovely – shall I drive there?'

'No, it's only a short walk from here. Give me your number. I'll meet you in the bar. The Royal Oak does great cider – I'm quite partial to a pint of Badger Spit.'

Selena scribbled her phone number on a piece of paper. 'I have a lot to learn about living in Somerset, but that would be lovely. I'll look forward to seeing you on Saturday.'

Laura said, 'My dad probably won't even notice I've popped out – he'll be in his office, on the computer. He's currently researching the Romans' time in Somerset. This morning at breakfast he was telling me all about how they mined lead, built villas and founded the city of Bath. I've persuaded him to do a talk with the primary children too, telling them about it all.' She led the way back to the door. 'But I'm so glad we've met. And thanks for the tea and the choccie biccies – I'm afraid I finished off half the packet.'

'That's not a problem — I was supposed to stop you, wasn't I?' Selena opened the heavy door and gazed into the garden. The trees by the gate were swaying in a strong breeze.

'I'll walk off the calories on the stroll home,' Laura joked. 'And you must come round for a cuppa to meet my dad. We live in one of the cottages near St Bart's, that's the church. He has such an extensive knowledge of the area and the history. He drives me mad with it sometimes, but I'm so glad he has a hobby.' She hugged Selena spontaneously. 'It's been lovely to meet you.'

'It has. I'll see you on Saturday.' Selena watched as Laura hurried away, through the wooden gate, turning left towards Ashcombe with a final wave of her hand. She waved back and was about to close the door as a gust of wind blew dust into the hall, a swirl of tiny particles landing by her feet.

Selena pushed the door closed and wandered back into the living room. She paused to sit by the fire, opening the doors of the wood burner, adding another log, feeling suddenly alone. Her phone buzzed in her pocket: it was Claire. Selena held the phone to her ear. 'Hi.'

Claire's voice came back to her quickly, a little breathless, as if she was in a rush. 'How's life in the sticks?'

'Great...'

'I have to say, I'm loving the paintings. The photos you sent are wonderful.'

'There will be plenty more where they came from. I'm enjoying it here.' Selena was filled with the desire to spend time with her oldest friend who knew her best. 'When are you coming to stay?'

'Well, I thought I'd drive down in a couple of weeks' time, on the first and second of May – the second is a Monday, a bank holiday, so I won't need to close the gallery. I can take some finished paintings back with me, if you like.'

'Perfect.'

'Selena...' Claire's voice had changed from excited to concerned. 'I got your text from earlier. So Veronica phoned you again?'

'Apparently she came to the gallery to look for me.'

'Did she? I must have been too busy to notice,' Claire said.

Selena exhaled sadly. 'I feel sorry for her. David is playing us off against each other...'

'I know. She should know the truth about him though.'

'I don't want anyone to know about, you know, the miscarriage... it'll take me some time to get over it.' Selena heard the wobble in her voice.

'Of course,' Claire replied quickly. 'So – what are you up to now? It's been so busy in the gallery; I've been rushed off my feet.'

'I feel guilty.'

'Well, don't. You're not to worry. You're painting cows and trees in the wilds of Somerset and I can cope here. If I can't, I'll buy in some help. I'm thinking of taking on an assistant anyway. An extra pair of hands would free me up to come and visit – and we can afford it.'

'That's a good idea...'

'Oh, I'd better go.' Claire's voice became suddenly softer. 'Some more customers have just come into the shop. We'll talk later. Take care. Lots of love...'

The phone crackled and was silent. Selena leaned back into the softness of the sofa and closed her eyes. It was comfortable, relaxing with her feet stretched out, her legs warmed by the blaze. She exhaled and thought about David, recalling sadly that his declarations of eternal love had only ever come from momentary passion; he'd never shared her serious plans for a future together. She knew she would have coped much better with his betrayal and the sense of being second best if she hadn't lost the baby. Then, from nowhere, her face was covered with tears and again she was filled with the familiar aching emptiness.

Selena snuffled, curling into the soft cushions of the sofa and a tendril of hair fell across her cheek. She stayed where she was, immobile, wet-faced, thinking. Then a touch, delicate as slender fingers, moved the strands back, a light brush of wind. Selena opened her eyes and sat up straight, putting a hand to her hair, smoothing it quickly. A gust of wind blew around her shoulders, a draught from the window, and she shivered. She leaned towards the fire and stretched out her hands: they were chilled, her skin goose flesh. Selena frowned; she would go back to the warmth of the kitchen, make a sandwich and then pull on her jacket and boots and go out for a walk. The fresh air outside, the trees and the farmland, were calling to her.

8

Grace lifted her chin high and stood up straight as Bett made some final adjustments to the cream dress festooned with embroidered blossoms. Her grandmother was chattering as she fitted the bodice. 'They say King Charles's Portuguese wife, Queen Catherine, can't produce an heir; I've heard tell that she's been with child four times and four times she's lost the baby or it has been stillborn. That's ill news.'

'So who will be King after Charles?'

Bett screwed up her face, tight as a walnut, showing disapproval. 'His brother, James, Duke of York could be next in line. It won't go well, I'm sure of it, with him being a Catholic. I'm glad we live here in the South West, Gracie – I wouldn't want to live in London. There's always trouble of some sort brewing there, and they say it's full of wagtails and kencrackers – women and men who are not fair company for the likes of decent folk like us.'

'But London's where the King lives,' Grace said, smoothing the cream linen with her fingers. 'Surely he doesn't surround himself with trollops and thieves...' She put a hand to her mouth.

'Let God be their judge. In London, they've had plagues, fires, three wars against the Dutch people, and they say you can't get a fresh carrot or a broad bean there. No, we live in the best place, Gracie, you mark my words. There, you're all done.' Bett stood back to survey her handi-work. 'Pretty as a picture, I'd say.'

Grace sighed. 'So, now I am ready for bringing in May today on the village green.'

'Indeed, and you must dance alongside all the other maids of the parish. But you will be the fairest of all, I'm sure. And let's hope you catch the eye of some proper gentleman.'

Grace shook her head. 'We have spoken of this...'

'We have...' Bett took her hand and led her to sit down at the table, where two mugs of mulled cider had been filled. Bett moistened her lips eagerly. 'But you have no mother now, Gracie, and so it befalls me to say this to you in her place. Your father is a good man, but he is made old by work and I have outlasted my years now. You do not want to be left alone when we have both departed this world. You want the comfort of a man to care for and protect you. You should have the joy of little ones clambering about your skirts.'

Grace put a hand to her cheeks, feeling them glow. 'I have never thought of such things. I have always imagined that I would stay with father.'

'Will Cotter has agues in his bones and a cough in his chest... I fear he will not last another winter.' Bett shook her head. 'We need to think of your future.'

Grace felt tears spring to her eyes. She reached for her mug but could not drink: the thought of life without her beloved father, without her grandmother too, was beyond her imagination.

Bett frowned. 'You are an innocent, my child. There are things in this world that you know nothing of...'

'Like being a wife, a mother?'

'Oh, those things come readily to a woman. No, I am talking of the wide world outside this village. Have you ever heard the tale of an old widow woman called Elizabeth Stile?'

'I can't say that I have...'

'You'd have been just a child. It was all the talk here for a while, some sixteen years ago. She was held in Taunton assizes, accused of witchcraft. The MP and justice of the peace over in Taunton, Robert Hunt, who died a few years past, had been on the lookout across Somerset for witches and he tried her in his courts. Everyone said she was a nasty piece of work. She bewitched a young girl, made her have fits of coughing every day until her lungs were shreds. Robert Hunt found a mark on Elizabeth Stile that looked like a morsel of beef. That marked her as a true witch. She died in the jail, and good riddance, I say. Women like that are to be avoided, Gracie. Even men have been accused of evil deeds and witchcraft. Around the same time, they hanged a man called Julian Cox – he bewitched a young woman, took her health away until there was nothing left of her but a single sigh.'

Grace shivered. 'What has that to do with me?'

'A young woman on her own is prey to such wicked creatures.' Bett shook her head. 'You need a husband to take care of you.' She took a deep draught of mulled cider. 'Now go on with you, my girl – get yourself over to the village green and enjoy the dancing and the music of the pipes and tabors. And perhaps today a certain young man's eye will settle upon you...'

Grace pointed to a garland she had brought in her basket. 'I have made my own coronet of blossom from my blackthorn tree.'

Bett approached, her eyes shining, and led her to the doorway, where she placed the garland on her granddaughter's head. She repeated lines from an old poem in a low voice:

'Here's not a budding boy, or girl, this day,
But is got up, and gone to bring in May.'

Grace smiled, performing a pretty curtsey, then she was on her way through the low door and off towards the village green.

Bett watched her granddaughter go, her wrinkled hand an open palm against her heart. Grace was inexperienced, in many ways a child still. Bett whispered, 'God keep ye from wanton sport at the hands of wicked men, my little Gracie, and find yourself a good man to dance with. You want no tosspot, no angler, no pudding-headed fellow. Find yourself a proper man, one who will have you yoked and bedded and joyful in his arms. If you can be as happy as me and my John, or Will and my Anne, God rest her, you'll be truly blessed.'

* * *

The village green was crammed with dancers circling the maypole, mostly young women wearing light-coloured dresses, their hair festooned with floral garlands. As Grace approached, she recognised Alice and Nancy Bryant. They were kicking out their skirts, colourful ribbons clutched in their fists. When they noticed Grace, they stopped, whispering to each other, then they rushed over.

Alice, the prettier of the two sisters, round-faced, rosy and dimpled, began to examine Grace's dress, touching the fabric with long fingers. 'Oh, look at these pretty flowers. How did you embroider all of them? It must have taken an age.'

'I suppose you have little else to do at Slaugh Cottage, other than looking after your father?' Nancy narrowed intensely blue eyes.

'But now is the time for us all to make merry.' Alice seized Grace's hands. 'Come and dance with us.'

Grace felt herself being tugged forwards.

Alice was laughing, her long hair tumbling across her shoulders, as she joined the throng. 'Everyone is here, Grace, even our little sister, Jennet. She and my mother made her a dress and she wove her own garland out of petals.'

'She is only fifteen,' Nancy said dismissively, an expression of scorn on her face as she whirled in the dance. 'We don't want her here with us.'

'She may distract us from our task of finding a handsome partner.' Alice's eyes shone. 'Today is the first day of spring, and with it comes fun, revelry and love.'

'Oh, I hope I can dance with someone today.' Nancy rolled her eyes dreamily. 'I have someone in mind, a man who labours on the farm, whose name begins with G...'

Grace danced on; she was light on her feet, moving nimbly, a ribbon between her fingers. Alice and Nancy laughed giddily, and their joyful mood was infectious. Grace found herself lifted on the breezy tune from the pipes and the beat of the tabor. Then she became aware that a group of men were observing her and, in the centre, wearing a crisp white shirt, tight breeches and a broad-brimmed hat was Nathaniel Harper. Grace looked away; she could tell from their demeanour that the men were discussing the young women. Their heads were together and, by the volume of their voices, they were merry, having drunk an ale or two in The Royal Oak.

Alice and Nancy had noticed the men too and they were both suddenly more carefree, dancing with abandon, their heads back, laughing loudly. Grace felt her cheeks tingle and she was unsure whether to leave the dance or whether to continue, to pretend she had not seen the group of jovial men.

Then Nathaniel was next to her; he pulled Alice into his grasp and she was shrieking with joy. Grace thought she sounded like a happy chicken, but she pushed the unkind thought from her head. She over-heard Nathaniel declare, 'Today, Alice, I intend to dance with the loveliest young women in Ashcomb.'

A young thick-set man had caught hold of Nancy and they were whirling round together in step, her eyes never leaving his face. The music continued to play and Grace danced alone, her mind spinning as quickly as the ground around her. Then Nathaniel shifted deftly from Alice to Grace, taking her in his arms. She inhaled the smell of him, sweet hops and something else, a warm heady scent, as he pulled her to him.

He said, 'Do not deny me this dance, Grace,' and swept her away in a tight embrace, his strong arms holding her so firmly that she couldn't help but move in time with him. They swayed closely, their eyes locked, Grace almost afraid to breathe. Then she felt a hand tugging at her sleeve and their dancing stopped abruptly.

She gazed at young Jennet Bryant, the sister of Alice and Nancy, a garland askew on her tousled head, frowning. 'Grace Cotter?'

'I am...'

'Mistress White says you are to go to her cottage immediately. She says there is a task you must do with her at once. She says you are not to tarry.'

Grace hesitated; she was still in Nathaniel's arms and he would not let her loose. His dark blue eyes met hers and he pulled her to his chest. 'Grace – do not leave – stay here with me.'

'I must go – my grandmother calls me...'

'I beg you to stay awhile. I do not want to dance with anyone else...'

Reluctantly, Grace slid from his grip and hurried away towards her grandmother's cob cottage, lifting her skirts, not looking back. She felt Nathaniel's eyes on her as she rushed across the village green, the music still bubbling in her ears. Then, almost at her grandmother's house, she paused, turning to look. She could see him in the centre of the throng dancing with Alice Bryant.

Grace scurried through her grandmother's open door to find Bett, a filled basket in hand, a bonnet on her head.

'Come, child – put on your kerchief and cap and follow me. We must go.'

'But I was dancing...'

'Then you must put that aside until another day. We have been sent for. We must go to Kitty Stokes' house, who lives near the church with her husband, Edmund.'

'Is the baby coming now?'

'It is, and we must help her. It is a first birth and I cannot work alone. Kitty is small and her husband is a tall man. I fear the baby will not come easily. It is time for you to learn about these things, Gracie. You are of an age now.'

Grace followed Bett as they rushed along the path; the light sound of the music and the steady drum beat carried on the wind from the village green and, briefly, Grace wished she could be back there dancing in the arms of Nathaniel. But her thoughts moved quickly to poor Kitty Stokes in the throes of birth. Grace was keen to help her grandmother, who was surging ahead despite her advanced years, her breath puffing from her mouth. Grace thought about her grandmother's request for help and she was filled with sadness: it was Bett's unspoken intention to teach Grace all she knew so that Grace would continue to help all birthing mothers after her death.

'I will teach you all I know.' Bett seemed to hear Grace's thoughts. 'Are you afeared of what you will see?'

'I am,' Grace answered honestly, glancing at Bett's basket and the implements in there which she couldn't name but she would surely learn to use over time.

'Gracie, you must keep everything clean as you can. And I have oil of sweet almonds for rubbing on Kitty's body to calm her. If it is needed, I will use an eagle-stone to hasten labour...'

'What will I do?'

Bett made a soft sound. 'You will watch what I do and assist me. I will ask you to cut the navel string. Pray God we can deliver Kitty safely of this child.'

'Were you afraid, Grandmother, when you birthed my mother?'

'Of course – all women fear that they will die during birthing. I bore three babies, Gracie – Anne was the only child of mine to survive – I lost two more, a girl and a boy, before she came to me. But it is the natural thing for women to have children and to redeem the sin of Eve.' Bett caught her breath; they were almost at the church. 'Most women are afraid of lying-in at first, for themselves and also for the child. Many women will have six or seven children, but less than half of their babies will survive to become men and women.'

Grace stared, round-eyed. They had arrived at St Bartholomew's church and stood in front of a row of cottages opposite. Grace immediately knew which one belonged to Edmund and Kitty Stokes. She could hear a woman's voice from inside, at first as loud as a lowing heifer, then came a sound that was not human, an agonised throaty yell. A young man appeared at the door, his eyes staring wildly, his hair dishevelled. He called out to Bett, 'This way, Mistress White. And come quickly, please, for I fear for my Kitty's life.'

9

Selena stood in the street outside St Bartholomew's church, gazing at a cluster of tiny cottages, all smartly renovated. She wondered if Laura and her father lived in one of them: she had said her home was near the church. The Royal Oak was a few minutes' walk away and it was not quite seven fifteen; she would be early. She continued on, hugging her jacket tightly against the evening breeze. It seemed strange to Selena that she was in a small village, miles from Manchester, where she had casually strolled into wine bars and clubs by herself to meet friends, but here, in this remote rural place, walking into a little pub alone made her feel nervous.

The Royal Oak was a white stone-built building set back from the road; it claimed to be an original seventeenth-century inn and its low doors and small windows showed its original dimensions, although, as Selena walked in to the bar, the interior was open, modern and extended, with painted beams, comfortable cushion-covered seating and bright lights.

Laura was nowhere to be seen; the clock showed that it was just after seven-twenty. There were only a handful of customers, mostly middle-aged men seated in groups, supping pints. A restaurant in the adjoining room was half-full, several couples sharing dinner at small tables.

Selena approached the bar attendant, a woman who was wearing a spotted blouse; she greeted Selena with a friendly smile. 'Hello. What can I get you?'

'I'll have...' Selena tried to remember what Laura drank. 'Half a pint of Badger Spit, please.'

The woman moved to a pump, pulling the long handle. 'Are you visiting Ashcombe? Are you here by yourself?'

'I'm meeting someone.' Selena watched as the fizzy drink gurgled to the top of the glass, bubbles rising and frothing over the surface. 'I'm staying locally.'

'She's living in Sloe Cottage, up in Chitterwell,' a deep voice behind her remarked.

Selena twisted round; she wasn't sure which one of the four men at the table had made the comment. She studied them; two were older men, wearing flat caps and heavy coats, huddled over pints of beer. The other two were younger, one slim with thinning hair and glasses, intellectual-looking, and one muscular, broad-shouldered, with a ready grin.

Selena nodded. 'Yes, I'm renting Sloe Cottage.' She assumed that, since they knew already, there could be no harm in saying so.

The slim, intellectual-looking man nodded. 'Ian Russell told me he had a renter. He says you're an artist, from the north.'

'Manchester, that's right.' Selena sipped from her glass of cider. The drink was sweet, fizzing on her tongue.

'It's a nice place, Sloe Cottage. Ian's done a lot of work to it over the years. I helped him build the conservatory.' The muscular man offered a friendly smile.

'It's very old though,' one of the cap-wearing men said, staring into his pint. 'There's a lot of history in there.'

'Yes,' Selena agreed. 'I'd like to find out more about it.'

'Oh, I'm sure that can be arranged,' the man in the cap replied matter-of-factly, glancing towards his companions.

'How are you finding life there?' The intellectual man's glasses shone. 'It's not everybody's cup of tea, Chitterwell being a walk up from the village.'

'Oh, I really like it,' Selena said, sipping her drink again. 'It's a lovely house and I'm feeling quite settled already.'

'Friendly folk here, mostly,' the other man in a cap agreed.

'So, welcome to Ashcombe and The Royal Oak.' The muscular man hadn't lost his grin as he lifted a half-pint glass.

'Thanks.' Selena glanced at the door; a woman with lilac hair had blundered into the pub, waving an arm.

'I'm so sorry I'm late, Selena.' Laura turned to the men. 'Evening, gents. How are you all?'

One of the men said, 'Evening, Laura. Not too bad. How's your father?'

'Hi, Scott. He's on the internet, roaming through Roman Somerset again, looking at the city of Bath, which used to be called Aquae Sulis apparently,' Laura breathed, her voice oozing patience. The bar assistant had already poured half a pint of Badger Spit. 'Thanks, Angie – shall we sit over here, Selena?' Laura pointed to a low wooden table and two armchairs, next to the hearth. The fire was unlit; a metal container of dried leaves had been placed in the grate.

The women sat down. Laura adjusted her glasses.

'Lovely to catch up again. I see you've met some of the locals.'

'They seem nice.'

Laura lowered her voice. 'Jack and Owen Jeffries are brothers – they own most of the farmland around here, including a lot of the fields up at Chitterwell. Matty Boswell does a lot of work for them – tree felling, hedging. And Scott Finch teaches in the primary school. They are all lovely people – they'll help you out if you need anything.'

'That's good to know,' Selena said.

Laura reached for her pint. 'So – how is the work going?'

'Great.' Selena's face shone. 'I've completed two paintings of the oak tree just beyond the gate of the cottage; one is a view from the trunk, looking up into the branches at acorns, and the other is a close-up of the bark. I managed to work in some interesting shades of the texture, the gnarled greys and browns.'

'I must come over and see,' Laura said. 'If I'm invited.'

'Come to dinner.' Selena was pleased with herself: she had been spontaneous in her invitation. It was a step forward to becoming more sociable, to healing.

Laura widened her eyes. 'Oh, I'd love to, yes please.'

'My friend, Claire, is coming to stay with me at the end of the bank holiday weekend – why don't you come then, on the Sunday evening? You could bring your father.'

'That would be fantastic – and it would be so good for him to get out socially – everything he does is with local history groups, which are mostly older men. So don't be surprised if he starts telling everyone all about the Roman cemetery unearthed in Somerton.'

'He sounds really interesting – and I'm always looking for new places to paint.' Selena cradled her glass. 'It's working out really well, being here.'

'Don't you miss your life in Manchester? Isn't it too quiet here in the sticks? I know I miss the life I had in Bristol sometimes, having friends round, the house parties.'

'I miss the gallery and Claire, yes, but…' Selena chose her words. 'I came here to get some peace and quiet.'

'I don't suppose there was a man behind your decision to get away for a bit, someone you don't want to bump into? There usually is, in my experience.' Laura pressed Selena's hand. 'Oh, I don't mean to intrude – how rude of me.'

Selena smiled. 'No, you're exactly right. David… I didn't realise he was married – then I did, and he told me it was over with his wife… he promised me it was, and I believed him. I was so wrong…'

'Oh, Selena…' Laura made a fist and rapped the table. 'How could he cheat on his wife and string you along like that? It makes my blood boil.'

Selena was surprised to hear herself blurt out, 'I was pregnant and that's why he left me. Then he told his wife I'd been pestering him, and she phoned me, wanting to know the truth...'

'That's awful.' Laura was full of sympathy. She spoke softly. 'And what about the baby?'

'I lost it...'

'Oh, you poor love, no wonder you came here for a break.'

Selena felt familiar tears cloud her eyes. 'I'm so sorry, Laura – I didn't mean to tell you all my troubles...'

'I'm glad you did. Now I understand why you came here, and anything I can do to help, don't hesitate to ask.' Laura's expression was full of concern. 'I really mean it.'

'You're helping more than you know,' Selena said slowly, realising the truth of her words. 'I feel a lot better, having told someone else besides Claire.'

'And is his wife still phoning you?'

'I've blocked her calls. She must feel so insecure – she keeps asking me lots of questions, but I'm not up to talking about David yet. She clearly loves him.' Selena shrugged. 'He is very persuasive, very easy to believe.'

'It must be so hard for you...' Laura jumped as her own phone began to ring. 'Oh, I'm sorry, I must get this.' She pressed the phone against her ear. 'Hello, ah, what's happened, Dad?' She frowned, listening. 'Oh, don't worry. I'll be on my way soon. No, it's no trouble at all, honestly – I'll be ten minutes.'

'Is everything all right...?' Selena began.

'That was my father.' Laura reached for her cider and drank the last quarter of a pint in two gulps. 'He's due to take his evening tablets and he can't find his medication. I know exactly where it is. He often loses things when he's busy researching. He can only concentrate on one thing at a time.'

'Is he very old?'

'Seventy-two – so no, and he's fit as a fiddle apart from the blood pressure being a bit high, but he can be very fastidious with his research and he gets so involved in it, nothing else seems to matter, and he loses things. I'm the same – I must get it from him.' Laura laughed, then sadness clouded her face. 'My mother was organised and sensible.'

Selena offered her a warm smile. 'Oh, well, we've almost finished our drink – you'd better head back and help him out.'

'I could have managed another. I'm so sorry to have to leave so soon – I feel awful.'

'Please don't worry. We can do this again...'

'Definitely.' Laura scraped back her seat and called across the bar. 'Jack, could you give Selena a lift home?'

'I don't need a lift, honestly,' Selena said. 'I can walk.'

One of the men in flat caps replied, his voice a deep rumble, 'I'm not going home just yet, Laura.'

'Oh, I just thought...' Laura waved a hand.

'I'll give you a lift – I ought to be getting back now.' The younger muscular man stood up; he was tall and sturdy in jeans and T-shirt. 'I've only had a half of Badger – I'll get you home in no time.' He jingled his car keys.

Laura smiled. 'You'll be all right with Matty.' She bent forward and kissed Selena's cheek. 'I'm really sorry to have to rush off. I'll make it up to you. I'll text. Bye, Selena.' She rushed to the bar and handed over some money, then hurried towards the door, turned to wave and was gone.

Selena glanced across the bar where the young man was already by the door, delving in his pocket for his keys. She left her drink unfinished and stood up, not wanting to keep him waiting. 'It's very kind of you to offer me a lift.'

'It's no problem at all,' the man said amiably.

Five minutes later, Selena was sitting in the tattered seat of a faded Land Rover. Matty had started the engine and it was rattling loudly. Selena was suddenly uncomfortable; she was alone with a man she didn't know and he was driving her home. She was unsure what to say and she realised that David had left her doubting her own instincts; she had lost her ability to trust people, especially men, and Matty was good-looking, dark hair falling over twinkling eyes, which made her feel uneasy.

She said, 'I hope it's not out of your way...'

He seemed surprised. 'No, it's only five minutes in the Land Rover.' They were moving from the car park, the engine drowning his words. 'I live in the opposite direction. I have a plot of land halfway up Wychanger Lane.'

'Oh.' Selena wasn't sure what to say.

Matty helped her out. 'So, what sort of paintings do you do?'

'Landscapes, mostly – trees and fields, that kind of thing.'

Matty raised an eyebrow. 'Like Constable?'

'Not really.' Selena imagined Constable's idyllic rural paintings and then her own alongside, stark and moody, turbulent skies, dusky rolling hills. 'Mine are a bit darker...'

'Do they sell well?' Matty's eyes were on the road. 'I mean, that's your living, you're an artist – nothing else? You don't work in a shop as well?'

Selena smiled. 'I have a gallery with a friend of mine – we sell our own paintings and other artists' work from there. So, yes, I suppose I do work in a shop too.'

'Did it take you a long time to learn to be an artist?'

'I did a Fine Arts degree at Manchester, years ago. That's where I met my flatmate, Claire.'

'It all sounds very nice,' Matty grinned. 'We folks have a quieter life here – working on the land, you get very attached to it, like it becomes a part of who you are. I suppose you do that through your paintings though, you know, you get to connect with a place as you paint it, then there's a sort of symbiosis.'

Selena nodded. She was impressed with the way Matty had made a simple but succinct comparison between his own work and her paintings. 'You're exactly right,' she agreed. 'It's a sort of bonding – the landscape becomes part of you while you're creating the painting.'

Matty said, 'Same with trees, plants and hedges – it's like we're all different parts of the same big picture. Well, here we are.' The Land

Rover slowed and was idling outside Sloe Cottage. He met her eyes and smiled. 'I hope you'll be okay.'

'Thanks, I will.' Selena unclipped her seat belt.

'You have a big stove in there,' Matty observed as she reached for the car door. Selena wondered if he was looking at the chimney or if he'd ever been inside the house and seen it.

'Yes, I do...'

'I'll bring you some wood sometime,' he said matter-of-factly.

'Thanks.' Selena clambered out and stood back as he turned the Land Rover round in the drive, reversing expertly, the engine knocking loudly, then he roared away in a cloud of diesel smoke.

Selena reached in her bag for the keys and began to walk towards the house. It was twilight now and the corners of the garden were full of shifting grey shadows. As she stood in the porch and pushed the key into the lock, the blackthorn tree swayed towards her in the breeze.

10

Selena walked into the house, closing the door behind her with a clunk. She could see very little as she fumbled for the round light switch. For a moment, she couldn't remember where it was and she stood still, her fingers groping against the rough stone wall. The corridor was gloomy and, as Selena breathed, the darkness seemed to breathe with her, as if another person was there, close by. Her fingers scrabbled against the wall; she felt almost sure that someone was standing in the shadows, watching her silently. She flicked the switch and as the hall was flooded with brightness, she was relieved that she was alone.

Her heart was still thumping as she walked into the living room. The flames glimmered in the wood-burning stove, but the corners of the room were cold, as if the warmth was not allowed to reach there. Selena switched on the table lamp and tended to the fire, throwing on a log, poking the embers. She flopped onto the sofa and as she leaned back, she felt the same sense of someone standing close to her, watching.

For a moment, Selena stayed where she was, afraid to turn, almost sure that if she swivelled round there would be someone there, waiting. She was conscious of her shallow breathing. She thought of calling out, and all of a sudden, she twisted and glanced round; the corners were crowded with leaping shadows cast by the fire, but she was alone. She gazed through the window and shuddered; it was dark outside now. The blackthorn tree pressed its branches against the glass like a palm. Selena pulled the curtains together with a swish and felt jittery. She decided to go to the kitchen; she had left the lights on there and it would be warmer, more welcoming, and she'd calm down.

Selena walked through the lobby, where the air brushed her skin like cold breath, into the kitchen, but there was no glow from the Aga. She put her hand on the ceramic surface and it was cool to the touch. Selena knelt down and checked the switch that controlled the oil feed; it had been turned off. She opened the little door to the burner and there was no flame. She frowned; she was sure she had not switched off the controls, but the Aga was stone cold, and she had no idea how to turn on the burner that started up the central heating as well as the cooker. She decided she'd phone Lesley tomorrow and ask for help, but for now she'd go to bed.

Selena switched on the light that illuminated the stairs before she turned off the kitchen lights: she didn't want to be left in a blackout again. She walked upstairs quickly, leaving the cold kitchen behind her. As she moved away, the darkness seemed to inhale and wait.

* * *

Grace held her breath as she walked back towards Slaugh Cottage along the darkening lane. She was sure someone was walking behind her; she could hear the thud of heavy footfall not far away. She quickened her pace. Her mind was still full of Kitty Stokes, images of the lengthy labouring while her grandmother coaxed her to be calm and take small gasps, her warm hands rubbing oil on her belly while Kitty roared, her face filled with anguish. Grace was surprised at the long number of hours she had watched the toil, feeling fearful that the baby would never come, that Kitty could not continue to howl and whimper in such a way, that soon her energy would fail. Grace had been in awe of her grandmother, who was composed and experienced, guiding the frightened young woman through the changing stages of birthing without showing signs of being perturbed or tired herself, although, afterwards, Bett had told Grace that she had been concerned that Kitty would not be able to manage to push out the large baby she was carrying.

And Grace was amazed by Kitty Stokes who, her husband banished to The Royal Oak, had been alone and appeared to be close to death's door; she had been pale and weak, the whites of her eyes wide with fear, then she had grunted and forced the baby out into the world. Grace had cut the navel string as instructed and swaddled the little boy in linen, wrapping him again in wool. The child had not cried quickly, his face had been puckered and red, unable to breathe, and Kitty had dragged herself upright, anxious, as Bett told Grace to put her finger into the baby's mouth and remove anything that was lodged there. She had loosened some mucus, placed the baby across her shoulder, patted his back gently and he had howled at the top of his lungs. Kitty had stretched out her arms then, her eyes soft and grateful, and Grace had placed the warm bundle at the mother's breast, surprised by her own tender feelings towards the child.

Hours had passed; Grace recalled the May dance she had attended earlier in the day, noticing spots of blood spattered on her freshly embroidered cream dress. She would try removing the stains with a little milk when she arrived home and, if that failed, she would soak the dress in urine overnight and wash it again in tallow and ashes.

The noise was still soft behind her, the repeated dull sound of footfall on soil. The moon was high; she was almost back at the cottage; her father would have taken himself to his bed hours ago, but if she needed to gather her skirts and run, she would be able to reach her home in a few minutes. Then she heard a voice call her name, one soft word, 'Grace,' and Nathaniel Harper was beside her, falling in step. She did not look up as he offered her an arm. 'May I walk with you to your door, Mistress Grace?'

Again, she wondered if his courteous tone was mocking her, but she threaded a hand through the crook of the elbow he offered and walked silently. His arm was muscled, firm and warm.

'I hear Kitty Stokes has a son. Edmund Stokes was in The Royal Oak while she was birthing. I believe you tended her, with your grandmother. Is that why you left me alone at the May dance?'

She did not look up at him. 'I was needed there to help.'

'I needed you by my side at the dance. You were the prettiest maid there.'

Grace was about to protest that she had seen him with Alice Bryant in his arms, but instead, she said, 'Perhaps next year I will be able to dance.'

'Before next year I must take a wife,' Nathaniel replied quickly. 'My father is anxious that I sire sons. A farming family must have men, and since my brothers died young, I am the only one, so I must do his bidding.' He glanced at Grace to observe her reaction. 'A young farmer needs a wife who will bear him sons, a wife who is modest, strong and wise and knows how to keep house.'

Grace nodded; she had no idea how to reply. Her arm was resting on Nathaniel's and she was conscious that he was walking too closely to her; he continued to watch her, judging her expression.

Then he said 'What do you think about that, Grace?'

'I think it is well,' she replied, unsure what to say. His words and the searching look he gave her made her breathless.

They had arrived at the wooden gate and Grace turned to walk into the garden alone, but Nathaniel held onto her arm, guiding her firmly towards the house. They stopped by the well, the blackthorn tree in shadow by the window shutter.

Grace faced him, meeting his eyes. 'I must go inside.' She was conscious that her heart was beating too quickly, that in truth she wanted to linger, to stay in his company.

'Your father will be asleep. It is late.'

'Yes.'

'My father owns Slaugh Cottage – he allows your father to live here because he is a hard worker.'

'Yes, I know. We are grateful.'

Nathaniel took her hand in his and held it up. 'Dance with me, Grace. On the village green you left me waiting for you and you did not return. We will dance now.'

He tugged her into his embrace, spinning her around so that she fell back into his arms again. Someone passed by the gate and Grace heard a shout go up, two men laughing together and a gruff voice called out, 'Master Nathaniel.'

Grace was alarmed. 'Who was that?'

'I think it was George Shears. He and his brother work for my father. I expect they have been making merry and will sleep in the barn.' Nathaniel held her at arm's-length, taking in her embroidered dress, her pale hair beneath the cap. 'You are indeed very lovely.'

Grace couldn't look away from him as he gazed at her, his eyes reflecting light. Then he wound his arms around her waist and pressed his mouth against hers, his lips insistent.

Grace pushed him away and stood back, breathing hard.

Nathaniel's eyes stayed locked on hers and he moved towards her again. 'Spare another little kiss for me.'

'I cannot.' Grace trembled with fear and desire; she was confused by the sudden power he had over her. She wanted to kiss him again; she felt strangely weak and strong at the same time and she had no word for it.

'Just a kiss.' His hands grasped her hips and he tugged her against him, his mouth on hers.

Grace wriggled away.

'You must not ask me...'

He laughed once. 'Would you prefer me to ask Alice Bryant?'

'No.' Grace could not help the words that slipped from her lips.

'You are the one I would choose, Grace. I know Alice Bryant would let me kiss her. I know she has eyes for me... and all the men on the farm think her a comely pippin...'

Grace's hands flew to her mouth, horrified. 'We should not talk of these things – it is wrong for them to talk of Alice.'

'Then let us not talk at all. I am a young man, you a chaste maid, and I have need of a wife.' He pulled her against him. 'Any man would wish to sample goods before he makes purchase...'

Nathaniel kissed her like he was taking a long draught of ale; his breath tasted of strong ale too, and Grace was surprised how readily her eyes closed, how easily she became intoxicated, lost in the embrace as he pressed her in his arms. He tugged her cap from her head, whispered her name into her hair, 'My own Grace,' then pulled her kerchief from around her shoulders. Grace felt the cool breeze on her skin and was about to protest, but he had stopped her mouth again with another long kiss.

Then Nathaniel tumbled to his knees, wrestling her onto the damp ground next to the well, and he crawled across her, his warm hands finding the hemline of her dress, caressing the flesh of her calves. Grace wriggled and protested, but his voice was soothing, his hands resolute, and she felt weak and unable to prevent what she knew would happen next.

He fumbled with his clothes, with hers, and she squeezed her eyes shut and allowed him to take control. He whispered her name, and at that moment, Grace believed that she truly belonged to him and that he would love her forever. She told herself that Nathaniel was the person she wanted to stay with for eternity; she had asked the chattering well to bring him to her, and now she was his and this moment would stretch to fill a lifetime. It was as if she and Nathaniel were the only people in the world, and the garden around them had dissolved away: only she and he remained. He groaned and she clung to his shirt, dazed; she loved him now, and she believed that now would never end. They stayed locked together for a moment longer, then Nathaniel pulled away. Grace did not move; her clothes were dishevelled.

Nathaniel stood up tall, beyond her reach, adjusting his breeches. He gazed down at her for a long time. She was sure he would speak, that he would swear to love her for all his days, that he would protect her with his life. Instead, he said, 'Well, it is late and I must go home to my bed now. I enjoyed our dance together. I will bid you goodnight.'

Then he turned away swiftly and was gone.

Grace sat up, puzzled, tugging her skirts, covering her shoulders with the kerchief, a hand to her hair, and she heard the muffled sound of his voice in the distance singing a little May song as he headed towards Hill Top Farm. Grace shivered, unsure about what had happened so quickly that she'd had no time to think, yet she was sure that what had just taken place between her and Nathaniel was not as she would have wished it.

She stood up with some difficulty and the world started to spin; she was suddenly dizzy. She reached a hand to press her leg beneath her dress and her fingers touched something sticky, like blood. Grace picked up the bucket by the well and began to wash herself. Overhead, an owl beat its wings and Grace remained fixed for a moment, listening for the familiar screech of recognition. The owl fluttered, settled in the branches of a tree at the end of the garden and was silent.

Grace held her breath; she was alone, not sure what to do. She was no longer as she was before: in the same moment that Nathaniel had possessed her, the moment that she had willingly given him her heart, she had lost the single precious thing that was her own and her life had changed forever.

11

Selena stood shivering in the kitchen in her pyjamas and dressing gown, thick socks on her feet, her phone in her hand. She had just called Lesley about the Aga not working, hoping that she or Ian could pop over and show her how to light it. Lesley had replied in a rush that she was sorry: she and Ian were on their way to Dorset to see their daughter for the day; it was their grandson's sixth birthday, so they wouldn't be able to fix the Aga themselves until late in the evening, but she'd have someone call round who would sort it out later today. Selena was puzzled; it wouldn't be easy to get a heating engineer or a plumber out on a Sunday, but Lesley had reassured her that she wouldn't let her down.

Selena took tea and a bowl of cereal into the conservatory where her easel was set up. It was bright, the warmest room in the house, but outside, the garden was wet and rain was slithering in rivulets against the blurred glass windows, the sky bleak beyond the fields where sheep stood still as if fixed in paint, their heads drooping and their wool soaked, staring at the ground. Selena knew how they felt. The damp April weather and the cold air had the effect of making her mood flat, dulling her optimism. She gazed at her latest painting: a branch of the blackthorn tree in black and white, starkly beautiful in its detail. It was a departure for Selena in terms of her style: she usually preferred sweeping landscapes, but the intricate blossom and the sharply pointed thorn had fascinated her, a contrast of beauty and spite.

She glanced at her phone and found two texts: one from Claire saying that she already had a buyer for the painting of the back garden of Sloe Cottage in sunshine, crammed with bluebells, tulips and daffodils. A customer had seen it on the website. Claire was excited, gushing that she was looking forward to seeing her in a week's time, and they'd have great fun together exploring the nightlife of the local village. Selena smiled, thinking about her visit to The Royal Oak last night: Claire would be baffled by the quaint old pub, the quiet drinkers, the empty seats.

The second text was from Laura, apologising for leaving so soon last night: her father's blood pressure tablets were exactly where he'd left them – in the bathroom. Selena replied that she was looking forward to meeting him and she reminded her that they were both invited to dinner at Sloe Cottage with her and Claire next Sunday, the first of May.

Her cereal unfinished, Selena took the bowl back to the kitchen and placed it in the sink. She wandered through the lobby into the living room. The fire was still glowing in the wood burner, so she placed another log inside and closed the doors, watching the blaze flare. She gazed through the window; rain dripped constantly from the blackthorn branches; beyond, puddles were filling on the drive. A lone pigeon waddled across the lawn and began pecking at something in the garden by the well.

Selena went back to the warmth of the fire and curled up on the sofa against the softness of the cushions. She closed her eyes and wondered if the baby would have been showing by now. She counted: she'd have been twelve weeks pregnant. She pictured how life might have been with David, with their baby. Images filled her mind: Selena holding a sweet bundle wrapped in a cream shawl, David looking on, his eyes shining with pride; both of them clambering into a car, the baby in her new seat at the back; late-night-time feeding, Selena smiling as she held her daughter close; David attempting to change a nappy and them both laughing together. She squeezed her eyes tightly at the thought; it was a dream; it could never have happened. She had been wrong about David; she'd misjudged his feelings for her, and now she didn't feel bitterness or pain. She simply felt empty.

Selena sat up, opened the doors to the wood burner and stared into the fire; the flames crackled and smoke swirled upwards to the chimney. She stretched out her feet in the fluffy socks and wondered if she should put on a coat and wellingtons, go for a walk across the fields or even into Ashcombe. She could photograph St Bartholomew's church; perhaps it might be a focus for another painting, an idyllic village scene in the haze of rain, surrounded by the little cottages.

A loud knock shattered the silence, two sharp raps, and she eased herself from the sofa and rushed into the hall, opening the door to see a man in a black anorak, hood up, his hands shoved deep in his pockets. Selena raised her eyebrows in question and he said, 'Hello. I believe your Aga doesn't work. Would you like me to take a look at it?'

'Did Lesley ask you to call?' Selena asked, staring over his shoulder to see if there was a car or a van parked in the drive, but there was none. He must have walked to Chitterwell from the village. He had a bag over his shoulder, clearly containing tools.

'Yes, she said the flame had gone out. I'm guessing it just needs a new wick. You'll need it working, especially in this weather.' He was standing just beyond the porch, the rain dripping onto his hood, a light rhythmic drumming.

Selena stood back. 'Oh, please come in.'

The man followed her through the hall, ducking slightly beneath the door frame into the living room. She noticed him glance around at the fire, then towards the plastered alcove and the bay window before they reached the kitchen. He took off his damp jacket; he was wearing an old sweatshirt, the sleeves rolled to his elbows, and jeans. He was probably close to forty, Selena thought; his light brown hair was ruffled, the beginnings of stubble on his face.

'It's good of you to come here on a Sunday,' she said, thinking that he looked like he'd recently dragged himself out of bed.

He moved towards the Aga, kneeling down next to the small door, examining the burner.

'Can I get you a cup of tea?' Selena offered.

'Do you have Earl Grey?' he replied from the floor.

'I'll check.' Selena emptied the contents of her tea caddy, searching among the mixture of tea bags. 'Is Lady Grey all right?'

'Just as good,' he said. 'No milk or sugar please.'

Selena bustled around with filling the kettle and clanking cups; she'd make herself another mug of tea. It was bitterly cold in the kitchen and she was suddenly conscious that she was still in pyjamas and dressing gown; the fluffy socks were not particularly becoming either.

She placed the mug of Lady Grey on the table and watched the man working, the muscles in his sinewy forearms moving as he held a pair of scissors. He didn't appear to feel the cold; he pushed a hand into his bag and pulled out a length of pale tape, then he grunted, 'Yeh, it just needs a new wick. I'll let the oil come through and we can light it in about twenty minutes and check it's good.'

'Thanks.' Selena sat at the table and cradled her mug of tea. The man joined her, sitting easily, picking up his mug and inhaling steam.

'I think that will do it. It's a cold house. You can't really do without the Aga.'

'It is cold – but I have the fire in the living room.'

He raised an eyebrow. 'It's cold in there too.'

Selena nodded, feeling awkward that they were having a conversation about heating. But then, he had come to fix the Aga, so what else would they talk about?

He changed the subject for her. 'I hear you're an artist?'

'I am.' Selena wondered how he'd known. Her paintings were not visible from the kitchen, but she supposed that everyone knew about everyone else in Ashcombe. It was a small community, and she was a newcomer, so it was no surprise that people talked about her. She offered a smile and said, 'Do you live in the village?'

He shook his head. 'No, I live just outside Exeter.'

'Oh,' Selena said. 'That's a long way to come on a Sunday...'

He shrugged. 'Not really – it's just a short trip down the M5. It doesn't take long.'

Selena wondered again where his car was; perhaps he had parked it beyond the gate. She watched him sipping tea, casually stretching his legs beneath the table.

Then he said, 'I'd love to see some of your paintings, if that's okay.'

Selena could smell the sickly-sweet oil soaking into the wick. 'All right – I'm set up in the conservatory.'

She pushed open the door to the glass room and he stepped inside, standing next to her, not moving, just scrutinising two pictures, the blackthorn branch, which was still on the easel, and the painting of the tree beyond the garden, which she had stood upright against the wall. He pointed to it. 'That's the old oak tree just outside the gate.'

'It is.' Selena was surprised he had recognised it.

'It's very good – you've captured how it's so solid – how it's been standing for years.'

Selena almost smiled; he clearly thought of himself as an amateur art critic. Then he was staring at the painting on the easel, the black and white one she'd almost finished.

'That's very dramatic. It's the tree outside, but you've made it really impactful – the creamy blossom and the spiky thorn, one contrasting with the other. I like that.' He gave her an appraising glance. 'I'm not sure I'd hang it on my wall though – it has a really eerie feel to it.'

'Does it?' Selena was almost affronted. She thought her painting was a strong representation; she was surprised he thought it eerie.

'Well, it is a blackthorn tree,' he replied simply. 'Do you know what it symbolises?' Selena shrugged and he continued. 'There are all sorts of myths surrounding the blackthorn, from way back to the time of the Celts. Death, misfortune – some people call it the witches' tree – it has a long association with witchcraft. It's about opposites too: spring and autumn, blossom and berry. The way you've captured the blossom is beautiful.' He thought for a moment, and murmured:

'*Into the scented woods we'll go and see the blackthorn swim in snow.*'

'Is that a poem?'

'Mary Webb. "Green Rain".' He nodded towards the huge panes of glass where water drizzled down in wiggly lines. 'That's just a perfect poem for today. Right. It must be time to light the wick.'

'I suppose so.' Selena followed him into the kitchen, wondering about the engineer who quoted poetry and analysed paintings. She wondered why he wasn't wearing a name badge, or, at least, why he hadn't said his name when she'd let him in. She ought to have asked or introduced herself. Selena pressed her lips together; the experience with David had left her flustered and awkward. She imagined the engineer visiting Ariel Art in Manchester, gazing at her landscapes, making comments about the sense of eeriness and foreboding in the dark brushstrokes of the hills and skies. The idea made her smile.

Then he stood up, pushed his sleeves further up his forearms and said, 'All done now. The new wick's lit – that was all it needed. You should feel the benefit in an hour or so.'

'Thank you.' Selena watched him reach for his damp anorak. 'How much do I owe you?'

He gave her an enigmatic smile. 'I think it's all taken care of in your rent.'

She smiled. 'Oh, I'm glad. I feel warmer already.'

'Well, thanks for the tea.' He was already on his way to the door. 'And for showing me your paintings. They are really good.'

'Thanks.' Selena opened the front door.

'No problem. And I'm glad you're settled in at Sloe Cottage. Enjoy the rest of your weekend.'

'I will.' Selena watched him pull up the hood of his jacket and walk towards the gate; it was still raining heavily, but he didn't seem to hurry as he turned to the right and began to walk in the direction of Hilltop Farm. Selena assumed he must have parked there.

She gave a light laugh; it was becoming interesting, living in rural Somerset. She had met a warm-hearted lilac-haired woman who was a supply teacher, a man who had given her a lift home in his Land Rover and offered to bring her logs despite never having met her before, and now an enigmatic engineer who drank Lady Grey tea, quoted poetry and expressed an interest in art and had fixed the Aga. Life in Chitterwell was full of surprises.

12

Despite it being the last week of May, the sunshine had stayed away and the cold rain poured, filling the fields with puddles of mud. Grace dug up the last of the weeds and straightened slowly. Her lower back had started to ache, and the hem of her dress was caked in filth, her fingers wet and stiff. She glanced over towards the strawed-down barn. Harriet Harper had told her to go and help with the milking; she had said that she was 'doing no good standing like a mawkin¹ in the fields getting soaking wet'.

Grace trudged sadly towards the barn, thinking about her father; he would be out in the next field, his shirt and breeches sodden. She imagined him at home later, his clothes steaming in front of the fire while she warmed ale for him to drink. He would be weary and she would need to find him clean dry clothes and a hot meal.

Grace found a stool and a pail, sitting down close to a lumbering cow, rubbing her raw hands to warm them before starting the milking. Alice and Nancy Bryant were close by, chattering as they tugged the cow's teats, their noses reddened with cold, their eyes glazed with boredom. Nancy greeted her with a nod and Alice with a smile. Grace smiled back and set to work, resting her cheek against the cow's side, closing her eyes and breathing softly as the cow gave a low sound of contentment.

Nancy stopped working. 'Jennet is starting here as a milkmaid next week. I'm hoping that soon after she arrives, I'll be able to finish.'

Alice leaned towards Grace. 'Nancy has a suitor, a young man who works here on the farm. She danced with him when we brought in the May. He is courting her now.'

'Oh, but he had eyes for me long before that, back since the wassailing of Twelfth Night. He is a good man, strong and hearty. It would be my wish to marry and to leave milking. Being a wife would be the life for me.'

Grace continued with her work. 'I am glad for you, Nancy. What is his name?'

'He is called George. He and his brother, Ned, work in the fields with your father. George wants us to get a room in Ashcombe – we could move in there, but a nice cottage like yours would suit us much better.'

Alice laughed. 'A single room won't do for me. I have set my sights on something much more comfortable.'

Nancy said, 'Like the farmhouse here on Hill Top? Alice fancies that she could be a lady.'

'Not a proper lady – but the wife of an important man, a farmer's son...' Alice's eyes shone.

Grace inhaled the warmth of the cow's scent and pressed her head against its flank as milk squirted into the pail.

'And you, Grace – do you not have dreams of marriage and a family? You are the same age as we...'

Grace did not look up. 'It is an honour I seldom dream of...'

Nancy snickered. 'Being a wife and having a husband, lying with him at night, practising the goat's jig – that is something I dream of all the time...'

'Shhh,' Alice hissed, lifting a finger in warning. The sound of footfall urged her to put her head down and jerk harder at the cow's teats.

Nancy copied her sister's actions. Then a man was in the barn, his hands on his hips, watching them. Alice raised her head coquettishly and met his eyes. 'Good afternoon, Master Nathaniel.' She smiled, all dimples, her cheeks pink.

Nathaniel gazed around the barn; his eyes sweeping over Grace, then back to Alice. 'How is the milking today, Alice? Do the cows yield well?'

'Oh, very well indeed,' Alice said. 'They always respond to my warm touch.'

'We've been milking all day, Master Nathaniel.' Nancy winked at her sister. 'But my sister and I are never too tired by night-time, if you catch my meaning, sir.'

Nathaniel spoke only to Alice. 'It is always pleasant to see a buxom milkmaid at her work. I must come in the barn more often and take away your pails for you. It pleases me a great deal, the sweet smell of milk and hay, and a rosy-cheeked maid.'

Nancy muttered under her breath, 'Some of us keep ourselves looking our best. Alice and I take a pride in ourselves. We are not draggles who work in the fields weeding turnips, our dresses clogged with muck.' She threw a glance at Grace and smiled slyly.

'I bid you good day, Alice.' Nathaniel gave a mock bow. 'Perhaps we will encounter each other later this evening, if the rain stops.'

Nancy watched him stride away, then she whispered, 'If the rain stops or if it doesn't, a man's maypole is still the same.' She placed a hand over her mouth and cackled. Alice pressed her lips together and made a soft sound of amusement. Nancy leaned towards Grace. 'It seems Master Nathaniel is most taken with my sister.'

'It does, indeed,' Grace said. Her pail was almost full, and her heart was heavy with sadness. Nathaniel had known she was seated nearby, but he had behaved as if she had not been there. He had spoken sweetly to Alice, knowing that Grace was watching, knowing that his words would pierce deep as arrows. She had not seen him since the night he had followed her home from Ashcomb. Grace had stood for a long time in her garden most evenings since then, waiting for him, hoping he would appear at her gate; she had whispered soft words of love into the chattering well for four weeks, but he had not come back.

She wondered if she should go after him and call him. She would ask him why he had spurned her, what she had done to make him treat her this way, but in her heart she knew the answer already. He had tossed her aside like a forkful of hay, and now he had set his sights on Alice. Grace recalled sadly that her Grandmother Bett had once told her that some men were 'nothing but danglers': they courted one woman and then, having won her, they began to follow another.

Grace sighed, her heart heavy, and whispered her thanks to the cow for letting down her milk. Then her mind drifted to her journey home. Grace knew a place on an exposed sunny bank where rue grew all year. She would pick some for herself when no one was looking. She had much need of it.

* * *

Selena stood in the warm kitchen, a glass of wine in her hand, and stirred the paella as Claire continued to rush around enthusiastically. 'And the kitchen is so modern, but the living room has all that period charm, and the oak conservatory, oh, I think I'm going to have to move to the countryside, Selena. You chose so well. The Aga, it's just incredible – I mean, the cooking smells are to die for. And the wood-burning stove in the living room is just so cosy. I love it here.'

'It's taken me a while to learn how to use it. I burned scrambled eggs the first time I tried to cook anything.' Selena took her first sip of wine. 'I'm glad you approve, though.'

'Do you like staying here? Is the place working its magic on you?'

'It is – I'm healing. I have space to paint—'

'Oh, and those paintings. They are some of the best ones you've done.' Claire refilled her glass. 'And they'll sell like mad. But the one you have done of the branch and the blossom – the detail is so incredible.'

'The engineer told me it was eerie...' Selena smiled at the recollection.

'Really? He must be mad. I think it's stunning.' Claire rushed over to the Aga, adding another grind of black pepper to the paella. 'This is making me feel a vibe of domestic bliss... What time are your new friends coming?'

'Half seven – so, in twenty minutes or so.'

'I can't wait to meet them. Ah, Selena...' Claire took a deep breath. Selena knew she was about to disclose something important. 'I have to tell you – last week, Veronica came round to the gallery again.'

'Oh?'

'I told her that she should look closer to home for someone to blame for David's misdemeanours. In fact, what I actually told her was that he was a serial womaniser.'

'Oh dear, what did she say?' Selena was anxious.

'I was a bit surprised by her reaction – she burst into tears.'

'Poor thing.'

'I think she knew; I'd touched a nerve...' Claire raised an eyebrow. 'I don't think it was the first time he'd, you know, played away.'

Selena exhaled. 'So, what did you do?'

'I gave her a tissue and told her to go home and talk to him,' Claire said. 'I just thought you should know. You can draw a line under that part of your life now and move on.'

'Thank you. You're just the best friend.' Selena hugged Claire and then paused. 'Was that someone knocking at the door?'

'You go,' Claire suggested. 'I'll check the table in the living room and give the rice another stir. I'm practising for the future when I buy my country retreat...'

* * *

The paella was a great success, and so was the fruit salad Selena served up for dessert. Laura enthused about the food all the way through the meal, helping herself to seconds, while her father, Rob, a charming man in a dark jacket and chinos, murmured that he hadn't had paella since he'd been on a family holiday to Andalucía twenty years ago when Laura had been a teenager. He smiled, his eyes misty, and Laura placed a hand over his reassuringly.

They were seated around the light wooden dining table in the corner of the living room, little tealight candles flickering in jars. Claire opened a second bottle of wine, pouring herself a full glass.

Laura reached forward, asking for a refill. 'I was telling my dad all about your wonderful paintings, Selena...'

Rob glanced from Selena to Claire. 'You own a gallery in Manchester?'

Claire smiled. 'It's more of a big shop, but yes, we sell our paintings there.'

'You paint too, Claire?' Laura raised her eyebrows. 'What do you do? Landscapes and scenery?'

'No, I do political things, gaunt faces, hungry families – Selena and I have styles that complement each other. Our work is totally different and that brings in a good mix of clients. But the paintings Selena has done while she's down here have been incredible.' Claire waved a hand towards the window where the branch tapped against the glass in the wind. 'For example, she's painted the blossom from that tree.'

'I can't wait to see it,' Laura said.

'It's a little eerie, the blackthorn,' Rob commented.

Selena met his eyes. 'That's exactly what the engineer said.'

'Why eerie?' Claire asked.

'Oh,' Laura waved a dismissive hand, 'Blackthorn has an old association with witchcraft.'

Rob gave a small cough. 'Witches apparently made staffs and wands from the wood of the blackthorn, and the thorns were used to prick wax images of those that they cursed. The crown of thorns that Jesus wore on the cross is reputed to have been made from the blackthorn.'

Selena shivered. 'That's certainly eerie.'

Laura looked around the room. 'The whole house is eerie. In fact, Chitterwell and Ashcombe are steeped in history of folklore and suchlike...' She noticed Selena's troubled expression. 'Oh, of course it's all hearsay and superstitious rubbish.'

Rob shook his head. 'I've read about the history of witchcraft in Somerset. They held witch trials in Taunton at one point, centuries ago.'

Claire drained her glass. 'Horrible. Those stories give me bad dreams. Shall I make us all some coffee?'

'I'll do it.' Selena was about to rise from her seat, but Claire was already on her feet.

'No, I'll get coffees and the chocolates – the minty ones I brought down, we could make a start on those.'

'I couldn't manage another thing,' Laura protested dramatically, then a laugh broke from her lips. 'Well, maybe just one.'

Claire rushed off into the kitchen and Selena moved to the window, Rob's words still buzzing in her mind, observing the blackthorn branch with an artist's eye. It was thin, jagged; it straddled half of the window. She gazed beyond, into the shadows. The moon hung low, a silver crescent shedding a narrow shaft of light.

Laura sipped her wine. 'Can we have Selena over to dinner soon, Dad? We could make curry. My dad makes a wonderful jalfrezi, don't you?'

'I love cooking with spices,' Rob said. 'Yes, you must come over, Selena. Do you like pakoras? I do enjoy making those...'

'His veggie pakoras are to die for,' Laura agreed.

'Mmm, that sounds lovely.' Selena was gazing into the garden: an owl crossed the sky, its wings beating silently behind the glass; she thought she heard the hollow echo of its cry. She looked towards the well and something moved; it was too big to be an animal. Selena stared harder, trying to discern a shape shifting in the shadows. It disappeared, and for a moment she thought she had imagined it. She glimpsed it again: at first a brief silhouette that slipped into shade, then she saw the outline of a slight figure, a woman almost shrouded in darkness, her back to the window. Selena held her breath as the woman in a thin shift stepped into the light and raised her arms to the moon.

Then she heard the scream as Claire's voice came sharp and high from the kitchen.

13

The entire cottage was suddenly dark: the only light came from the little flickering candles that threw tall shifting shadows against the walls. Claire came blundering in, breathing hard.

'There was a flash and all the lights went out.'

Selena wrapped a comforting arm around her shoulders, despite feeling decidedly jumpy. 'What happened?'

'I plugged the coffee maker in and there was a bright flash, then the whole room was plunged into total blackout. I couldn't see my hand in front of my face.' Claire was shaking.

'Oh, it's a really intense dark here in the countryside...' Laura's voice was a soothing whisper. 'These old cottages are so isolated: there's not much light outside.'

'I expect it's just the trip switch that flipped,' Rob said matter-of-factly.

'Yes – do you have a torch?' Laura asked. 'Where's the fuse box?'

'It's above the front door – in the hall.' Selena thought for a moment. 'I think I've seen a torch on the floor there, in a box of tools.'

The four of them trooped into the hall in a line, one behind the other, fumbling in the grainy blackness. Selena's fingers found a small torch and she aimed the beam at the fuse box, while Rob, the only one tall enough to reach, pushed a switch upwards and the lights were immediately restored.

Back in the kitchen, they discovered the fault: the coffee machine had blown a fuse and would no longer work.

'I have instant?' Selena suggested hopefully. 'Or tea?'

'Tea would be lovely,' Laura replied.

'Instant coffee for me,' Claire said. 'I'm in need of a stiff brandy, to tell you the truth.'

'Coffee for me, please,' Rob added.

'We can take it into the conservatory if you like – I'll just move my paintings.'

'Oh, yes please, Selena.' Laura clasped her hands. 'I just love that conservatory – it's so warm and bright.'

'It's the nicest room – I have to sleep in that spare bedroom...' Claire's mouth turned down. 'It has such an eerie atmosphere in there. So cold...'

Selena frowned: that word, eerie, again. 'We can swap rooms if you like...'

'Oh, no sorry, Selena – I shouldn't have said that – you have to live here.' Claire was all smiles. 'I'll be fine – seriously, I'll sleep like a top if I have a large brandy with my coffee.'

'Brandy for everyone?' Selena asked.

'I wouldn't say no: I'm partial to a small one after such a lovely meal,' Rob said.

'I'm on driving duty, so not for me...' Laura mumbled as she picked up the tray of mugs.

Claire pounced on a box of chocolates and Selena found a bottle of cognac and glasses.

'Let's go into the warmest room in the house and chill out,' Claire said eagerly.

'Good idea,' Selena smiled and followed them towards the conservatory. She was still on edge, thinking about the shape she had glimpsed outside by the well, a slim young woman, her arms raised high. She was sure she hadn't imagined it: the long dress, a grey shadow in the moonlight.

Selena shook her head, trying to banish the thoughts, and joined her friends on the sofa in the corner. They were already chattering happily. She gazed through the huge window into the back garden towards the fields. Outside, everything was a jumble of shifting dark shapes.

* * *

June 1682 was a hot month, each day suffused with intense sunshine. The toil in the fields during the week was long and hard, but at weekends there were celebrations involving most of the villagers in Ashcomb. Two summer weddings took place, two sisters with very different ceremonies. On the sixth, Nancy Bryant exchanged rings in a fallow field with farm labourer, George Shears, a thick-set man who wore his brother's best patched breeches; the bride flounced joyfully to meet her groom in a pretty brown dress, which had been kept in good condition since her mother wore it for her own ceremony over twenty-five years before. The groom had already guzzled several ales in The Royal Oak and was in a merry mood, and the whole village attended, dancing to the pipe and tabor before many of the menfolk disappeared into the inn again to raise a mug of ale or two to the happy couple.

Bett White had commented to Grace that she thought George Shears was 'a bacon-faced man and a tickle pitcher, who would lead poor Nancy a merry dance' as he was already spending most of his meagre earnings in The Royal Oak. She reminded Grace that wedlock meant that a woman would be under the rod of her husband and if poor Nancy Bryant was unlucky enough to find a man who would beat her and treat her ill, as many others would, then that was her lot and she must bear it for the rest of her days.

But at the end of the month, on the twenty-seventh, Nathaniel Harper's marriage to Alice Bryant was a grander affair. The bride wore a white gown, her rosy cheeks dimpled, smiling as she stood at the altar in St Bartholomew's church. Joseph Harper had spared no expense for his only son's wedding: even Harriet, in a new bonnet, had smiled and told everyone around her that Alice would provide them with at least six grandchildren, and the farm would grow and prosper under Nathaniel's instruction. She'd likened their union to that of Puritan leader, Oliver Cromwell, and his wife, Elizabeth: it would be a marriage of duty, prudence and hard work, although Alice's expression as she gazed at Nathaniel was one of besotted adoration.

Grace and Bett waited outside the church in the throng of villagers to throw wheat at the head of the bride, so that she would thrive and have many children. Grace gazed around at the smiling faces; the cheering was loud in her ears, and the happy bride and groom had eyes only for each other. She desperately wished she could have stayed at home. The sun shone overhead as the couple emerged, Alice all smiles, Nathaniel more serious, the expression of a man already considering his responsibilities, as they were showered with grain and cheered. Grace, a posy of lavender stalks and daisies in her other hand flung the wheat, which landed softly at the bride's feet, and then turned away, full of sadness, as the couple embraced. She glanced at Bett, who was shouting and waving along with everyone else in Ashcomb. Grace slunk towards the churchyard, tracing familiar steps through the identical graves to a small hump in the ground, surrounded by other mounds of a similar size.

Grace knelt next to the grave, placing the posy on the green turf; she bowed her head, closed her eyes and whispered a small prayer. Then she whispered, 'May you rest in His everlasting peace, dear Mother.' She was still awhile, thinking. The sunlight was bright, the strong rays warm on her back. Grace felt too hot, a little dizzy in her scrubbed cream linen dress and a bonnet and kerchief. Images of the happy couple, rosy-faced Alice and Nathaniel, his brow creased with an air of maturity and respectability, swayed before her eyes: she could still hear the merry cheering and the tune of a pipe and drum.

'I truly do wish them the best in their marriage,' A sob caught in her throat. 'Oh, if only you were here.' A tear trickled down her cheek. 'If you could help me – each day I am sick to my stomach and I cannot speak of it to my poor father. Even now, he is at home in his chair; although this is a day of sunshine and much joy, he would rather be at the hearth warming his bones. And I... Oh, Mother, I am an unfortunate...' Grace paused: someone was standing behind her. She could feel the presence of someone close by, watching.

She turned round to see Bett White, her arms folded, considering her granddaughter's expression carefully as one who knew letters might study a book.

'Grandmother...' Grace's cheeks were pink. 'I was talking to my mother... I often come here to unfold the secrets of my heart...'

'You do not need to explain, child.' Bett's voice was kind. She stretched out a hand. 'Come home with me now. Let us share a cup and have some food. I think we have much to say to one another.'

Grace eyed her grandmother nervously. 'What will we speak of?'

Bett offered a smile, a wrinkling of the skin around her eyes. 'When women meet to jaw together, often more is made than just the noise of chatter. Besides, I am hungry.'

Back at the small cob-walled cottage, they sat at the table.

Bett leaned over, placing her hand on Grace's.

'How is your father?'

'He rests at home. He was weary today and did not want to come to Alice's wedding. I have left him some bread and meat, and some ale.'

'Have you eaten today, Gracie?'

Grace shook her head. 'I have not been hungry, Grandmother.'

'You are becoming thinner...'

Grace seemed surprised: Bett examined her closely, the tired eyes, the glazed stare, the softness of her chin.

She sighed. 'You are thinner in the body, but fatter in the face, I think...'

Grace folded her hands in her lap. 'I have no one to speak to, Grandmother. But I have an imbalance of humours, a melancholy on me that will not pass.'

'Is this because of Master Nathaniel?'

'I must put him from my mind. He is married to Alice now.'

'Indeed, you must forsake all thoughts of him...' Bett said thoughtfully, giving her granddaughter an appraising stare. Then she inhaled sharply. 'Gracie, have you been taking a hot mixture of laurel, madder, pepper, sage and savin? You know why I say this to you. It is a potion that many a maid will take when she has the need to rid herself of—'

'No, not that...' Grace looked up, bashful, her eyes round. Her voice was soft. 'I have been swallowing an infusion of rue.'

'Rue can be dangerous, taken in quantity. But did it work?'

'I thought, at first, that it was the rue made me ill, but now I think it is not. I am sick most mornings and I cannot eat.'

Bett lifted Grace's hands in hers; her eyes gleamed, intense. 'What passed between you and the farmer's son?'

'I have not spoken of it to anyone, Grandmother.'

'You must speak of it now – there is but me here, and I think I can help you.'

Grace looked into her grandmother's gaze and saw only kindness and sympathy there. She was longing to confide in her. She took a shuddering breath. 'I misjudged Nathaniel. I believed he loved me... but now I have been undone.'

Bett nodded, her voice soothing. 'I can see it in you, the changes are clear to those of us who notice such things. When did it happen?'

'After the May Day dance – after we had delivered Kitty Stokes of her baby. He walked home with me and then he would not go.'

'You have taken rue as a remedy, but it has not worked; so, you have had no flux for two moons now, am I correct?'

'It is so.' Grace moved her head once; her eyes were full of tears. 'There is nothing more I can do.'

'Then we must abide with the consequences and make do and mend,' Bett said firmly. 'The winter months will come and you will have to let out your dresses, they cannot be laced tightly. But we need to keep this a secret from Farmer Harper as long as we can, for you must work. It will be cold in November and December, so you can cover yourself with a warm shawl, then perhaps Mistress Harriet will not notice your condition and you may still milk the cows after the baby quickens in Michaelmas; you may even continue unnoticed at Yuletide. I think the baby will come in February, in late winter. Pray God that I am still here on this earth to deliver you.'

Grace's hands shook. 'Grandmother, please forgive me, I have done much wrong...'

Bett placed a soft hand beneath her granddaughter's chin. 'No, not you, my Gracie – it is you who have been wronged, and you have no mother at home to warn you of these things.' Her brow creased with anger. 'Oh, it makes me vexed.'

'But what will become of me – and the child?'

'Have you spoken to Nathaniel Harper?'

'I dare not, Grandmother. And he will not look my way; he is yoked to Alice Bryant now and if he is asked, he may say the child is not his.'

'Oh, Gracie.' A sigh shuddered through Bett's small frame. 'We will do what we can. Meanwhile, we will have to think of how we can keep you strong. I will make you some tea from ginger to take home with you, to drink each morn, and then, in August, some raspberry leaf, which will make you ready for the lying-in.'

'I will be shunned by others... I will be despised...'

'Gracie, do not think of these things – we will find a way by ourselves. There are simples, charms that I can help you make, the old ways are with us even now to keep you safe, and the child too. We can use the spindle and sew, use our time well to make clothes for the child. I will help – and together we will pass through this time of difficulty.' Bett squeezed Grace's fingers. 'Maybe we can even make it a time of joy.'

Grace met her eyes. 'I will try my best. But what of my father? How shall I tell him? He will be disappointed with what I have brought upon him – he will be troubled that there will be another mouth to feed...' Tears welled in her eyes; her throat became constricted and Grace let out a sob, followed by another, then she pushed her face into her hands and wept softly.

'Peace.' Bett moved from her seat and cradled Grace's head in her arms. 'Peace now. Don't concern yourself with Will. If need be, I will explain. Between us, we will find a way – we will discover love and joy where there is now sadness and despair. God help me, Gracie, I give you my word on that.'

14

Selena's brow creased; she nibbled her lower lip as she concentrated on the canvas. Brush in hand, she stood in the warm, sweet-scented garden, her easel in front of her, painting the old stone well and the fields rising beyond the garden wall. The weather was warm for the first week in May, bees buzzing in the long grasses, and the skin on her bare arms and legs glowed as she loaded her brush and brought colour to the canvas. She was unsure about the composition of her picture; the well was almost central, the fields behind were golden, bathed in bright summer sunlight. But it was somehow incomplete: she could not put her finger on the elusive detail that would make the scene jump into life. Selena concentrated instead on her brushstrokes, adding a creamy grey light to one side of a cloud.

She pursed her lips, thinking about Claire, who had left four days ago on Monday morning, saying how much she'd enjoyed herself and that she'd be down at the end of June for a second visit. In fact, as a result of her stay at Chitterwell, Claire was determined to employ someone to help in the gallery so that she could paint more pictures herself and visit again soon. The only downside was, Claire had said with a grin, that the second bedroom gave her bad dreams, and Selena understood. The room held an unnatural chill.

Selena had received a text from Laura too, an effusive invite to meet again for drinks at The Royal Oak soon, and to come to dinner at the weekend. Selena had accepted straight away; she was enjoying the perfect life, the solitude of painting for most of her time, but the reassuring promise of a social life. The chance to interact with others was something she wouldn't do often enough left to her own devices.

She returned to her painting. The pretty pastoral scene was in harmony with her emotions; she felt positive, uplifted, buoyed by the sunshine around her and on the canvas, but the overall picture lacked something. She glanced again at the little stone well, positioned to the right of centre; perhaps it wasn't enough of a focal point; perhaps it had become lost in the expanse of green fields and azure skies.

Selena was tugged from her thoughts by the sound of a chugging engine as a Land Rover rumbled through the gates. She recognised the driver; she remembered his smile, his cheery wave: it was Matty, the man who had given her a lift back from The Royal Oak. There was a young woman next to him, wearing colourful clothes, her hair was swept back in a ponytail.

They clambered from the Land Rover and rushed across, Matty calling, 'Hi.'

'Hello.' Selena put her brush down.

Matty glanced at the painting. 'Oh, that's very idyllic, very calming.'

Selena realised immediately what had been bothering her about the picture; as Matty had said, it was too peaceful, and now she thought it needed some turbulence, a brooding atmosphere.

She turned to the woman, who was standing next to Matty, a brown leather bag crossed over her body; she was wearing a long flowery dress and ankle boots. Selena stuck out a welcoming hand. 'Hello.'

'Hi,' the woman said. 'I hope you don't mind me coming over here with Matty...'

'I brought you some logs,' Matty pointed towards the vehicle with his thumb.

'... Only I wanted to meet you and say hello, and I believe there are a lot of interesting herbs in the garden and I'm so keen to take a look.'

'This is Joely Doran, my partner,' Matty added by way of introduction.

'Of course – pleased to meet you.' Selena watched Joely gaze round the garden, towards the herb patch. 'I don't know much about herbs – but please, help yourself.'

'Oh, Joely will tell you all about them – she's a bit of an expert,' Matty grinned. 'Meanwhile, shall I put your logs in the shed around the side of the cottage?'

'Yes, please do.' Selena turned to Joely. 'So, tell me about the herbs...'

Joely led the way towards the patch of land beyond the well, a raised bed and a further small garden where a variety of plants grew. She pointed a long finger wrapped in silver rings. 'Well, you have all the good culinary ones here, growing really well.'

'I recognise thyme and mint, sage, some parsley.'

'And lovely varieties – that looks like pineapple sage, lemon thyme, and you have some chocolate mint. You're really well stocked.' Joely smiled. 'This is tidier than my garden – mine is wilder, and I have lots of really useful medicinal herbs on our patch of land.' She pointed beyond the raised bed. 'But you have some great healing herbs here too – look, chamomile, feverfew – oh, you have valerian and a huge crop of comfrey. What a great garden.'

Matty was lifting a sack of logs on his back, hauling them around the side of the property.

Selena smiled at Joely. 'Would you like to come in for a cup of tea?'

'I'd love to.' Joely called out to Matty, 'We're going indoors for a cuppa.' They walked through the hall and Joely asked, 'Do you make tea from your own herbs?'

'No...'

'I expect you're so busy painting, but I can bring you some nettle tea if you like – I've just dried some leaves at home.'

'Thank you.' Selena replied. 'What is nettle good for?'

'It's a diuretic, so it helps flush away toxins. Also, it is full of polyphenols, which can help prevent chronic diseases such as diabetes and heart disease.'

'Oh,' Selena said with a smile. 'I'd better have some then.'

'Plus, it's really refreshing.' Joely was standing next to Selena in the living room. Warmth came from the wood burner, but it was much cooler indoors.

Selena saw her shiver, so she asked. 'Shall we go into the kitchen?'

'This is a strange room, isn't it?' Joely shook her head, her ponytail swishing across her shoulder. 'Can't you feel it?'

'The cold?' Selena frowned.

'The cold, yes, but something else – there's definitely a... presence.'

'Oh?' Selena felt her body tense and wished Joely would follow her into the kitchen, but she was staring blankly towards the fire, then out of the window, beyond the blackthorn tree. The white blossom had faded now, leaving a greyish forlorn flower.

'Yes, there's definitely a sort of sadness,' Joely said, then she noticed Selena's troubled expression, so she smiled cheerfully, 'but I'm sure you'll bring so much happiness to the house. Shall we have that cup of tea?'

Selena was on her way to the kitchen as Matty joined them, closing the front door behind him with a dull clunk. She smiled at them both. 'I can only offer you tea or instant coffee. The coffee machine blew up at the weekend. Lesley says she'll replace it but I told her not to rush as I don't drink coffee much.'

'Any fruit tea for me, and Matty will have the same. Honey in it would be nice if you have some.' Joely gazed around the kitchen. 'Oh, this is a lovely welcoming room, and the new conservatory is so nice.'

'We live in a caravan,' Matty explained. 'Joely's not used to all this space.'

Joely met his eyes, her own dancing with happiness. 'Our space is outside, Matty. We have the field to grow and cook and do whatever we want.' She took the mug Selena offered her. 'We have our own plot of land halfway along Wychanger Lane, just outside Ashcombe. It's really beautiful up there, we have huge views across the Blackdowns. You must come over.'

'I'd love to.' Selena handed Matty a fruit tea. They sat at the table quietly together and Selena realised how much she was enjoying the chance to invite people into her home and make new friends. She cupped a mug in her hands thoughtfully, watching Joely's calm expression, Matty's easy smile. She envied the way they both seemed so comfortable in their surroundings; it was as if they belonged to the countryside and it belonged to them. A question formed in her mouth. 'I'd be really interested to know more about herbs. I only cook with the basic ones, but you can use them for all sorts of different reasons, can't you?'

Joely was delighted. 'Oh yes – I make face masks from aloe vera and basil, ginger, turmeric... I can give you an aloe vera plant or two. And I make a tisane from feverfew for headaches...'

Matty laughed. 'She also makes great bread and stew and delicious cakes, so you'll have to visit for lunch sometimes.'

'That would be lovely.' Selena considered how much she'd enjoy a visit to their caravan, the wide outdoor space, the wonderful views. She imagined herself painting a landscape of muted green and earthy red, creating a patchwork panorama. Then she noticed that her visitors had finished their tea, and she dragged herself from her thoughts. 'By the way, there's a bread oven here. Apparently, it's not used now.'

'Oh, can I see it?' Joely said. 'This is such an interesting house. It must be great to be living here – Matty says you're renting it for several months while you paint. That's wonderful.'

'This way.' Selena pushed her cup away and leaped up, leading them both into the living room, pointing to the side of the hearth. 'The old bread oven is on the right, just set back.'

Joely squeezed past the sofa, her long dress catching against a cushion, and peered into the bread oven behind the chimney breast. 'Oh, this is incredible,' she purred. 'Look, Matty – the bread oven's still so warm because the log burner is on – it would be great to prove bread in here.' She turned to Selena. 'Imagine, hundreds of years ago, women had nothing to cook on but the open fire and the bread oven. This house is so fascinating. Do you know much about the place, Selena?'

'Not really.' Selena shook her head. 'I know this part of the house was built in the seventeenth century – Lesley said there used to be a staircase where that alcove is and it led to the second bedroom, which was divided into two rooms then.'

'It's so interesting.' Joely's eyes were wide with excitement. 'And the cottage has such an atmosphere.'

'You're welcome to visit whenever you want.'

'Oh, I will, thanks, Selena – and I'd love to take a cutting of the pineapple sage next time, if that's all right.'

'We should be going,' Matty said. 'I have logs to deliver up to Hilltop. But we'll pop round soon, if that's all right.'

'And I'll see you in the pub, perhaps?' Selena accompanied them to the door. 'I ought to get back to my painting...'

They strolled into the garden.

As Joely hugged Selena goodbye, Matty yelled, 'Oh, no. Your painting...' He rushed over to Selena's easel, which had toppled over on the ground. 'The painted side is face down.' He lifted the canvas; Joely and Selena were setting the easel upright, collecting brushes. 'It must have blown over in a gust of wind.'

Selena shook her head. The air was completely calm, still as held breath. She replaced the painting and gazed at it, disappointment in her eyes. A lot of the wet paint had been smudged, the green of the hills had run into the azure sky, rendering it a messy dark grey.

Joely was anxious. 'It's not ruined, is it?'

Selena pushed a hand through her hair, thinking, then she said. 'Oh, it'll be fine – I can paint over the top. Yes – don't worry.' She offered them her brightest smile. 'Thanks for the logs, Matty – and lovely to meet you, Joely. I hope we can catch up soon.'

'I'd like that.' Joely hugged her again briefly. 'And thanks for the tea.'

'See you, Selena,' Matty called, but her thoughts were on the painting and she hardly heard him. She was aware of Matty's Land

Rover starting up, the engine rattling; it chugged away and then the garden was silent apart from busy insects. Selena stared at the painting, her thoughts coming one after the other: she understood exactly how to put it right. She mixed some colours: midnight blue, silver, smoky white, inky black. Then she stared at the smeared canvas and started to paint thick layers of dusky colour at the top, over the blue, where the azure sky had been. The hills now became an ominous dark green, the sky crepuscular, then darker still. Selena added a moon, lurking shadows beyond the well.

Time passed, but she didn't notice the air grow cool as the sun sank behind Hilltop farm. Her arms and legs were no longer warm and sun-kissed; she painted on until the sky became grey and the light had completely faded.

Then she stood back and gazed at her picture with a smile. The well was almost central in the picture, the looming fields darker behind. There was a hooked moon, its light glinting onto grey clouds in the sky. An owl was overhead, in mid-flight, its wings wide. And in the middle of the picture was a slender figure in a long dress, a translucent grey shadow, her arms raised.

15

Selena waved a warm goodbye as Laura pulled out of the drive: she had insisted on dropping her home after dinner. They'd had a wonderful evening, which seemed to go by in a flash.

Selena pushed her key into the lock, glad that she had left all the lights blazing inside Sloe Cottage – she didn't intend to come home to a dark house again. She walked quickly through the living room, where the air was icy despite the glowing fire, and into the kitchen, taking off her jacket and shoes, stretching her legs. It was past midnight, Sunday morning already, so she'd go straight up to bed and have a shower when she woke up.

Selena rushed upstairs, two steps at a time, keen to enjoy the warmth of her bed: she'd only had one glass of wine with dinner. Laura, generous to a fault, had insisted that she try several of her father's pakoras, by which time she was too full to eat much of the huge portion of chicken jalfrezi that was placed in front of her. She walked down the landing between the two bedrooms: the door to the second bedroom was ajar. Selena pulled it crisply closed.

Ten minutes later, she was in bed, the room lit by a soft glow from the lamp. She considered reading a book for twenty minutes, but then she changed her mind, switching off the light and closing her eyes. As she tried to sleep, shreds of conversation from the evening came back to her. Rob and Laura had entertained her with anecdotes connected with Rob's love of history. Laura thought that it was hilarious that Rome was founded by two brothers who were nursed by a she-wolf: her pupils always loved to act out that story. Rob explained excitedly that he was a member of several local societies, that he had recently been to Taunton Museum to see the largest collection of Roman coins which had been found in a single container, in Frome. Selena thought that Rob was fascinating: she liked the way his eyes shone as he spoke with such enthusiasm about his research. They had chatted for a while about Selena's paintings, and she had mentioned meeting Joely, who, according to Laura, was well known in Ashcombe as a herbalist who was always in demand, particularly for her incredible natural skin creams.

Selena breathed deeply, trying to calm her mind so that sleep would come; she thought wryly that she could do with some of Joely's valerian or chamomile tea to help her drift off. She opened her eyes: the room was intensely dark, the granular blackness made it impossible to see a chair or a wardrobe in the corner of the room. Selena tensed as she recalled the shadowy form she thought she had seen beside the old well, the slender figure, her arms raised as if in salutation. She told herself firmly that it had been simply her imagination, a trick of the moonlight and shadow. There had been no one there. She was enjoying living and painting in Sloe Cottage and just because it was old, it creaked a little and it had an atmosphere, she wasn't going to let that spoil her stay. She was painting good marketable pictures, she was benefiting from the peace and quiet, she was healing, and she had started to think less about David and everything she had lost.

Selena rolled over on her side and exhaled, feeling sleep start to swamp her. She was safe and warm, her toes curled beneath a soft duvet, and she began to drift. Her breathing was deep and rhythmic, she was almost asleep, when she heard a sound, a distinctive noise coming from outside the room. It woke her immediately; she was alert, listening. It was a single sob, soft, but definitely a throaty moan. She was sure she had heard it: it had been outside the door on the landing, or beyond.

Selena held her breath, wide awake now, her ears straining for any sound. She wondered if an intruder had managed to sneak in while she was out, but it was unlikely: the house had been locked. Her mind raced, wondering what to do. For a while there was nothing, deafening silence in her ears, then she heard the click of a latch, the creak of a door opening. She recalled the second bedroom, how she had closed the door earlier, and now she had just heard it open; she had heard *someone* open it.

Selena couldn't move; her breath rasped in her chest as she listened hard. Her skin prickled with cold and fear; she felt a rivulet of perspiration pool at the bottom of her spine. She huddled beneath the duvet and waited. Then she heard a soft footfall on the landing, hardly a sound at all, but Selena was sure someone was there. She opened her mouth to call out, but the words stuck in her throat. She was sure that there was someone just beyond the bedroom door: she felt that at any moment, the door would be pushed open. Selena wished she had the courage to get up, to switch on the lights, flood the room with brightness, fling open the door and prove to herself that there was no one there. Her mind was playing tricks.

Then there was another noise, a slow dull metallic scrape: the door latch to her bedroom was being lifted. Selena felt her body stiffen, bracing herself, and time stretched as she held herself tense and coiled. She strained her ears to listen, but there was no sound other than the thud of her pulse.

Selena cowered beneath the duvet and squeezed her eyes closed, shaking, hoping that sleep would soon come.

* * *

The next morning, Selena woke unusually late: it was after eight thirty. Once she had fallen into slumber, she had slept surprisingly well. She slithered from beneath the duvet in pyjamas, about to rush to the shower, then she changed her mind. She stood in front of her bedroom door: it was closed, as she had left it: nothing had changed. In the bright daylight, Selena knew that her imagination had played tricks on her last night; she had heard the wind and believed it was something else, something supernatural. Perhaps Joely's words about the house having a presence, the constant repetition of the word eerie, had got to her. This morning, her mind was calm, focused. She had imagined the sound of a sob and the rest had followed: the natural creaks of the house, movement from the wind.

She placed a hand on the door latch, hesitating for a moment before thrusting the door wide and stepping onto the landing. The air was cool, the space was gloomy, but nothing was amiss. She stepped cautiously towards the second bedroom and caught her breath. The door was slightly ajar. She knew she had closed it firmly last night, but now it was open, a gap revealing the shadows beyond. Selena took a breath and pushed the door open: it banged against the interior wall, creaking back towards her. She stepped into the bedroom. The air was ice against her skin through her thin pyjamas. She gazed around: the bed was exactly as Claire had left it a week ago, the duvet smooth, the pillows plumped. The curtains were parted, revealing a clear glass vase. Nothing had changed. Selena resolved to wash the bedding today, to open the windows wide and let in some fresh spring air. But first, she'd have a shower.

It was past nine when she emerged from the shower, her hair dripping. She paused, listening, hearing the sound of rapping: there was someone knocking at the front door downstairs. She wriggled into clothes and rushed down, barefooted beyond her jeans, her hair soaking into the fabric of her top.

When she shoved the door ajar, she was surprised to see the engineer, now smarter, tall and lean in jeans and T-shirt instead of the black anorak: he was standing there, smiling broadly.

'Has something else broken down?' she asked, puzzled. 'Only, it's a bit odd to get another visit from an engineer on a Sunday.'

He laughed, thinking she was making a joke, and held out a box containing a coffee maker. 'I've brought you this, since the old one doesn't work. And also...' His other hand held a paper bag of croissants. 'I brought these too – I hope you haven't had breakfast yet.'

Selena was even more puzzled. 'Thank you...'

He smiled. 'My mother asked me to bring the coffee maker over and I thought the croissants would be a useful addition.'

'Your mother?' Realisation dawned on her slowly. 'Do you mean Lesley?'

'I should have introduced myself last time, but I thought you knew. I'm Nick Russell. Ian and Lesley are my parents.'

Selena smiled shyly, feeling a little awkward that she had assumed he was the engineer. But now it all made perfect sense.

She opened the door wider. 'Would you like to come in? Have you had breakfast? I mean, there are too many croissants for one.' She put a hand to her mouth, wondering if she was being forward.

'Thanks, and no, I haven't eaten already – breakfast would be nice. And we can check the coffee machine works...'

* * *

Half an hour later, they were sitting at the kitchen table with small cups of perfectly brewed coffee and a plate each of warm flaky croissants. Selena was glad she had asked Nick Russell to stay. He was good company, and the presence of another person was exactly what she needed to bring her back to normality after her imagination had played tricks last night. She watched him from across the table, his fingers wrapped around the small cup, and she smiled. 'The new machine makes great coffee. It was kind of you to bring it over.'

'Mum and Dad are busy in the garden this morning. I usually drive up to see them at some point over the weekend,' he said. 'Coffee makes a nice change. I'll have to start drinking it again.'

Selena remembered. 'Oh, you usually drink Earl Grey tea.'

'This is Sunday breakfast, though.' The skin around his eyes crinkled as he grinned. 'But why are we talking about breakfast when I've wanted so much to talk about your paintings?'

A smile spread across Selena's lips. 'The painting is going really well. I'm having such a great time here – it's so inspiring.' She leaned forward. 'I've painted fields, cows, trees, and I've even painted the old well.'

'I'm glad you're enjoying Sloe Cottage.' Nick raised his eyebrows. 'Many people just find it a bit cold and a bit eerie.'

'That was the word you used last week.' Selena wondered whether to mention to him the silhouette she'd glimpsed standing beneath the moon, or the sob she'd heard last night from the spare bedroom. She decided not to: he hardly knew her and she didn't want him to think her foolish.

'It's an old house,' Nick said by way of explanation. 'Especially the front part, the original seventeenth-century rooms. It has an atmosphere and not everyone feels comfortable here. But you clearly do.' His gaze was one of admiration. 'You seem to be really at home, painting and sketching, having a great time.'

'That's what I came here to do,' Selena replied.

'On that note,' Nick pushed his half-finished coffee cup away. 'How would you like to go for a walk? There are some great places around here – woodland, farmland, hills. It's a lovely day and you could bring your sketch pad. From the Blackdowns, you can see for miles. And there's a lovely walk up to an old beacon, one of a chain of beacons built in Elizabethan times to warn of advancing enemies, the Spanish Armada. From the top, you can see villages, hills and farms, the motorway and the Wellington monument. It's a stretch of history, the old and the new.'

'Oh, that would be great. I'll take some photos, and perhaps I can paint some of the scenes later.' Selena's voice was warm with enthusiasm. It would be a perfect Sunday, being outdoors exploring, looking for new landscapes to paint. And Nick had local knowledge; he knew the best places to visit. She would pull on some walking boots and a jacket, then they'd set off into the sunshine.

Selena smiled: she was looking forward to the rest of the day: it was glowing with all sorts of new possibilities.

16

September brought the rains and, thankfully, Grace was moved to the strawed-down barn to milk the cows every day. Since Nancy and Alice had left to be married, their younger sister, Jennet, had taken their place and a new milkmaid had started, a girl in her teens whose name was Margaret, who seemed indifferent to Jennet's chatter and tended the cows quietly, her head down as milk splashed into the pail.

Grace huddled inside a sheepskin cloak her grandmother had acquired for her from a local woman who owed her a favour; she and Bett had spent evenings together sewing, letting out her skirt and bodice at the seams so that her clothes hung loosely. Grace's belly had swollen a little, but so far no one had seemed to notice and neither Grace nor Bett had taken an opportunity to speak to Will Cotter about the baby that would arrive at the end of winter.

Grace paused momentarily from milking; she removed her woollen mittens and blew on her hands, rubbing them together, both for the comfort of the cow and for herself. Her toes were brittle with cold inside the thin boots; she stamped her feet every few minutes to thaw them. Outside, beyond the barn, the rain was incessant, pooling in the fields; it drummed on the ground with a repetitive drone and dripped constantly from the timber frame.

Grace wondered what her father was doing, whether there was any work inside the barns for him to do or whether he'd be outside, tilling the soil, surrounded by puddles. She thought of the quiet of the evening, sitting by the hearth, cooking his pottage, and felt sad; she would not be able to visit the garden, or pluck herbs, or share the thoughts of her heart with the chattering well. More than ever, she felt alone.

Jennet made a long sound of discontentment. 'I do not know what is wrong with this cow, why she won't let down her milk for me. Perchance she has a bad humour on her, like Nancy.' She scowled. 'Nancy is always out of temper nowadays; she would make the milk sour if she was here.'

Grace looked up from her work. 'Why? What befalls Nancy?'

'She is with child already. It will come next spring and her husband is a pudding-headed fellow who is always in his cups – he loves the taste of ale more than he loves my sister: she knows it is true herself. He spends each evening in The Royal Oak, playing Noddy and Penneech with the other men from the farm, and he comes home each evening with an empty purse. They have little money between them and they do nothing but exchange cross words.'

'Poor Nancy,' Grace said.

'Oh, she must lie on the bed she has made for herself,' Jennet replied carelessly, sounding much older than her fifteen years. 'It does not come near me. I will never take a husband.' She thought for a moment. 'Even Alice does not seem in a good humour now she is wed.'

Grace did not reply. She was afraid to cross Nathaniel's path: she had avoided him since the wedding and the thought of meeting him terrified her. Her heart knocked as she imagined speaking to him, what he would say if he knew about the child she was carrying. She had seen Alice occasionally, her head bent as she followed Harriet Harper, who always spoke loudly and incessantly, Alice constantly under her instruction. She thought it must be difficult, to be firstly a milkmaid and then the wife of a farmer. There was so much to learn about running the household and, despite her new position, Alice's duty was to obey both Nathaniel and his parents. And it was said that Harriet was quick to judge and quick to disapprove.

Jennet was still talking quickly. 'No, none of this will come near me, for I shall never marry. I have no intention of being a big-bellied fussock like my sister, Nancy, or a farmer's mother's maidservant, like Alice.' She turned to Margaret, who was working hard, her head down, and laughed. 'What do you think of it all? You are the same age as I, Margaret, maybe a little older. Do you not dream of being yoked to a tosspot like George Shears?'

Margaret shook her head. 'It touches me not, Jennet. I work by day, and in the evening, I do my close work by the light of the tallow. That is enough. Mother and I need to sew and take in washing to put food on the table for my younger brother and sister. I have no time for jawing and idle gossip. I must work all hours.'

'Oh, I do beg pardon,' Jennet replied, her voice heavy with sarcasm. She thought for a moment and then turned her attention to Grace. 'But what about you, Grace? You live with your father. It is not much of a life for a woman your age. And I recall seeing you at the May dance – Nathaniel Harper danced both with you and with Alice. Did you not think yourself his favourite then?'

'I did not.' Grace looked up. 'And there is but little milk in your pail. I fear you will be scolded, Jennet. Here, let me help.'

Grace eased herself from the stool and moved to where Jennet was working. She wrapped her hands around Jennet's, her chapped skin covering Jennet's soft plump fingers, and she began to pull at the udders gently, a strong rhythm, a new pressure. Jennet watched, amazed, as milk squirted into the pail.

'You must have enchanted hands, Grace,' Jennet said. 'I have heard you have all sorts of skills with plants and herbs. Can you teach me that too? Then perhaps I will learn to use some of your magic for myself.'

Grace returned to her work. 'The plants and simples teach me, not the other way.' She resumed milking. 'But if you speak kindly to Mistress Cow, Jennet, then she will yield her milk willingly.'

Jennet barked a laugh. 'And that is how it is with menfolk – they speak women fair only for them to yield willingly too. Then they become a wagtail, like Nancy, or ill-tempered, like Alice – one already big with child and the other married into a family of vipers. They will both be out of humours for the rest of their days.'

She stopped: light footsteps were approaching and the three women worked in silence as Alice Harper came into the barn. She was wearing a pale grey dress, the bodice laced tightly, and a cream-coloured cap over her hair. Her eyes searched the barn as Jennet called, 'You look very becoming today, sister. Has your husband's father paid for another new gown?'

Alice frowned, ignoring her, and turned to Grace. 'I would speak with you, Grace.'

'Of course.' Grace rose from her work and Alice pointed to the fields where the rain still fell.

'We will speak here, at the edge of the barn.'

Grace followed Alice until they were at a distance from the milk-maids, sheltered from the downpour, then Alice lowered her voice.

'I have heard it said that you are skilled in the use of plants and herbs.'

Grace nodded. 'I learned from my mother and my grandmother, Bett White, who has many skills.'

'And it has been said that you can make a poultice that can stop a woman's cramps?'

'I can...'

Alice seized her arm, her grip tight. 'And can you make a powder or a potion that will make a woman quickly get with child?'

Grace met Alice's sad blue eyes. She noticed her rosy cheeks had become sallow.

'You have been wed but three months. There is yet much time...'

'I need to be with child soon. Please, Grace, can you help me? Nathaniel and my mother-in-law grow impatient with me.'

Grace's expression was soft with sympathy. 'I have some nettle infusion at home and the leaves of raspberry may help, too.' Her voice was low. 'Do not fret yourself. I will bring it here to you tomorrow.'

'Thank you, Grace. I have thought to seek a physician, to find tinctures and purges. There is no limit to what I will do. I must give him a son, and soon.'

'I will do my best to help you.'

Alice's fingers still circled Grace's wrist. 'And I beg of you, say nothing to anyone of this.'

'I never shall speak of it.' Grace was about to return to her stool and pail, but Alice grasped her hand.

'If I do not bear him a son, I am undone. Nathaniel and his mother expect it of me. Every day, she asks me when I will do my duty by the family. Promise me you will help.'

'I can but promise to try,' Grace said.

Alice sighed and swept away back to the farmhouse, slender as a branch. Grace moved a hand to her belly, closing her eyes, feeling the rounded shape beneath. For a moment, she was overcome with sadness for Alice and for herself.

* * *

'Culmstock Beacon is incredible.' Selena was relaxing in a soft seat in the bar of The Royal Oak cradling a glass of tomato juice, her booted legs stretched out in front of her. 'What an exhilarating walk. Thank you so much, Nick.'

He smiled. 'I enjoyed it – I'd like to have made a day of it, but I have to help my parents this afternoon: there's some lifting to do, an old wardrobe in one of the bedrooms needs chopping up, and if I don't help my dad out, he'll do it by himself.'

'I'm really grateful that you showed me around this part of Somerset,' Selena said. 'I have some wonderful photos. So, while you're busy helping out at Hilltop Farm, I'm going to start a new painting, and I know exactly what I'm going to do first.'

'The panoramic view from the Beacon?' Nick asked. 'Or the walk through the woods with all the tall trees?'

'Neither,' she smiled. 'On the way here, when we looked at the view across the Blackdowns, I took a photo of a solitary cow in a field. The sky behind was really ominous, all greys and blues, rainclouds coming in. I'm going to paint that.'

'Sounds perfect. I think you're right about the weather, Selena.' Nick finished his half-pint of cider. 'It looks like we're in for a downpour this afternoon. Maybe we ought to be getting back to Chitterwell.'

'Okay.' Selena reached for her coat.

'How about doing this again next week, weather permitting?' Nick asked. 'We could walk along the canal paths or go further afield. Perhaps we could even stop somewhere nice for lunch?'

'I'd like that.' Selena was ready to go. 'That will give me something to look forward to when I'm hard at work all week.' She glanced at the wall clock. 'Almost one o'clock already? That gives me plenty of time to start my painting this afternoon.'

'I can't wait to see it.' Nick opened the door and they stepped out into the village street. The skies were overcast already, dark clouds hanging low. 'We'd better hurry up – it's definitely going to pour down soon.'

As they walked, Selena's phone buzzed: it was Claire. She glanced at Nick. 'Sorry, I ought to get this.'

'Of course.'

'Hi, Claire – how's it going?' Selena listened while Claire's voice bubbled in her ear.

'Good news – I think I've found the perfect person to help out in the gallery. Do you remember Gulliver Ocasio, who was in our year at uni? I haven't seen him since we left, but he came in the other day to see if we could feature some of his work. He's a graffiti artist and I'm tempted to take him on for a trial period. He could look after the gallery and sell some of his paintings with us at the same time. But I wanted to check that it was okay with you first.'

'Of course – I trust your judgement completely,' Selena said. 'Tell me about him.'

Claire was excited. 'I've seen some of his work. He's amazing – he does oversized, garish faces, stunningly bright colours. And he's a really nice guy. Don't you remember him? Originally from the Caribbean, tall, lean, great sense of humour...'

'Take him on, Claire. He sounds perfect.' Selena had left the village behind her and was walking towards Chitterwell, Nick by her side. 'So, he'll get a trial period first?'

'I think so. And he's good-looking too.'

Selena smiled. 'I thought that might be the case.'

Claire's voice was loud in the earpiece. 'I'll ring him today and see if he can start first thing tomorrow. Once he's got the hang of it all, I can leave him for a while. It will free me up to visit you. By the way, how's the painting going?'

'Really well.' Selena glanced towards Nick who offered her a conspiratorial wink.

'Oh, and one more thing.' Claire's tone changed: she was suddenly quieter, more confidential. 'There's something I ought to tell you. It's not great news.'

'Oh?' Selena frowned.

'David came in the gallery today. He was asking about you, about the... about the baby.'

'What did you say to him?' Selena's voice rose and Nick glanced at her, checking her expression, raising anxious brows.

'I told him to go away. I said you didn't want to talk to him.'

'Thanks, Claire.' Selena breathed a sigh. 'You're right, I don't want any contact with him.'

'Don't worry, I'll keep him at arm's-length, I promise. Right, I'll ring Gulliver now. Talk to you later.'

Claire hung up and Nick met Selena's gaze. 'Is everything all right?'

'That was my flatmate, Claire – we own the gallery together. She was just giving me an update.' Selena paused at the gate to Sloe Cottage, the fields rising to Hilltop Farm in the distance. She wondered if she should have mentioned David, but the moment had passed and she wasn't ready to talk about the miscarriage, not yet. Another opportunity would present itself in time and she'd feel ready then to talk to Nick about her past. She opted for a simple reply. 'Yes, things are going really well at the gallery.'

'I'm glad to hear it.' Nick grinned. 'Right – well, I'll say goodbye here. Shall I call round next week?'

'Come to breakfast,' Selena said. 'I'll get the croissants this time, and we'll have them with Earl Grey tea.'

'Perfect,' Nick agreed. He waved a hand and began to walk away. 'I'll look forward to it all week.'

'Me too.' Selena turned towards the cottage, smiling at the thought of seeing Nick again, rummaging for the keys as her phone rang again. She tugged it out of her pocket without thinking and answered the call. 'Hello?'

'Hello.' It was David's voice. 'Selena. Where are you? I have to talk to you.'

Selena pulled the phone from her ear as if it had shocked her, pressing a button to end the call. It had started to rain, fat drops spattering on the ground. She found the keys and pushed the front door open, rushing inside. Her heart was thumping: the last thing she needed was David Marsh to create turbulence in her new-found calm.

17

It was late one Saturday afternoon; grey December rain thudded against the wooden window shutters in Bett White's cob cottage as she sat at the spindle, Grace at her shoulder, watching the yarn twist and lengthen. Bett was calm, almost hypnotised, as her eyes followed the turn of the yarn, and she recited to herself.

> *'If the maids a-spinning go,*
> *Burn the flax and fire the tow;*
> *Scorch their plackets, but beware*
> *That ye singe no maidenhair.'*

Grace frowned. 'What are these words, Grandmother? Is it a poem?'

'It is, and a famous one. The poet, Robert Herrick, was a cleric, and he lived to an old age. He died some years ago, in '74, I think. Have you not heard of his poem that begins "Gather ye rosebuds while ye may"?'

'I have not.'

'Ah.' Bett sighed and for a while there was no other sound than the thrum of the spindle. 'The poet warns maids to marry while they are young. Time passes and we are too soon left old.' She was quiet again.

'I like his wise words. "Gather ye rosebuds while ye may, Old Time is still a-flying; And this same flower that smiles today, Tomorrow will be dying."'

Grace inclined her head. 'Wise words, and sad ones too.' She watched her grandmother, the side-to-side movement of her cap as she spun the yarn. 'You must have seen many a change in your lifetime, Grandmother.'

'I have, indeed.' Again, Bett was thoughtful. 'I was born in '21. Four years before, King James died of a tertian ague and his son, Charles, came to the throne. And before I had reached ten years, King Charles had dissolved Parliament. I was just married to my John when the Civil War began. That was a bloody time: the castle at Taunton was damaged over and over. Men came to fight from all corners of the land; they used to say that the Cornishmen were some of the king's toughest soldiers. And by 1645, the New Model Army was a proper force to be reckoned with and Sir Thomas Fairfax was appointed its Lord General. Oliver Cromwell was his second-in-command, and we all know what happened after that. The king went to the scaffold in '49. They say he held his head up high before it was chopped from his body.'

'I have never known any king other this King Charles.'

'You have lived but a few years. Pray God that when you are my age, Gracie, all you will have known is a time of peace.'

'By the time I am your age, Grandmother, my child will have children too, and I may be made a happy grandmother just as you.'

Bett was troubled by a sudden thought. 'And may God keep you all safe. I have heard whispers of witchcraft from some people in the village and once the talk starts, it is not long before someone is accused. Although Robert Hunt has gone from Taunton now, there are many more men keen and willing to do his work. I heard that a woman was seen dancing on the Devil's Stone in Holcombe Fitzpaine and the next day, her mother-in-law was struck to the ground and took numb down one side.'

'What happened to her?'

'They set fire to the young woman's thatched cottage. Have you not heard tell, if you set fire to a witch's thatched roof, she'll come running? And, sure enough, she ran from the house and confessed all.'

'She said that she was a witch?'

'Oh, and it was true. She had turned herself into a hare, as many do, so the farmer could not catch her when she came to curse his farm. And, of course, she will hang now and they will bury her in an unmarked grave at Dead Woman's Ditch.' Bett's tone was hushed, grave. 'Once they have breathed the word *witch*, Gracie, there can be no unsaying of it.'

Grace shivered and Bett turned to meet her eyes, her hands still busy twisting yarn.

'The child flutters?'

'Oh yes – I feel it constantly. It brings me joy to know that the baby quickens and is strong.'

'And your father – does he know yet?'

'I am sure that he does – I see him watching me as I cook, when I bend over slowly, his eyes are sad, but he says nothing.'

'Then you must speak to him of it yourself.'

'I dare not, Grandmother. I am ashamed of what I have done.'

Bett sighed and suddenly her hands were still. 'Let me make you a raspberry infusion, and we will sit at the hearth and talk of names for the child. I am eager to know what you will call the baby.'

'I put such things from my heart in case it brings bad luck.'

'But you must not think such thoughts. Being with child is a time of contemplation and joy: it is a good time when we must use our hands wisely, making ready for the day he comes into the world.'

'I have been making a string ladder, just as you told me, Grandmother, with knotted rope and feathers, and I have been saying the words over that you taught me. Then if I should die when I am birthing, it may lead me to heaven to be with my mother.'

Bett took her hand, soothing the rough skin with gentle pressure. 'I would rather eat a pincushion as have you worry yourself about what will happen when you are bringing forth the baby. I will be there with you.'

'I have never seen a pincushion, not a real one like the fine ladies have.'

'They keep them to ward off evil. Do you know, a lady will put a tomato on the mantel of a new house to make the family prosper and to keep away evil spirits, but when tomatoes are out of season, she will use a round ball of red fabric filled with sand, and that is how the pincushion came to be.'

Grace smiled, a slight curve of her lips. 'You are so wise, and I always love to hear your stories, Grandmother. And you must promise me that you will be by my side when the time comes...'

'Nothing will keep me from the birth, Gracie. You have my word on it.'

Grace smoothed the fabric of her skirts. 'I must leave now. It is already dark and Father will be in need of his supper.'

'That you must,' Bett said sadly. 'How I wish you could stay here with me and I could take care of you and the child, when he comes.'

Grace kissed her cheek. 'You're the best of grandmothers. But the walk to Slaugh Cottage from here is good for me and the baby. It warms us, and there will be a fire in the hearth and a pot of food warming over it. Now I must bid you goodbye.'

Bett accompanied Grace to the low door of her cottage. 'And how goes the milking at Hill Top Farm?'

'I am a good worker; I fill pails more quickly than anyone and I think that is why they keep me there.' Grace shrugged. 'They look at the milk that I get the cows to yield; no one notices me while I am seated on the stool milking cows.'

'And Master Nathaniel? How goes Mistress Alice?'

'I rarely see Master Nathaniel; he busies himself with the menfolk on the farm and in the fields, and I am seldom disturbed. As for Alice, I see her each week, and she asks me for more potions, nettle infusion, oil to rub on her skin, but there is no change in her condition. It seems she cannot get with child.'

'She has been wed for six months. It is not unusual to take a year, more, oft times. Perhaps the yuletide will be an occasion for her to put her mind to festivities; these things often come to pass when a woman does not fret over them.'

Grace agreed. 'I hope it does, for her sake. She tells me that both Mistress Harriet and Nathaniel are out of temper with her; they long for sons to fill their farm.'

'It is their folly to make so much fuss. It will not help poor Alice.'

'Alice's sister Nancy is big with child now. I believe the baby will come in March. I rack myself about how I can help Alice, Grandmother. Especially since I have a child coming and she has none yet.'

Bett shook her head. 'Think of yourself, Gracie. Take care of yourself and the little one. And come and see me tomorrow – we must not miss church on Sunday.' Her expression changed to one of concern. 'May God keep you safe.'

'And you too.' Grace waved her hand and was on her way, the old sheepskin cloak wrapped tightly around her shoulders. She hurried as fast as she could through the grey drizzle, her head down against the gusty wind. She was almost outside Ashcomb when she heard a low voice call her name.

'Grace.'

Grace walked on, quickening her pace.

'Grace, tarry awhile. I would walk with you.'

The voice was quiet, a man's, urgency in the tone. She recalled with a pang of sadness what had happened when Nathaniel had walked her home. She had trusted him and he had misled her.

'Grace.'

She turned. 'Who's there?'

A young man was level with her; he was thick-set, with rough brown hair, honest hazel eyes. 'It is me, Ned, George Shears' brother, George that married Nancy Bryant.'

Grace continued to walk, and he was at her side, speaking quickly. 'Tonight, I sleep in the barn in Hill Top. Oft times, I stay with my brother and his wife, but they are ill at ease with me there.' He continued to chatter, his expression amiable. 'Nathaniel Harper knows I like to sleep in the straw – he pays me no mind. I have been to The

Royal Oak, drinking with George and the others. The walk back is pleasant – even more so in your good company. Please, allow me to walk with you as far as Slaugh Cottage.'

Grace did not look at him. 'I have no need of anyone to walk with me, Ned. Thank you, but I am quite well alone.'

Ned kept up with her pace, moving closer to her side. 'I won some money from my brother tonight – we were playing Noddy and Penneech. George is not skilled with his cards. He has ill luck. I think he has ill luck with his wife too –most times I am there, they quarrel and bicker. He is in his cups and she is a scold.'

'Do not speak ill of Nancy,' Grace said softly.

'Speak kindly to me then, Grace. I have seen you working in the strawed-down barn. I often wonder if you have need of a good man, one who will care for you.'

'Thank you, Ned, but I have need of no one.' Grace was walking as fast as she could. She was aware that, months ago, she could have broken into a run and left Ned Shears behind her in a moment. Now her gait was lumbering, slowed.

'Pretty Grace, do you not like me?' Ned was insistent. 'I am hard-working, strong, God-fearing. I would make a young woman a good husband...'

Grace heard the plea in his voice and felt sorry for him. She paused, catching her breath, and turned to look at him. 'I am not in need of a husband.'

Ned misunderstood her intentions; he thought she had stopped to talk, that she feigned disinterest in order to persuade him to court her, and he seized his opportunity and clasped her in his arms. 'Dear Grace.'

She pulled away, but Ned's arms had circled her waist, then he jerked back in shock. Grace saw the horrified expression.

'No, Grace Cotter, you have no need for a husband. It is too late for that, I fear. You have already been tumbled.'

Grace put her hand to her mouth. 'Ned, I pray you say nothing of this.'

'I will not speak of it.' Ned stepped back, his eyes on her. 'For it is not mine to speak of. I am no village gossip.'

Grace took a breath. 'Thank you, Ned. I am in your debt.'

'Your belly is big with child. Who fathered it?' Ned caught his breath, taking a step back. 'You are no jade. I know you for a simple village girl who works hard. How did this come to pass?'

'I cannot say.'

He was staring, mouth agape. 'I recollect back in May, after the dancing, when I was walking back to the barn from the inn, I saw you in your garden with a man. Was it then that this happened?'

Grace recalled the evening she had stood in the garden with Nathaniel. Two men had passed the gate on their way to Hill Top Farm; one had called out his name in jest, 'Master Nathaniel,' and laughed. Grace wondered if Ned would remember and if later he would speak about it in the village. Grace thought of Alice, desperate to have a baby of her own, and she thought of Nathaniel and his mother, angry because Alice had not conceived. Grace made up her mind and spoke quickly. 'It was no one you know. No one from the village. And I beg you, Ned, to say nothing.'

Ned took another step back. 'No man from the village? A stranger, then? An outsider. Was it an outsider, Grace?'

Grace shook her head. 'I cannot speak of it...'

'I have said it already – I will breathe no word to anyone.' His eyes were wide and his expression strange. 'I want nothing to do with any stranger who stands in your garden at nightfall and tempts you. I am sorry you are no longer in need of a husband. I would have treated you well and we could have been happy. But it is no matter now. I bid you goodnight.'

Then he began to walk away, to run at a pace. Grace watched as he pounded up the path towards Hill Top Farm. Ned had discovered that she was with child and it had frightened him. Grace wondered what would happen when other people knew about her condition: her father, Alice, Nathaniel. She shivered, passed a damp hand across her brow and was suddenly filled with despair.

18

Selena stood in the conservatory, her hair tied in a knot, brush in hand, and gazed at the painting she had started several days before. It was a perfect image of a black and white cow standing in an open field; in the distance, there were more fields, yellow and ochre, rising towards a blustery sky. A heavy storm was brewing; clouds hanging low, dark as bruises. Selena was pleased with the composition. She'd leave it a while and go back to it with fresh eyes.

She gazed through the glass panelled windows into the back garden. It was illuminated with sunshine. It was already a hot morning, the twelfth of May, and there were bright bluebells lodged between stones, a pink flowering apple tree and, beyond, the fields of Hilltop Farm. Selena looked around: the view was idyllic. Sloe Cottage was an inspirational place to live: strange, yet somehow inspiring, as if she was almost connected to the people who had lived there before, who had been immersed in the harsh beauty of rural Somerset.

Then the brush twitched in her hand and she plunged it into pale paint and began to sketch in a figure. To one side of the cow, she drew the outline of a woman sitting on a stool. She was bent over, milking, deep in thought. Selena painted in the outline of a long skirt, an apron, a cap on her head and a kerchief across her shoulders. She wondered, as she began to compose the milkmaid, why she had chosen the clothing, where she had seen the image before, but it was clear in her artist's mind's eye and she transferred it to the canvas.

Selena paused, thinking; she would make the milkmaid lost in thought, as if her mind was tugged elsewhere, not on her labours. Her cheek rested against the cow's hindquarters, but her expression was troubled about the mouth, as if her life brimmed with problems that she could not resolve. Exactly, Selena thought: she was a peasant woman whose life revolved around making ends meet. She had little power and her troubles were caused by others, by those who ordered her simple life and made it even harder.

Selena added detail to the figure, the dull cream dress, the soiled apron, the modest cap, the sad eyes, a hint of pale red hair below the bonnet. She was amazed how easily the figure fitted the picture, as if it had always been intended there. Selena wondered where the poor girl might shelter when the rains began to pelt down; there was no barn. She would paint Sloe Cottage in the background, but it would be smaller, the roof thatched, the garden full of the mixed green shades of various herbs. She would add the well and the dark shadow of a barbed blackthorn tree where the window would have been.

Selena felt the warmth of breath on her neck, a light exhalation. It was as if someone was standing behind her, watching her at work. She stood still for a moment; someone was a few inches from her, she could feel it. Her skin became cold. Selena held her breath. She felt a person leaning close, the prickle of proximity, of another body. Selena exhaled lightly, waiting. It was there, still. She shivered and felt her body tense.

For some reason she couldn't explain, Selena raised her voice and spoke out, shakily. 'I hope you like the picture.'

Then the person was gone. Selena whirled round and stared into the empty conservatory. Despite the warm sunshine streaming through the glass, Selena's skin was still ice cold and she was trembling.

Her phone buzzed: she examined the caller ID before answering as she had done with every call she'd received since Sunday afternoon, and she was glad it was not David. She held the phone to her ear. 'Laura.'

'I hope I'm not interrupting your work.'

'Not at all.' Selena was relieved to hear the rattle of a friendly voice.

'Only I'm off to Taunton shopping – the Thursday market is really good. And I thought you might like to come with me.'

'Oh, yes please.' Selena jumped at the chance to go out; the presence of an unseen observer had shaken her more than she wanted to admit. The painting would wait: the milkmaid was poised on her stool and Selena knew exactly how it would look when she finished.

'I'll be at your gate in ten minutes,' Laura said.

'Great,' Selena replied. 'I'll grab a jacket and my bag.'

* * *

An hour later, Selena and Laura were wandering around the market stalls set up in front of the sumptuous wisteria-clad Castle Hotel, once an old Norman fortress. Laura was raving about the organic fruit and vegetables she bought each week, the delicious range of cheeses and a stall which sold gluten-free bread and cakes. 'You'd never tell their produce was gluten-free, Selena. The sponges are so light and the bread is to die for. I have to buy gluten-free for my dad because if he eats wheat, he gets a horrible bloated stomach.' Laura tucked an arm through Selena's. 'Of course, I end up eating it all, but, ah, what the hell.' She laughed.

'Oh, look.' Selena paused to gaze at a stall selling crystals. She reached out, touching a pendant necklace with a smooth green stone.

The stallholder was a tall woman wearing a silk headscarf and a long dress. She pointed a finger. 'Does that stone draw you to it?'

Selena was a little surprised. 'Yes, I suppose it does. It's a gorgeous deep green colour, and so smooth. What is it?'

'Malachite,' the woman replied simply.

'You should buy it,' Laura said. 'If it's drawn you to it, there must be a reason. Nothing is drawing me to it, but maybe that's because I'm completely skint, so I can't splurge on myself. I'm so hoping a job will come up at Ashcombe Primary soon – I can't exist forever on supply work.'

The stallholder inclined her wrapped head. 'The stone is malachite; the chain is sterling silver. It's thirty-six pounds, but I'll sell it to you for thirty.'

'It's lovely,' Selena held it up, enjoying the gleaming light that bounced from the polished stone.

'What is malachite good for?' Laura asked.

'It absorbs negative energies and pollutants,' the woman replied. 'Malachite also clears and activates the chakras and attunes the wearer to spiritual guidance. It opens the heart to unconditional love.'

'Oh, that's just perfect for you,' Laura clapped her hands.

'It drew you to it. I noticed how quickly you picked it up.' The stallholder stared at Selena, frowning. 'Malachite wards off evil. It is worn over the heart to rebalance and to keep it open to new experiences.'

Selena plunged her hand into her bag and brought out her purse. 'Thirty pounds?' She handed over her card. 'Do you take cards?'

'Of course. Shall I wrap the pendant?'

'Oh, no – she'll wear it now,' Laura said. 'Won't you, Selena?'

'I think I'd better – my heart needs all the balancing it can get,' Selena smiled, wrapping the pendant around her neck and fiddling with the clip. 'There. How is that?'

'Lovely,' Laura breathed.

'May it bring you joy and keep all negative energy from you,' the stallholder said in a quiet monotone as she handed the bank card back to Selena. 'Have a wonderful day.'

Then Laura grasped the sleeve of Selena's jacket and started to tug. 'Look at the stall over there – it's all the natural creams and lotions, and there's Joely.'

They reached a stall which smelled of sweet oils and heady scents, where Joely and another woman, who was tall and wore a long coat, were selling pots of cream to a woman with a toddler in her arms.

The woman took her purchase and hurried away and Joely turned her smile on Laura and Selena. 'Hello. Great to see you both.'

Selena was looking at rows of little muslin bags that held herbal teas. 'Do you have anything that will help me to sleep?'

'Oh, aren't you sleeping well?' Joely raised an eyebrow in concern.

'I'm fine – but it's an old house and I'm all alone. It does feel a little strange there sometimes, so I thought a warm drink before I turn in...'

'I have some chamomile and some valerian.' Joely offered her the small pouches. 'Try both and see what you think. If you like them, I'll bring you some more round.'

Laura picked up a simple pot of cream. 'I'll take some of this for my wrinkles if I may, Joely. I'm thirty-four and I swear I look at least ten years older...'

'You look lovely, Laura,' Joely said. 'But this stuff is really good – it's avocado, calendula and clary sage. It's the one I use myself.' Then she turned to the woman who was helping her behind the stall. 'Lucy, will you be okay by yourself for half an hour?'

'Of course,' her friend replied.

Joely reached behind the stall for her handbag. 'Do you fancy a quick drink? I haven't had lunch, so a liquid one might just do me for today.'

'What a lovely idea,' Laura said. 'Why don't we go to the Gallows?'

Selena gasped. 'Go to the Gallows?'

'Don't panic,' Laura grinned. 'It's an old pub round the corner. It does the most amazing cheese and onion pies.'

The Stonegallows Inn was a white-fronted building that had been completely renovated inside to include cream-painted wood surfaces and gold flock wallpaper. The jukebox played a selection of lively pop and the bar staff were all young men and women wearing black polo shirts with a noose logo above the name of the pub. The only other reference to its gloomy history was a silver plaque proclaiming that the inn had been a site for executions from 1575 until 1810.

Selena, Laura and Joely huddled round a square table, each with half a pint of cider and a cheese and onion pasty. Selena fingered the malachite pendant around her neck. 'So, I wonder who was executed on this site all those years ago?'

'You can be sure they were poor and probably innocent,' Joely said cynically.

Laura shivered. 'It'll be to do with Judge Deed, I expect. He had loads of people hanged at the end of the 1600s here in Taunton. They rebelled against James the Second – wasn't it the Monmouth Rebellion? I think the Crown took a dim view of rebels in those days.'

'The Pitchfork Rebellion, 1685, the Revolt of the West.' Joely grinned. 'Matty was talking about it the other day – he loves local history. He was going on about the Battle of Sedgemoor – he said twenty-seven Royalists were killed there and they were all buried in the church at Westonzoyland, near Bridgwater.'

'It's strange...' Selena shook her head. 'All the hangings that took place here on this site, yet the pub doesn't feel at all spooky.'

Laura reached for her cider. 'Perhaps all of the ghosts have been chased away by the drinkers.'

'Unlike your house, Selena.' Joely frowned. 'There's a really weird feeling in Sloe Cottage.'

'Don't tell her that – she has to live there.' Laura sat up straight.

'You're not telling me you haven't felt it?' Joely said. 'I mean, there's a sense of sadness, or, I don't know, unfinished business.'

'It's real things that scare me.' Laura gave a high laugh, trying to make light of Joely's comments. 'The other night, when Claire blew a fuse and the lights went out, I was terrified.'

'Joely has a point – there is definitely a sense of something or someone...' Selena's eyes gleamed. 'I have felt, you know, a presence, someone else in the house.'

Laura shuddered. 'Oh don't – you'll give me nightmares.'

'It's more pronounced in the old part of the cottage, where there are shadows and creaks, although I felt someone watching me in the conservatory. It was quite chilling.' Selena leaned back in her seat. 'And the front garden has a strange atmosphere near the old well. I suppose it's just my imagination.'

'Well, I think houses hold their history,' Joely said. 'I think there's some sort of memory of the people who have lived there before, a trace of them having been there, left in the fabric of the house. Perhaps that's why we live in a caravan!'

'Like DNA?' Laura suggested.

Selena agreed. 'Like the people who have spent whole lives in a house, and an essence of them remains behind. You know, a house feels happy if people were happy when they lived there...'

'And that's why Sloe Cottage feels so sad,' Joely said.

'Do you think something horrible happened there?' Laura's eyes were wide.

'Something unfinished, that's why there's a restless spirit?' Joely replied.

'Perhaps. There is a feeling of being... not alone – sometimes, which is quite scary.' Selena reached for her glass for the first time and forced a grin. 'It's definitely inspiring my moody paintings though, my imagination is really fired up – I'm creating all sorts of shadowy shapes, stormy skies and unforgiving country scenes.' She saw Laura's anxious expression. 'I'll be fine. And Claire's really pleased. She's put the paintings I've sent her on the website and there's loads of interest already.'

'But are you sure you're all right there, by yourself?' Laura's eyes glowed with concern behind her glasses.

'Maybe that's why you bought the malachite necklace?' Joely asked. 'For protection?'

'I'm all right most of the time, honestly. I just concentrate on painting.' Selena deliberately changed the subject, trying to appear more casual. The topic of a ghostly presence in Sloe Cottage worried her more than she wanted to believe. She smiled. 'The protection I really need is from my ex, back in Manchester. He rang me at the weekend and I picked up the phone without thinking.'

'The man who...' Laura paused, choosing her words carefully. She wasn't sure if Joely knew about the miscarriage. '... Who you came here to get away from?'

'That's right.' Selena's fingers touched the gleaming stone around her neck. 'If he rings me again, I'm going to talk to him directly and tell him to leave me alone. I won't run away from him, not now.'

'Good for you,' Joely offered an approving smile. She lifted her glass. 'To being strong.'

Selena and Laura raised their glasses and they chorused, 'To being strong.'

Selena took a sip of cider and breathed out slowly. 'I can't help but wonder, though, what happened to the people who lived at Sloe Cottage all those years ago. I find myself thinking of it more and more. I'm sure there must be a story behind all the – what's the word everyone keeps using? – the eeriness.'

19

Selena wasn't thinking about the eerie atmosphere in Sloe Cottage on Sunday morning as she sat across the kitchen table from Nick Russell over a pot of Earl Grey tea and a plate piled with croissants. She was enjoying herself too much. Nick had a map on the table and was pointing out areas of outstanding natural beauty that they might visit to take photos for her paintings.

She leaned back in her seat. 'So, we can visit Hemyock or the Iron Age forts, or we could go to Staple Hill? Which has the best scenery for painting?'

Nick placed a finger on a spot on the map. 'Let's go to Staple Hill. The views from there are incredible – it's the highest point of the Blackdowns. The 800-metre circular walk won't take us long, so, if you like, we can drive on to somewhere else afterwards.'

'And end up at The Royal Oak?' Selena grinned encouragingly, touching her malachite pendant.

'Why not? I think we'll deserve it,' Nick said. 'There's a marshy place just beyond Staple Hill called Deadman which might become a really dramatic painting. It's well known by locals for the willow trees and the St John's wort that grows there.'

'I'm sure Joely uses it – I must ask her.' Selena met his eyes. 'You must love this part of the world.'

'Of course – I grew up here; I went to school in Taunton.' Nick was thoughtful. 'Then after uni and spending a few years working in Bristol, I came back again and found a job in Exeter.'

'What do you do there?'

'I work in the English department of the university – I teach literature, stuff from the medieval period to the present day.'

He grinned and Selena was reminded that she'd assumed he was a heating engineer when they'd first met. She liked the fact that he'd never mentioned her mistake. David had always enjoyed repeatedly reminding her of her flaws. She realised she was smiling. 'It sounds wonderful.'

'I like it – it was a really good move for me.'

'How long have you been there?'

'Three years. I moved on from Bristol after...' Nick ruffled his hair. 'I decided to come back after my girlfriend and I split up. We'd been together a long time and it was the right thing for me to move away.'

'Oh, I'm sorry.' Selena put a hand to her mouth. 'I didn't mean to pry – it sounded like twenty questions...'

'Not at all.' He stretched out his legs beneath the table. Selena decided that it would be easy to spend the whole day in his company and not set foot outside the cottage. But she was looking forward to being outdoors. She pushed back her chair.

'Well, I suppose breakfast is all done now – should we get going?'

'If you like.' Nick didn't move. 'I just wondered if I could have a quick look at your paintings again. I'm fascinated by them, so many contrasting pieces.'

'Of course.' Selena pushed back her chair. 'They are all in the conservatory.'

Nick stood at her shoulder as Selena showed him the painting of the woman milking a cow beneath stormy skies. As he gazed from behind, she was reminded of the nerve-wrenching sensation she had felt as she'd painted it, the presence of someone watching. Nick exhaled.

'Well, that's certainly very dramatic.' He thought for a moment. 'There's something of the victim in the milkmaid, isn't there, her head bowed, acquiescent. Then there's the brooding weather, as if there are consequences for her that are bound to happen and she's in the centre of it all, tossed on life's turbulent storm.'

'Wow,' Selena said. 'You've summed it up perfectly. You should be an art critic.'

Nick grinned. 'I suppose analysing poems and novels isn't that different to discussing art – we all look for symbols to interpret and to guide what we think.' He stood back. 'It's wonderful. Can I see some more?' His gaze fell on a painting standing against the far wall. 'What's that one?'

'Oh, I'm not sure about this one at all – it started out as a picture of the old well in the daytime and then suddenly the moonlight took over.' Selena lifted the painting and placed it on the easel, moving the picture of the cow to the side. 'It's a bit of a departure from my usual style. I'm not sure if it will sell.'

'Someone will find it captivating – it has a hypnotic quality.' Nick indicated the shadowy figure beneath the moon. 'What is this? A woman...'

'Yes...' Selena gazed at her own work, trying to explain her thoughts. 'It's the garden at night and the person is outside, where she feels most at home.'

Nick gave a soft laugh. 'Do you know what I see when I look at this?'

Selena shook her head. 'Not me, I hope.'

'No... but I think this is a companion painting to the one we just looked at, the milkmaid and the cow. I think that's her, the same woman, but here she's not subservient. This time she's in her own territory, she's strong and in charge.'

'Goodness,' Selena shivered. 'I hadn't thought of that. It's made me go cold; you know the sensation people have when they say someone has walked on their grave.'

Nick wrapped an arm around her. 'Sorry, I didn't mean to unnerve you.' He took the comforting arm away too soon. 'Maybe we should go. A nice drive, a couple of interesting walks and then we can come back to The Royal Oak for lunch.'

'That would be great,' Selena said. 'I'll just get my coat and we'll be off.'

She was thankful to turn her back on the paintings and move back into the warm kitchen. Her skin had turned to ice, just as if it had been touched by cold fingers.

* * *

Grace's fingers were frozen as she sat on her stool in the barn, milking another cow. She quivered inside the sheepskin cloak wrapped around her shoulders, stamping her feet to bring her toes back to life.

Jennet nodded her head. 'It's proper yule weather, I'd say. This cow's paps feel like icicles.'

'Yuletide's no special time for me,' Margaret grumbled. 'There's still the washing to do and the mending. There will be no joy in our house – the young ones are gutfoundered, yowling or fighting over crusts. My poor mother doesn't know how she will feed the children – we can hardly feed the fire in the hearth.'

'You should get wed, Margaret.' Jennet tugged harder at the cow's teats. 'That's what I'm going to do. Find yourself a husband who works hard and will take care of you.'

Margaret looked up. 'You change like the wind,' she mumbled. 'You told me you'd rather be dead than wed.'

'The wind blows more gently now,' Jennet said slyly. 'I have a new suitor. And I am turned sixteen years. It is time for me to think about being a bride. And he is a handsome man, and strong, and kind. He is eight years older than I, and he will take good care of me so that I won't need to come milking each day.'

'Who is he?'

'You know him, Margaret. He is called Ned Shears. He is Nancy's husband's brother and he works here, at Hill Top Farm. He lives with my sister, Nancy, and her husband now, but he will find us a small room and we will live together there once we're wed. He is no drunken tosspot like George. He is a fine man and I will be very happy.'

Margaret rubbed her hands together and resumed milking. 'I think there will be thunder soon. The sky is dark as pitch.'

'It may not come yet.' Grace looked out of the barn towards the hovering clouds. The temperature had fallen. Her pail was almost full and she blew on her raw hands to warm them.

'What about you, Grace?' Jennet called across. 'What will you be doing this yuletide? It is only two days away.' Grace didn't answer, so Jennet raised her voice. 'Will you be in Slaugh Cottage, cooking your father's food and washing his clothes?'

Margaret shook her head. 'It seems to me the same thing, Jennet, whether Grace waits on her father or I wait on the children in our family or you wait on a husband, we are all still working our fingers to the bone.'

'Ah, but my Ned is handsome and he is a good man. We want to find our own little cottage one day and live happily there together, just me and him, a pitcher of ale and a vicious mousing cat to keep the vermin away.'

Grace sighed and rubbed her belly with a gentle circular movement. The wind that whistled around the barn was bitterly cold and it cut through her clothing. She felt the child moving and she wanted to keep him warm. In the distance, a single crow swooped to peck at the muddy soil. Grace's pail was full and she rose to lift it, her shoulders swaying, moving heavily. She took a step forward as Harriet Harper rounded the barn, Alice just behind her. Grace paused: she felt instinctively that something was wrong. Harriet's brow was puckered with anger and, in contrast, Alice appeared hunched, drawn and pale. Outside the barn, the rain began to spatter.

'Grace, will you come here?' Harriet pointed a finger, indicating that she wanted Grace's immediate obedience.

Grace pulled the sheepskin cloak around her and shuffled forwards.

'Mistress Harriet?'

Harriet's voice was a low hiss. 'Alice tells me you have been giving her potions.'

Grace gazed at Alice, who hung her head low, and then back to Harriet. 'I meant well.' Silence hung in the air so Grace added, 'It was only some nettle infusion... some raspberry leaf...'

Harriet threw an angry look towards Jennet. 'Why have you stopped work?'

Jennet and Margaret lowered their eyes and appeared to be milking with all their energy.

Harriet grabbed Grace's arm. 'What evil mixture have you given her?'

'I have done nothing wrong.' Grace replied softly.

'So why can she not get with child?'

'It is not Grace's fault...' Alice began.

'You will stop your mouth, Alice, it is to Grace that I speak,' Harriet snapped. 'Is it because of you that I still wait for a grandson?'

'No, it is not,' Grace said honestly. 'I was trying to help, and only where I was asked to do so.'

'You hussy.' Harriet pulled Grace hard, tugging at her arm, and the cloak fell from her shoulders onto the straw.

Grace stood still for a moment, her dress loose, the fabric around the belly stretched and round. As she turned to pick up her cloak, Grace glimpsed Jennet's wide eyes, her mouth open in surprise.

'What is this?' Harriet shrieked. Then her voice became even louder. 'Ah, so now I see your tricks. You are belly-up, you have no husband at home, and Alice is living here with nothing to show, while you feed her potions to make her barren. Is that it?'

'No,' Grace protested.

'So, tell me, who is the father of your child, Grace Cotter? Tell me, are you a left-handed wife, a mistress of some foolish man already married to another? Say what befell you.'

'I cannot,' Grace lowered her head. 'I do not know the man now – he is gone.' Her voice trailed off.

'And you must be gone too,' Harriet raised a hand and for a moment Grace thought she would strike her. Then, her arms firmly folded back across her chest, Harriet said, 'Go home now, Grace. We no longer have need of you here.'

Grace gazed at the rain. The blustering wind blew clouds overhead. She turned to Alice. 'I am sorry for you.'

Alice's cheek was streaked with tears. She swallowed hard, then she whispered, 'And I for you, Grace. I did not wish it this way.'

Grace lifted the cloak from the ground, hugging it around her, and stepped out into the rain. The rain tumbled, dampening her face and cap and the sheepskin cloak. She continued to walk the descending path towards Slaugh Cottage without looking over her shoulder, even when she heard Harriet shriek after her, 'And do not come back here, Grace. You are not welcome.'

Grace continued to plod towards home, her head down, the hem of her dress trailing in the mud. She was bitterly cold, shivering inside her own skin. It would be Christmas in two days' time; next year, at the end of winter, the baby would be born. Grace had no idea what she would do to help herself. Her whole body began to tremble, then the tears came in throaty sobs. She felt utterly alone.

20

Later that Sunday afternoon, Selena curled up on the sofa in the living room, closing her eyes. The fire warmed her feet, and she rested her head against the cushions. She had some thinking to do. The walk and lunch with Nick had been pleasant and Selena was reliving moments in her head, attempting to analyse their relationship. She recalled the moment their gaze locked, just after he had pointed out a wonderful view from Deadman, beyond Staple Hill, and told her he'd love to see her interpretation of it on canvas. There had been something in his eyes, but Selena wasn't sure what it was, professional interest, admiration or something more. He had quoted some lines from one of his favourite poets, Selena couldn't remember the man's name, about the beauty of the fields: she recalled the soft tone of his voice as he had murmured;

'Fresh-firecoal chestnut-falls; finches' wings;
Landscape plotted and pieced – fold, fallow, and plough.'

It had stirred something in her heart.

Nick was intelligent; he seemed sensitive, considerate; he was attractive – very much so – and he was a deep thinker. But she didn't know if he was a friend or a potential lover. The signs from him weren't clear and Selena wasn't sure that she wanted a lover. Besides, at the end of June she would return, fresh and strong and resilient, with a carload of new paintings, to her old life in Manchester.

Her fingers touched the malachite pendant as her thoughts turned to the new friends she had made; she'd enjoyed the impromptu lunch at The Stonegallows Inn with Laura and Joely on Thursday. In their own different ways, they were both delightfully spontaneous and brimming with enthusiasm, a perfect foil for her own tentative approach to people she hardly knew. The time she'd spent in a relationship with David had done that to her: she hadn't been so unsure of herself, so insecure and withdrawn before she'd met him. But she was recovering.

Her mind drifted back to Joely's suggestion that she and Laura should come up to the field on Wychanger Lane where she lived with Matty and stay for lunch: she was sure Selena would find the panoramic views that stretched for miles well worth photographing. Then, in the car on the way home from Taunton, Laura had asked her if she'd be free on Thursday afternoon the following week to go with her into Ashcombe Primary School. Scott Finch, a friend from her supply work there, was the Year 6 teacher and he had agreed that it would be lovely if Selena would go in to his class and show them her sketchbook, a slide show or a few paintings. Selena had said she'd be delighted. It was another opportunity to build up her shaken confidence.

Selena sighed happily. She felt at home in Sloe Cottage at this moment, cocooned, safe and warm. She drifted into a hazy dream where she was in the oak conservatory painting a picture. Soft words, a distant breath, whispered in her ear, telling her what to paint: a landscape, the image of a hill in the countryside, the colours all reds and russets, a bloody sun. There were clumps of gorse in the foreground, scrubby yellow bushes, and a dry-stone wall, a patchwork of grey and brown slabs stacked horizontally. The voice told her to imagine that she was travelling slowly along a dirt track. She saw an elm tree, heavy branches of sprouting green leaves above a sturdy trunk and beyond, the copper sky was hung with heavy clouds, as if a storm loomed. The picture's point of view, as Selena dreamed it, was that of a woman, Selena herself, who was riding along a bumpy road, gazing at the landscape from a kind of primitive wagon pulled by a plodding carthorse. Her heart felt heavy, as if she had lost someone dear to her, as if her chest was constrained by anxiety.

Then the dream whisked her back to the conservatory where she saw herself engrossed in her work again, her brush loaded with mulberry paint; the scene was now a gloomy twilight. In her dream, her painting was interrupted by a single knock at the front door. Selena left her painting and her brush and rushed towards the door, but she was gliding through the air, her bare feet not touching the ground. She tugged the door open and a small child stood facing her, a girl with pale red hair and no face. Selena jerked back, shocked, and the faceless child spoke words that were soft as cotton.

'I will come back to you.'

Selena flinched as if stunned by a strong electric charge, then she was flung upwards towards the ceiling, powerless to stop the impetus that carried her through plaster and wood into an attic that had once been thatched, threads of straw sticking from beams. She hovered, stuck in time, unable to descend. She called out in her dream, but the power that held her fast would not let her go. She was high in the eaves of the house, and something scurried in a corner beneath her, a squirrel, and she was so high that she feared whatever held her would suddenly let go and she would fall. Then it happened, the grip slackened and she was released, tumbling, dropping through the air, sure she would hit the ground with a hard bump.

She opened her eyes. She was awake, on the sofa again; the fire had died down, the room was gloomy and the air was chilly. Selena glanced over her shoulder; shadows clung to corners and she blinked, shivering, afraid. No one was there. She breathed out slowly, stretched her arms and legs, placed another log on the fire and pulled out her phone. It was almost six o'clock.

Then the phone burst to life. Selena checked the caller, held the phone to her ear, took a deep breath and said, 'Hello, David.'

His voice came back quickly, insistent. 'Selena, I have to talk to you.'

She said nothing, waiting. Her heart was banging hard, thundering in her ears; he still had the ability to do that to her.

He tried again. 'Can we talk?'

Her tone was flat. 'I'm listening.'

'Can we meet?'

'I'm not in Manchester.'

'Then where are you?' He was clearly incredulous.

'It doesn't matter where I am,' Selena said. 'What do you have to say to me?'

He sounded frustrated, annoyed. 'I need to talk to you about the baby, of course. Our baby.'

Selena swallowed. 'There is no baby.'

He was louder in the earpiece, fierce. 'You had a termination?'

'A miscarriage,' Selena replied quietly.

'Oh,' David was momentarily stunned, then he said, 'I didn't know.'

'There was no reason why you should.' Selena's words were tinged with bitterness.

'It was my child...'

'You walked away.'

David's voice took on a wheedling note. 'Selena, I want us to try again. Since we... parted ways, I've realised I want to be with you. I miss you. Veronica's impossible to live with.'

Selena shook her head. 'I don't blame her. You told her I had been chasing you. You lied.'

She could hear him thinking what to say to her. Then his voice was almost a whine. 'I've realised it's you I love, Selena. Please, let's try again...'

'No.' Selena was surprised how quickly the word flew from her mouth.

'Where are you? I'll come round and we can talk.'

'I don't want to talk...'

'You owe me that much.'

'I owe you nothing.' Selena was amazed at her self-control: despite her thumping heart, she was quiet but firm. 'I don't think we have anything else to say.'

His voice became cracked and emotional, as if he might cry. 'I won't give up on us, Selena. I will find you and make you understand – I know it's what you want too.'

Selena held the phone tightly in her fist. 'Go back to Veronica, David. Please, I don't want to talk to you again.'

With a press of her thumb, she blocked his calls. Selena was shaking. Talking to him had uncovered the old wound he'd left when he walked away, but she was making progress. She was sure of that now: her head was ruling her heart, she never wanted to speak to him again.

Her instinct was to phone Claire, then Laura, and tell them both what had happened. The solidarity of other women was so important now. But her hand holding the phone still trembled and her body was rigid with the tension of the conversation. She touched the malachite pendant on its long chain. She'd breathe deeply, make a cup of tea and return to the fireside. Then she'd call upon her friends for some moral support.

* * *

Christmas 1682 was a quiet day at Slaugh Cottage. Will Cotter sat at the hearth, his head in his hands, while Grace moved slowly around the room, lifting the blackened vessel of pottage and heaving it over the fire, filling his cup with mulled ale, putting a taper to the tinders, coaxing the fire to leap into flame. Then his eyes were on her, watching as she sat on a stool in the corner, her sewing on her knee, letting out a dress by the light of the candle. Finally, he spoke.

'She is an ill-favoured woman, Mistress Harriet Harper. What she has done has put me out of sorts. I never did take to her. She had no business sending you home.'

Grace nodded agreement in his direction. Her back ached and she was tired.

Will continued. 'I will beg them to take you back to work at the farm after... after the lying-in. They know you are a strong worker. You fill your pails quicker than any other milkmaid. It avails them to have you at Hill Top.'

'I hope you are right.'

Suddenly, he stood up, tall and sinewy, his legs shaking. 'I have failed you, Grace. You had no mother to teach you and I have let this thing happen when I should have protected you. Now we have nothing but ill fortune.'

Grace looked up from her sewing. It was the first time her father had spoken openly of the baby; for several weeks she had noticed him staring at her, his expression miserable, and she could not bring herself to mention it. Now his words filled Grace with fresh sorrow and she hung her head. 'Father, it is not your fault. Please do not say such things.'

'If I had been a good father and taken more heed, then you would not be shunned in this way. But I allowed you to wander by yourself, to do as you will, and now this has befallen us.'

Grace put down her sewing and moved to sit next to him. 'Do not blame yourself. It is I who have wronged you.'

'Who knows what our fate will be in the new year?' Will stared into the blaze, one side of his face illuminated in the flames. 'If Harriet Harper should talk to her husband, if Joseph Harper should listen to his wife's sharp tongue, what then? Will I too be sent away? Will we no longer have a home here in Slaugh Cottage, but be cast out instead? You, me and the baby, Grace?' He looked haggard. 'We are beset with ill fortune, we both. It has been this way since your mother died. And now you are with child, what will become of us?'

'Do not fret.' Grace stood up, stretching her aching back, and then she placed her hands together, thinking. When she spoke, her voice was clear and strong. 'It is Yuletide, and a new moon shines over us. Let us do our best to eat and drink and make merry. Trust me, Father, there are ways and means to prosper, to change our fortune, and I will seek them out. We will have another mouth to feed, and we cannot turn back time to change that.' She gazed at her father's troubled expression and she was suddenly determined. 'I will pour you a glass of ale and then I will go out for a while. I will not let you down.'

Grace watched her father staring silently into the flames: he was deep in thought, not listening. She poured ale from a pitcher and placed it in his hand, then she wrapped herself in the sheepskin cloak and left the house quietly, wandering in the direction of the old oak tree beyond the gate. Across the road beneath the tree, she would find acorns: planted in the light of the new moon, they would be sure to bring luck and abundance in the new year. She would make herself an amulet from a polished acorn to wear over her heart for when the baby came; it would keep them both safe.

She stood beneath the oak, picking up fallen bark for the fire to bring good health and healing when burned. Then she moved to her beloved blackthorn tree. The plump purple sloes were already stored in a jar in the larder, steeped in gin and sugar. But Grace wanted to pluck several of the spines which she hoped could protect her; she would dry them, keep them in a basket. They were sharp and fierce, and would be sure to ward off anyone who would wish to do her or her baby harm.

She tugged several barbs carefully, snapping them free of the branch, clutching them in the rounded palm of her hand, then she knelt silently in front of the old stone well. Her head bowed, she whispered low words into the water. She heard her voice come back to her, a resounding echo from the well's throat, and she closed her eyes and stood up to face the thin sliver of moon. She wished from the depths of her heart that there would be no more bad luck, not ever again.

21

December the twenty-eighth, 1682 was a Monday, a bitterly windy day that cut through thin clothes to the bone, and Will Cotter was back at work in the fields. Grace had risen early, prepared warmed milk and bread for him, then she swept the downstairs room and ventured into the garden to dig potatoes and parsnips, her cloak protecting her from the wind's blast. Back inside, comforted by the warmth of Slaugh Cottage, she busied herself with preparing the stew, using a scrag end of mutton she had kept back and adding vegetables, heaving the blackened pot over the fire and placing heavy logs in the grate to catch and burn.

She felt suddenly weary, so she sat in her father's seat by the hearth, shifting position until she and the baby were comfortable, and she closed her eyes for a moment. Grace cupped her hands around the curve of her belly and began to sing softly.

> 'Cares you know not, therefore sleep,
> While mother here a watch will keep,
> Sleep, pretty darling, do not cry,
> And I will sing a lullaby.'

Grace felt the little one wriggle and turn around, an elbow poking out, and she rubbed the place with the flat palm of her hand, smiling. She promised the baby silently that he would never go hungry. She wanted the best for the child's future, wishing him more prosperity and affluence than she had known in her life. Grace knew only how to write the letters of her name; she could not read or write any other letters, but she hoped that he would be able to learn and would never want for food or shelter. And she hoped more than anything that her child would love and be loved back.

Grace thought again, as she did almost constantly each day now, about the birth in February. Her grandmother had promised that she would be there to assist her, but Grace had seen birthing before – she recalled Kitty Stokes' labours – and she was afraid. She remembered her grandmother saying that Kitty's labour would be hard: her exact words had been, 'She is very small and her husband is a tall man.' Grace took a breath; she was slender and Nathaniel was broad and muscular. She feared that she too, would find the birth difficult. But she would be strong: she was determined to bring a healthy baby into the world, to hear the first lusty cry of life break from powerful lungs before she held her child in her arms for the first time. She wondered if he would have her pale red hair, or if it would be dark, like Nathaniel's, like her own mother's.

She thought about a name for her child: in her heart, she had always wanted a daughter to be called Mercy or Martha. And she liked the sound of the name Charity Cotter. She was unsure which to choose: she would talk to her grandmother and ask her for her thoughts. But she believed in her heart that she'd have a son and she'd name him Gabriel after the angel who announced the birth of Jesus to Our Lady. She was sure of her choice; the name Gabriel Cotter was strong and upright, just as her child would be.

Grace's eyelids were heavy; in the warm firelight, she began to doze, her body slumped in her father's chair. Sleep crawled over her as she basked in the fire's orange glow, and for a moment she let go of all her cares.

Then there was a sharp knock at the door, a second followed quickly. Grace roused herself, rubbing her eyes, easing her body from the comfortable chair until she stood upright.

When she opened the door, she was surprised to see Alice Harper standing there, anxious. Grace recalled how she used to be before she married, all rosy cheeks and dimples, Alice dancing, bedecked in ribbons at May Day. Alice was thinner now, and her brow permanently creased with worry.

'Can I come in?' Alice asked, glancing over her shoulder. 'Harriet does not know I am here, or indeed Nathaniel. They think I am feeding chickens.'

Grace nodded, leading the way into the dark room, lit only by the glow of the fire and a single candle. She moved to the pitcher by the hearth. 'Can I pour you a warm drink? You must be cold.'

'Thank you. I am.' Alice put down a basket. 'I wanted to speak to you, Grace, and I have brought some things for you.'

'For me?' Grace handed her the cup. 'Will you sit yourself down at the hearth?'

Alice shuffled to sit in Will Cotter's chair, placing the basket on the ground at her side; she put out her palms to warm them. 'It is cosy here. You keep your home very comfortable.'

Grace moved to the stool opposite and eased herself down slowly. 'It is good of you to come to see me.'

'I have brought a basket with some milk, eggs, cheese and a rabbit.'

Grace was puzzled. 'How did you come by them?'

'I stole them from Harriet's kitchen. She has plenty, especially now, left over from the Yuletide festivities. And I must say sorry to you, because you were put out because of me, because you helped me.'

'Not at all,' Grace said firmly. 'I was put out by Mistress Harriet's bad temper and because I am with child.' She lifted the linen cloth and inspected the contents of the basket. Her eyes gleamed. 'I am very grateful to you, Alice.'

'And I to you.' Alice sipped from the cup. 'I envy you.'

'You envy me? But why?' Grace was surprised. 'I have no husband, no means to work. Why would anyone envy me?'

'What I want most in the world is a child.' Alice's face was sad. 'But I have a cruel mother-in-law who constantly upbraids me and a bad-tempered husband who seldom shares a soft word. My life is not my own – I must do everyone else's bidding. And Nathaniel does not love me, not really – he thinks me still a milkmaid. He says as much when he is out of temper. I was charmed by his smile and now I am racked with regret.'

Grace nodded slowly: she understood.

'He spoke very prettily to me before we were wed; he told me he chose me above all others and that he loved me. But I see now that was just a springe to catch a woodcock. Once we were wed, he turned his back on me and I was a maidservant again, fit only to clean his boots.' Alice was forlorn. 'And to warm his bed.'

Grace sighed. 'You must have hoped for so much more.'

'Do you think, Grace, that it is possible for there to be true love in this world between a woman and a man?'

'I do. My own father loved my mother, and my Grandmother Bett speaks so fondly of my grandfather. I believe that a husband and wife can follow each other through life, speaking only kind words, and with love as deep as the seas.'

'Then I am undone in a loveless marriage.' Alice's eyes were full of tears. 'It is my folly and now I have no children and I am alone.'

'I too, am alone,' Grace said sadly. 'No man will want me now I will have another man's child.'

'No one knows who fathered your child, but many people in the village have spoken of it. Some think it to be Ned Shears' child, but I think not.'

'You think right.'

'So who is he? Is he a man from this parish who is already yoked to another? Is that why you will not tell his name?'

'I do not want to say, because...' Grace swallowed. Lying to Alice was difficult, but she knew she must. 'Because it is a man whom no one knows. He is not of this parish. He was passing through Ashcomb during the May Day dance. I was swayed by his charms but one time, and I must pay for it for the length of my life.'

'Perhaps having no husband is better than a bad marriage, no matter how people speak of you.' Alice sighed. 'I too will pay fulsome for the rest of my days for foolishly yoking myself to Nathaniel and his family.'

'I think it must be hard to be a wife,' Grace agreed. 'To bear children and run a household is endurable if you have love in your life, but without it, all that remains is drudgery each day.'

'My sister, Nancy, has made a dreadful marriage; her life too is all toil, but she delights in telling me that she is with child and her baby will come in March, then she will have one more each year until she is thirty-five, but I fear I will still be barren then.' She grasped Grace's hands. 'Do you think that is so, that I will never have a child? Mistress Harriet tells me she believes it is so.'

'I think not.' Grace's voice was soft. 'Sometimes these things can happen if we believe strongly enough that they will. You are an upright woman, Alice, and kind, and good fortune will come to you if you allow it.'

'Do you really believe that?' Alice asked. 'I hope for a child with all my heart.'

Grace moved her fingers to her neck and tugged an acorn tied with a piece of ribbon that she wore beneath her dress. 'Alice, this is for you. Wear it always.'

'Nay, I cannot...'

'You have brought me food. I wear this because it will bring luck and now I can return the favour. I wish you what your heart desires, truly I do.'

Alice took the ribbon with the little acorn tied in it and pushed it over her head, hiding it beneath her kerchief. 'May it bring me blessings. You are a true friend. And I promise you, each week I will come here with some things in my basket for you – cheese, milk, a chicken.'

'Thank you, Alice. I am grateful.'

'And I too.' Alice stood, reaching for the basket. 'Now let us put these things in your larder, then I must go. I will be missed, and Mistress Harriet is always ready to beat me with a birch stick. To tell truth, Grace, I dislike her. She is a curd-faced old crone.'

'You must forget her and think of helping yourself.' Grace eased herself up straight. 'You must find some oak bark as you return home, from the tree beyond the gate. Make sure your husband is the one who will put it on the fire first, then you must do the same. It will bring fertility to you both.'

'Thank you.' Alice wrapped her arms around Grace. 'It has taken me too long to realise what a good friend you are.' She pulled back, examining Grace carefully. 'And I think it will not be long before your child comes.'

'February, my Grandmother Bett says. And you must not worry,' Grace's eyes were kind. 'A baby will come to you when ready to do so. Perhaps next year.'

Grace accompanied Alice to the door and watched her walk away, leaning against the sharp wind through the gate, bending down by the oak tree to pick up a piece of fallen bark. At the top of the hill over the farmlands, a soft mist was gathering and the skies were overcast. Twilight would come early.

Grace closed the door with a firm thud and returned to the hearth to warm her hands. The stew in the pot that hung over the fire had started to bubble and she would be able to doze in the armchair for another hour or so before she visited the well to draw water. She thought of the gifts Alice had brought: the rabbit would last her and Will almost a whole week in the stew pot, and the eggs would be useful, helping to fill her father's belly before he left in the mornings.

Grace closed her eyes, filled with relief: she was so lucky to have Alice as a friend. She had no idea what she would do without her kindness and gifts of food, and she was determined to do all she could to help Alice in return.

22

Selena wanted to transfer the vivid images of the landscape in her dream straight onto the canvas. The scene was still fresh in her mind: a hill in the countryside, the colours all warm coppers and russets, a crimson sun hidden behind the peaks, a storm looming. She recalled the clumps of gorse in the foreground, scrubby yellow bushes, the elm tree and the dry-stone wall, a patchwork of grey and brown slabs stacked horizontally.

She loaded her brush with paint and waved it across the canvas, making broad strokes, defining the hills, the skies, the wall. The dream was playing over in her mind, the emotions still alive, buzzing through her veins: she still felt the loss and sadness she had experienced as she'd opened the door to the faceless child; she was still gripped by the sense of powerlessness as she had been hurled up through the ceiling into the attic. But Selena felt instinctively that if she painted the land-scape scene from the viewpoint of herself, the person riding in a horse-drawn wagon on the road gazing at the surroundings, the act of creating the scene would allow her time to put her thoughts into place.

Selena was amazed how easy it was to render the scene exactly as she had visualised it in the dream. She knew Claire would love it; she'd put the painting on the Ariel Art website in no time. And Nick would be impressed with it too: he'd love the colours she was using. Selena thought about Nick while she was painting; his easy-going nature appealed to her: he was unhurried, undemanding, thoughtful. She found herself comparing him to David, who had always been persistent, obstinate, inclined to sulk if he couldn't have his way. Selena realised she was frowning: her relationship with David had taken her to a place where she had been continually striving to please him, trying to find new ways to make him love her; then, once she'd found out about Veronica's existence, she was desperate for him to commit. He had doled out his affection by degrees, so that she would sometimes feel adored and at other times unworthy. She promised herself she would never allow herself to be in such a situation again, not ever.

An hour passed, two. She had started to fill the canvas and the scene was bursting into life. The hills were bathed in pink light as if the sun was setting; the overall impression was an unchanging landscape, forever constant; day might become night and one year, one century, might lead to another, but little else would change, as if the land was an anchor and could be relied upon not to alter when everything around it was whirling forward blindly.

Selena felt the buzz of her phone in her pocket and held it to her ear. 'Claire. I was just thinking of you. How are you? How are things going at the gallery? I'm painting a picture I know you'll love.'

'Oh? All's fine. Somewhere local you've visited?'

'No, it was an image from a dream. It's a sunset, a country scene.'

'Great. I have some good news for you too. Can you put me up in your cottage for a whole week?'

'Oh, lovely – yes, of course.'

'Only, I thought we could both paint together in your conservatory.' Claire's voice was rushed with excitement. 'Then I could take the pictures back and we'll have such an incredible stock to sell. We could even organise an exhibition.'

'Great. When are you coming down?'

'I thought I'd come on Monday the thirtieth. It's a bank holiday. I'll drive down really early, first thing, and travel back on the Saturday if that's okay.'

'It will be wonderful to have you to stay. What a great idea. What about the gallery?'

'Well, I think Gulliver is ready to take over – he'll be fine by himself. He's very confident, and we get on really well. We went for a drink together yesterday and we were talking about uni days, some of the people we both knew, and those we've lost contact with. He remembers Flynn, your ex: apparently he's married with kids now.'

'Oh?' Selena took a breath, not sure how to reply. Then she said, 'I can't wait for you to come down.'

'I thought we could have barbecues in the garden and walks in the woods. You can take me to some of the great places you've visited – and the village pub too...'

Selena laughed. 'And between all that we'll get lots of painting done.'

'It will be so good to see you. I miss you.'

'You too.' Selena thought for a moment about how she'd grown to love the solitude of Sloe Cottage, but how pleasant it would be for her to spend time with her friend again. 'So, Monday the thirtieth it is.'

'That's so exciting,' Claire said. 'It's a shame I can't bring Gulliver with me – I'd love you to meet him, but I took him on to mind the gallery. Maybe another time...'

'That would be nice, Claire.'

'And send me photos of any new paintings – send the sunset you're working on now.'

'I will.'

'Right, well, I must crack on. I'll give Gulliver a ring and tell him the good news. Lots of love, Selena. See you on the thirtieth.'

There was a click and Claire was gone. Selena turned her attention back to her painting, feeling calm and happy as she loaded her brush and applied thick strokes. She wanted to recreate her dream exactly as she remembered it, making the colours vibrant and alive. But as she painted, the picture took on a more brooding tone. Amid the blood-spattered sunset, dark undulating fields and turbulent clouds crowded the canvas and it stirred a new uneasy feeling within her.

* * *

The next morning, Laura called round to Sloe Cottage in her car; they were going to Joely and Matty's place for lunch. Laura was gripping the steering wheel with excitement.

'I've driven past their field so often but never stopped there; the location in the hills is incredible and both Joely and Matty are great foragers, so I'm sure we'll get something wonderful to eat.'

Selena leaned back in the passenger seat. 'It's nice to have some time off. I worked into the early hours to finish a painting. I sent a photo of it to Claire just before I came out. It's great to have time out and relax.'

'You do look a bit peaky. The fresh air up at Joely's will do you the world of good.'

'I had a weird dream while I was dozing by the fire yesterday and I can't stop thinking about it. I didn't sleep well after that. It shook me a bit, if I'm honest.'

'Ooh,' Laura glanced towards her. 'I love dreams. Do tell me about it. I always try to interpret dreams – I did psychology A level and that left me full of the joys of analysis. I'm always dreaming that I'm in the classroom dressed in a clown costume and all the children laugh at me.' She was suddenly serious. 'So what did you dream?'

'The worst bit was that I saw a child with no face, a little girl, and she spoke to me. She said that she would come back. Then I was whizzing through the air as if propelled like magic and I couldn't stop myself.'

'Classic dream, falling, flying, out of control.' Laura turned the car into a narrow lane, travelling up hill. 'It means there are areas of your life you can't do anything about and you feel powerless.'

'Yes, I'm sure you're right.' Selena was thinking of David, relieved that she would hear no more from him now that she had blocked his calls. 'And what about the child with no face?'

Laura sighed. 'I think that's to do with the miscarriage, Selena. Perhaps the yet-unknown child is telling you that you'll meet again, but it won't be this time.'

Selena shuddered, suddenly cold. 'Oh, my goodness – do you believe that?'

'I don't know.' Laura slowed the car; the hill was becoming steeper, pale green in the strong sunlight. 'I hope so. You'll meet someone nice one day, and you'll start a family, if that's what you want.'

'I think I might...' Selena said.

'Well, good luck with that.' Laura glanced at her, glasses flashing. 'I've never thought about having kids of my own. I suppose I haven't made my mind up yet. And I'd have to find a man first, although I'm not sure I want to lose my independence. I always love the kids I taught at school best – which reminds me, Selena – I hope you're still up for the art class at Ashcombe Primary on Thursday.'

'Yes, definitely.'

The car bumped along uneven ground, then Laura moved the steering wheel sharply to the left and they drove through open gates into a large field surrounded by overhanging trees. A caravan was parked to one side, beneath the shelter of a sweeping willow, and Matty was chopping wood in a vest and jeans. He waved a hand as the car came to a halt, then put down his axe and walked over.

'Hello, both. Nice to see you. Joely is in the caravan. She's just finished making lunch, so you're bang on time.'

They sat in the open field at a wooden table set for four, with ceramic tumblers and a flagon of water with mint and lemon. Joely placed bowls of salad and pasta in front of them. Laura inhaled, smiling. 'The food smells absolutely heavenly. What is it?'

Joely sat down. 'It's home-made tagliatelle and a pesto I created: chickweed, garlic, olive oil and walnuts. And the salad has sorrel in it and some mallow. I love using fresh mallow. The leaves are full of protein, calcium, iron, vitamin C.'

'I've never had mallow before...' Selena helped herself to salad.

'It's great to treat all sorts – everything from coughs to constipation.'

'That's fascinating. Were all the ingredients foraged around here?' Laura asked.

'No, November is the best month for foraging,' Joely replied. 'I grew the garlic and the sorrel – the chickweed is from the woodlands.' She pointed into the distance.

'And all this land around the caravan belongs to you?' Selena wondered.

'It does.' Matty poured water into the tumblers. 'This field, the surrounding woodlands, as far as the hedgerows over there, which are great for blackberries and sloes in the autumn.'

'You have a sloe tree, don't you, Selena?' Laura stopped munching. 'That's why the place is called Sloe Cottage.'

'It's a blackthorn tree,' Joely explained. 'It's a shame you won't be here in November, Selena. You could pick the sloes and make sloe gin.' She pointed to a tree in the distance. 'My elder tree over there is so wonderful to me. I make elderflower cordial and champagne in May, then elderberry wine in the late summer.'

'You should try some.' Matty raised an eyebrow in jest. 'Although you won't want to drive after the elderflower champagne. It's strong stuff.'

'Claire's coming down to stay soon and we'll have a barbecue – you will all come?' Selena glanced from face to face. 'Maybe we can try some elderflower champagne then?'

'Oh, I'd love that,' Laura said, rubbing her hands together. She patted Joely's arm. 'How did you learn so much about plants and trees and things?'

'Some of it's been handed down from my mother and gran – some of it is my own research.' Joely leaned back. 'For example, I was just talking about the elder tree. Did you know that people once believed that if you burned elder wood, you'd see the Devil, but if you planted elder by your house, it would keep the Devil away?'

Laura shuddered. 'Some of these old beliefs are really scary.'

'Living around here, we're steeped in the old traditions, and it's important not to forget them. They belong to the people who went before us,' Matty said thoughtfully. 'Sometimes, especially at sunset, you can feel it in the air. Joely and I often sit down and watch the sunset and we both say there's a real sense of time standing still, as if all the old ways are still here with us, as if the past somehow seeps through into the present.'

Selena's eyes widened. 'That's so true – do you know, I just painted a sunset picture, and that describes exactly the atmosphere I wanted to create...' She recalled Matty's words. 'Just like you said, the old ways are still here with us – at times, the past somehow oozes through.'

'I'd love to see the painting,' Joely said.

'It's here, on my phone – I sent a picture of it to Claire this morning.' Selena passed her phone to Joely and, as she stared at it, Matty moved to gaze over her shoulder.

'I know where that is,' Joely said suddenly.

'It's up the lane, just before the road becomes the crossroads, the border between the two counties,' Matty added.

Joely pointed with her finger. 'The stone wall's quite ancient in your painting, but it's been recently rebuilt, and it looks much tidier now.'

Matty was amazed. 'And you've never been up the lane here before, Selena?'

'No, never.' Selena suddenly felt cold. She thought of how she had dozed in front of the fire; a voice, just a whisper, had described it in her ear.

Laura had joined Joely and Matty to stare at the picture. 'Oh, yes – it's the view across the top of Wychanger Lane. This part is Somerset and that is where Devon begins. It's a really pretty sunset...'

'But the painting has a really eerie feeling,' Matty said.

Selena frowned: that word again, *eerie*.

'It's mournful, I think – the setting sun is like an ending,' Joely added. 'But it's so beautiful. I love it, Selena.'

'Oh, I wish I could buy it – I'd put it in my bedroom.' Laura's face shone with admiration. 'This is a local beauty spot.'

Selena shook her head. She was mystified that she'd painted a place she'd never been to. Despite the warmth of the early summer sunshine, her skin was chilled. She glanced from Matty to Laura, then to Joely. 'Do you think we could go up there, to the crossroads between the two counties, and look across the countryside?' She was intrigued. 'I want to see the place for myself...'

23

A hoar frost frothed in the corners of the garden of Slaugh Cottage, illuminating spiders' webs, glistening on the iron blackthorn branches, making the grass sparkle and the bushes gleam white in the morning dew. It was the sixth of January, 1683, a Wednesday, and Grace stood in her garden digging up vegetables for the evening stew. She would dine alone tonight. It was Twelfth Night and her father would not break with a time-honoured tradition; there would be wassailing up at Hill Top Farm, the farmworkers congregating together in the ox barn to toast the animals and the crops to encourage fertility. There would be feasting, singing and plenty of drinking from the wassail bowl.

Grace recalled being there last year, watching men sup from the upturned bowl and singing with them:

> 'Love and joy come to you,
> And to you your wassail too;
> And God bless you and send you
> a happy New Year.'

Nathaniel had been amongst the throng watching her then, his hands on his hips, his dark blue eyes luminous.

It seemed so long ago now; so much had come to pass in just one year. She wondered what the next one would bring and she smiled.

Grace gathered potatoes and turnips in her apron and gazed up at the sky. It was white, heavy with snow, a full belly just like her own. She rubbed the baby beneath her dress with the flat palm of her hand and murmured, 'It will snow today, little one, and we must go to the farm for milk.'

She deposited the vegetables in a bowl on the table, wrapped herself in the sheepskin cloak and set off with a pitcher towards the farm. A few single flakes of snow twirled in the air and held, before falling to the ground and dissolving. Grace leaned forward, struggling against the biting wind, her eyes watering, her cheeks becoming numb in the cold. She crossed a field where some men were working with a flock of sheep, bringing them closer to the farm because of the imminent snow and putting out hay. She recognised Ned and George Shears amongst several other men and Ned waved a hand and called to her.

'How now, Grace?' He approached her warily, standing a few paces away. 'I hope you are well.'

'I am, thank you, Ned.' Grace cast her eyes down, uneasy, as the other men stopped working to watch them talk together. 'I go to the farm to fill my pitcher.'

Ned hesitated. 'You have heard of my news? I am to marry Jennet Bryant this coming summer.'

'I am glad to hear it. I wish you both many blessings.' Grace noticed how he stared at her, tentative, a little nervous around the mouth.

Then he said, 'And – do you have all you need to keep you warm and well fed at Slaugh Cottage?'

'I do. My father and I have enough food.'

'Will you come to the wassailing up in the ox barn this evening?'

Grace's hand rested on her belly. 'I will not. I must rest.'

Ned inclined his head. 'Then farewell to you, Grace.'

'Farewell.' Grace moved away slowly. Above her, the clouds were still thick with snow, but only the occasional flakes fell, landing on her eyelids. She pulled the sheepskin cape tightly around her, hearing the men's low chatter drifting on the wind from behind her, a guffaw from a hearty voice that she believed must be George Shears. Then something caught her eye. A black sheep had overturned in a ditch by the edge of the field. It lay on its back, completely still, its legs sticking upwards.

Grace called over her shoulder, 'Ned, make haste. There is a sheep fallen in the ditch. I fear it may be dead.'

Grace reached the animal and knelt down; damp earth seeped into the material of her skirt. She wrapped her arms around the sheep and heaved, struggling to turn it carefully, always mindful of the baby she carried. Ned was at her elbow as she pushed the sheep back onto its legs. It wriggled for a moment and then rushed away to join the flock.

Ned gaped. 'The black-woolled sheep was dead and now it is alive.'

'No, I turned it – it had fallen on its back and couldn't right itself without help.' Grace inspected her muddy hands. 'It will be well now.'

Ned grasped one of her hands, helping her up from where she had knelt in the mud. His eyes held a tender expression. 'Even the sheep do your bidding, Grace.'

'Thanking you kindly.' Grace removed her hand from his. 'I must be on my way, for I fear the snow will come soon.'

'I will tell the others how you saved the sheep. I will tell Farmer Harper of your good deed, and he will recompense you.'

'Oh, I beg you do not,' Grace said. 'I wish only to fill my pitcher with milk. Good day to you, Ned.'

She left him watching her. She felt sad momentarily; Ned Shears was a good man and she believed he was probably a little in love with her. But he was promised to Jennet Bryant and there was only love for her child in her heart now; there would never be space for a man. She knew that was true: she had even promised the chattering well beneath the new moon that her entire life would belong to her child if he came into the world hale and whole, if he would be blessed with good fortune.

Grace reached the farm and knocked on the door. She noticed the familiar marks above it: a circular daisy wheel and two letters etched into the woodwork. Grace recognised the A in Grace and knew the engravings had been carved there to ward off evil.

The cold wind made her shiver and she knocked again. Then Alice appeared, an apron over a pretty linen dress, a cap on her head. She smiled happily when she saw Grace. 'Come in, come in and warm yourself by the hearth.'

'Oh no, I am here only for a pitcher of milk,' Grace began, but Alice's arm was around her shoulder, tugging her into the spacious square room with an inglenook.

Alice set her on a chair before a roaring fire. 'Old Mother Harper is busy with the festivities for the wassailing tonight. She is in the kitchen. She will not come here to disturb us.' Alice knelt at her feet. 'Your dress is dirty.'

'I helped a sheep that had fallen on its back into a ditch. As I knelt, my skirts became muddy.'

Alice took Grace's raw, icy hands and rubbed them gently. 'You have made yourself cold, Grace, and it is not good for the baby. Rest awhile – I will fill your pitcher and bring some posset to warm you.'

'Thank you.' Grace closed her eyes for a moment and her skin begin to thaw again. The baby turned, pushing out a strong foot, and Grace rubbed it, a soothing circular movement. She hummed the lullaby she believed the child recognised already; she was sure he knew the comforting sound of her voice.

Steam rose rise from the damp skirts of her dress; her feet inside the thick boots began to dry. Then Alice was beside her, placing a cup of posset in her hands. Grace inhaled the smell of warm spices, nutmeg and cinnamon, the milk curdled with wine. She sipped it gratefully.

Alice placed a basket beside her on the floor. 'Here is your pitcher of milk. And I have put in a few things to take with you – some cheese, bread, butter, a piece of pie, some bacon. My mother-in-law will not miss them. Will you be able to carry them to Slaugh Cottage? If not, I will gladly walk there with you.'

'Oh, Alice, you are most kind.'

'Finish your drink and we will go together.' Alice's blue eyes twinkled. 'For I have much to speak about: since you gave me the acorn to wear against my heart for luck, life here is much improved. And I am hopeful for my marriage.'

Grace finished the posset and handed the cup to Alice before easing herself upright. 'Then we will leave together. It is not good your mother-in-law finds me here.'

'Oh, she is an ill-tempered, heavy-footed stamp-crab.' Alice covered her mouth with a small hand and smiled, a little embarrassed at her boldness, almost believing that if she had dared to speak ill of her mother-in-law, her words would surely be heard. 'Come, let us not tarry.'

Alice wrapped Grace snugly in her cape and pulled on a cloak of her own, then lifted the basket in one hand and threaded the other through the crook of Grace's elbow.

'Let us walk down the hill.'

As they stepped outside, it had started to snow, the flakes falling thickly.

Alice cheered. 'God is eating goose tonight for the Twelfth Night Feast. Look how the snow tumbles, fat as feathers. Someone in heaven is plucking them and letting them fall to earth.'

Grace smiled. 'You are in a better humour, Alice. I am pleased to see it.'

'You have brought me good luck with the acorn you gave me.' Alice allowed Grace to lean against her as they walked down the hill. 'Nathaniel pays me more attention now. He has bought me a new dress for the festivities tonight and this morning he called me his pretty Alice. I am sure that he and I will have a child soon.'

Grace felt the snow settle against her brow; she looked up towards the heavens, enjoying the icy softness against her skin. 'I am pleased for you.'

'Besides, if I do not get a child this year, I will have one soon. I believe it. And you are my dear friend now.' Alice squeezed Grace's arm. 'And next month you will have your baby, and at Hill Top I am secretly making a blanket to keep him warm. I will visit you at Slaugh

Cottage whenever I can once he is born, and we can watch him grow together. Perhaps you will let me hold him and stroke his cheeks, and it will bring me luck to conceive a baby of my own.'

'Perhaps I will bring forth a girl?' Grace said.

'Perhaps you will, but whether it is a boy or a maid, I will help you in any way I can. You have shown me such kindness and I mean to do the same for you.'

'Thank you, Alice – I am truly happy to hear it.' They were approaching Slaugh Cottage and Grace pointed to the old oak tree. 'Look how heavily laden the branches are on the tree. The snow is heaped so high, I fear they may break and fall.'

Alice stooped, picking up a handful of snow. Flakes danced around her head, settling on her cap, sticking to her eyelashes, making the tips white. 'If you were not with child now, or if your baby were already born and walking, we would make a big snowman. You, I and the child could make one almost as tall as the house.'

'A man made of snow is a good thing,' Grace agreed. 'I once heard my mother say that white snow is God's forgiveness of our sins. The circular snowball shows the everlasting life God promises us. It would be pleasant to make such a man.'

'Just imagine, Grace – next year we will be here in the snow, and the year after. Your child will laugh, his little cheeks red, and you and I will laugh along with him. And maybe I too will have a child of my own, and the four of us can make one together.'

'I hope for it.' Grace clasped Alice's hand. 'For I wish you much happiness.'

Alice lifted her skirt in a pirouette. 'Tonight, Nathaniel and I will dance together in the ox barn, and perhaps our union will be blessed...'

A sudden thought came to Grace and she grabbed her friend's wrist. 'Come with me, Alice.' She picked up the basket in her free hand, tugging Alice towards the well. 'You must speak your heart's desire into the well. Then whatever you wish for will come to pass.'

'The chattering well – I have heard others speak of it.' Alice's eyes shone.

They rushed towards the well, kneeling down, leaning into to the depths.

Alice squeezed Grace's hand and whispered, 'Shall I say it now?'

'Speak that which you want more than anything else,' Grace said softly.

Alice leaned forward, Grace's fingers folded tightly in hers, and murmured, 'More than anything in the world, I would like a baby boy of my own.'

'And I wish on my own life that it will come to pass.' Grace's voice trembled, and her words mixed with Alice's in a soft echo at the bottom of the well, the sound returning to them as a single voice from the depths.

They smiled and threw their arms around each other.

'So be it,' Grace embraced Alice again and when they pulled apart their cheeks were damp with melting ice or warm tears, they were not sure which.

24

'I didn't expect to feel nervous, but I'm truly terrified.' Selena hugged her sketchbook, hauling her portfolio carry case and her laptop in her free hand as she and Laura made their way through the main entrance of Ashcombe Primary. The familiar smell hit her straight away, sweaty gym shoes and steamed cabbage, reminding her of her own school-days, and she felt a sudden apprehension.

Laura laughed and ran a hand through her hair. 'Do you know, I feel most alive when I'm in front of a class of youngsters. My dad was the same when he was a history teacher. I used to love it when I was in Bristol, singing with the children, story time, craft classes, drama and PE in the hall. Oh, I do miss teaching.'

'You can do my talk for me,' Selena joked. 'I might be useless. I'm sure I'm going to stammer or clam up. It's ridiculous isn't it, being scared by a bunch of ten-year-olds.'

'I'll be right next to you,' Laura said. 'If you get stuck, I'll just impro-vise and tell them how brilliant you are. And you are, you know.' She raised her eyebrows over the glasses, an expression of encouragement. 'You're marvellous to do this, and the kids will really appreciate it.'

Selena and Laura signed in at reception, a secretary in frameless glasses and a crisp white blouse giving them a lanyard each to wear.

Laura waved a hand. 'I know the way to Scott's year six class, Julie. Lovely to see you again.' Then she breezed down the corridor; Selena following her, a feeling of dread in the pit of her stomach.

The children were already grouped around tables, identically clad in dark blue, excited, notebooks in their hands, as Scott Finch greeted Selena and Laura. He was wearing glasses, a tie, dark jacket and smart trousers. He held out a hand for Selena to shake, but she had none free, so she simply grinned, 'Pleased to meet you.' The eyes of the children seemed to burn into her skin as she placed her laptop, portfolio and sketchbook on the table that had been prepared for her. She gazed up hopefully and saw thirty faces staring back in anticipation.

One little boy waved to her and called out, 'Hello. Are you famous?'

Selena immediately felt self-conscious; she had worn a long dress and arranged her hair in a chignon – it was too formal; she was a visiting artist in a rural school; perhaps she should have worn jeans and a sweatshirt.

Scott Finch took over. 'This is Selena Cain. She is a professional artist and she's here because she's painting the beautiful landscapes of Somerset. We are lucky to have her with us today.'

The children broke into spontaneous applause and Selena felt the skin on her face tingle.

Scott continued. 'And you all know Ms Fletcher, who comes in to teach different classes from time to time. It's good to have her here with us too.'

'Good afternoon, Ms Fletcher,' the children chorused as one and Laura replied, 'Good afternoon, everyone. It's so nice to see you all again.'

'So...' Scott lowered his voice. 'It is okay to call you Selena? Not Ms Cain?'

'Selena's fine,' Selena mumbled in reply, her head down as she arranged A4-sized pictures, opened her sketchbook and set up her laptop for a slide show.

Scott raised his voice. 'Right, I'll hand over to Selena and she'll talk to you for a while, then, if it's okay with you, Selena, maybe the class can ask you some questions.'

'Of course. Thanks.' Selena stood up, her eyes wandering from one expectant face to another. 'Well, who can tell me what an artist does?'

Every hand shot up. Selena raised her eyebrows towards a small boy who was pumping the air with his fist, immediately regretting the fact that she had responded to the most persistent, attention-seeking child. She recalled, with a pang of sadness, being the small child at school who sat in the middle and was always invisible.

The little boy had a front tooth missing. 'Miss, they paint pictures.'

'That's right.'

Another boy chimed in, without being asked, 'There are lots of artists, Miss. Van Cough was nuts because he cut his ear off. Then there are artists who drink beer all the time. My dad calls them...'

'Charlie...' Scott gave him a warning glance and the boy lowered his head.

'Right...' Selena took a breath. She tried again. 'I trained to be an artist in Manchester, where I live most of the time when I'm not here. I paint mostly landscapes – paintings of trees and hills and skies. Here are some examples.' She showed them several slides on the laptop: the garden, rising hills, trees spreading tall branches.

'Miss, isn't that a bit boring? Just trees and scenery?' A cheeky-faced girl with tousled fair hair spoke as she raised her hand.

'Not at all.' Selena clicked the mouse and more images of landscapes appeared. 'I get to sit outside in the sunshine and sketch things all day– for example, this is the oak tree across the road from where I live, and this is a blackthorn, and here's a well in the garden.'

The children leaned forward in unison, their faces puckered with interest.

'And do you get paid lots of money for doing it?' Charlie called out.

'It's not bad. I can make a living.' Selena thought a simple answer would be best. 'Here are some larger paintings I've done.' She showed them one from her portfolio. 'This is a painting of the flowers in the back garden, and this one here is of a cow being milked by a milkmaid.'

'Is that you?' The boy with the missing front tooth gave a wide grin.

Scott raised a finger. 'You can see the costume the milkmaid is wearing. Clearly, Selena has researched it, and we've just been studying that time period in class, Charles the Second and Oliver Cromwell. Who can tell me the dates the milkmaid might have lived?'

Arms were raised at once, some pupils pushing their fists towards the ceiling and calling 'Sir!' as if in pain.

'Phoebe?' Scott pointed a finger. 'Phoebe Shears, not Phoebe Davis.'

'The sixteen hundreds, Sir.' Phoebe, the girl with the tousled fair hair, replied. '1666.'

Another girl replied sulkily, '1666 was the Great Fire of London.'

Scott waved a hand. 'The costume is what an ordinary woman would wear in the seventeenth century, so yes, the sixteen hundreds. It's a beautiful painting of a milkmaid at work.' He nodded encouragingly to Selena.

Selena took a breath and gazed around at the children's faces. 'So, I paint the pictures and then they go to my gallery in Manchester, which is called Ariel Art, and that's where people come in and look around, and then they buy the ones they like.'

'Are your paintings worth a lot of money?' Charlie shouted out.

Selena smiled. 'Not as much as Van Gogh's. But it's a great life being an artist. You get to be independent, and work at your own pace, and you choose what you want to paint.'

Another girl wearing blue glasses pushed up her hand. 'Miss, why would you want to paint a cow? If I was an artist, I'd want to paint ponies.'

'Good question,' Selena said, her face shining with approval. 'I paint things that relax people. Often people buy pictures of the countryside because of the sense of tranquility they bring.'

Scott intervened. 'Who can tell me what tranquility means?'

Several faces were screwed tightly, as if in deep thought. Then one girl raised her hand and said, 'Peace and quiet.'

'Exactly.' Selena smiled. 'Now, if anyone would like to ask me some questions about being an artist, I'd be happy to answer them.'

A dark-haired boy threw up his hand. 'What's the hardest thing to paint: people or scenery?'

'Both are equally exacting. It's about practice, and trying to improve,' Selena replied. 'Everything gets easier if you practise it a lot.'

More hands shot into the air. Selena indicated a small girl at the front. 'Miss, have you ever painted any famous people?'

Selena said, 'In my final year at university, I did a scene from a rock concert, the Arctic Monkeys. It took me weeks to finish it because there were so many people in it.' She shrugged. 'After that I stuck to landscapes.'

A frowning boy threw his hand into the air. 'Do you paint men and ladies in their nude?'

Scott was about to intervene, but Selena replied, 'As part of an artist's training, we have to study everything, from the human body to the dimples in an orange. We paint everything that is out there – still life, figures – in detail so that we can learn, but it's like a science, because we want to improve and get it exactly right.' She raised her eyebrows in the direction of the boy. 'Does that answer your question?'

'Miss, yes,' he mumbled.

'Any more questions?'

Selena turned to the girl who had spoken earlier, Phoebe Shears, who had raised her hand.

'You live in Sloe Cottage in Chitterwell, don't you, Miss?' Phoebe smiled, a brash confident grin. 'My dad says that place is haunted. My dad says our family have lived in Ashcombe for hundreds of years and Sloe Cottage is a bad place and no one will live there because it's haunted by a ghost.' She gave Selena a bold stare. 'Have you seen the ghost yet?'

'No, I haven't.' Selena tried her best to keep her voice calm. 'To be honest, I don't really believe in them.'

'I do. My dad's seen it; it's a lady. He went there once to sweep the chimneys and he saw her looking at him. She was horrible—'

'Enough, Phoebe, please,' Scott said calmly. 'Now it's almost time to pack up tidily and go home, but first I think we need to thank Selena for being our guest.'

Applause sounded and Selena breathed out, relieved.

* * *

Selena sat in the warmth of the kitchen of Laura's cottage, sharing a cup of tea: the walk back from the school had been chilly and the sky was overcast. Rob was upstairs in his room, having a nap and Laura was glad of the company. Her eyes shone behind the glasses. 'You were great with the kids today, Selena. Really calm and confident.'

Selena shook her head. 'I was rattled by the questions a couple of times.'

'When the boy asked about painting nudes? I thought you handled that brilliantly.'

Selena shook her head. 'It was the question about the ghost that threw me.'

'Why?' Laura leaned forward. 'Do you think Sloe Cottage is haunted?'

'Almost certainly,' Selena replied and Laura caught her breath, taken aback. 'Do you know the painting I did, the one that I showed you, Joely and Matty...'

'The one of Wychanger Lane?' Laura said. 'Even though you've never been there? I thought that was a bit odd...'

Selena's voice was low and confidential. 'I was sure someone whispered it in my ear as I slept. When I woke up, I put it down on the canvas, just as I remembered it in the dream.'

Laura looked doubtful. 'It's probably a coincidence – are you absolutely sure you haven't been past there and not remembered?'

'There are other things though...' Selena pressed her lips together. 'More than just an atmosphere – I've heard noises on the landing.'

'Oh, this old house creaks too,' Laura waved a hand, then she saw Selena's serious expression and paused. 'Are you sure you're all right living there alone, Selena?'

'I'm fine, most of the time,' Selena said. 'There's something about the solitude I actually like. And it's really working for me, being there and painting, but, you know, I often have the sensation that someone is watching me or standing behind me...'

Laura was staring at her, her eyes shining behind the glasses. 'If I lived somewhere like that, I just couldn't stay there by myself...'

'I've had a few moments where I've felt really shaken, but...' Selena forced a smile. 'I'm okay. I just work all the time, and I have great visitors like you and Joely, and Claire is coming down to stay next week. I'm not really too worried.' Laura's expression was still horrified, so Selena continued. 'It doesn't feel like an evil presence, just... a bit unsettling.'

'I'll have nightmares tonight now.' Laura glanced at the wall clock and frowned. 'Right, Selena – I'll run you home.' She placed a hand on her shoulder. 'Now, are you sure you'll be all right?'

'Absolutely, yes,' Selena said, in an attempt to convince herself. 'And thanks for the cuppa. I'm shattered after just one hour of being in the school today. I think I'll go back and have a shower and get an early night.'

Laura reached for her car keys and shrugged on a jacket. 'Okay, let's get you back.'

Selena protested. 'I can walk, it's not far...'

'The wind has picked up outside – it looks like it might rain,' Laura suggested.

Laura drove down the narrow lane to Chitterwell and they paused in the drive to Sloe Cottage. The wind blustered and stirred the garden. Overhead, clouds gathered and the sky was brooding and heavy with rain. Selena hugged Laura briefly, pulling keys from her pocket, her other hand holding the laptop and the portfolio case, her sketchbook under her arm, then she wriggled out and watched Laura's car swivel round, disappearing towards Ashcombe.

Selena opened the door and stepped inside the hall. The evening gloom swallowed her, enfolding her in its arms, as she fumbled for a light switch. In the sitting room, the fire glowed amber and she dropped her portfolio and laptop on the table, flopping down on the sofa for a moment to warm her hands, staring into the flames as if in a trance.

In the garden, something moved by the well. The shape of a slender woman shifted silently towards the blackthorn tree. She stayed, pressing her hand against the window as if she was watching Selena by the fireside. Her face touched the glass and she paused for a moment, but there was no mist from her breath.

25

On the afternoon after Twelfth Night, Grace picked her way carefully to her grandmother's house across packed snow, a basket in her hand. She had walked the twenty-minute journey to Ashcomb many times since she had been a child, but this time she felt achingly tired. Her Grandmother Bett met her at the door, her face crumpled with concern.

'You are only weeks from lying-in and you have walked here through the cold and the snow? You make me fret...' She shepherded her indoors and sat her down in the chair at the hearth. 'I will bring you something warm to drink. You must rest, Gracie.'

Grace was glad of the opportunity to relax in front of the fire, and she handed over her basket dutifully. 'I brought these things for you.'

Bett lifted the linen cloth. 'Eggs, pie, a good slab of cheese. Did your father bring these back from wassailing at Hill Top Farm?'

'No, Alice Harper – Alice Shears as was – took them from the farm kitchen. She said they had plenty there for the family and a little left over. Alice is my friend now.'

Bett watched her a moment, concerned: Grace appeared exhausted. Bett placed the basket on the table and poured warm cider from a jug, handing it to Grace, who closed her eyes. Then Bett crouched down, taking her granddaughter's hands, rubbing them between her palms to warm them. 'Did you see the fallen branch of the oak tree when you left Slaugh Cottage? Is it still across the lane?'

'I know not of what you speak – there was none fallen when I left.' Grace's eyelids were still closed. 'Did the oak branch snap? I said to Alice that it would. It was laden heavily with snow. I expect someone has taken it away to burn in their hearth.'

'Oak wood burns slowly to bring fertility,' Bett said. 'But a high branch snapped late last night and crashed to the ground, just after the feasting for the wassail. Did you not hear about it? Everyone in Ashcomb is talking about Ned Shears' accident after the wassailing in the ox barn.'

'An accident has befallen Ned?' Grace gasped. 'How did it happen?'

'Did your father not tell you this morning?'

'He returned early from the wassailing. He was tired and took to his bed.'

'I have heard this story several times today from many people in the village. Ned Shears and his brother, George, and several others were walking back towards Ashcomb late, after midnight, and as they were beneath it, the branch broke in half, falling down on Ned and his leg was trapped and twisted beneath him. The other men had to lift off the branch and then carry him to his home.'

'Is he recovered?'

'I fear he will not.' Bett shook her head. 'I have heard the leg is much damaged. I do not think he will work for many weeks. This morning I spoke to Mary Cook, a woman who lives in one of the cottages by St Bartholomew's, and she told me that a splint was put on his leg, and that he was racked in terrible pain. I promised to call round later with a comfrey poultice to help knit the bone.'

'Poor Ned.'

'Of course, if he cannot work, then what will he do? He lives with George and Nancy, and Nancy has a child coming in March. Ned was to marry Jennet Bryant this summer, but he cannot wed her if he cannot afford to wive. He has suffered much misfortune. The wassail

festivities did not send good luck to knock on his door this year, I
fear.'

'I am sad to hear about this, grandmother. I like Ned. He is a kindly
man, and he has a good heart.' Grace sighed, recalling how she had
only spoken to him the day before. She remembered the gentleness of
his voice, and the tender light in his eyes. 'I wish him well,' she
muttered.

'There is much sadness in this world,' Bett said. 'But there is also
much to rejoice this coming year. I hear that Kitty Stokes is with child
again, that she will be delivered of it in the autumn. And you will soon
be safely delivered too, then you will need to lie in for a while to
recover.'

'I hope you will be there with me when the child comes. I fear I
cannot do it alone.'

'I have promised it, Gracie. And I hope all will be well; you are
sturdy and strong, if slight, and you are carrying the child high, but you
are a good girl and I hope it will not be a difficult birth.'

'I hope so too, with all my heart,' Grace said. 'The little one turns
and stretches every day and I fear that soon he will be too big for me to
carry.'

Bett laughed. 'I may be furrowed with old age, but I have delivered
many women of their babes. You need not fret, for you are safe in my
hands.'

'I do not doubt it.' Grace stretched out her legs in front of the fire
and sighed deeply. 'And, indeed, I am looking forward to holding my
child. He will come soon, I know it.'

'But meanwhile we must keep ourselves strong...' Bett stood up
slowly. 'My back aches today and I need a cup of warm cider to ease
the pain.' She began to laugh. 'Do not think me a swill-belly, Gracie,
but I need to pour myself another cup. Let me get us both something to
quench our thirst and I'll cut us a piece of the pie you brought, then we
can sit together and tittle-tattle the hours away...'

Bett stopped, moving softly towards Grace, whose small face was
illuminated in the orange blaze, her eyes closed. There was a sweet

smile on her lips, and she was breathing gently. Bett gazed at her fondly. Grace was sound asleep.

On Sunday morning, Selena was awake and dressed by seven o'clock, bright-eyed and smiling. Nick arrived at eight: they shared breakfast and were ready to leave at nine, her sketch pad stowed safely in the back of his Dacia Duster. Intense sunlight streamed through the windscreen, a warm honey-gold beam, but there was a sharp bracing wind; it was a perfect day to visit the coast, driving through Taunton and onto the sleepy A358 and then the busy A39.

'So, where are we going first?' Selena asked.

'The weather is due to be dry all day, so you choose,' Nick said, his eyes on the road. 'We can either go to Dunster Castle, which is beautiful and packed with history, or we can walk through Dunster itself and see the thatched yarn market, the ruins of a Benedictine priory, a working watermill and the packhorse bridge.'

Selena clapped her hands. 'All of those, please.'

'But then the artist in you might want to go to Dunster Beach, which is all sand and shingle, it's great for a long walk. Or we can drive up to Exmoor, where the views are stunning. I can imagine you painting the panorama of the moors, with all the folklore, pixies, ghosts. Even the Devil himself is said to lurk on Exmoor. It's a wild place, with changeable weather and vast skies. Have you ever read Blackmore's novel *Lorna Doone*?'

Selena shook her head. 'No, I don't think so...'

'It's a love story between a kidnapped aristocratic girl and a young farm lad who has a grudge against the notorious Doone clan; it was written in the late seventeenth century. The story is set in a hidden valley on Exmoor.'

'That sounds so romantic,' Selena blurted, then stopped herself, her cheeks tingling. 'I mean, it might be nice to go there...'

'I was thinking about the sort of places you might want to photograph so that you can paint them later,' Nick explained. 'If we can feed your creative imagination on a Sunday, then maybe it will help you to paint during the week.'

'It certainly will.' Selena felt a surge of gratitude; Nick was so thoughtful, seeking out inspirational views for her to use in her painting. She was about to suggest that he should decide where to go since he knew the area so well, but she stopped herself. In the past, she had allowed David to make all the choices; she had often been passive or ambivalent. It was time now for her to become more decisive. 'Can we go to Exmoor first and see the moorlands, then perhaps we can visit the beach, then if there is any time left, we can go to Dunster?'

'Perfect,' Nick replied, then he offered, 'However, there is one small problem, which means we might run out of time. My mother made me promise to bring you over later this afternoon for tea at Hilltop.'

'Tea? As in a cup of tea and crumpets?' Selena asked nervously.

'My mother likes to bake. She'll be at home right now whisking up a sponge or making some scones.' He glanced across. 'Is that all right? My mother knows I'm showing you round the sights and she's been grumbling that she hadn't seen you in ages.'

'Of course – that's wonderful.' Selena tried to sound pleased, but she was unsure about having tea with Nick's parents. Immediately she told herself she was being silly; she was Lesley Russell's tenant and Nick's friend, that was all; it wasn't as if they were the parents of a new boyfriend. She was worrying unnecessarily.

Nick glanced anxiously towards Selena, then back at the road ahead. 'Are you okay? You're a bit quiet today...'

'Am I? Oh, sorry...' Selena said. 'It's been a busy week. I've done lots more work in the conservatory, lots more local scenes, and then I visited the primary school to show some paintings to the ten-year-olds.'

'Impressive.' Nick raised an eyebrow. 'I'd love to see the latest paintings you've been doing.'

Selena thought of the sunset view from Wychanger Lane that she had painted, and decided not to say anything about her visit to Joely and Matty, and what they had discussed. Instead, she said, 'I'm even more excited about the ones I'm going to paint this week. Exmoor sounds wonderful and I haven't painted an ocean in years. What I'd really like to do is paint the sea at night, you know, the moonlight and the reflection on the water...'

'We can come back one evening, drive to somewhere like Bossington Beach and take lots of photos...' Nick replied and Selena wondered if he was teasing her. No, she decided, he was genuinely offering to give up his time to help her with her paintings. He seemed to read her thoughts as he added, 'I really look forward all week to the places we visit together on Sundays, going round the county and finding some of the best places for you to paint. It's great to be outdoors, walking. If I was back in Exeter, I'd be either reading or working at home, or having a pint down the pub with a mate.' He grinned. 'This is much more fun.'

'I'm glad.' Selena gave him a warm smile. 'I have to say, I'm really grateful for everything you're doing to help me.'

'It's a pleasure.' Nick pointed through the windscreen as he turned the car left to climb up a steep hill. Selena gazed out of the window at tufty grass, shades of green mixed with yellow gorse and wild purple heather. 'And we're almost here. I think you're going to love Exmoor.'

26

They walked for over an hour, Selena taking dozens of photos of the landscape, stark outcrops of jagged rock, wild expanses of gorse, layered fields and trees in shades of green stretching towards a sky crammed full of pleated clouds. Then they arrived at a path that dissected purple heather and a criss-cross of fields, dropping down to the deep blue sea and fading eventually into pale hazy sky. Not far away, ponies grazed freely, their heads down nibbling long grass. Selena said, 'Oh, this is incredible. I want to paint it all.'

Nick looked pleased as she snapped away, taking more photos. 'We could spend days here and not see everything. I'd love to go on to Valley of the Rocks, but we won't have time today. There are some great costal paths to walk, streams – the ancient "clapper bridge" is fantastic, and you can't come to Exmoor and not visit Porlock Weir.'

Selena whirled round. 'I want to see everything,' she gushed. 'Can't we visit all of them? There's so much I want to paint. It's paradise.'

'You might have to stay on for another month,' Nick suggested. 'I'm sure the colours will be even more striking in the autumn and in the winter – imagine the sight of a stag standing on the top of a rock.'

Selena smiled. 'Maybe I should stay for a whole year.'

Their eyes met, and they were both quiet for a moment, thinking.

Selena imagined being with Nick in a cosy thatched cottage over-looking the sea, morning mist rising outside the windows, the sun warming the pale sand. Then Nick said, 'We can walk the half a mile back to the car, then drive to the clapper bridge. You could take some photos there. It will be a complete contrast to Exmoor, all overhanging trees, and then we could take the road back via Tiverton in time for afternoon tea at Hilltop.'

'It sounds perfect.'

They walked side by side, Nick talking to her; she could hear the gentle cadence of his voice, but she was lost deep in her own thoughts. She realised that Nick had asked her a question, and she shook her head, apologetically.

'I'm so sorry... what was that?'

'You were miles away,' Nick said.

'Yes, sorry, I do that sometimes,' Selena explained. 'My head becomes full of things I'm going to paint and I start composing pictures and I get lost in my own world.' She smiled ruefully. 'I'm not great company, am I? Typical obsessive artist.'

'You're wonderful company,' Nick insisted. 'I wouldn't be out walking on the moors if you weren't here. And it's fascinating, getting to understand the mind of an obsessive artist.' He smiled. 'I could get used to it.'

Selena felt the blood rush to her face; she covered her embarrass-ment with a laugh. 'But you're creative too. Doesn't it happen to you?'

'I get lost in a book, yes, all the time,' he said. 'I can open something to read in the evening, start at chapter one, and before I know it, time has flown by, I'm halfway through and it's past midnight. It's so easy to get lost in another world.'

'It is.'

They had reached the car. Selena stretched her legs towards the footwell and settled into the warmth.

As Nick drove along winding roads, she became enveloped in thoughts again; her mind was sucked back to Sloe Cottage, the gloomy living room with its warm hearth, the bright conservatory where paintings seemed to flow from her brushes thick and fast, the homely kitchen. She wondered what time Claire would arrive tomorrow, and her thoughts shifted to the spare bedroom where Claire would stay. Selena planned to open the windows straight after breakfast, put a scented candle in there, so that the room would be welcoming and fresh.

They arrived at Tarr Bridge, walking from the car park towards the river. Selena stopped and caught her breath. Huge slabs of uneven grey stones stretched across the stream, shards of sunlight sending silver ripples wriggling on the surface. Trees hung thickly over the stone bridge and, as they crossed slowly, step by step, Selena thought about clutching Nick's arm. She stopped herself: she would not grasp anyone for support again. She was balanced now and sure-footed: she had survived David's betrayal and the loss of her baby. She was stronger than ever.

She tugged her phone from a pocket and began to take photographs. Sunlight filtered through the trees, making starburst rays flood through dappled leaves and branches. They reached an expanse of space and turned to look back at the steps.

'Why is it called a clapper bridge?' Selena asked.

'I think clapper is from the Latin *claperius,* meaning pile of stones.' Nick made a mischievous face. 'Or maybe I'm just making it up.'

'It sounds feasible.'

'I read somewhere that there's an old belief that the Devil built the bridge. But it's far too beautiful to come from something evil.'

'I'm not sure. My paintings are often about just that... the beauty in nature that has the power to change, to become wild, tempestuous, dangerous even.' Selena shook her head.

'So, who is your favourite painter?' Nick asked. 'Let me guess... Van Gogh? Cézanne?'

'I love O'Keeffe and Turner, Berthe Morisot, but my favourite of all is John Martin. Do you know his work?'

'Did he paint one of Macbeth? I recall there being tiny figures and overwhelming sky, as if the heavens are enveloping Macbeth and Banquo on the moors...'

'That's it exactly.' Selena took a breath. 'John Martin makes nature so potent and awe-inspiring, as if it could crush humanity by its sheer power – which it can.'

Nick was gazing at her, his eyes shining. 'I think that's perfect.'

'So...' Selena took her turn. 'Who's your favourite poet?'

'I have so many.' Nick smiled. 'But Yeats comes to mind right now, looking at the stream.'

'Why do you say that?'

'Yeats says that the impact of water stays with you, similar to what you were saying about the effect of nature in your paintings,' Nick murmured;

'I will arise and go now, for always night and day
I hear lake water lapping with low sounds by the shore;
While I stand on the roadway, or on the pavements grey,
I hear it in the deep heart's core.'

'I like Yeats too, now I've heard that,' Selena said.

'I hope you like sponge cake as well,' Nick grinned. 'My mother will have made heaps of food and we ought to be getting back for tea...'

When they arrived at Hilltop Farm, Selena was struck by the extensive view beyond the flower-crammed garden across the fields down to Sloe Cottage and into the distance. She took more pictures on her phone and pointed at the panorama. 'That must be the Blackdown Hills over there. Is that the beacon we walked to? Oh, and look – there's the monument.' She turned back to Nick, her eyes shining. 'I want to paint this – look at all the fields and hills, the bright yellow of the rapeseed standing out against all the ochres and greys.'

Nick said, 'I love the way everything captivates you as an artist. The enthusiasm is totally infectious.'

They turned to go inside, and Selena pointed to deep marks scored in the wood over the door, the letters A and M etched above a circular pattern. 'What are those?'

'Witch's marks,' Nick explained. 'The daisy wheel shape is a hexafoil.'

Selena frowned. 'Did a witch live in this farmhouse?'

'No, it would have been the superstitious people who lived here in the seventeenth century. I think they made the marks to ward off bad luck.'

'Why A and M?'

'I'm not sure,' Nick said. 'Maybe that was the initials of the residents, or perhaps the person they suspected of being a witch?'

'No, it's something completely different.' A tall man with pale hair and a green waxed coat stood at the doorway; Selena noticed that he looked like an older version of Nick: the twinkle of his eyes, the curve of his mouth. The man smiled. 'Nick is right, it is the witch's mark, but the AM stands for Ave Maria. The people who lived here were asking the Virgin Mary for protection.' He held out his hand. 'Ian Russell. Glad to meet you at last, Selena.'

Selena shook his hand: she liked him immediately.

Inside the square kitchen, Lesley was pouring tea into china cups. She was wearing a pretty flowery dress and the table was set out with glass cake stands, cakes on plates with doilies, scones, jam, cream, sandwiches.

Selena couldn't help herself: 'I should have dressed up.'

Lesley was delighted to see her. 'Oh, no, you two have been walking all morning and I dare say you haven't had any lunch.' She glanced at her son. 'Sit down, tuck in.'

'Thanks, Mum.' Nick offered a sheepish grin as Lesley loaded sandwiches onto a serving dish.

'So where have you been to today?' Lesley addressed Selena directly. 'Or should I say where has he dragged you to?'

'Oh, I've loved it – Exmoor, Tarr Bridge. I'm going to do so much painting next week,' Selena replied enthusiastically and Lesley seemed thrilled.

Nick reached for a sandwich. 'This is a great spread, Mum.'

'Oh, I like to make a proper tea on a Sunday nowadays. The men in this family are all sinew and bones and I need to fatten you all up. Look at my Ian – there's not a pick on him.' Lesley winked at Selena. 'I garden all week and I never lose a pound.'

'You don't need to.' Ian patted his wife's arm affectionately. 'Selena was just asking about the witch's marks over the door.'

'I haven't seen any marks like that above the door at Sloe Cottage,' Selena replied cheerfully.

Ian's expression was mischievous. 'How are you finding it at Sloe Cottage? Has the ghost been behaving itself?'

'Ian!' Lesley admonished him. 'You'll frighten the poor girl.'

'Not at all,' Selena protested. 'I love it there.'

'What Ian means...' Lesley said, 'is that the house is very old; it comes with an atmosphere.'

'We've had people stay there who have claimed to have heard all sorts of bumps and creaks.' Ian seemed to find it mildly amusing. 'One couple flat refused to pay the rent; they said the place had terrified them.'

Nick glanced at Selena, his face filled with concern. 'I think you're fine, aren't you? It's an old place, but it doesn't seem to bother you much.'

'I try not to think about it.' Selena sipped her tea. 'It is a bit creepy at times, and I have an artist's imagination, which isn't always a good thing, but I think if I knew more about the history of it, maybe then I wouldn't feel so jumpy when I was alone. I just tell myself that all the creaks and bumps are a natural part of the house's past.'

Lesley nodded agreement. 'This farmhouse and the cottage belonged to my great-grandfather, and my father sold off most of the land to Jack and Owen Jeffries, who are local farmers. I think there's a box of really old paperwork in the attic, which I keep meaning to look through. I've lived at Hilltop Farm since I was a child and Sloe Cottage has been a rental for much of the time, but it used to be a farmworker's cottage and was updated over the years. We put the conservatory in and extended the kitchen and the main bedroom. An old couple lived in the cottage for five years when I was in my teens; they were a bit odd and never really complained about ghosts and such nonsense. But Ian's right, we've had a few people who've stayed for a holiday and found it less relaxing than they'd hoped... I suppose I ought to sell it at some point in the future.'

'I'd like to know more about the house. Who would know about past residents?' Selena asked.

'There would be parish records,' Nick suggested.

'You'd definitely find a lot of information in records. For example,' Lesley held her fork in the air, 'this area is called Chitterwell now. And that comes from the history of Sloe Cottage. Did you know that, Nick? It means chattering well. There's a well in the garden.'

'There is.' Selena shivered: she had painted it, and the shadowy apparition standing just beyond, in the moonlight.

'There's a local family, the Shears, who seem to know a lot about Ashcombe – they've lived here for generations.' Ian seemed pleased with his idea. 'I'll ask Jonathan Shears to drop by at some point, shall I? Then you can ask him all about the place for yourself.'

'That would be great...' Selena said. 'I think there was a girl in Ashcombe Primary called Phoebe Shears who said something about the cottage being haunted. It seems to have quite a reputation locally.' She sipped tea thoughtfully. Claire was arriving tomorrow, but once she'd gone back to Manchester, Selena would ask Nick if he'd help her to do some research.

Again, he seemed to read her thoughts. 'It would be good to discover more about Sloe Cottage. It's hundreds of years old, so there must be some fascinating facts.'

'Oh, definitely.' Selena met his gaze. 'Perhaps it would explain the odd atmosphere, because the place holds so many memories. It would make me feel a little less edgy.'

'Right – shall we start next week?' Nick was enthusiastic. 'What do you think, Mum? It's your cottage.'

'You know I've never believed in ghosts and hauntings. It's an old cottage and it's bound to creak a bit,' Lesley said. 'I've been in there so often and, yes, it's a bit cold and a few doors slam, but that's due to the age of the place and the draughts.'

'I hope you're right.' Selena felt relieved.

'Then we'll fix a date and make a start.' Nick grinned.

'Wonderful.' Lesley looked from her son to Selena and her expression was one of clear joy as she held out the glass cake stand and purred, 'Anyone for angel cake?'

27

Grace didn't feel at all hungry. She watched her father break his fast, wrap himself against the cold and leave for work, then she stared at the crust of bread and curds on the table that she had prepared for herself and wondered what to do. It was the first day of February, a Monday, and she thought she might begin the new month by cleaning the hearth, sweeping out the room, then moving upstairs to the bedrooms and brushing out the dust. She always kept the besom broom behind the door, and she set to pushing it across the rough dirt floor rhythmically, shifting dry mud and leaves. She stretched up towards the ceiling by the stairs, wafting an empty spider's web from a corner, and then she stopped, standing still, a hand to her back, which felt hollow and tired. The baby hadn't moved, not this morning or during the night when he was usually most active, and she hoped all was well. She had risen five times during the night to fill the chamber pot and she had slept fitfully, her spine had ached badly; she had twisted and turned all night, but today she felt energetic, keen to be busy.

Grace resumed sweeping again, then she heard a familiar knock at the door and stopped to listen. 'Alice,' she whispered, knowing that the young farmer's wife often called round on a Monday morning with some eggs in her basket.

When she reached the door, Alice was huddled beneath a warm cape, a basket in her hand.

'Come inside, warm yourself,' Grace said. 'The wind will blow all the dust in again.'

Alice scurried inside, placing the basket on the table. 'I have brought eggs, cheese, some fish, a piece of Twelfth Night cake that was left over and some fruit pie. I also baked some jumbles – I thought you might like the spice in them. I make jumbles all the time now – the little mouthfuls of sweetness seem to keep Nathaniel happy with me.' Alice clapped her hands excitedly. 'There, you see, Grace, I can weave spells too.'

Grace frowned. 'I weave no spells...'

'Oh, I didn't mean to suggest that.' Alice took two jumble biscuits from beneath the linen cover of the basket, handing one to Grace and nibbling the second. 'I was jesting.'

Grace held the biscuit to her nose, inhaling the warm smell of cinnamon and nutmeg. 'I have my simples, my plants and herbs, and that is all I use for the good of others.'

'I did not mean to offend you. People are very grateful for the remedies you make. Your Grandmother Bett has made a poultice for Ned Shears and I believe he improves on it.'

'I am glad,' Grace replied. 'Then his leg is mended?'

'Oh no, it will never straighten. I fear it will not bear his weight well again. But the poultice does ease the pain.'

'Will he be able to work at the farm?'

'Nathaniel has said he will find him some work to do, although he will not labour with the other men in the fields. Nathaniel feels sorry for him. It was not his fault the branch was laden with so much snow that it broke. I told him you and I had seen it that very day and that you had foretold that it would break.'

Grace nibbled the jumble biscuit. 'I wish I could have forewarned him.'

'But you could not,' Alice said. 'And there is more bad news. I brought this basket from the kitchen this morning and on the way my sister, Jennet, saw me with it, and she asked me why I often bring food down to Slaugh Cottage. I told her to mind her mouth, but I fear she will tell Mistress Harriet. I will have to take pains that she does not see me again. Jennet has become like Nancy; they are both often in a bad humour. And old Mother Harper is still a shrew. She stares constantly at my belly to see if it has grown. She thinks me an ill match for her son.'

'And what about your news, Alice? Will there be a child soon?'

Alice's pretty face crumpled. 'Not yet, but I wear the acorn against my heart constantly and I burn oak bark on the hearth, and I put plenty of the foods you told me to on my plate: parsley, hazelnuts, pepper, ginger. I have not tried the rabbit's womb you urged me to eat, but I fear I must be brave and mix it into my dishes for the sake of a child.'

Grace wished that she had some words of comfort. She was filled with sympathy as she reached for Alice's hand. 'Can you stay and have some warmed ale with me before you go?'

'I will, but I must leave soon. My mother-in-law has sent me to the strawed-down barn to milk today. She says since you left, there is not enough milk from the cows and now I must work. None of the milk-maids have charmed fingers to coax the milk from the teats as you do.'

Grace handed Alice a cup of ale, and Alice settled herself in front of the hearth.

'It would be a nice life, to feel your baby grow and sit by the fireside dreaming of all the moments of happiness to come...' She stretched out her palms to warm them in front of the blaze. 'I do believe Nathaniel would love me more if I gave him a son.'

'He should love you most in the world, Alice, for you are a good person.' Grace moved to the linen-covered basket on the table. 'I am grateful for what you have brought. I will use the eggs and the fish later to—'

Grace did not finish her sentence; she slumped forward onto the table, the eggs smashing against the dirt floor, shells and yolk spreading. Then she groaned, a muffled sound of pain.

Alice was at her side. 'What ails you? Is it the baby?'

Grace looked up, her face contorted. 'It may be coming now.' She gripped Alice's arm. 'Can you send someone into Ashcomb to fetch my Grandmother Bett? She promised that she will be with me and help me with the birthing.'

Alice's eyes were wide. 'I must go myself, Grace. There is no one from the farm who will go in my place. If old Mother Harper beats me, then so be it. I will run as fast as my legs will carry me and fetch Mistress Bett for you.'

'Go quickly, please.' Grace bent double again, catching her breath. 'Bring her as soon as you can.'

Then Alice was gone and Grace stood alone in the room. She leaned over carefully to clean up the broken eggs. When she stood up, there was an intense pain in her back and she felt dizzy. She wondered what she could do to get ready and she tried to recall the time she had helped her grandmother deliver Kitty Stokes' baby. Everything would need to be clean.

Grace looked around the room. There was a black kettle steaming in the grate, a pile of dry linen scrubbed with ash and urine; she wondered whether she should go to her bedroom and wait there. She felt another pain clutch deep in her belly, and she dragged herself towards the fire, resting against her father's chair, groaning through tight lips. Grace thought about her father, what he would eat for supper; he would be cold and hungry when he returned from the fields and she did not want him to go without.

She eased herself away from the chair, her hands on her belly; she was not comfortable sitting down. Another pain grabbed her, forcing the breath from her body. Her forehead was damp with perspiration, even though the room was cold as she walked away from the fire to lean against the wooden table. She took a small breath, and then began to walk around the room slowly, squeezing her eyes closed each time a new pain held her.

Grace felt the urge to go outside, to feel the cool wind against her face. She rushed towards the door – Alice had left it open – and she stumbled towards the chattering well. The wind was strong, grass blown flat, the oak tree rustling its branches, the blackthorn rattling twigs against the window shutter.

Grace dropped to her knees and leaned over the well, whispering into the murky depths. 'Please remember the words we spoke to each other – let my baby thrive. Whatever comes to me, I am contented as long as my child is whole and strong.'

Her words echoed in the dark water at the bottom of the well and she eased herself upright. A pain shot through her abdomen and she wrapped her arms around herself, moaning until it left her. The wind took her cap into the air, across the grass, and her hair blew around her face; the droplets of sweat on her brow cooled and Grace shivered. A crow landed in the oak tree and called out, a harsh cry.

Grace breathed shallow gasps, and hoped that Alice would arrive soon with her grandmother. Then a magpie landed in the herb garden, pecking at the soil. Grace stared at it and spat over her shoulder to ward off evil: a magpie was a harbinger of bad luck. She knew that one bird was an omen: death would follow.

She cradled her belly as another pain came and felt a trickle of liquid beneath her dress.

A second magpie landed in the herb garden, foraging with its beak for worms. Grace whispered, 'Two for joy.'

She began to shiver; her entire body was convulsing with cold beyond her control, and she staggered back towards the cottage.

A third magpie landed next to its mate. The baby would be a girl.

Grace leaned against the doorpost; she was gripped by a pain that held her there, she could not move. She felt water splash from her body onto the ground. She was not sure what was happening to her, but she needed to be inside the house, to be warm, to hunker down on the dirt floor and wait for the next overwhelming ache to envelop her.

She glanced again at the herb garden; four magpies were there now. One glanced towards her: four, a boy.

Grace stumbled inside the house, leaving the door ajar, and managed to reach her father's chair before doubling over in agony, grunting through her teeth. She knew the baby was ready to come. She breathed rapidly, panting hard, then she was down on all fours, teeth bared like an animal, waiting for the next wave of pain to clutch her.

* * *

Less than an hour later, she heard voices at the door, Bett gasping, Alice's high cry behind her. Grace sat on the dirt floor leaning against the table, holding her son in her arms; he was suckled, almost asleep, wrapped tightly in a woollen blanket for warmth. Her eyes glowed in the dark room; Grace's face was soft with love, but there was something else in her expression now, a defensive set of her jaw, the new knowledge that she would protect her child at all costs; she would kill, if need be, to keep him alive.

Bett was by her side. 'How are you, Gracie? How is the child?' She turned to Alice. 'Fetch a warm drink, some posset, something to keep up her strength. And bring me some clean linen and a pitcher of hot water from the kettle. Quickly to it.'

Grace spoke quietly, easing herself into a comfortable position. 'I am well, Grandmother. And the baby, too, he is well.'

'You have done this by yourself.' Bett busied herself with Grace and the baby, speaking as she worked. 'You have had a good birthing. The baby is strong. It is a wonderful sight, when both mother and child are hearty.'

Then Bett stood slowly, placing a hand on Alice's shoulder, moving her away from Grace, her voice low and confidential.

'In truth, Alice, I had not expected the baby to come so quickly. It is not usually this way the first time. But Gracie and the child thrive and I am full of gladness for it. My own sister, Mary, had six children, but only two survived. The first died within half an hour of the birth; the second, at eighteen months. The third, a boy, died during the birth – a terrible time Mary had of it – and the fourth gave her haemorrhages and it died forthwith. The fifth I delivered for her, and the sixth, both safely born. But Gracie has managed it by herself, and my heart is happy to see her so swiftly recovered.'

'And thank God the child is well.' Alice turned to gaze fondly at the baby held tightly in Grace's arms. 'He is perfect, and so strong. And look at his deep-set eyes and dark hair, his noble brow. He is going to be an important man, I know it.'

'I know it too.' Grace's lids fluttered and closed for a moment. 'I am sure of it.' She accepted the cup that Alice placed in her hand and sipped gratefully.

Bett placed her hands on her hips. 'Well, Gracie, you have a fine son. Alice and I will help you upstairs to your room and you and the baby can rest awhile.'

Grace frowned. 'I need to prepare my father's tea.'

'I will do that,' Bett said firmly. 'I will stay here tonight and make sure Will has breakfast tomorrow and I will see that you are warm and comfortable and well fed. After all, you must suckle your son, so you need to eat and drink heartily.'

'I will bring some things from the kitchen at Hill Top Farm,' Alice added. She stroked the baby's round cheek; Grace noticed the soft expression on her face as she gazed at his dark eyes and long eyelashes. Then Alice took Grace's hand in hers, pressing her fingers fondly. 'I have sewn a blanket to keep him warm and I will embroider it with the initial of his name and the year of his birth. Bett has promised to help me to copy the numbers from a page, and then I can stitch them. I will bring it to you tomorrow or the day after, once I have finished my chores and milking.' She laughed softly, placing a hand across her mouth. 'I know my mother-in-law will be angry with me today, but I am truly happy that I am here with you now, Grace. And your son is so sweet-faced, so handsomely favoured.'

'He is,' Grace replied; she noticed her grandmother's sharp glance, and she knew Bett's thoughts. The child did not look like Grace; he had tufts of dark hair; he was broad-shouldered, not slender as she was. But Grace had vowed never to talk again about the child's father.

Bett patted her hand, urging her to drink. 'And what will you call your son, Gracie? What have you decided to name him?'

Grace pulled the child close to her, smelling the warm, sweet scent as her eyes closed in sleep. 'His name is Gabriel,' she said. 'Gabriel Cotter.'

28

Monday the thirtieth of May was a bright, glorious day. Selena threw open the windows of the second bedroom, gazing out at the clustered flowers in the garden, the newly growing herbs, the well. Cool fresh air and sunlight thick as honey flooded into every corner. In the centre of the room, the bed was freshly made; the bedcovers were crisp and white, newly washed and spotless, arranged over plump pillows. A fragrant candle flickered on the bedside table. Joely had recommended one in a jar, scented with sage: she said it was an uplifting aroma promoting wisdom, and sage was apparently the perfect way to cleanse the house of any negative energy. Selena was delighted; in the daylight, the second bedroom was pretty and welcoming. With its clean white walls, curtains billowing like sails in the breeze, a clear glass vase of bluebells in the window, it looked perfect. Selena was sure Claire would be both comfortable and relaxed there during her stay. It was hard to imagine, she decided, that the bedroom had once been two small rooms, which, coupled with the living room, had been home to an entire family centuries ago.

Selena wandered downstairs, taking a cup of tea into the conservatory with the intention of organising her paintings into some kind of chronological order. She'd enjoy showing them to Claire, who would take them back to Manchester to display in the gallery. Selena was pleased with the number of paintings she had finished; Sloe Cottage was very conducive to creativity.

She gazed again at the picture of the red sunset over Wychanger Lane and decided that she would tell Claire about how the painting had come to be, how it was whispered in her ear during a strange dream. In fact, she was going to speak openly about the eerie atmosphere in the cottage from now onwards. She hoped it would make her feel less on edge; she wanted to find out everything she could about the people who had lived here when it had been a simple dwelling. She was mystified by so many things: the strange witch's marks over the door at Hilltop Farm, Ian's tales of other people who had rented the cottage having had bizarre experiences, and the little tousle-haired girl at Ashcombe Primary who had declared in front of the class that Sloe Cottage was haunted. Nick had appeared similarly fascinated by the history of Sloe Cottage, and she was looking forward to seeing him on Sunday, when they'd plan a strategy for uncovering the cottage's secret past. The idea made her skin tingle with excitement.

Selena sorted through her paintings, gazing again at the picture of the garden in moonlight, and had to admit the garden held an almost magical atmosphere at night. She felt the impulse to go there in darkness, to look up at the moon, to listen to the bubbling water at the bottom of the well and to breathe in cool air.

She was tugged from her thoughts by a distant knocking on the front door and she rushed to open it. Then she was hugging Claire and grinning.

Claire held Selena at arm's-length, smiling at her. 'Wow, you're looking so good. How fresh-faced and healthy are you? I must look awful. The drive was horrendous – all congestion and queues and traffic cones. I left at six in the morning and it's taken me until now – what time is it? Well past lunchtime.' She indicated her luggage, two bulging cases. 'And I've brought all of this. You'd think I was going out on the town for a week, not enjoying a rural retreat. But you know I've never mastered the art of packing light.'

'Let's take lunch into the back garden. It's a perfect little suntrap out there,' Selena said. She lifted one of Claire's cases and they both stepped through into the hall. The door slammed behind them with a bang, as if an unseen hand had closed it.

Claire shivered. 'Oh, I'd forgotten how chilly it is once you step inside. It was nice and sunny in the front garden, but it's like a freezer in here.' They were in the living room and she pointed at the wood-burning stove. 'I can see why you keep a fire on all the time. It does take the chill off the air.'

Selena was already in front of her, calling over her shoulder. 'Come on, let's put these cases in your bedroom and then we'll sit in the garden and have lunch.'

Claire pulled a face. 'I had to leave the light on all night last time I slept in that room. And I drank half a bottle of brandy so that I'd forget where I was. It gets incredibly dark in there and everything creaks.'

Selena's voice was light. 'I've aired the whole room and made it smell gorgeous. You'll sleep like a log this time.'

* * *

They sat in the back garden, bowls of salad on their knees. Claire was still chattering, her voice excited. 'The gallery is doing so well. Three of my paintings have sold this week, and four of yours. And Gulliver has even sold one of his. Selena, he's amazing. People who come in to the gallery flock to talk to him – he's like a magnet, and such a persuasive salesman.'

'I can't wait to meet him,' Selena said, enjoying Claire's excitement.

'I'm sure you'll remember him from uni. I knew who he was as soon as I saw him.'

Selena shook her head. 'I'm not sure I would. I was a bit self-absorbed in those days. Flynn and I were, you know, wrapped up in ourselves.'

'I remember. Like an old married couple.' Claire leaned forward. 'To be honest, I need to talk to you about Gulliver. I think there's a chance that he, well, how can I put it? I think he likes me. There's an attraction there and I'm not sure whether to go for it...'

'Oh?' Selena raised an eyebrow. 'Well, you could wait and see what happens...'

'The thing is,' Claire said. 'I had all those years with Ross and I was completely disastrous as a wife. He was really only interested in his music and I was only interested in my art, and once we were married, I knew it was a mistake for both of us. We tried, but, you know the rest, we failed miserably. And I always saw myself as a good-time girl after that, parties and fun and no commitments. And focusing on painting and our gallery.'

Selena examined Claire's face: there was something different, something calm about her friend's expression, a new warmth in her voice when she mentioned Gulliver. She couldn't stop herself from asking, 'So why is Gulliver special?'

Claire didn't hesitate. 'He's genuinely interested in me. He's thoughtful, considerate. We talk, we understand each other. We sort of gel.' She laughed, a short sudden sound of triumph. 'And besides, he's gorgeous.'

'I do understand.' Selena was delighted. She was thinking of Nick. She wondered whether to confide in Claire, to tell her that she'd met someone who was similarly caring and unselfish, the opposite of David. But she decided to say nothing, not yet; she was unsure if Nick would ever be more than a friend. She exhaled. 'Gulliver sounds perfect. And just play it by ear – if it's going to happen, then it will.'

'Oh, I hope so.' Claire agreed. 'He's so nice. And brilliant to work with. He's in the gallery right now.'

'It's a bank holiday today,' Selena said, surprised.

'I know – but he's keen. He's setting up some of his new paintings and ours: he's changing the window display. He is marvellous. Oh, and he's looking after the flat, too.'

'That's great.' Selena realised that she had forgotten all about the flat: she had begun to think of Sloe Cottage as home. Memories of her old life in Manchester surfaced for a moment and with them, the dull ache of sadness.

Claire smiled. 'He's currently living in a poky terrace with his sister, her husband and two kids in Moss Side, until he can find a place of his own. I've told him he can flat-sit while I'm away. Don't worry, Selena, he's absolutely trustworthy.' Claire patted her friend's hand, noting her troubled expression. 'He's staying in my room. Your stuff is all locked away.'

'Oh, I didn't mean...'

'It's a perfect arrangement.' Claire fished a slice of tomato from her salad bowl and pushed it into her mouth. 'Even the food tastes better out in the countryside. And I can't wait to meet all your new friends. Aren't we having a dinner party one night?'

'Thursday. I'm borrowing Matty's barbecue – he's going to set it up in the front garden. I've invited lots of people.' Selena wondered for a moment if she should invite Nick. But he'd be in Exeter, probably working late at the university, and she had the distinct feeling that Claire would become very protective of Selena if she mentioned the possibility of a new man in her life: there would be a great deal of questions. She decided she'd save telling Claire about him until later, until she was sure about the status of their relationship. She added, 'I'm so looking forward to spending some time with you this week. So, once we've had lunch, how would you like to look at all the work I've done? Then maybe we can do a bit of painting ourselves. I have some wonderful photos of Exmoor to show you.'

* * *

Late that evening, after supper, Selena and Claire sat on the sofa in front of the wood burner, their toes stretched out. Claire cradled a large glass of brandy in her hand and Selena was sipping tea.

Claire yawned. 'The drive has taken it out of me – I'm exhausted. I think I'll turn in soon.' She heard a sudden slapping at the window, a crack of knuckles, and she sat up abruptly. 'What's that?'

'The blackthorn branch.' Selena returned the yawn. 'It's always doing it.'

'It sounds like someone's knocking...' Claire was clearly unsettled.

'It keeps me company,' Selena said calmly.

'Oh, that's so creepy.' Claire shook her head as if pushing a thought away. 'But being here has clearly helped you flourish as an artist. I can't get over your new paintings. They are so vivid. The landscape just jumps out at you.' Claire sipped her brandy. 'What's happened? Your style has changed, shifted a bit – it's more surreal.'

'It's definitely the effect of living here, you're right,' Selena admitted. 'The house seems to affect my paintings. I feel isolated and a bit edgy; sometimes it's as if someone is watching me when I paint. And my work is becoming influenced by that.'

'You're making me shiver.' Claire stared at Selena. 'And there was that incredibly moody painting you did of the hills in the sunset...'

'Wychanger Lane?' Selena began. Then she sat absolutely still: there was a dull thud from above, a single crashing noise as if something had fallen in the bedroom.

Claire couldn't speak.

Selena frowned. 'I've no idea what that was.'

Claire shook her head. Then she found her voice. 'It was in my bedroom, wasn't it?'

'Did you leave your case on the bed? Could it have dropped off?'

'No... I packed everything away and put the case underneath the bed.' Claire shook visibly. 'You were there with me. It was like ice in that room too.'

'I left the windows open to air the room... but I know I shut them before we had supper.' Selena stood up. 'Right, let's go and check.'

'Really?' Claire gasped.

Selena held out a hand and Claire gripped it. They walked slowly through the lobby and the kitchen, treading quietly up the stairs. Then Selena heard another thud and stopped, holding her breath, listening.

'What is it?' Claire whispered.

Selena climbed two more steps, heaving Claire with her; they were almost at the top. Then she put a finger to her lips.

The muffled sound came from beyond the landing, from inside Claire's bedroom. It was a woman's voice, just audible, singing the tender notes of a lullaby.

> 'Cares you know not, therefore sleep,
> While mother here a watch will keep...'

Selena tugged Claire's hand; Claire held back, terrified, as they moved from the top step onto the landing. The door to the second bedroom was ajar.

The song continued, the voice now hollow and desolate, the tenderness replaced by sadness and loss.

> 'Sleep, pretty darling, do not cry,
> And I will sing a lullaby.'

Selena knew she had shut the door. She recalled being there with Claire, closing the windows, pulling the door to with a crisp click. But the door was open, and the voice was murmuring from inside the room, almost a whisper.

Claire froze where she was, shaking her head frantically. She couldn't move forward.

Selena took two steps, then another. She was almost level with the door. A sound came from inside the room, a hushed voice, words flat and toneless, the incantation of a spell. Selena put out a hand and touched the door latch, staring into the room. The windows had been flung open and a draught blew cold air in her face. The pale ceiling was gone; there was darkness, emptiness, rafters, straw and a high roof space. Then, in the corner of the room, something moved, a hazy shifting of light in the gritty darkness, a huddled shape. The silhouette was still for a moment, then it loosened, became mist and was no more.

Selena blinked, staring into the gloom; she could see the bed, the windows open, the corners cluttered with shadows. On the floor, bluebells were strewn; the vase must have toppled from the windowsill. She closed the door with a soft clunk and turned to Claire, who was cowering a distance away, a hand to her mouth. She would not go in.

29

The next few weeks were some of the happiest Grace had known. Gabriel was close by all day long, resting in her arms or slumbering in the hollowed-out barrel stuffed with soft straw and linen. She suckled him whenever he was hungry, her body responding immediately to the vigorous cry of his lungs, all the time watching his eyes on her, his lashes against his cheek as his mouth puckered and he slipped into contented sleep. Nursing him was always precious; she was astonished by the rush of love she felt every time she lifted him, the warmth of his skin against hers; Grace had never known such complete devotion. As she worked around the house preparing food, she sang happy little ditties that would make him smile and gurgle. And at night-time, she would snuggle in her pallet bed, holding him in her arms, listening to the soft rhythm of his breathing as he slept, inhaling the sweet warmth, pressing her lips against his cheek, so many kisses.

As March approached, new herbs started to push through in the garden and Grace slipped outside while Gabriel dozed, lingering to coax them to grow and to reply to the crow's loud call. There were hares loitering in the garden, hedgehogs, and a vixen roamed, calling for her mate. Grace whispered her thanks to the well daily; gratitude filled her heart like a blossoming flower. She knew that her beloved blackthorn bush would bloom soon, heralding the arrival of May and she could take the baby outside to sit on the grass and she would make a daisy chain for him.

It was a Friday, March the twelfth, a fresh day with the promise of spring. Grace was working indoors, but she left the door ajar, aware of the birdsong, the sweet smell of new grass and changing seasons in the air. The blackthorn tree brushed against the shutters and Grace greeted the sound with a smile; she thought of her father working out in the fields and she was thankful for the heat of the logs crackling in the grate. She had prepared the evening meal – a hearty mutton stew was cooking in its pot on the hook; a loaf of bread was baking in the little oven – and Grace sat down to relax in her chair, Gabriel nestling in the crook of her arm. She murmured to him, telling him a story about a handsome young man who rode on a horse and brought treasure back from far-off lands. His eyes were on hers all the time, listening as if he understood each new word, his little fist clasped around her finger. Grace marvelled at the pudding softness of his hand and it saddened her to think that one day it would be calloused and rough as her own, raw like her father's after he had ploughed fields each day. She wished with all her heart that she could save him from the hardship she and her father had known.

Watching Gabriel deep in slumber, Grace knew that she had named him right: he had the sweet flushed face of an angel. She placed him in his barrel crib, covering him with the blanket Alice had made for him, embroidered with the letter G which Grace knew well, it being the first letter of her own name. Alice had sewn four numbers onto the blanket, 1683, and Grace was pleased that the year of her son's birth was chronicled in the stitches.

She gazed at her baby as he slept, then she reached for her own sewing work in a basket. She had a dress that needed patching, some breeches of her father's to mend, but first she would finish the little doll she was making for Gabriel. She had worked a piece of linen into the shape of a boy with dark wool for the hair and eyes and for the buttons on his shirt, stuffing the cloth with new herbs, mint and sage, rosemary, lemon balm and parsley. She imagined Gabriel holding it in his tiny fist and inhaling the fresh scents, chattering to it like a companion: he would never have a brother or a sister.

She looked down at Gabriel again, and her thoughts turned to Alice: she was so kind, a true friend. Since the baby was born, Alice had visited Slaugh Cottage whenever she could, bringing gifts she'd pilfered from the kitchen at Hill Top Farm. She'd insisted on bringing curds and making posset to build up Grace's strength; she'd baked more batches of spicy jumble biscuits and stolen eggs and fish, bringing them to Grace hidden beneath a linen cloth in a basket. Alice spent more time in the barn now, milking the cows, as Harriet was short of milkmaids, but she would slip down to see Grace whenever she could.

Grace knew how fond Alice was of Gabriel too; her face would relax and her eyes would fill with tears whenever she saw him, and she would beg to pick him up, and cradle him in her arms. Grace would always say yes, even if Gabriel was sleeping; Alice would lift him with such tenderness, never waking him, laying her cheek against his face and offering Grace a look of pure gratitude and affection. Grace hoped that Alice would find herself with child soon: she deserved to share the same happiness that filled Grace's waking moments and her sleeping hours as she held her son in her arms.

There was a loud rap at the door. Grace's first thought was to hope that the abrupt noise wouldn't wake Gabriel. She wondered if Alice had come to visit early, if she had managed to slip away from her chores and from the keen eagle-eye of her mother-in-law. Her eyes moved to the baby, adjusting his blanket, then she pushed her needle into the linen of her sewing, dropped it into the basket and slipped from the room towards the front door.

Grace caught her breath. Nathaniel Harper stood in the opening facing her. Grace gazed over his shoulder; small birds fluttered in the leaves of the oak tree. She met Nathaniel's dark-eyes and suddenly realised she was without her cap and her kerchief. Her pale hair hung around her shoulders and her dress was loose. She waited for him to speak.

'Can I come in, Grace?'

Grace wished she could say no; the baby was inside, asleep; she was busy, but Slaugh Cottage belonged to Joseph Harper so she could not refuse his son.

She nodded and Nathaniel strode inside, into the living room. He stopped when he reached the cot, staring down at the sleeping child, taking in the dark tufts of hair. Then he turned to Grace.

'So, the baby is well?'

'He is.'

'And I hear you have named him Gabriel?'

'I have.'

Nathaniel did not take his eyes from her and Grace felt uncomfortable; he was in her house, a threat in the place she felt most safe.

She took a breath. 'So – what can I do for you, Master Nathaniel? Was it my father you wanted to see? You know he is at work in the fields and will not be home until late.'

'I wanted to see you, Grace.'

There was an urgency in Nathaniel's tone that made Grace feel uneasy. 'What is it that you want?'

Nathaniel looked at the baby again and a moment's tenderness smoothed his furrowed brow. Grace wondered if he would lift the child from the cot and she was ready to tell him to leave her child alone; Gabriel was not Nathaniel's to touch.

Nathaniel exhaled. 'You know that my wife cannot get with child?'

'She has much time before her. You have not been wed a year.'

Nathaniel shook his head. 'I fear she cannot conceive. Alice is key-cold, not a warm-blooded maid like you.' He gazed again at the baby. 'And I need a son.'

Grace felt her heart start to knock in her chest; she was seized with the fear that Nathaniel would try to take the child from his cot, that he wanted to steal him away from her. She thought of her sewing tools in a basket next to her father's chair; she imagined herself reaching for scissors or a bodkin. She would stab Nathaniel before she would allow him to snatch her son. She replied, her tone flat, 'Gabriel is mine.'

Nathaniel's face was immediately filled with regret. 'Perhaps I made the wrong choice when I wived?'

'You abandoned me.'

'You bewitched me, Grace, and I was unwittingly charmed...'

Grace did not reply. Her gaze moved from Nathaniel to her baby, who was asleep in his cot, oblivious to the tension that hung in the air.

Nathaniel took a breath. 'I'm here to speak to you for my mother. We are short of milkmaids in the strawed-down barn. And you are a skilled milkmaid. I have heard it said that your fingers have the power to make the cows let down more milk than any other maid. I want you to come back to work at the farm on Monday morning.'

Grace said, 'And what of my child?'

Nathaniel shrugged. 'It is spring. Wrap him well and bring him with you. He can sleep while you work.'

Grace stared at him, amazed that she had been called back to the barn: it was Mistress Harriet who had put her out. But the extra money would help. She would find a way to look after her son and to work. She offered a brief nod. 'Very well. I will be there on Monday morning.'

Nathaniel turned, as if to leave. Then his eyes fell on the sewing. 'What is this?' He reached into the basket and picked up the little doll. 'What have you made here, Grace? Is it an enchanted poppet?'

'It is just a little herb-scented doll to comfort my son.'

Nathaniel turned it over in his fingers and then cried out in pain, 'I have been pricked by a thorn.'

Grace reached for his hand without thinking, taking the doll from his fist, examining the palm of his hand where a bead of blood bloomed. 'It is only my needle, it made just a small wound. If you like, I can clean it with water from the pitcher.'

Nathaniel tugged his hand away and took a step back. 'It is no matter.' He stared at Grace for a while. Outside, the sunshine illuminated fresh grass, buds of new blossom on the blackthorn. Nathaniel was still looking at her and Grace turned her gaze away.

He sighed. 'I am sorry for what happened between us, Grace.'

Grace glanced at the baby asleep in the barrel cot. 'I am not sorry for it.'

His brow creased. 'Alice was my mother's choice for a wife. Neither she nor my mother know this baby is mine.'

'I will not mention your name. I have told no one.'

He drew himself up, taller, more self-assured, then he said, 'Very well, Grace. You will start on Monday morning. I will bid you good day.'

Grace did not move. 'Good day to you, Master Nathaniel.'

He watched her for a moment and she thought he might put out a hand and touch her hair, or speak a fond word, but he turned away. 'I wish you well, Grace, you and the baby.'

Then he was gone; she heard the click of the door latch and she imagined him walking back up the lane to Hill Top Farm. She doubted they would ever speak again.

Gabriel was sleeping, making soft snuffling sounds as if dreaming, and Grace settled herself in the chair to finish her sewing. She picked up the doll she had been making, carefully extracting the needle from where she had tucked it in the fabric. She turned it over in her hands and saw the tiny spot of blood from Nathaniel's hand on the cloth, like a little red heart. She lifted her needle and began to make careful stitches, finishing the doll, tying a knot in the thread. The flames leaped and crackled in the hearth and her face glowed in the orange light. Grace stretched out her legs, feeling the heat spread through her boots to her toes, and she sighed contentedly.

30

Selena watched from the garden seat as Ian Russell and Rob busied themselves like strutting bantams, poking sizzling sausages on the barbecue, flourishing long-pronged forks. They were both wearing aprons; Ian's was a blue and white striped affair and Rob wore a thick canvas one with a dagger design and the slogan *I've Got Your Back, Caesar, (Brutus 44BC)*, which he was showing off to everyone with far too much enthusiasm.

Selena smiled and wondered why men loved to preside over a barbecue so much; it was the same at her parents' house in Buxton: her dad would always stand over the flames and smile broadly as if he was Hades in charge of the underworld. She reminded herself that she should call her parents soon; they had been worried about her after the split with David. Of course, she hadn't told them about the miscarriage: her mum would have wanted to rush over at once and she'd have been furious with David, whom she'd met twice and disliked instantly. Her dad was more like Selena: a little reticent, more tolerant and laid-back, but she knew that both she and her father were resilient, strong at the centre when it was most needed.

Selena sipped wine and gazed at the other guests who were sitting around a table on wooden chairs: Joely was talking to Lesley about a lotion she'd created using lady's mantle, which was perfect for the skin of older women. Lesley had just demanded a bucket of it, complaining that her face was always dry once the summer arrived. Claire was chatting to Matty and Laura, telling them in a low, confidential voice that sleeping in the same bed as Selena each night had been a lifesaver; she hadn't had to stay in the scary second bedroom, which terrified her now. Besides, Selena's bedroom window opened on to the back garden where the birdsong at dawn was so peaceful: being in the cottage was so different to her life in Manchester, where she would wake at night to the sounds of the busy city.

Then Joely refilled their glasses and Lesley rushed over to sit next to Selena, who was staring up at the sky where the white disc of a moon was just rising.

'I love the garden at this time, don't you, Selena? Dusk, or, as the locals say here, when it gets dimpsey.'

Selena agreed. 'Especially this part – the grass and the herb garden and the well. It just feels so calm.'

'Have you heard the well bubble? If you get close enough, you can hear the sound of the water moving. The chattering well.'

'It's lovely. So relaxing.'

'It's a shame Nick was working tonight. I'm sure he'd have enjoyed being here.' Lesley nodded towards Selena meaningfully. 'He has a PhD student, Sara, who always asks him for help after hours and then tries to persuade him to join her in a wine bar. I think she's a little bit in love with him.'

Selena smiled: she knew Lesley was trying to gauge her reaction, so she said, 'I'm sure he can take care of himself.'

'She's not his type, but she seems desperate to talk poetry to him all the time.' Lesley raised an eyebrow. 'And what about you – you're single, aren't you? No boyfriend up in Manchester?'

'No one.' Selena decided to keep her response simple. Then she added, 'It's so nice to be here, where I'm able to paint and spend time by myself.' She wondered if her words made her sound stand-offish or rude, so she continued, 'But I've made some lovely friends in Ashcombe – it's such a treat to spend time with you all.'

'And you'll be seeing Nick at the weekend.'

'Oh yes – we're going to do some research on the house.' Selena couldn't keep the enthusiasm from her voice. 'I'm so keen to discover the names of the people behind the history of Sloe Cottage.'

'I must remember to find that box in the attic for you – I'm sure there will be something of interest.' Lesley seemed pleased. 'And Nick enjoys spending time with you – I can tell.'

'He's nice,' Selena replied, then she was concerned that she had let her guard down.

Fortunately, Ian turned from the barbecue waving a fork, and called, 'Grub's ready, everyone. Time to dig in.'

Selena smiled with relief and rushed forward: she was not hungry, but she was pleased to avoid talking to Lesley about her son: she was sure there was a glint in her eye that implied matchmaking and made her feel a little awkward.

Selena piled salad onto her plate and accepted a sausage and a piece of sweetcorn from Rob, resolving to sort out her love life at her own pace.

Then a Transit van drove through the gate, wheels crunching on gravel, and Ian waved a hand. 'Oh, look who's here. Just in time.'

Laura saw Selena's confused expression and grabbed her arm. 'It's Jonathan Shears. Ian said he was going to invite him. Don't you remember his little girl at the primary school, Phoebe?'

'The one who claimed the cottage was…' Selena's voice trailed off as she watched a tall tousle-haired man leap from the van and walk quickly towards the group seated around the table near the barbecue: he carried a six-pack of beers in his hand and was smiling.

'Hello,' he called. 'I hope I'm not late.'

Ian held out a hand. 'Good to see you, Jonathan. This is Selena, our talented tenant – and her friend, Claire, and I suppose you know everyone else.'

Jonathan nodded towards Selena and selected a can of beer,

ripping off the ring pull, pushing the foaming liquid to his lips. 'I'll only have the one beer – I'm driving,' he announced. Then he accepted a plate of food from Rob and murmured, 'Lovely. Thanks, Rob. Nice to see you out and about – I must pop over and do your chimney before the winter sets in.'

'Jonathan is our local chimney sweep,' Lesley told Selena. 'He comes up to Hilltop every year to sort out our flues. How are Katie and the kids, Jonathan?'

'All fine.' Jonathan wiped beer foam from his mouth with the back of his hand. 'My eldest one, Phoebe's a handful – she's turning out to be a right little madam. And Mae, our little one who's just six, she's her mother's little princess, both girls are spoiled rotten.' He shrugged. 'I keep saying that one of them will have to take over Dad's business one day, but neither are keen.'

He was devouring a sausage as Laura said, 'Your girls are lovely. Adorable.'

Jonathan rolled his eyes, drew up a wooden chair and sat down. 'Expensive habit, having three women at home to keep. I'm glad to be able to get out once in a while, to give myself a break.' He glanced at Selena. 'Thanks for inviting me.'

'If you need a job, Jonathan, you can come over and sweep the chimney in Sloe Cottage,' Ian said. 'I don't think you've done it for a couple of years.'

'I might.'

There was the quiet sound of munching; Laura refilled her glass, then Claire's and Lesley's.

Jonathan handed beers to Ian and Rob and said, 'It's nice out here in the garden. Better than inside. I don't much like being inside the house, especially the old part.'

Claire exchanged a look with Selena, raising an eyebrow, and said, 'We've had some strange experiences in there too.'

Jonathan replied. 'The upstairs bedroom's the one that bothers me – the old one. The chimney flue goes right through behind the wall, up to where the old thatch roof must have been, and I can't say I like the atmosphere in there. I thought I saw a woman's face peeping out the window once.'

'It is creepy,' Claire agreed. 'I can't sleep in that room. There's definitely a presence – both Selena and I heard a voice in there. It was quite harrowing.'

'I suggested lighting some sage candles,' Joely said. 'To purify and smudge...'

Lesley held up a hand. 'The cottage has been in our family for years. It's all a bit old and stale in the original part, that's why we renovated it, and a few people have said that it's, you know, cold in the downstairs room, that it has a bit of a strange feel to it, but I can't say it's bothered me much.'

Selena sipped wine. 'It's nice to sit in the conservatory.'

'After those noises the other night, I couldn't live here alone.' Claire shuddered. 'I don't know how you do it, Selena.'

Ian gave a short laugh. 'I've met a couple of people who have stayed for a week and said that they wouldn't want to come back.'

'Ian,' Lesley protested. 'Don't scare Selena.'

'I don't think our Selena is scared,' Laura said.

Selena sighed. 'I've had my moments – and I'm glad Claire was here a few nights ago when we thought we heard a voice in her room. Having so many visitors really helps. But I'm really enjoying painting here, all the peace and quiet.'

'The painting you did of Wychanger Lane was wonderful,' Joely added.

'But what of the ghost?' Claire turned to Jonathan. 'Tell me I'm imagining the sounds we heard the other day from that room...'

'I don't expect you imagined it.' Jonathan had finished his beer. 'My family have lived in Ashcombe for generations. My grandma told me about an old woman who lived in Sloe Cottage, centuries ago. She used to say that her ghost still haunts the place. We'd sit round Granny Shears' fire and she'd tell us kids all the spine-chilling tales that were handed down – it used to scare us something terrible.'

'What stories?' Laura asked. 'Selena – are you all right with this?'

'I'm fine,' Selena said, feeling a mixture of curiosity and uneasiness. 'It's just stories...'

Lesley grinned optimistically. 'It might help you and Nick with the research.'

Claire elbowed Selena and mouthed, 'Who's Nick?' She was smiling in a way that Selena found a little troubling.

Selena winked and hoped that would satisfy Claire for now: it was harder than she'd thought to tell her best friend about her growing feelings for Nick. She knew the reason was entirely to do with how badly David had treated her and how subsequently Claire would be loyal and over-protective.

'Yes, tell us about this so-called ghost...' Rob leaned forward.

'Go on,' Matty urged. 'I've heard something mentioned in the pub about a ghost here, but I never heard any real details...'

'Hundreds of years ago...' Jonathan took a breath, his eyes gleaming. 'There was an old woman who lived here called Granny Cotter. She was a bad old woman, a witch, like – she'd put spells on people in the village and terrible things would happen to them.' He noticed his audience listening, rapt. 'No, not Granny – Old Mother Cotter, she was called. Apparently, her ghost is still here. She can't rest.'

'What happened to her?' Laura breathed.

'My grandmother used to say that she got what she deserved – she came to a sticky end. She was old and ugly, all warts and bad teeth...' Jonathan noticed that Lesley was losing interest; Joely was gazing around the garden and Rob was staring at his empty plate, keen to go back to the barbecue for seconds, so he continued with added enthusiasm, 'The ghost of Old Mother Cotter has been seen loads of times. People have noticed her staring out the window, a pale face, and she's been seen floating or standing by that tree.' Jonathan shot out a finger, pointing towards the window.

'The blackthorn?' Rob said.

'The witch's tree,' Laura added, her voice soft.

Jonathan's eyes gleamed. 'Ah, well, she would be next to a witch's tree, wouldn't she?' He lowered his tone for effect. 'Because she was a real witch.'

Selena cradled her glass. 'I think I've seen her...'

'Have you?' Ian sounded surprised.

'I saw what I thought was a woman in the garden under the moon-light. She was standing by the well, her arms raised. She was just a shadow...'

Ian laughed. 'That was probably Lesley, sleepwalking.'

Lesley shot him a look, unamused, then Claire whispered, 'Is she the woman in the painting you've done? The woman beneath the moon?'

'Yes, I painted what I saw,' Selena said softly and there was silence for a while, everyone lost in their own thoughts. The sky was dark now, starless, smudged with grey clouds. A chill had settled on the air. Then, from the distance, there was a low yelp, another, a muffled screech.

Claire sat up straight. 'What was that noise?'

Jonathan smiled, his eyes sparkling, still the storyteller. 'The witch knows we're speaking about her – it was probably Old Mother Cotter screaming from the bushes.'

Claire's eyes widened and Laura said quietly, 'Stop it, Jonathan. You'll frighten people. Selena and Claire have to sleep here.'

Then it came again, a distant cry, desolate and soulless.

Claire reached for Selena's hand. 'Did you hear it?'

Everyone listened intently, then Matty said, 'It's just a fox barking.'

Joely shook her head. 'That's not a vixen – it's past mating season...'

'It's a dog fox – they often scream at each other as a territory warn-ing.' Matty winked at Selena. 'Most things usually have a down-to-earth explanation. It's just nature.'

'That makes sense,' Selena replied.

Laura looked anxious, her eyes wide behind her glasses. 'Are you sure, Matty?'

'He's right – it's a fox,' Lesley agreed. 'They'll have cubs now. They are very active at night. If we're upwind of them, they stray into our garden sometimes...'

The fox barked again, an eerie yell from a field beyond the garden, and Joely smiled. 'There, it's just a fox. Nothing to worry about.'

Selena met her eyes. 'Claire and I will be fine.'

Claire was still nervous. 'I'll have some more wine though.'

Rob stood up. 'There's plenty of food left on the barbie. Who's for seconds?'

'I am.' Ian and Jonathan said together.

'I'll have a small helping, Dad, please.' Laura watched as her father began serving food from the smoking coals.

Selena leaned over to Claire. 'Are you all right with all this talk of ghosts?'

'I'm fine,' Claire offered a brave smile. 'Since that weird episode in the spare bedroom, everything has been perfect. And we are okay, sharing the same bed – I feel much safer with you around. Besides, I'm going back to Manchester the day after tomorrow.' She rubbed her hands together. 'I'll be able to tell Gulliver all about the excitement.'

Selena smiled and sipped the last mouthful of wine in her glass.

Laura asked everyone if they had any plans for June. It was already the second of the month, and she had heard on the television that a heatwave had been forecast. Joely suggested that everyone should come up to their field for a huge barbecue soon and Jonathan grumbled that his wife, Katie, intended to drag the family to the Costa Del Sol once the schools broke up, and that he'd prefer living with the ghost anytime to a holiday with his three females. Matty changed the conversation, opening a bottle of Joely's elderflower champagne, filling glasses. Contented chatter and laughter rippled.

The group ate, drank and talked together, their voices rising on the night air, as the smoke from the barbecue coiled towards the sky. No one noticed the outline of a woman framed in the window of the downstairs room, her fingers against the glass, watching them. Then she was gone.

31

There was frost sparkling, bright against the dark earth, as Grace walked up the hill towards the farm. It was Monday the fifteenth of March, not yet dawn, the first coils of pink light visible beyond the hills. The ground was iron-hard. Grace held Gabriel close beneath her cloak and stumbled forward; he was swaddled in linen, then wrapped in a woollen blanket to keep him warm and, as she held him, Grace could feel him curved against her, trusting, asleep. Across the field, a vixen slunk away, dragging her drooping belly towards a den. She would give birth to cubs soon; blind for the first fourteen days, they would be warmed by their mother's body heat for four weeks until the spring air was mellow and kind. Grace called softly to the vixen, wishing her well. She understood the keen expression in the eyes of the she-fox, the sharp sixth sense that sought the warmest safest place to bring her cubs into the world where she could guard them fiercely against predators.

Once she reached the barn, Grace found Alice already seated on her stool, ribbons in her hair beneath the white cap. Next to her was a makeshift cradle, a wooden box stuffed with fresh hay, soft blankets tucked snugly over the top. She reached out her hands in welcome. 'I persuaded Nathaniel to find me a box so that I could make the baby a crib. He can sleep between us all day. We can both take care of him.'

Grace noticed the concerned gleam in Alice's eyes. 'I am grateful to you, Alice,' she said. 'I have been worried for my baby's welfare. I do not wish him to become cold – the weather is not yet warm enough for spring.'

'Oh, he will not catch a cold – I have brought extra blankets. And I thought that when he wakes and you suckle him, I could take over your milking and give you a chance to spend a few moments with him until he sleeps again.'

'Thank you, Alice. You are indeed a good friend.'

Grace arranged Gabriel in the cradle, then she and Alice set to work to milk the first cows just as Jennet and Margaret arrived. Margaret peered into the crib at the baby, grunted and went about her business, but Jennet lingered, pausing to peruse the child's face and then Grace's, making a snorting noise that clearly meant Gabriel did not resemble his mother, before she found a stool and sat down.

The morning passed slowly; Grace tended each cow with special care, patting their warm hides, offering them gentle words of sympathy because they too were mothers and full of milk. But she gazed constantly towards the crib, desperate to pick Gabriel up, aware of every small sound, every movement, wondering if he needed her to hold him, to nuzzle his soft skin and to whisper tender words into his ear. Then, a few hours later, he began to make small noises and Grace dried her hands on her apron, plucked him from his crib, opened the front of her dress and settled herself down to feed him.

Jennet watched closely, peering from behind the cow. Margaret showed no interest, but Alice slid from her stool and crouched next to Grace, touching the baby's skin with a gentle finger. Grace sighed as she felt little Gabriel suckle; she closed her eyes, filled with tenderness, and Alice wrapped the sheepskin cloak around them both closely so that the cold air that whipped through the barn would not chill them. Grace smiled and Alice whispered, 'I think it will not be too long before I have a son of my own.' She saw Grace's interested expression, and murmured, 'I am not yet with child, but I am hopeful.'

'I pray it will be soon,' Grace replied. 'Being a mother fills me with so much joy and I wish the same happiness for you, Alice.'

Jennet watched as Grace tucked Gabriel back into his crib, tracing the curve of his cheek, placing a kiss on his brow, then she grunted, 'It is to be hoped that he survives this cold weather. There are many babies who don't. The wind is raw and it may settle into his lungs and bring on a fever.'

Grace's brow wrinkled with concern and Alice spoke loudly. 'Hush your mouth, Jennet, or speak well to Grace. Our sister, Nancy, will be delivered of her child soon and we do not wish to bring bad luck by talking of sickness.'

'Nancy has bad luck already – she is yoked to George,' Jennet said.

'Will you deliver Nancy's baby?' Margaret asked Grace. 'I believe you help Bett White with birthing.'

'If I am needed, I will gladly do so.' Grace made sure her fingers were warm before gripping the cow's teats. The sound of splashing milk came from her pail.

'There's typhus fever over in Hockholler. My mother said that two children had died of it.' Margaret did not look up. 'She said that's two less mouths to feed in the family.'

Grace glanced at her baby and shuddered. His face was flushed pink and she hoped he was warm and comfortable.

Alice's pretty face was full of hope. 'Ashcomb is a small village; we are a blessed community. That's what Reverend Walters says in church on Sunday and I believe every word.'

Jennet shook her head. 'Nonsense, Alice. You are so green. You have lived many more years than I, but you have always been foolish. We have nothing but misfortune from the day we leave our mother's womb to the day we gasp our final breath.' She glanced towards the baby and her face was sullen. 'And that is the truth of it.'

'I am of gentle disposition and you are not,' Alice said. 'Our mother always says as much.'

'I have every reason to feel anger. Ned and I were to be married and now it may not come to pass because his leg is blasted.'

Margaret laughed. 'His leg is not the working part you have most need of...'

'And I am truly sorry for what has happened,' Alice cried out. 'But Nathaniel will find him work here on the farm and...'

'It will be women's work,' Jennet snapped. 'And now his leg is lame, since the time the men returned home from the wassailing in January, Father says I must wait and see if I can make a better match. But Ned was the man I wanted to wed.'

'And it still may come to be...' Alice protested.

Jennet turned to Grace, her brow creased. 'You foretold it, the breaking of the oak branch. Alice told me and I told Ned. You knew it, Grace.'

'In truth,' Grace said, 'I saw the branch laden with snow and I feared it would not hold the weight of it.'

Jennet folded her arms, glaring angrily. 'And now my Ned cannot walk, and it is due to your words.'

Grace was astonished. 'How can that be, Jennet? I wish Ned no harm.'

'He says as much,' Jennet scoffed. 'But I do not believe him.'

Jennet's constant scowl made Grace feel troubled and she glanced at Gabriel, checking that he was sleeping comfortably. She wanted badly to pick him up and hold him close: Jennet's ill mood had made her anxious for his safety, although she had no reason to suspect that Jennet would do him any harm. Hurriedly, Grace led the cow into the field and another cow approached her, its head bent, docile. She took the cow back to the barn, seated herself and rubbed her hands together, looking at her slumbering son again.

Jennet watched Grace as she began to milk the cow, her brow now a deeper frown. 'Ned always speaks you fair, Grace. I think he carries a torch for you. I cannot think why. What power do you hold over him?'

Grace shook her head. 'I only wish him well, Jennet, and I wish you well too.'

'Jennet is angry because she cannot wed him this summer,' Alice soothed. 'But be patient, sister, because he is a goodly man and you are blessed with him. Ned Shears is not like his brother, George, who fights each day with Nancy – they are angry as two cats...'

'That touches me not,' Jennet said spitefully. 'I wonder about Grace, and how she came to be with child and no one knows who the father is. I do not think it is my Ned, because he has brown hair. And I wonder who will marry you now, Grace Cotter. You have had a child and now you are no better than a strumpet, some man's whore.' Her face had taken on an expression of malevolent satisfaction.

Margaret turned abruptly. 'Hush your mouth, Jennet, or the cow's milk will become curds before it leaves the udder.'

Alice leaned forward. 'I beg you, Jennet, do not say these things of Grace.'

'I am not afraid of her, even though she may make my teeth fall out for the words I have said.'

'Jennet,' Grace began, but a sharp cry escaped from the crib and she rushed over to Gabriel, picking him up, rocking him in her arms.

'He is hungry yet again,' Alice said. 'He will grow to be a fine strong man.'

'He will – harken to those lusty lungs,' Margaret agreed.

Jennet watched as Grace loosened her dress and began to feed the baby, whose cries quickly became snuffles of contentment. Her face clouded with anger. 'So, tell us the truth, Grace, who is the baby's father? Everyone here wants to know it.'

Alice looked up abruptly from her milking. 'Grace has already said – he is no one we know. He is someone from another parish.'

'So, how did you and he meet, Grace?' Jennet's voice became louder, determined to make her point. 'Did you meet him in Ashcomb? Did you dance with him on the village green at the bringing in of the May?' Her eyes flashed with spite. 'Did he tumble you on the grass outside the cottage, or was it here in this barn?'

'Be silent, Jennet,' Alice spat through her teeth. 'If you continue in this vein, I will strike you.'

'I am not afraid of you, Alice, with your pretty ribbons and your fine manners and your airs, as if you were the wife of a gentleman. It is clear your husband cares not a jot for you, or he would not have you still working here a milkmaid in his barn.'

Grace's head was low, listening to the sounds of her suckling baby, stroking his cheek with a gentle finger. She shuddered: she was sure Jennet was about to say something that would cause trouble. She had no idea what to do to remedy the situation, but her skin prickled in anticipation; she was ready to flee with her child if the situation demanded it.

Alice raised her voice. 'You have gone too far, Jennet...'

'No, sister, I tell the truth because you are foolish and weak. Look at Grace, holding her bastard child, and you cannot get one yourself.'

'Do not you speak ill of my son, Jennet,' Grace said, but Alice stood up shaking, her fist clenched.

Margaret watched from her stool in surprise, convinced that Alice would strike her own sister. Grace hugged Gabriel close to her and watched the sisters as they opposed each other, both quivering in anger.

Then Jennet said, 'Look at the child, Alice. He has no look of Grace, with her pale hair and her slender limbs. He is hearty, and dark of hair and eyes. Who does the baby favour, do you think? Not her.'

Margaret frowned. 'They say the Devil is a dark-haired man.'

'And some men in the parish have dark hair too...' Jennet began, a smirk on her face, and Alice took a step towards her.

'Hold your tongue, Jennet, or I will make you hold it.'

'But look at him, Alice – it is clear who the baby resembles. You have eyes and you can see it for yourself, but you will not.'

Then they heard a low voice call sharply, 'What is all this noise?'

The four women turned to see Nathaniel striding into the barn, dark hair tumbling over deep-set eyes, frowning, looking from face to face. Grace watched as she clasped her child, the warmth of his skin next to hers. She saw Alice's smooth brow cloud as she glanced from

Jennet to Nathaniel, then to the baby and then back to Grace, her eyes glinting with tears of realisation.

In one movement, Alice caught her breath in a single sob and rushed from the barn.

32

Claire drove back to Manchester on Saturday morning, her car stacked with paintings, clearly keen to see Gulliver but protesting that she would miss Selena and she couldn't wait for her to come back to the flat at the end of June. By the evening, Selena had tidied the house, started a new painting of a view of the sea from the cliffs on Exmoor and aired the spare bedroom, which currently smelled of fresh sage from Joely's candle. Now, early on Sunday morning, she was feeling cheerful and positive, laying the table for breakfast. Nick would arrive at any moment and they would make plans to find out more about the house's history.

Selena set the table carefully: pretty cups and a china teapot for the Earl Grey tea, a basket for the croissants, a pot of jam with a small spoon. She was looking forward to spending time with him. Again, she thought about their relationship: he was unlike any man she had known before. He had never tried to persuade or cajole her to do what he wanted, as David would always do, and David would invariably sulk if he didn't have his way. Even Flynn, who had been with her for the longest time, had taken the lead in most decisions, including being the one to end the relationship. But Nick consulted her on everything: they decided together where they would go, what they would do. She liked his easy confidence; he was intelligent without arrogance, unlike David, who could be pompous; he was warm, kind-hearted, and he had a wonderful sense of fun: David was often stubborn and aloof.

Selena smiled: perhaps she was ready for a relationship. It was clear that Nick was very different to David; there was mutual trust and affection in his relationship with her, an equality, and he was prepared to take things at Selena's pace whereas David had been assertive, elusive, non-committal, supercilious. It occurred to Selena in a flash of light that she was over David. The hurt he had caused her was in the past now and she could move on. She knew that the memory of the miscarriage would be with her forever; it still kept her awake at night and haunted her dreams when she slept, but she was learning to live with the constant hollow ache. She told herself that she was healing; at least tears didn't flow so readily now.

There was a knock at the door and she rushed towards it eagerly. Nick was pleased to see her; despite the bags he carried, he enveloped her in a warm hug and she led the way to the kitchen. After a leisurely breakfast, they moved to the sitting room, lounging on the sofa in front of the fire, and Nick handed her a book wrapped in tissue. Selena eagerly tore away the paper and clapped her hands.

'*Turbulent Exmoor*, what a great title,' she said, leafing through the pages. 'Look at the pictures – paintings, landscapes, beautiful water-colours. Oh, and there's poetry too – I didn't know Coleridge was from Somerset.'

'He rented a cottage just like you do now, to work on his poems. He stayed in Nether Stowey for a few years at the end of the eighteenth century – he wrote "The Rime of the Ancient Mariner" there.'

Selena hugged the book. 'Thanks Nick – I'll treasure this.' She was about to add that it would help her remember her time in Somerset when she returned to Manchester, but the words wouldn't come.

His eyes sparkled. 'And I've brought something else – my mother sent this.' He indicated a box file that he'd placed on the table. 'She found these papers in the attic. There are all sorts of old documents that go way back, apparently. They might give us some clues about the cottage, and the people who lived here.'

Selena took the box file over to the sofa, her face was flushed with excitement. 'I can't wait to delve in. This is so exciting. Do say thanks to Lesley for me.'

'I will.' Nick gave an apologetic grin. 'She's fond of you – I think she sees herself as a matchmaker too...'

'I have noticed...' Selena's smile was almost flirtatious. 'Well, we're both single...'

He smiled broadly. 'And we're enjoying spending time together...'

Nick's words hung in the air.

Selena deliberately turned her attention to the box file. 'Right – what are we looking for?'

Nick watched her flip the lid as she gazed with fascination at aged documents, crinkled handwritten parchments. 'Mum thinks the farmhouse was built in the mid-1600s, and the cottage too, so we're looking for anything from the seventeenth century. We could do with some family names to follow up...'

'Cotter.' Selena's eyes flashed. 'Jonathan Shears, the chimney sweep, said that the cottage was...' She lowered her voice. 'The ghost was called Mother Cotter. So, if we can find the family name, we might be able to discover what happened to her.' She lifted a pile of documents and placed them on her knee, passing the file to Nick.

For the next two hours, they were quiet, leafing through bills of sale, copies of Land Registry documents, letters to relatives.

Nick said, 'I've found an old birth certificate in here, dated 1892. It's for someone called Marion Tucker – Tucker was my mother's maiden name – and this baby was the child of Cornelius and Mary Tucker: she died at the age of three weeks, of scarlet fever.' He met Selena's eyes. 'It's quite incredible – this box contains the lives of so many people who are connected with me and I know nothing about them. Their stories are just paper in this box now.'

Selena nodded, her face serious. 'And as we go further back in time, what remains of those people, of the Cotter woman and her family? It makes you realise how transient we all are.'

'Hopkins says it perfectly, that life isn't for long.' Nick was thoughtful, his voice soft;

'Leaves, like the things of man, you
With your fresh thoughts care for, can you?
Ah! as the heart grows older
It will come to such sights colder.'

Selena sighed. 'That's so moving.'

Nick placed his hand over hers. 'We have to touch the earth lightly and maybe try to be kind to others and enjoy life to the full while we're here.'

'We do...'

Nick grinned. 'Right, let's see if we can find our Ms Cotter and I'm sure we'll discover that she was a sweet old lady who lived in Sloe Cottage until a ripe old age...'

'I hope so.' Selena said. 'If she's the ghost of the woman standing in the moonlight, I feel I know her a little bit already.'

Selena and Nick pored over their paperwork again.

Then Selena said, 'I've found something here... it's very faded, but it looks like a letter, dated 1706, and it's about the cottage, but it's spelled differently – Hill Top Farm, not Hilltop as it is now, and Slaugh Cottage not Sloe, and Ashcomb has no letter e.'

Nick looked up. 'What is it about?'

'I'm not sure.' Selena said. 'A hand-written letter from someone called G Harper who lived at Hill Top. It doesn't make much sense... *"Yet that I could very well have disposed with to serve soe good a freinde as I allwayes esteemed you to be, & had that summe of money I am in disburse for you been 4 times as much more to have sent you 2 or 3 yeares with a farthinge interest..."* It might be some sort of business letter.'

'Well, G Harper must have owned the farm and the cottage, I

suppose, so we can add the name Harper to our search list. Maybe we're getting closer to our ghost—'

'I've got something else,' Selena exclaimed excitedly. 'It's a really old document about a Joseph Harper of Hill Top Farm, naming the residents in Slaugh Cottage as William Cotter, Anne Cotter and Grace Cotter. It's dated 1672 and – oh, this is interesting. It says that Anne Cotter has just died of something described as the King's Evil...'

'Scrofula. It's mentioned in Samuel Pepys' diary. I use Pepys a lot in teaching because he's a primary source about life in London in the seventeenth century. People once believed that the king could cure it just by touching the person. I think the practice started in the time of Edward the Confessor, well before 1066. Apparently, King Charles the Second restarted the ceremony – I read somewhere that during his reign he touched almost 100,000 people.'

Selena smiled. 'It's a wonder he didn't catch it himself.'

'He died of a stroke,' Nick said. 'Samuel Pepys writes in his diary about watching the king touch someone with dignity and the person recovered. People really believed he could heal.'

'People had faith in all sorts of healing in those days.' Selena held out the letter she had found to Nick. 'But I think we've found her. Anne Cotter. That must be the woman Jonathan was talking about, the ghost.'

Nick examined the letter. 'Yes, especially if she died in this cottage – we certainly have a clue of her dates and her first name.'

Selena frowned. 'Do you think she was really a witch?'

'So many women were accused of witchcraft, and for no reason. Usually, it started with jealousy or superstition from the local people.'

'I wonder what Anne Cotter's story was? She had a husband, William, and a child, Grace. Just saying their names makes me feel a little bit uncomfortable.' Selena gazed towards the ceiling. 'Do you think she's still here with us?'

Nick shrugged. 'We'll find out all we can about her from here on. But it's a lovely day, and we've worked hard this morning – why don't we take a stroll to The Royal Oak and get some lunch?'

'I'd love to.' A smile spread across Selena's face. 'I'm developing a taste for Badger Spit.'

'We'll turn you into a Somerset maid yet,' Nick teased. 'Right. We'll come back to Anne Cotter and her hazy past later.'

There was a loud knock at the front door.

Nick glanced at Selena and said, 'Shall I get it?'

'Please – I'll grab a jacket and we'll go...'

Selena reached for her bag, shrugged on a jacket and froze. She could hear Nick's calm voice and another, more persistent tone. She recognised it immediately. Her eyes were already wide with shock as Nick returned, accompanied by a tall, slim man wearing an expensive jacket and black-framed glasses. She caught her breath.

'David.'

'I left Manchester early this morning – we have things we need to discuss.'

'How did you find out where I was?'

'I went round to your flat a few days ago. Claire wasn't there. There was a man flat-sitting and I saw your name and an address on a piece of paper pinned to a noticeboard.'

Nick looked enquiringly at Selena. 'Do you want to do lunch another day?'

Selena noticed David glance furtively at Nick, his chin thrust out aggressively. She nodded, then shook her head, unsure what to say. In truth, she wanted Nick to stay and David to leave.

David pretended to have just noticed Nick. 'I think it might be a good idea if you left. Selena and I have a lot to talk about.'

Nick ignored him, talking to Selena. 'We can catch up next week, if you like.'

'Look,' David's voice was deliberately assertive. 'Selena and I need to discuss our relationship. It's been very difficult for us both, especially since she lost our baby.'

Selena put her palm to her face as if she'd been slapped.

Nick's expression was one of both surprise and sadness. He placed a hand on her arm. 'Message me.' She felt him press her shoulder tenderly. 'Thanks for this morning. Stay in touch.'

'I'll come to the door...'

'No, I'll see myself out.'

Selena watched him leave and wished she was going with him. The news of the baby had certainly shocked him. She whirled back to David, noticing the arrogant set of his jaw, and she saw him for the cold, selfish man that he was.

David's eyes were intense, his expression accusing, then he raised an eyebrow. 'Who was that?'

'A friend.'

'A boyfriend?' David grasped her shoulder and Selena immediately noticed the difference between his possessive grip and Nick's affectionate touch. She ignored his question. Then he said, 'You blocked my calls.'

'I did,' Selena said.

He didn't wait for her to say anything more. 'Selena, I miss you. I want us to start again. We can find a place, move in together.' He still held her shoulders. 'We are good, you and me.'

Selena closed her eyes. She waited for the familiar sense of weakness to flood over her, the compliance that would seep into her bones whenever he held her in his arms. But nothing happened: she felt nothing at all.

Her lids flickered open and she said, 'Please go, David.'

The pressure on her shoulders increased and he smiled, playing his trump card. 'I've left Veronica. It's you I need, not her.'

'I think you should go, David. There's nothing here for you.'

'Come back to Manchester with me now. It's where you belong, not here in some tumbledown place in the middle of nowhere.' His voice was wheedling. 'You're an artist, a talented woman. You must be stifled here in this backwater...'

'I love it here.'

'Selena, you're not being sensible,' he said.

'I am,' she replied calmly. 'I want you to go.'

He bristled, suddenly irritated. 'I came all the way down here to bring you back.'

'I don't want to go back.'

'Have you lost your senses?'

'No, I've found them. Please, can you leave?'

'And what about us? What about the baby?'

Again, Selena recoiled. 'I lost the baby. I was alone, and it was the hardest time of my life...'

'We can have another...' He wrapped his arms around her, pulling her against him, his lips pressing against her ear. 'I'll make it up to you, I promise.'

'David, no.'

His expression was one of surprise. 'Why don't I take you to lunch? I can drive us somewhere...'

Selena shook her head.

'All right then, we'll have lunch here and you can show me around.'

'I want you to leave.'

David took a step back. 'I've come here all the way from Manchester, for God's sake...'

Selena said, 'Please, just go.'

'Not even a coffee and a chat?'

'No.'

'Selena...?'

'No.' Although her voice was hushed, Selena felt confident now, in control, and it was liberating. She met his eyes. 'There's nothing more to discuss.'

David pushed a hand through his hair, as if adjusting his thought process. 'Right. Well, before I go, may I use the – facilities?'

Selena pointed towards the lobby. 'Go through into the kitchen and upstairs. The bathroom is at the top, before you get to the bedrooms.'

He nodded curtly. 'Thank you.'

Selena turned to the ancient documents on the sofa and began to collect them, aware that David was still watching her. Then he seemed to lose patience and he left; she was alone in the room. She needed to concentrate on something, to be methodical in order to stay calm, so she arranged the papers that she and Nick had been examining and put them back into the box file, closing the lid. Then she picked up the book Nick had given her, *Turbulent Exmoor*, and sank onto the sofa by the glow of the fire. She opened the pages randomly, looking at a watercolour painting, pale skies and hedgerows, greens and yellows. She read some lines by Coleridge.

> *'All in a hot and copper sky,*
> *The bloody Sun, at noon,*
> *Right up above the mast did stand,*
> *No bigger than the Moon.'*

Selena wanted to go out into the garden, into the fresh sunlight. She wanted to be away from David; his presence in the house made her uncomfortable, and she wanted him to leave; she wanted to breathe again. She was free of him now.

Then he was back, standing in the doorway, watching her, his face composed.

'I suppose there's no point in trying to persuade you.'

'No.'

David shook his head. 'I think you're making a mistake.'

Selena stood up. 'I'll live with it.' She indicated the door. 'I'll see you out.'

'It's a long drive back...'

Selena shrugged. She was not going to apologise. She opened the door; bright sunlight flooded in, illuminating the cold hallway. Selena felt calm: there would be no more weakness and dependence. She was stronger now, level-headed. She noticed David's Audi parked by the gate.

'Well, this is goodbye, Selena.'

'Yes.'

'By the way...' He met her eyes. 'Who's your house guest?'

Selena frowned. 'House guest?'

'A slim girl in a cap and a long frock. I passed her on the landing and she walked into one of the bedrooms without even speaking. A strange young woman.'

'Oh...' Selena held her breath for a moment, then she met his gaze deliberately and replied, 'That's the resident ghost.'

David gaped at her in confusion; his eyes widened, a moment of panic gripped him and he turned, striding rapidly towards his car.

Selena touched the malachite necklace around her neck and recalled the words of the woman who had sold it to her. '*May it bring you joy and keep all negative energy from you.*' She smiled; she was sure she'd never see David again.

33

Grace, wearing her best dress and cap, was huddled in the farthest pew in the nave of St Bartholomew's church, Gabriel in her arms, Will on one side and her Grandmother Bett on the other. Reverend Walters was speaking the words of God from the lectern in a voice of thunder, quoting Deuteronomy Chapter 23: Verse 2. 'No one born of a forbidden union may enter the assembly of the Lord. Even to the tenth generation, none of his descendants may enter the assembly of the Lord.'

Grace felt small, she and her baby hunched inside her cloak, as the rector's furious eyes fell on her and several members of the congregation twisted round to stare in her direction. Will coughed, wrapping a protective arm around his daughter and Bett folded her arms, hissing between her lips, 'Let he who is without sin cast the first stone.'

Outside, the pale sun glimmered in a grey sky as the parishioners made their way from the church, many loitering to talk together. Someone brushed past Grace, spitting a comment about a strumpet and her fatherless child not being welcome in God's house.

Bett pressed Grace's arm. 'Will you come back with me for a cup of posset?'

Will smiled. 'Go, Grace – take time to be with your grandmother. You know how she dotes on the baby.'

'But I have to prepare for Lady Day on Friday next. I like a fresh start, to sweep the house clean and make sure we have all we need in the larder.'

'Come home with me, Gracie.' Bett patted her cheek.

'Father needs me to prepare him something to eat...'

'And you need to rest,' Bett insisted. 'I will dangle the baby on my knee while you close your eyes for a while. I am so fond of him, and I have so little time left on this earth, it is my pleasure to spend it with him.'

'And I will sleep this afternoon; I am aweary,' Will said. 'All week I have been working the oxen at the plough and helping with the calving. I am for resting in my chair until the evening, and we can sup together then, Grace. Go, be a good girl and keep your grandmother company.'

'Very well.' Grace touched her father's hand, a soothing tap of her fingers. 'Gabriel will want to feed soon, and it will be nice to sit at my grandmother's hearth with him.'

Grace heard a light shout and suddenly Alice was next to her, wearing a pretty blue dress, cap and ribbons, calling her name.

Grace greeted her with a smile. 'Alice, it is good to see you so hale.'

'I must talk to you.' Alice tugged her arm, moving her away from Bett, then she lowered her voice. 'I have been unwell since Monday. It was the time of my monthly courses, and I took to my bed; my back ached so badly and Nathaniel does not like me to be near him when I am that way...' Her cheeks flushed pink. 'I wanted to say to you, Grace, that I do not believe the things that Jennet was saying about the baby's father. She has become a shrew, because of the accident to Ned Shears. But you and I are best friends, and she will not come between us. Besides...' Alice's lips were next to Grace's cheek, her whisper confidential, 'I believe that Gabriel was fathered by a man not of this parish, as you have told me. I was vexed to hear otherwise from my sister – she seeks only to cause trouble betwixt us, but I will not listen to her words again.'

'I thank you for your kindness,' Grace said, embarrassed to lie to Alice, who was so trusting.

'I am sorry you have to sit at the back of the church now.'

'But I have Gabriel, and he is everything,' Grace blurted, then she saw the sadness in Alice's face and regretted her impulsive words, adding, 'And you too, praise God, soon...'

'Gracie, can you come here?'

Grace heard the urgency in her grandmother's call. Bett was talking to George Shears, who was red in the face and waving his arms. Grace scurried towards her grandmother, Alice at her shoulder.

'Gracie, I must ask for your help.' Bett caught her breath. 'George tells me Nancy's pains have begun and we must go to her.'

'And what of my baby? I must bring him with me,' Grace replied.

Alice's voice was suddenly loud with enthusiasm. 'I will come with you, to help my sister and to hold Gabriel if you need me to, Grace. Oh, please let me come. I would see the child born and assist you and not return to Hill Top Farm and bear my mother-in-law's sharp tongue.'

Bett nodded. 'It may be good for you to be there, Alice. Gracie, you will go ahead and do what you can for Nancy and I will go home and collect all that I need for the birth. Do not forget, make sure everything nearby is as clean as it can be.'

Grace and Alice arrived at the room Nancy shared with George to find Nancy bunched in the corner wrapped in a blanket, her hair dishevelled and her eyes wild. George had left in haste, protesting that he would find someone who would offer him warm ale and a game of Penneech. He wanted no part in the birthing; it was women's work and he would not return until morning.

Grace gently handed Gabriel to Alice, rushing to Nancy, speaking in a comforting voice, filling the kettle from a pitcher of water. Nancy's face was red; she was groaning loudly, and suddenly Gabriel began to cry out, despite Alice rocking him in her arms.

Grace took her baby and began to unbutton her dress. 'Can you give Nancy a sip of water, Alice, and let her get herself comfortable? I will feed Gabriel and then he may sleep while we help poor Nancy with her labours.'

Alice nodded, and rushed to her sister's side; Nancy's yells became louder and Alice was suddenly nervous, calling to Grace, 'Will my sister live through it?'

Grace looked up from suckling her baby, her expression calm. 'I think perhaps it may not be long before the child comes. Tell her to rest when she can between the pains.'

Then Bett arrived with her basket and sat down by Nancy, placing firm hands on her belly and whispering soothing words. Nancy writhed, roaring again, and Bett turned to Grace. 'It's almost time for us to greet this small one. Gracie, fetch linen and hot water.' She reached into her bag and found some oil, smearing it on her hands. 'Now, Nancy, I want you to do just as I bid you. Do you understand me?'

Nancy nodded, then wailed, 'God help me, for I fear I will die.'

Bett said, 'The baby is on her way. Everything is as it should be.'

* * *

Half an hour later, as Gabriel dozed, enfolded in a blanket, Nancy bellowed and grunted in turns. Alice squeezed Nancy's hand, her eyes bulging with horror as the baby was pushed out into the world. Bett and Grace placed themselves at Nancy's feet, Grace cutting the umbilical cord. Bett nodded, satisfied. 'It is good that the navel string is cut now. Can you clean the baby and wrap her up warm? I am busy here still.' She wiped Nancy's feverish brow. 'Well, Nancy, as I thought, you have a baby girl.'

'Nancy, your baby is well.' Alice peered over Bett's shoulder. 'What is it that you do now, Mistress Bett? What is happening to my sister?'

Bett spoke as she worked. 'It is just the caul, the bag of waters that must come out soon after the birth.'

'What must be done with it?'

Bett replied, 'I'll give it to Gracie to take away. Many believe it can make a woman who is infertile quickly get with child if eaten. But we must dispose of it, because such practice goes against the will of the church.'

'I will help Grace with it,' Alice insisted. Her usually open face was cunning as she held out her hands to take the thin membrane from Bett.

Grace put a tentative finger in the baby's mouth, her brow furrowed. She called anxiously, 'Grandmother, something is amiss here.'

Bett wiped her hands on a piece of linen and scurried over, taking the child and examining her.

Grace whispered, 'The child has a cleft lip, the lip of a hare.'

'She has. I didn't see it. My eyes are becoming weak.'

Grace was puzzled. 'I have not seen the like before. What can be done?'

'Nothing can change it,' Bett said. 'Some people say a child with a cleft lip will come from a parent who has the same affliction. But I have heard that it is due to the incurable bone-ache, the infinite malady.' Bett noticed Grace's confused expression, so she breathed her next words softly. 'A man who visits many strumpets, or the strumpet herself, will oftentimes get such a thing on the face of a child.'

'Why are you whispering together? How does my baby? Does she live?' Nancy croaked from her bed. 'Bring the child to me.'

Alice rushed over, swept the baby in her arms and gasped. 'What is this? Why is the baby's mouth so?'

Nancy reached out to clutch the child then, as she saw her face, she screamed.

Bett crouched next to her, rubbing her back with a soothing palm, clucking, 'Rest, Nancy. You have a healthy girl. You must lie in for several days now. All will be well if you rest.'

'All is not well.' Nancy's face was red, swollen with anger and tears. 'Can you not see the child's mouth?'

Alice joined her, touching the baby's soft cheek with a delicate finger, tracing the raised lip. Her voice wavered with emotion as she tried to cover her shock with comforting words. 'Look, Nancy, she has my dimples. What will you name her?'

'I have chosen the name Agnes for her. I think it a beautiful name.' Nancy was tired and tearful. 'But I fear my daughter will never be beautiful.'

Grace lifted Gabriel from his cot; he had begun to snuffle and she opened her dress to feed him.

Bett spoke in a gentle tone. 'Will you feed little Agnes now, Nancy? I'm sure she will suckle – why don't you put her to the breast?'

Nancy lifted the child, unlacing her shift, positioning the baby as Bett was adjusting her position, placing a blanket around the shoulders and beneath her elbow. The baby latched on, then turned her face away and began to cry. Nancy grasped Bett's shoulder. 'She cannot suckle. What will become of her if I cannot feed her?'

'Try once again – she will soon discover how.'

Nancy lifted little Agnes, clearly exhausted: the baby found the nipple and Nancy winced. Then, she fell back against the folded blanket behind her and closed her eyes. 'I am weary – I will sleep now. I do not think George will be back tonight. Agnes and I will rest here until he returns.'

'I will stay awhile and clear up,' Bett said. 'Nancy, here is some posset Grace prepared for you. I will leave it here beside you for when you wake. You will need to eat to be able to feed little Agnes here.'

'I will not eat it if Grace has touched it,' Nancy grumbled. 'It may poison me. She has placed a finger on my baby, and she has cursed Ned's leg, and my George told me what happened in the field when she put her hands on the dead sheep. I should not have let her near me...'

'Do not say such things – they are folly,' Bett chided. 'You must rest.'

Nancy's eyes were closed, her arm around the baby who was still suckling.

Bett put a finger to her lips and whispered to Grace and Alice, 'Get you both off home before it is dark. Alice, your husband will be troubled – I'm sure you are waited for at the farm. Gracie, your little one will need to rest in his crib. I will make sure Nancy sleeps and the baby is wrapped warm in her cradle. Get you both gone.'

The scattered light of the evening sky was diffused with orange and blue as the sun sank behind Hill Top Farm. Grace hugged Gabriel beneath her cloak as she and Alice walked home together. She was lost in thought, thinking about the twist of little Agnes's mouth and how it had come to be. Nancy's angry words repeated in her ears: Grace was troubled that anyone could believe she would harm a baby or that she had caused Ned's accident. But Alice wanted to chatter.

'Are you sure I cannot carry him for you, Grace? He must be a burden in your arms.'

Grace smiled, thankful. 'He is no burden.'

'Watching my sister bring forth her child – it was not as I imagined it would be.'

Grace plodded along slowly. 'Did you think labouring would be easy?'

'I do not know what I thought.' Alice sighed. 'It is the curse of Eve that we must bear. But I am not afraid when it becomes my turn.'

'Amen to that,' Grace said. 'And I wish it may be soon.'

'As I do.' Alice's eyes glistened, thinking of the caul she had hidden in the folds of her apron. 'And I want you with me when I have my baby. Will you be there?'

'If I can.'

'Even after what happened to Nancy, I do not think my child will come to harm at your hand.'

'I would harm no one.' Grace frowned. 'Please do not fear it, Alice.'

'There are gossips in Ashcomb – but I do not listen to them. George Shears is among the worst. He blames you for Ned's shattered leg.'

'It was not I who broke the branch – you know that.'

'I do. But there is the tale of you and the dead sheep.'

'It was not dead. I turned it and it ran off.'

'And then, George says, after you had brought it back to life, you turned into a hare and scuttled away.'

Grace was alarmed. 'That is not possible. How could I have done that?'

'By magic, I suppose.' Alice shook her head.

'It is all gossip, Alice – you know it. I do not understand why people speak this way.'

Alice's brow creased. 'But baby Agnes has the lip of a hare in the place you touched her.'

'I would not harm the child, or Nancy. Not ever would I wish anyone ill fortune.'

'I know it, and tomorrow my sister will be thankful that you were there at the birthing and gave her good assistance. You are a gentle person, Grace. Everyone knows – you are mild and kind. I am sure that once George has filled his belly with ale and returned safely home to Nancy tonight, they will be joyful that their baby is healthy and all this talk will be forgot.'

'I wish it with all my heart.' They paused by the oak tree outside Slaugh Cottage and Grace felt Gabriel wriggle beneath her cloak. 'And I am late to make supper for my poor father. Will you return to the barn tomorrow to milk the cows?'

'I may not. I have persuaded Nathaniel to let me rest in the house a week or two longer. I have told him that I must build up my strength to get with child. Mistress Harriet is always complaining that she is weary – she has a disposition of old age on her now, which makes her in a constant bad humour, so I will play the farmer's wife. Nathaniel and his father are much concerned with the calving and he has a hedge and a stone wall to build, so I will stay home and make cheese and cook the supper and bake bread and cakes. It suits me well, much better than milking cows.'

'Then I bid you goodnight, Alice.' Grace smiled. 'I hope we shall meet soon.'

'Indeed – I will bring some fish to the house for you one evening before dark. And perhaps you will let me dangle little Gabriel on my knee.' Alice threw her arms around Grace, and her voice was soft. 'For I love that baby as much as if he were my own. And you too, Grace. I am your constant true friend, I promise. Never fear otherwise.'

34

Selena parked the car at the entrance to Jubilee Woods at the top of Wychanger Lane and scrambled out, followed by Laura, a huge straw hat over her lilac hair. It was a hot Wednesday morning, June the eighth, and Laura was desperate to show Selena around the woodlands, convinced that she would want to paint the trees and flowers and the views down into Ashcombe.

Laura pointed at a tree covered in creamy blossom. 'Look – the elderflower is in bloom. Can you smell it? It's divine.'

'The smell of summer...' Selena inhaled deeply, then took some photos on her camera.

'The damp ones smell of cat's pee,' Laura said. 'I bet Joely is picking some this week to make wine. Her sparkling elderflower is absolutely nectar – I drank half a bottle of it at your barbecue.'

'I think we'd been through several bottles between us by the end of the evening.' Selena smiled, then she pointed to a thick carpet of nodding blue flowers. 'Bluebells – how lovely – so many of them.'

'They are quite late this year.' Laura grinned. 'Hark at me – I'm a proper country woman now, aren't I? And to think that not that long ago I was a Bristolian who practically lived in the local wine bar, who didn't know my sneezewort from my mother-in-law's tongue.'

'What's that tree?' Selena snapped away at a tall, bare skeletal tree with no foliage. 'It's quite dramatic.'

'It's dead, sadly,' Laura said. 'I always imagine that it was hit by lightning during a raging storm, but it probably just died of natural causes – I'm just a hopeless romantic.'

'And look,' Selena pointed. 'A blackthorn tree, just like the one at Sloe Cottage. The blossoms have all gone now, but it's still beautiful. The thorns are like sharp claws. I want to paint the one at the cottage through the window, the view to the outside from the living room, framed behind glass. It bangs on the window constantly.'

'I've heard it – I find it quite scary.'

'Oh, just look.' Selena gasped. 'This is what I want to paint too.' She pointed at the treetops, sunlight filtering through the leaves casting mottled blotches on the grass. 'I just love those muted shades and the bright shaft of light, the dappled effect.' She adjusted position and snapped more photos.

'I'm so glad we came here, Selena – I knew you'd love it.' Laura clapped her hands. 'And I so wanted to share my good news. I have a job. I'm really excited about it. It's just what I need, starting in September.'

'A job?'

'In Ashcombe Primary; Cheryl Clark, the year five teacher, is leaving and I applied for the post and got it. I'm so thrilled.'

Selena hugged her. 'That's wonderful – well done.'

'We must celebrate. Of course, my dad's delighted I'm working full-time again. He says he needs a break from my constant fussing, although he really appreciates having me around.'

'You're both so sweet.' Selena suddenly wanted to confide in Laura; she was touched by her frankness and she had the urge to reciprocate. 'I wanted to tell you – David came down to visit me from Manchester – he turned up out of the blue on Sunday.'

'David? The ex?' Laura shuddered. 'What happened? Did you send him packing?'

'I did...' Selena said. 'He got my address from Claire's flat-sitter. I mentioned it to Claire on Monday and she was horrified. So, I told David to leave – he thought I'd fall into his arms, but I'm over him now. In a way, it was good to see him. I realised I feel nothing at all now.'

'And his wife?'

'I think they've split up.'

'That's a shame,' Laura said sadly. 'Good for you, though. Now you can find someone decent and put dastardly David behind you.'

'I might have found someone already...' Selena was amazed to hear herself sharing her secrets with such self-assurance.

'Oh, who? Someone I know? Do tell.' Laura gripped her arm.

'I've been seeing Nick Russell, Lesley and Ian's son – we've just had a few dates, well, not even dates, just friends really. We've been out around the area – Exmoor, Culmstock Beacon. He's very nice...'

'Oh, yes – I met him once, just after I arrived in the village. He was in The Royal Oak on New Year's Eve with Ian and Lesley – his sister was there too, and her husband. Nick's quite gorgeous, Selena.'

'He is.'

'So – what's holding you back? Surely not David?'

'No...' Selena felt a pang of sadness. 'He was there when David called, and he did the polite thing and left us to talk. But before Nick left, David mentioned that I'd had a miscarriage – Nick knew nothing about that – I hadn't told him.'

Laura's face was suddenly stern. 'And why should you? It's your life. And David had no right to mention the baby. Ooh, if he was here, I'd give him a piece of my mind – he clearly wanted to ruin anything you had with Nick...'

'But what if he has spoiled things? Nick might not be keen on me any more – if he ever was.'

'Have you talked it over?'

'No...'

'Then you must.' Laura's glasses flashed. 'It's time for you to put your cards on the table.'

Selena nodded. 'I think you're right. Yes, I'll call him.'

'If you haven't contacted him since Sunday, he'll think you're back with David, or that you don't care.'

Selena pressed her lips together, anxious. 'To be honest, I've been a bit nervous about phoning him – should I message now?'

'There will be no reception up here,' Laura's mouth turned down at the corners, 'we're in the back of beyond. But you must get hold of him and soon.'

'I will.' She paused. 'We were working on the history of the cottage – you know, what Jonathan Shears said about the ghost of old Mother Cotter haunting the place.'

'Oh, goody – did anything interesting come to light?'

'I think so.' Selena took several more photos of a glade of trees, the stippled sunlight filtering through boughs. 'Yes, the farm was originally owned by someone called Harper back in the 1600s, and I think the Cotters must have been labourers who lived in the cottage – William Cotter and his wife, Anne. So, I assume Anne must be our Old Mother Cotter, although I think she died before her husband. It was probably in 1672.'

'And did they have children?'

'Grace Cotter. But I haven't found out about her yet, how old she was or what happened to her.'

Laura gave a soft laugh. 'I expect she married one of the locals and had ten children. That's what they all did in those days, poor women.'

'I wonder if Anne really was a witch?' Selena was thoughtful. 'Do you know, when David was in the cottage, he thought he saw a young woman on the landing, wearing a cap and a long dress. Do you think that was Anne Cotter?'

'Or Grace?' Laura said. 'If the woman was young...'

'Could be,' Selena agreed. 'Nick and I are making inroads into the research and I really want to find out what happened to all of the Cotter family.'

'I can help,' Laura piped up, all enthusiasm. 'I'll ask my dad what he knows about the parish records. They go way back, don't they, and I think you can access them online. He'll know how to research the

Cotter family's births and deaths – it's all written down, I'm sure. 1672, you said?'

'Yes, oh, that would be wonderful.' Selena was thoughtful. 'Would they be buried in the graveyard of St Bartholomew's?'

'They probably were.'

They had arrived at an open patch of grassland surrounded by holly bushes and Laura pointed.

'There's a beautiful beech tree. It's quite special – it has purple foliage.'

'I could paint that.' Selena rushed over, moving her phone at different angles. 'I have so much material now, I could paint for months.'

'I have an idea.' Laura's eyes twinkled. 'It's such a beautiful day. Come back with me and I'll make us a sandwich – we can eat in the garden. I'll ask my dad later if he can find out anything from the records. He's in Taunton at the moment: there's a meeting of the archaeology society, so I'd be on my own for lunch anyway.' She offered a hopeful look. 'In fact, while I'm slaving over the sandwich, you could give Nick a call. Then everything will be resolved and we'll all be happy.'

'You're right.' Selena exhaled slowly. 'I'll ring him. I ought to at least let him know David's out of the frame...'

'So that he can step into it?' Laura replied mischievously. 'Oh, I do love a good romance.'

* * *

Selena was in the garden arranging plates on a small wooden table, listening to Laura in the kitchen. The window had been flung open wide and Selena heard the whirring of a food mixer, then Laura swore and shouted, 'It wasn't a good idea to make my own mayo – the whole thing has just hurled itself out of the food processor up the kitchen wall.'

'Do you need any help?' Selena asked hopefully.

'No,' the muffled reply came from the kitchen. 'I need you to ring lovely Nick and sort everything out.'

'Right,' Selena said. She had been nervous, putting it off.

She walked away from the window, out of Laura's earshot, and held the phone to her ear. It rang for a few moments and Selena thought about ending the call; Nick was probably in a meeting or with students; he might be in a lecture hall talking to a fascinated audience about the poetry of Coleridge, and she didn't want to interrupt. More to the point, she didn't want to discover that his interest in her had dwindled, thanks to David's arrival. Then his voice was in the earpiece, light and cheerful. 'Selena?'

'Is it okay to talk?'

'It's fine. I'm in Exeter. I've just nipped outside for a breath of fresh air.'

'Okay.' Selena's voice shook and she wondered what to say. She decided to take the plunge. 'I'm really sorry about Sunday.'

There was a pause, then Nick said 'Are you all right?'

'I'm fine, thanks. David has gone.'

'Back to Manchester?' Nick's voice was quiet.

'I asked him to leave. We've been over for a long time.'

'As long as you're okay…'

'I am.' Selena's words came out in a rush. 'I don't want to see him again and I told him so. I feel stronger now, more in charge, and that's because I came down to Sloe Cottage for a break and to recover and… and I think I'm slowly starting to get my old self back.'

She could hear Nick's easy laugh, then he said, 'I'm so pleased.' There was a moment's quiet, then he added, 'Can I come and see you?'

'I'd like that.' Selena knew she'd answered too quickly, but honesty was the way forward: she was sure of her feelings now.

'How about Saturday afternoon? We could do a bit more research on the house then – afterwards, we could go out to dinner.'

'Oh, that would be lovely.' Selena was relieved; Nick sounded as keen to see her as she was to spend time with him.

'That's good – it was fun researching the history of the cottage and we can discuss where we can go next to discover more about the Cotters.'

'Laura's going to see if her dad can check the parish register.'

'That's a great idea. So, I'll find somewhere for us to eat on Saturday evening. What sort of food do you like?'

Selena was about to say 'anything', but she stopped herself. She wasn't going to be acquiescent any longer: she had a mind of her own. 'I love Greek food – and Indian. You choose between the two – pick somewhere nice.'

'I know exactly the place,' Nick replied and Selena could tell that he was smiling. 'I'll see you around two on Saturday then?'

'It's a date,' Selena said eagerly.

'I look forward to it.'

Selena's face was flushed and happy as she pushed her phone into her pocket. She turned round to see Laura standing behind her holding out a tray with two salad sandwiches and glasses of sparkling water. She raised her eyebrows, a grin on her face.

'I'm not the greatest cook in the world, but here's your lunch – make the most of it.' Laura winked mischievously. 'At least you and Nick will be able to get a decent meal on Saturday night.'

35

Selena had worked on the painting throughout Friday, her easel set up in the sitting room not far from the window, outlining the shape of the window frame and the blackthorn tree. She had stopped for lunch at two o'clock, sitting dreamily in front of a plate of rye biscuits and a piece of brie, thinking about the date tomorrow. Perhaps Nick would book a table at an intimate taverna somewhere in nearby Taunton, but, again, he might take her closer to his home in Exeter and Selena wondered, her thoughts racing, if he would invite her back to his place afterwards. She imagined that his living room would be crammed with bookshelves, packed with piles of books: so many novels, thick ancient tomes, modern literature, philosophy. She could picture the spines lined up alphabetically, Dickens next to Dickinson, Pratchett next to Proust. She visualised his bedroom, wooden floors, a thick patterned rug, the walls cream, the duvet grey, a Basquiat or Picasso print on the wall. Their first kiss might be on the sofa, poring over a book, or he might take her in his arms before that, as they stepped from the car and hesitated by the door. Or perhaps she'd kiss him first. Then she stopped her thoughts abruptly and told herself that she must take things slowly. She and Nick would spend a cordial afternoon together researching the history of the cottage, they'd pop into the nearest town for a pleasant meal and then he would drop her off and go home.

By three thirty, Selena was completely absorbed in her painting of the blackthorn tree. The outline was sparse, thin twigs jutting from thicker branches curved towards the frame of the glass. She worked on into the evening, ignoring the hunger that gnawed at her stomach. She mixed silver and cream-coloured paint to highlight the tips of the twigs, indigo to create the heavy shadow and the sinister curves in the foreground. She was pleased with her work, but she needed to make the blackthorn tree stand out, to show its potency. She began to paint in the night sky behind it, thin silver brushstrokes illuminating the branches from the moon's glow, thicker layers for the inky darkness behind, spattered with silver stars. She stood back and considered her work: it was almost there. She glanced at the clock – time had flown by: it was past ten and she knew that she ought to go to bed. She placed another log on the fire: she felt warm beside the grate, but beyond the easel, the windows were cold, a mist of condensation on thin glass.

Selena's phone rang and she twisted away from the fire and her painting to answer it: it was Claire, her voice hurried and full of apology. 'Selena. It's just me. I'm sorry – is this too late? It's been bothering me all evening. I just wanted to say again – I feel so bad about David getting hold of your address. I feel really awful.'

'Don't worry,' Selena said. 'It worked out for the best – it brought me some closure.'

'Gulliver feels awful too – David was very persuasive about needing your address and poor Gulliver's such a trusting soul – he believed David's rubbish about you wanting him to get in touch. He says he'll make it up to you. He can't wait to see you again. It's less than three weeks until you come home and we'll put up all your paintings in the gallery. I was thinking about names for the exhibition – the Somerset Collection, the Mystic Collection...'

'Home,' Selena repeated flatly, thinking about Manchester. She was suddenly tired.

'And I wanted to tell you – Gulliver and I are together, we're a couple, as from yesterday.'

Selena grinned. 'Oh. That's great.'

'It is,' Claire's voice was bubbling with excitement. 'We both think this could be it; we've found the *one*. We're just so compatible.'

'That's brilliant, Claire.' For a second, Selena wondered whether to mention her date with Nick, but she held back; it was too soon to be certain about what would happen between them and, besides, this was Claire's moment and Selena wanted her to revel in it fully. She took a breath. 'I'm so glad everything is working out well for you.'

'Oh, it is...' Claire lowered her voice. 'In fact, he's staying here at the moment...'

'I'm so pleased for you.' Selena said. 'I'd better let you go now...'

'Thanks, Selena. See you soon – take care, love you lots,' Claire replied, and she was gone.

Selena turned back to her painting of the tree. All of a sudden, the room felt cold, her skin prickled with it. She was aware of the sensation of icy breath on her neck, a light touch on her shoulder. Someone had just walked past her, brushing against her hair. She shuddered, her legs suddenly weak, the phone clenched hard in her fist, then she looked towards the window. The blackthorn tree drummed lightly in the wind. There was something written on the window, strange shapes on the glass. Selena stared, her heart pounding: five letters had been scrawled untidily in the condensation, as if unpractised fingers had tried to form them for the first time. She saw it clearly, the word inscribed in moisture.

A name: *Grace.*

* * *

Grace stared at the shutters, wishing she could be outside gazing at the moon, breathing in the fresh night air. Her father was sitting in his chair by the fire, dozing in the warmth. She glanced towards the wooden stairs; Gabriel was upstairs, asleep in her room. She would go up soon and join him; she always looked forward to lifting him in his blanket, the bundle of warmth next to her skin, listening to the light rise and fall of his breath.

Her father gave a cough, waving a hand to beckon her. 'Come and sit with me by the fireside a moment, Grace.'

She moved to the grate dutifully, sitting on the low stool. 'How are you, Father?'

'I am weary – all day I have been cleaning out the stables and barns with some of the men. April is no easier than any month on the farm, but I am glad the air is a little warmer.' A smile flickered on his lips and was gone. 'What I would give to rest my bones on a stool, sitting miking a cow.'

'It is better than being a weeding woman – I am happy that the cows let down their milk for me so readily or I would surely be back to plucking weeds.' Grace raised a hand to her head, pressing the temple that had begun to ache, a tight band around her head. 'No one will speak to me in the barn now, not since Nancy's baby, Agnes, was born, and that was four weeks since. Jennet turns her back to me; Margaret says little most of the time and the new girl, Joanna, is afraid of Jennet and looks to her for what she should do.' Grace sighed. 'But it is no matter to work alone. I have my son with me all day and he cheers my heart. I miss Alice, though. She is the farmer's wife now that Mistress Harriet rests all day, and I see her only when she comes to the barn to check our milk pails.'

'Grace…' Will chose his words carefully. 'I believe I am not long for this world…'

'Father, do not speak like this—'

'Hear me, child. I would go gladly to be with my Anne in Heaven, were it not for the fear of leaving you and Gabriel behind. If I were to die, Slaugh Cottage would surely go to another labourer at the farm. I know George Shears has already asked Master Nathaniel about it for himself.'

'He has a family of his own now, and they live in one small room.'

'There is much talk between the men each day, Grace.'

'Between the women, too. I have heard Jennet tell Joanna that Master Nathaniel is buying a new horse for himself. He will bring it to the farm soon. It is a fine beast and he will ride it out to Taunton and in the fields when we are working.'

'I have heard it.' Will met her eyes. 'But the talk is often of you and little Gabriel, and that he has no father named.'

'I am sorry, Father.'

Will's face was etched with anxiety. 'You have grown to be a fine woman, Grace, but you have not had a mother to guide you, and I have been of little avail. It is I who am sorry.'

'Gabriel is mine. I would not change it now.'

'I have seen you with the child. You are a good mother. Your mother was just so with you. It warms my heart to see it.' Will closed his eyes. His face in the orange firelight was furrowed and tired. When he opened his eyes again, he said, 'People ask me who is the child's father. There is much talk of it, and some of it is jealousy, spleen and malice. But I do not like to hear it.'

Grace took a breath. 'I cannot speak the name of Gabriel's father. I have vowed to myself that it will not pass my lips.'

'Then who knows what will come?' Will said. 'Take heed, Grace. There are some who do not speak you fair and I have tried my best to stop them. George Shears is the worst. And you know that once a word has been uttered, it cannot be unsaid...'

Grace was thoughtful for a while, staring into the flames. Sparks swirled up the chimney and away into darkness. A high pile of logs hissed and smouldered in the grate among blackened twigs like charred, snapped bones. Grace put out her palms and warmed the span of her hands until they were too hot, placing them over her face, her fingers pressing her temples. Beyond the window, a breeze blew hard, seeping through the rickety shutters. She smoothed her skirt and stared into the hearth. Then she exhaled slowly. 'I will go outside into the garden, Father. I will not be long.'

Grace wandered from the house, leaving the door ajar; the hooked moon glimmered in a starless sky, casting silver light, tinting the edges of leaves. Her headache was gone now. She moved on silent feet to the well, staring into the blackness of the water, whispering words in a low voice that floated down to the depths. Then she stood slowly, turning to the blackthorn tree and smiled. It was her favourite tree at all times of the year, but now, in April, its branches were crammed with blossom, and she reached out slender fingers, murmuring her request. 'May I pluck a bloom or two for myself and wear them in my hair?'

Grace touched the creamy petals, stretching to pick a tiny flower, selecting the largest bloom, then she jerked back, her hand caught in the thorns; the blackthorn tree had answered her. She felt a stabbing pain in her finger and, in the moonlight, she saw the dark bead of blood rise and spread across her flesh. The indentation of a sharp curved thorn had lodged in her skin. She tugged the blackthorn out, putting her fingertip to her lips to stop the flow of blood. For several moments, Grace trembled from the shock of the spike: a sharp puncture from the blackthorn was a bad sign.

She turned to gaze up at the moon. It slipped from behind a cloud, leaving ragged grey clouds in its wake. She breathed in the sweet smell of the garden, the damp grass, the fragrant herbs, and pulled off her cap to feel the breeze separate the strands of her hair and lift them, cool on her neck. Then she closed her eyes, raising her arms towards the moon, whispering soft words in the hope that all would be well, that she would be safe. Beyond, in the hedgerow, a hare scuttled into the shadows and, in the distance, a fox screamed.

36

Selena and Nick sat at the kitchen table, piles of papers spread out, a notebook each in front of them. 'So,' Selena tapped her pen against her lips. 'Seventeenth century. What kind of background do we have for the Cotters?'

'The early part of the seventeenth century would be before our Cotters were born, I would imagine. So, to give them a context, Queen Elizabeth died in 1603 and the Gunpowder plot was in 1605. It was a time of unrest.' Nick thought for a moment as Selena scribbled, then he said, 'Shakespeare died in 1616. The Civil War was in 1642.'

'Would the Cotters have known much about all that, living in Somerset?' Selena asked. 'Didn't everything happen in London?'

'I think Yeovil and Street were at the heart of a huge battle between Cavaliers and Roundheads. Many of the Somerset men were involved – but I dare say William Cotter was too young.'

'So, what happened after that?'

Nick frowned. 'The Great Plague was in 1665; the Puritans had been a strong influence in the country for about a hundred years, trying to purify the Church from all Catholic elements until around 1660, then Charles the Second was on the throne from 1660 to 1685; James the

Second ruled from 1685 until William took over in1688. So, the Cotters might have known some changes during their lifetimes.'

'How do you know all those dates?' Selena was impressed.

'The history is parallel with the literature of that period: the latter part of the century was all about Milton, Molière, Dryden, Racine...'

'It was the time of the Baroque movement in art,' Selena said as she jotted in her notebook. 'Rembrandt, then later, Vermeer.'

'And by 1687, Isaac Newton was published. So that tells us a little bit about the shifting times the Cotters lived in – what had come before them, what changes were happening. But then, being in this rural community as low-paid farm labourers, I don't expect their lives improved much; they probably rarely travelled as far as Taunton.'

'I think they must have lived a simple life in this cottage, one room downstairs, plus the lobby and the pantry out the back. Then upstairs...' Selena pointed to the alcove. 'The original stairs were over there, leading to two bedrooms, your mum said, which is now all opened up into the second bedroom. That's a very cold room...'

'So...' Nick put his pen down on the table. 'Anne Cotter. What do we know about her except that she died in 1672? And we think that she was called Mother Cotter and she might have been considered a witch?'

'Nick...' Selena took her phone from the table. 'I need to show you something.' She handed him her phone. 'I was painting last night and then – this happened, so I photographed it. It's a name. It just appeared, written in condensation on the window...'

Nick examined the photo. 'It says *Grace*. It's a very rough, untrained hand.'

'Yes, I thought the same thing. And just before that, I'm sure someone touched me...'

'Are you all right? I worry about you here, by yourself.' He placed a hand on hers, a comforting warmth, then took it away too soon. 'You must have been terrified.'

'I was really shaken... The room became icy cold.' Selena shuddered. 'It was quite unsettling – I took myself off to bed as quickly as I could and then I couldn't sleep for thinking about it. Perhaps Grace is our ghost, not Anne. We'll never know if she was trying to tell us that, but it's very strange that her name appeared on the glass.'

'Let's have another look at Grace...' Nick picked up the documents from the box file, sifting through them. He found the one he was looking for. 'So, Anne Cotter died in 1672, therefore Grace and her father must have stayed on in the cottage together.'

'It doesn't say when she was born or how long she and her father lived here.'

Nick was thoughtful. 'Perhaps Rob can help us with that.'

'So, do you think Old Mother Cotter is in fact the daughter, Grace? Do you think she lived to a ripe old age and people just thought she was a witch because she lived longer than her father and, well, you know how prejudiced people were about older ladies who lived alone or with a cat?'

Nick took a breath. 'Something you just said about the layout of the original cottage...'

'What are you thinking?'

'Let's go and explore. Have you got a torch? Comfortable shoes?'

Selena nodded. 'Where are we going?'

'Up into the attic, where the old roof space used to be, where it was thatched, above the second bedroom. I don't expect we'll find much; there will have been so many changes – a new tiled roof, some restructuring – but who knows what clues might be there? I think we should take a look.'

'Great idea,' Selena stood up, her face bright with enthusiasm. 'If we need information about the past, perhaps it's a good idea to start in the present, and then go backwards?'

* * *

As Selena climbed the stairs towards the landing, she thought of the ghostly young woman that David claimed to have seen, dressed in a long skirt and a cap. She recalled hearing the soft voice from the bedroom singing a lullaby, beneath straw-filled rafters, and Claire's terrified expression, the footsteps on the landing and the soft clunk of the door she had shut being opened again. Nick at her shoulder, she pushed open the door to the second bedroom and immediately felt the chill of the air despite the June sunshine outside.

Nick gazed up at the ceiling where there was a hatch leading to the loft. 'I wonder how we can get up there? Is there a ladder anywhere?'

Selena said. 'There might be one in the shed round the side of the cottage, where Matty puts the logs.'

'I know the place.' Nick winked and was gone.

Selena clutched the torch in her hand, conscious of being alone. She had been alone in the room before, but she had always been busy, making the bed up for Claire, cleaning. She could smell something, the faint whiff of lavender, sweet and comforting. Selena was confused; she had burned a sage candle in the room, but not lavender. She whispered, 'Grace... I wonder who you were... and why you are still here?' She half expected a whispered reply, or an unseen finger writing an answer on the window, or that a young woman wearing a white cap would float in, but she was only aware of the chill on the air and the strangely calming scent. She waited, the silence all around her, then Nick's quick footsteps could be heard and he was in the room with a stepladder.

'Right. So, let's take a look upstairs in the roof space.'

Selena handed the torch to Nick and he moved nimbly up the steps to the top, easing the hatch up and away, then he disappeared into the attic. He called down, 'Do you need a hand to come up?'

'No – I'm fine.' Selena would have relished the warmth of his skin against hers, but she could manage the ladder alone.

She followed him, climbing almost to the top step until her head poked through into the darkness. The smell was musty; it caught in her throat, a stink of age and dampness and something else, possibly straw.

Nick shone the torchlight into the shadows across the loft space.

'This attic is huge, it goes back and back; it covers the whole house, but it's this part we're interested in.'

Selena eased her body up through the hatch until she was sitting on the edges of the opening, then she swung her legs and she was in.

Nick took her hand. 'It's best to step on the joists – just in case. Who knows how old the timbers are up here?'

'What's that at the end?' Selena blinked in the darkness.

'That A-framed structure? It holds up the roof – it was probably the divide between the two original bedrooms. If we crawl through it, we'll be above the second part of the bedroom, then the house ends at the chimney breast on the flat part of the wall.'

'I'm right behind you,' Selena said. The smell of the attic was thick in her nostrils; the air was stone cold.

They crawled through the wooden structure, the light of the beam guiding them into darkness. As Nick shone the torch above them, strands of straw were visible in the roof space. They stood and gazed up into the eaves.

Selena frowned. 'Why is there still straw here?'

'Debris from the thatch – I don't think slate roofs were a thing in the countryside until the 1800s...'

'So – this would have been the roof of Grace's bedroom – or her father and mother's.'

Nick nodded. 'Almost certainly – someone would have lain in bed and looked up into this space at a thatched roof.'

They edged forward into darkness, led by a single thin torch beam.

'What are we looking for?' Selena asked as Nick aimed the shaft of light at the wooden joists below them.

'I've no idea. Anything that gives us a clue. It might not be from the Cotters at all – lots of people will have lived here since, and I don't think my parents will have been up in decades, if ever.'

They paused, watching the torchlight swivel up and down, into corners. Selena pointed. 'What's that on the floor?'

She bent down, lifting a sheet of newspaper. Nick aimed the beam at the yellowed page, the faded print, the sepia photo so that she could see better.

'It's just a piece of old paper, dated 1956. A picture of Marilyn Monroe stepping out of an old car – apparently, she visited the UK to film *The Prince and the Showgirl* with Laurence Olivier.'

Nick shook his head. 'Maybe someone came up here in the fifties to fix a slate?' He gazed up at the roof. 'Everything's just about hanging together in the roof.'

'I'll leave this where I found it,' Selena said. 'Maybe someone else will come up again in the future and find it, and it will be a real treasure.'

Nick took her hand; his was warm, dry and the connection filled Selena with a new feeling of belonging. 'Shall we move on? I think I can see the end of the house, the chimney breast against the wall.'

They continued to take small steps forward, carefully moving across the rafters, then Nick called, 'Wait. Don't move, Selena.'

She heard the tension in his voice. 'What have you seen?'

'Please – just stand where you are a moment.'

Selena stood still, watching Nick creep over towards the corner of the sloping roof, crouching down. Then she heard him catch his breath.

'What is it?' Selena asked.

'It's an animal – it's not very nice. I hope we don't find any more. I'm not dealing with it now – it's been there for a long time and it'll stay there until another day.'

Selena held her breath as Nick crept back towards her, the beam shining down. She gazed at his face, trying to discern an expression; in the darkness, he seemed serious and a little troubled. 'What was it?'

He exhaled. 'A squirrel. I'm not usually squeamish, but it's mummi-fied. It might have crawled in beneath the thatch, so it could have been there for over two hundred years.'

Selena shivered. 'Oh...'

'I hope that's the only one.' Nick took her hand again. 'Right, let's see if we can find anything useful.'

They moved towards the chimney breast, a formation of stones jutting from the wall.

'This is from the fire below, the one that's always lit?' Selena spoke quietly. 'This is original, isn't it?'

Nick bent forwards to avoid the overhanging beams, shining the light at the chimney breast, placing a hand against the rough surface. 'Yes, it keeps the place warm and dry. This would have been a great source of heat in the bedroom, that and the thatch.'

'There's something... look.' Selena pointed to a wide gap between the stones. 'What's the thing wedged in there?'

Nick aimed the torch towards the space. 'There's something hidden – some sort of box. Can you reach it?'

'I think so...' Selena tugged an old wooden box from the gap in the stones. 'There's some stuff inside.' The beam illuminated the box, a sharp brightness revealing folded material inside, fabric, something else. 'Should we take it downstairs and look at it?'

'Definitely,' Nick replied. 'I hope it's very old, and if it is, we'll have to be careful with it.'

'It's probably nothing – just some rags someone used to clean up here,' Selena suggested, but her voice was filled with hope.

Nick met her eyes, his own gleaming with interest. 'Let's have a quick check round for anything else. Then we'll go back downstairs and take a look.'

They crept tentatively through the attic, closed the loft hatch, leaving the ladder in the chilly bedroom, and took the wooden box to the kitchen table.

Selena held her breath. 'I feel like I should be wearing plastic gloves...'

'Whatever it is seems fairly intact.' Nick watched over her shoulder. 'There's some sort of fabric, it could be linen...'

'Look!' Selena was excited. 'The material has some embroidery on it – some numbers.' She stared at the stiff fold of cloth. 'If I get it out, will it fall to pieces and just become dust?'

'The box has been up in the roof, beyond the fire; it's been away from sunlight and damp – it's well preserved, but just ease it out.'

'I'm afraid to touch it in case it comes apart.' Selena laid the brittle linen on the table, inspecting it closely. 'Does the embroidery say some sort of date?1680? 1688?'

'And a letter has been stitched on – is that a C or a G?'

'C for Cotter? G for Grace?'

'And what's underneath?'

'Oh!' Selena lifted the cloth out carefully and stared at a piece of disintegrating rope, wispy spines of shapes attached. 'It's a piece of knotted string with things tied on it.'

'And what's that tiny bit of material next to it?' Nick pointed to a piece of twisted cloth. 'The small scrap – what do you think that is?'

'It has eyes and tufts for hair… it looks like some sort of primitive doll.' She met Nick's eyes as a door slammed upstairs, a loud bang from the second bedroom. 'That wasn't the wind…'

'I think you may be right. Is this what happens here all the time? Selena, there's definitely a feeling of… something very troubled.' Nick frowned.

'There's a presence, yes,' Selena said. 'It's part of the fabric of the house.'

Nick's eyes shone. 'And how do you manage, living here alone?'

'There have been moments where I'm really nervous.' Selena admitted. 'But I feel something else now. It's not an evil presence. It's as if she's asking us to help her.'

'Can I make a suggestion? We keep this stuff in the box intact. I know someone at the university, Colleen, she's an archaeologist. She's extremely experienced – she's spent almost forty years studying all sorts of relics from the past. If she doesn't know all about it, she'll know someone who will. I'll give her a call. Maybe she'll be able to take a look next week.'

'That's great. So, what shall we do now?'

Nick looked up towards the clock: it was almost six.

'You have time to show me some of your latest paintings – then we're going out for dinner.' He offered an arm. 'I think we deserve it.'

'We certainly do.' Selena threaded her arm through his, feeling warm and contented. 'It feels like we're moving forward, uncovering the past and I hope we can help a troubled soul to rest. I'd say we've had a good afternoon's work.'

37

Selena and Nick spent the evening in a country inn at Holcombe Fitzpaine where the chef, a friend of Nick's, had prepared a delicious meze of vegetables, cheeses, dips, fruit, nuts, seafood and pita bread. They began the evening seriously, talking about the Sloe Cottage ghost and their findings, Selena admitting that she'd felt very afraid after Grace's name had appeared on the glass. But later, they relaxed, chattering excitedly over coffee, discussing the breaking traditions of art and literature in the 1920s. Nick was passionate about Gertrude Stein's 'Lost Generation', authors such as F. Scott Fitzgerald, Ernest Hemingway and Virginia Woolf. Selena found herself interrupting him, bursting with enthusiasm about how much she loved Surrealism and Art Deco, how Hopper and Dali had been favourites for so long. It crossed her mind how often she'd listened to David as he'd dominated conversations, before pushing the thought away, staring into Nick's eyes and devouring his words, matching them with her own. Each time she met his gaze, Selena found it hard to tug away.

On the way home, they were both quiet, listening to a sultry voice on the radio singing a love song. Selena closed her eyes, enjoying the warmth inside the car, the low humming sound of the engine. It was past ten: she wondered whether to invite Nick in for another coffee. It would be a nice way to end a perfect evening and she didn't want to let him go, not yet.

He pulled up in the drive of Sloe Cottage and they both looked towards the house: Selena had left lights on in every room. She was about to ask him in, but something stopped her; there was an expression on his face she hadn't seen before, a question. Instead, she said, 'Thanks for a lovely evening.'

'I had a great time,' Nick replied.

'And I'm really looking forward to hearing what your friend at the university says about the things we found in the loft.'

'I hope it will shed some light on our ghost.' He met her eyes, suddenly serious. 'Selena...' She waited for the moment, although she had no idea what it contained. Her heart started to bump with anxiety. 'I have to ask you...'

'Anything,' she told him, her tone deliberately bright.

'You came to Somerset to paint – but I think you also came here to get over the relationship with the man who came to visit you the other day.'

'Yes, you're right,' Selena said slowly. 'David's in the past now.'

'And the miscarriage must have been so difficult...' Nick's voice was soft with kindness.

'Yes, it was tough.' She nodded, registering the fresh sadness that always clung to her when she thought of the baby. 'It's been therapeutic, coming here and concentrating solely on my painting, being in a different place, meeting new people.' Selena looked at him hopefully.

Nick exhaled. 'So, I'm assuming it will be a while until you're ready for another relationship?' He took her hand. 'I think we get on really well, you and I...'

'We do...'

'But I don't want to dive in and spoil things when you're still healing. What I'm saying is, several months ago you were with someone who meant a great deal to you, and it would be presumptuous of me to ask you to start something new so soon.'

Selena was stunned, unsure how to reply, so she nodded.

'We can take things slowly.' He was still holding her hand. 'I'd like to see you next week? Maybe we can do the same as we did today, catch up on the history of the Cotters of Sloe Cottage and then go for dinner.'

'I'd like that.' Selena reached for the door handle: she was unsure how to explain her feelings of disappointment; she felt the need to dash for safety. 'That would be lovely. Next Saturday, then?'

He kissed her, a gentle brush of their lips. 'And I'll text you.'

'Great. I'll see you then.' She smiled as widely as she could, then rushed into the dark night air, pulling her keys from her bag as she watched him reverse. She waved a hand energetically and hurried inside.

Selena locked the door and paused in the hall. She'd imagined herself and Nick together by the fireside, seated on the sofa, in each other's arms. Now she wondered if she had just pushed him away. She'd admitted the end of her relationship with David had been devastating: she had lost the baby, which had knocked her sideways. But now she was developing strong feelings for Nick, he'd suggested taking things slowly and she'd just agreed. Yet in less than three weeks, her tenancy on the cottage would end and she would be going back to Manchester. She was confused and annoyed with herself: it would have been easy to say no, she was over David, he didn't matter now, and she was ready for a relationship with a much sweeter, kinder man who had already started to mean a lot.

Selena threw several logs on the wood burner to keep the room warm overnight and walked upstairs, past the landing and the second bedroom, barely noticing the door was ajar again. In her own bedroom, she pulled on pyjamas, cleaned her teeth and face and flung herself into bed, turning off the lights and plunging the room into shadows. She rolled over, her mind crowded with thoughts, wishing she'd asked Nick to come into the house so that they could talk things over together. She should have taken the opportunity to explain her feelings and allow him to share his own. Now she was full of regrets, and the idea that Nick might think she wasn't ready for a relationship or that she wasn't keen on him troubled her.

The door to her bedroom creaked; Selena heard it open slowly and she held her breath. There was silence for a while, then someone was inside the room. She inhaled the sweet traces of lavender on the air, then it became a stronger scent. Selena's eyes were closed, screwed tight now, but she knew instinctively that there was someone standing by the side of the bed, watching her. She wondered whether to open her eyes: whether she would she see the outline of the slender woman in a long dress, or if there would be no one there. Her heart thumped, blood pounding in her ears, and it was suddenly hard to breathe. She shivered beneath the duvet, tucking her legs up, her body in a foetal curl, pushing the cover over her head, but she was still quaking. She would not look; she would stay where she was until morning and hope that sleep would come and, when she opened her eyes, the sun would be streaming through the window and she would be calm again.

* * *

May Day 1683 was a Saturday, a gloriously warm day; the village green was crowded with brightly clothed dancers, the light music of a pipe and tabor lifting on the wind. Grace stood with Gabriel in her arms, watching. Jennet Bryant had found a new dancing partner, a sinewy young man who bounded around energetically with her in his arms; the smile on her face showed that she was enjoying herself. Grace recalled the previous May Day when she had danced with Nathaniel; so many changes had happened in one year. She hugged Gabriel close, jiggling him to the music, then she glanced towards her grandmother's cottage. She would watch the festivities a little longer, then she would visit Bett. She longed for her grandmother's warm hearth and kind, encouraging words.

Nancy and George Shears stood together, watching the couples dance; baby Agnes was in her mother's arms, writhing and yelling as Nancy wrestled to calm her. George glanced towards The Royal Oak, then he said something to his wife and wandered away. Nancy met Grace's gaze but did not return her smile, deliberately looking back to the young women in pretty dresses, garlands in their hair, circling around the maypole.

Grace looked around for Alice, expecting to see her in the crowd wearing her best dress, cheerful on Nathaniel's arm, but neither of them had arrived yet. Kitty Stokes and her husband, Edmund, were also in the throng; Kitty was just noticeably pregnant now, holding her child in her arms. Grace recalled the boy would be one year old today. Grace wondered whether to go over and ask her how she was keeping, and to say that she was looking forward to helping her grandmother deliver the second child.

Grace felt a light pressure on her shoulder and she turned to see Ned Shears, his face shining with enthusiasm. He was leaning to one side, a stick supporting his weight. He reached out a hand and touched Gabriel's cheek.

'Your son thrives, Grace. He is well-favoured.'

'Thank you,' Grace replied.

'And you are looking pretty today...' Ned seemed a little flustered. 'The embroidered dress becomes you well.'

'You are kind.' Grace smiled. 'I have just seen your brother, George, going towards The Royal Oak. Will you not sup there with him today?'

'Oh, George would sell his soul for a pot of ale,' Ned joked. 'I am not of the same metal. I would rather be bringing in the May.'

Grace saw him move his gaze to the dancers and she muttered, 'Jennet is here.'

'I have released her from any promise of marriage,' Ned said simply. 'She is free to dance with who she will.'

'I am sorry to hear it.'

'I am not sorry.' Ned indicated his leg. 'She was not so keen to wed me since the accident and I have realised that she is not the one for me.' His gaze came to rest on Grace. 'My feelings are for another.'

'Then you should talk to the maid and tell her...' Grace paused; she saw the expression on Ned's face and she understood.

'I wish to marry you, Grace. I am not troubled by the gossip from the villagers; I would care for you and the child as if he was my own.

And I will work – my leg becomes stronger now and I am unafraid of labour, especially if I have a wife and children to feed.'

Grace was unsure what to say. 'I am not a good choice for you...'

'But why?' Ned's face was flushed with excitement. 'You are young, lovely; you have the hands of a healer, and you are sweet and kind and mild in disposition.' He put a hand on her arm. 'You and I could have many more children; I could live with you in the cottage and your father could rest. I would work for all of us in the fields all day behind a plough just to come home in the evening to your sweet smile.'

'Thank you, Ned.' Grace felt her throat swell with emotion. 'You are too kind and I do not deserve such gentleness. But I am afraid I must say no.'

Ned's eyes widened. 'Do not say anything, Grace, not yet. Think about my words. Believe me, I will make a good husband who will care for you each day.'

'I do not doubt it...'

'Is there another you wait for? Are you hoping the baby's father will return?'

Grace shook her head. 'He is not in my thoughts...'

Ned leaned towards her, his lips touching her cheek. 'Then think about my offer, sweet Grace. I will not rush you for an answer, but do not say nay, not yet. You know I would be good to you and to little Gabriel.'

Grace lowered her eyelids. 'I will think on it. But I believe my answer will not change.'

'I pray that it will,' Ned said, then he turned and was lost in the crowd.

Grace pressed her lips against Gabriel's soft cheek and bounced him in her arms to the rhythm of the dance. She thought about Ned's words; she did not doubt that he would be kind and that he would cherish her. It would be convenient to have a husband, one who cared so much for her and the child; it would stop the chattering of tongues in Ashcomb. But Ned deserved a woman who would love him in return, whose love would equally match his, and she could not promise that. She had trusted Nathaniel, she had loved him and he had hurt her. Now the love in her heart was only for her child. Besides, Grace thought sadly, Ned was the sort of man who warranted more than she could give him.

Grace heard someone call her name and Alice rushed towards her, a flurry of ribbons and frills. They hugged and Alice said, 'I hoped to find you here. It is good to share the company of a true friend.'

'Where is Nathaniel?' Grace was puzzled.

'Oh, he has gone to bring a horse back to the farm, a stallion he has bought in Taunton. It is all he talks of, how he will ride it across the Blackdowns and enjoy the expanse of countryside.' Alice lifted Gabriel from Grace's arms. 'May I hold him, just for a moment? You must be weary and he is such a delight to rock in my arms.'

Grace nodded, happy to see the joy on Alice's face. She looked for a sign that Alice might be expecting a baby herself, but nothing in the sweet dimpled face showed any change.

Alice hugged Gabriel, kissing the top of his head. She guessed Grace's thoughts. 'I am not yet expecting...' She put her face close to Grace's and whispered, 'But I took the caul after the birthing, the bag that held the waters from Nancy's labours. Your grandmother told you to have it but I kept it. She said it would make a woman who is infertile get with child if cooked and eaten. It was not pleasant, but I put my feelings of sickness to one side. I hope yet that it may work.'

'I was distracted with baby Agnes. I did not notice...' Grace frowned: she had not thought Alice to be capable of cunning. 'I promised my grandmother that I would take it away. Such practice goes against the church.'

'I did not tell you – I wanted to keep it,' Alice insisted, her face hardening. 'I will do anything to get myself a son, you know it. And please say no more of it – I know you are a good friend to me, Grace.'

Grace sighed. 'If it is God's will, it will come to pass. But I pray that it will work.'

'I am sure that it will,' Alice clenched her small fists, determined. 'This next year will see me a happy mother made. I am certain of it.'

'Alice!'

Grace and Alice turned towards a sharp voice that came from the crowd.

'Alice, come and stand with me here.'

'It is Nancy.' Alice waved a hand to her sister. 'Come and join us.'

Nancy shook her head, gripping baby Agnes tightly. 'I will not. I will not stand near Grace Cotter. She has already harmed my baby.'

'That is not true, Nancy,' Grace said.

'Grace did nothing wrong, she helped to deliver Agnes – I was there,' Alice agreed.

'She put the finger on my baby's mouth and now it twists like a hare's.' Nancy's face was furious. 'I dare not speak to her for fear she will curse me.'

'Nancy, I wish only good for you.'

'You have blighted my child's life,' Nancy spat between clenched teeth. 'I will never forgive you.'

'What you say is true.' A young pregnant woman with a child in her arms moved next to Nancy, jabbing a finger in accusation towards Grace. It was Kitty Stokes. 'You will not be there at my next lying-in, Grace.'

'I do not understand...' Grace frowned. 'Your baby thrives...'

Kitty spoke to Alice. 'I saw Grace Cotter put the finger on my child's mouth – she was trying to do the same to little Edmund, to give him the lip of a hare...'

'I did not.' Grace raised her voice. 'The baby could not breathe and I cleared his mouth as instructed by my grandmother. I sought only to help him to live.'

Kitty turned to Nancy. 'I saw her do it. I put out my arms and called for the child to be brought to me. Otherwise, he too would have the mark on his face.'

Grace was aghast. 'Please do not say such things...' She reached for Gabriel, lifting him from Alice's grasp.

Alice pressed her shoulder and whispered sweetly, 'Do not heed them, Grace. They are foolish women. I will go and talk to Nancy and tell her to hush her mouth. She will listen to me.'

'Thank you...' Grace's face flooded with relief. 'It is not good, especially where others may hear their words.'

Alice's expression was bright as she flounced towards Nancy. 'Sister, let me hold baby Agnes for you. You must be weary. And, Kitty, how well you look.'

Grace watched as Alice stood between the women, Nancy's baby in her arms; they were soon laughing together, their expressions bright. Grace marvelled at how eagerly Alice chattered to the other women. She did not glance back and smile complicitly, as Grace hoped she might. Grace gazed around at the crowd who were watching the dancing; two women had heard the comments Kitty had made and were shaking their heads, frowning. One of them pointed. 'That's Grace Cotter, here in Ashcomb for all to see with her bastard baby. She knows no shame.'

Grace held Gabriel even closer. For a reason she could not understand, she was suddenly afraid for his safety; she wondered if the women might try to pluck him from her grasp. She pushed through the crowd and ran towards her grandmother's cottage, her heart beating in her throat, desperate for shelter, wanting only to hear the words of wisdom and comfort that her grandmother would offer.

38

'Sit yourself down in the chair and rest, Gracie.' Bett handed her a cup. 'Your face is flushed. And give the little one to me to hold. It pleases me to look at him – he has the smile of an angel.'

'Thank you, Grandmother.' Grace settled herself on a chair and Bett scooped up Gabriel, rocking him gently.

'To hold him reminds me so of my own babies, and I remember what pleasure it gave me to nurse them. Now that is all in the past and I am alone and old.'

'You have me, Grandmother. And Gabriel.'

Bett sighed and reached for her cup with her spare hand, moistening her lips and swallowing greedily. 'I spend too much time alone. It is not good for the soul. And now all my children are gone. I fear it will be my turn next, Gracie. My bones ache and my heart grows weak.'

'You will outlive us all,' Grace smiled.

'This helps.' Bett swigged again. 'Ah, you have a fine boy here. You are a fortunate girl.'

'I know that I am.' Grace closed her eyes, weary. 'But some people have much to say about me. Outside, while the crowds were watching the bringing of May, more was spoken about Nancy's baby, that I harmed her at the birthing. Even Kitty Stokes does not trust me now.'

'It is foolish prattle,' Bett said, making soft clucking noises, returning Gabriel's smile. 'But we should be wary of people's loose tongues.' She rocked the baby a little longer, then she turned to Grace, her eyes narrowed. 'Do you have anything kept in the cottage that might cast suspicion on you? What did you do with the string ladder you made before the baby's birth? Do you have other things, charms and potions?'

'I still have the ladder, yes...'

'Hide it,' Bett said urgently. 'For who knows how suspicion works when fingers are pointed. As you have heard many times, once a word has been uttered, it cannot be unsaid.'

Grace nodded. 'I will.'

'And Gracie,' Bett's expression was troubled, 'I think you should stay inside Slaugh Cottage when you are not working. Stay far from Ashcomb for a while, away from gossips' tongues. And on Sunday when you are come to church, sit at the back in the corner, out of the way of straying eyes. Perhaps people may forget their idle chatter soon.'

'Yes, Grandmother.'

'Ah, it's a pity you haven't a husband, someone to protect you. I know Will Cotter does his best, but he is too tired now to be of much use. Since Anne died, he has been in continued melancholy.'

'I have had a proposal of marriage...' Grace said.

'From a good man?'

'Ned Shears. Yes, I think him a good man. He is thoughtful and kind and he is always sweet to Gabriel.'

'Then marry him, Gracie. It will save your name and all may be well.'

Grace sighed. 'I cannot. I do not love him.'

'Love?' Bett gave a muffled cackle. 'Marriage is not about soft matters such as love. If you can find a man who works hard, puts meat on the table each day and does not beat his wife and children, you have a marriage made in heaven.' Her face became serious. 'You should accept him. It will avert suspicion. In but a little time after you are both wed, no one will remember Gabriel has no father. Then tongues will no longer wag.'

'I will think on it,' Grace agreed, stretching out her arms to receive the baby that Bett was holding out.

'Take him from me, Gracie – my back does ache. I must stop awhile for all this talk has made me weary.'

Grace struggled to her feet, the baby in the crook of her arm, and smiled. 'Sit and rest your bones, Grandmother. I will hold him now.'

'You are the best of girls.' Bett smiled, easing herself into her chair. 'And you have the most beautiful baby. You mark my words, he will grow into a fine man and perhaps, when you are old, he will be the joy to you that you are to me now.' She chuckled softly. 'Yes, Gabriel is going to grow to be handsome and strong and make his mother very proud, you'll see.'

* * *

Selena struggled along a stony footpath as it twisted up a hill between clumps of trees. She paused for breath, opening her backpack and bringing a metal water bottle to her lips to quench her thirst in the heat. 'This is a great walk – I'm certainly working up an appetite.'

Matty was next to her with Joely, Laura a few paces further behind. He grinned. 'The barbecue will be the perfect temperature for cooking on by the time we are back.' He turned round and pointed back down the hill. 'Can you see our field from here? There's our caravan and the barbecue smoke curling up?'

'I think this is the hottest day we've had.' Joely wiped perspiration from her brow. 'It's not far to the top of the hill though.'

'At least it's downhill on the way back,' Laura puffed her way towards the group. 'And the view from the top is spectacular.'

'I love this place.' Joely's face shone. 'Just standing here and looking at our home, and up to the treetops, before it flattens out to scrubland, and you can see for miles.'

'Just a few more steps, then a few more,' Matty said encouragingly as he surged forward. Joely was level with him, then ahead.

Laura sidled closer to Selena. 'When we come out at the top and the path leads to the flatter terrain, you'll recognise the view again – it's the sunset landscape you painted after your dream, the one you did in those amazing colours.'

'I remember it well.' Selena smiled. 'Claire has put the picture on our website and there are two clients interested.'

'Fantastic,' Laura was breathing hard as she walked. 'So, how is life at Sloe Cottage?'

'Great – I've been working on a painting from a picture I took on Exmoor – the heather and the gorse. But I have had an idea that I want to paint the blackthorn in the garden again, this time from another viewpoint.'

'And the ghost?' Laura pushed lilac hair from her face. 'Any more sightings of her?'

'I think she visited me a few nights ago when I was in bed.' Selena exhaled. 'I was scared, to tell you the truth. I didn't look, but it felt like she was there. The entire room smelled of lavender.'

'Oh, my goodness,' Laura gasped. 'I'd have been terrified.'

'I was,' Selena admitted.

'Now's the best time for lavender – the flowers tend to come in June and stay for a few months,' Joely called over her shoulder. 'I'm currently working on a lavender cream for stretch marks. I know it will be popular on Thursdays at the market.'

Laura leaned closer to Selena. 'And what about Nick? How is the romance blossoming?'

'Slowly...' Selena wondered whether to say any more, so she added, 'I'm seeing him on Saturday.'

'Come to my house for lunch, both of you – my dad is wading through the records and he'll have something for us to look at by then. He's loving it, looking through all those names and dates. Besides, it would be nice to spend time in the garden. I promise I'll do better than a sandwich this time...'

'A sandwich is fine,' Selena said. 'It's the company that counts.'

'We're nearly there,' Matty shouted over his shoulder. 'Get your camera ready, Selena. The view from the top is incredible.'

'It is – this is the best place to see two counties,' Joely added. 'Devon and Somerset in all their glory.'

They reached the top of the hill, the view intersected with paths and scrubland, willow trees, the occasional oak and private land hidden behind a wire fence. They stood still, gazing around at the panoramic view. Peaks dropped down to pretty villages on one side; the blue horizon stretched to the other, houses nestling between dipping valleys. The slicing grey line of a motorway could be seen in the distance and then there was field upon field of farmland. The air was filled with the soft hum of bees, the chatter of birds and the distant rumble of cars. Selena took out her camera, moving one way and another to take snaps of the views.

'How far have we walked?' Laura asked, her face flushed with heat.

'About a mile, up the hill.' Matty grinned. 'It is the same distance back down, but it will seem shorter.'

'And look – there's Ashcombe, about a mile and a half from here, and Chitterwell half a mile the other side,' Joely said.

Laura laughed. 'Oh, that's wonderful. I can just imagine me dragging a group of schoolchildren up here next term to write poems about the landscape.'

Joely pointed. 'Can you see that tall piece of wood, over there, where the road ends?'

'Yes.' Laura's eyes were small behind her glasses. 'It's just a post stuck in the ground with a huge hunk of stone next to it, isn't it?'

'The post and the rock show the place where a tree stood, the one that once marked the crossroads between the two counties. What tree was it?'

'An elm.' Matty touched Joely's arm, a casual brush of affection. 'There aren't many elm trees left now since the disease in the 1960s, but the country used to be full of them, way back to the Bronze Age.'

Selena frowned. 'So, what's the significance of the border? Is there a particular reason why this part of it is marked?'

'I've no idea,' Matty replied. 'It's just the line between the two counties, I assume.'

'It seems likely to be more significant than just a random place on the boundary, though,' Joely said. 'There's a kind of magic to it, isn't there, the place where the crossroads meet?'

'It's romantic,' Laura sighed. 'It makes me think of handsome highwaymen stealing jewels from rich ladies in a coach and four...'

'Or perhaps it's something else...' Selena took a photograph as an oily-feathered crow swooped down and perched on the post. Other crows circled overhead, a dark halo of hovering birds. She recalled what Nick had said about Exmoor, that the legend claimed that pixies, ghosts, even the Devil himself lurked there. The crossing of the roads, segmented by a dark post that stood upright as if perpetually waiting, and a heavy stone boulder placed on the ground, seemed to mark a cold, sinister place hung with shadows. Despite the intense sunshine, Selena shivered.

* * *

Two hours later, they were sitting outside the caravan on chairs around a table, drinking home-made mint lemonade and eating barbecued food. Joely and Matt had prepared a feast: baked potatoes and salad, grilled peaches, cauliflower, leeks and avocado.

Laura licked her lips. 'I never knew you could barbecue some of these things – it's incredible.'

'You can bake anything that's edible and it will taste better,' Matty grinned. 'My Grandma Boswell used to bake hedgehogs in clay, although they are protected now. She baked bacon rolled in suet too, which was a family favourite. I've even heard of people baking squirrels.'

Selena pulled a face, recalling the mummified squirrel that Nick discovered in the loft at Sloe Cottage.

Joely poured more lemonade into tumblers and said, 'I suppose whatever meat you eat, it's all the same process, except you have to take into account how rare the creature is.'

'Oh, I couldn't eat horse flesh,' Laura shuddered.

'I love the idea of barbecuing fruit though,' Selena said. 'I've learned so much since I've lived in Somerset.'

'When do you go back to Manchester?' Joely asked.

'The end of the month. Today's the sixteenth, so I have exactly two weeks left on my tenancy.'

'Are you looking forward to going back?' Matty said.

Selena shrugged. 'I haven't thought about it. My life is there, the gallery, the flat I share – well, it's Claire's flat really and she's found the love of her life now, so I suppose things will be a bit different.'

'Then stay here in Ashcombe,' Laura's eyes were large. 'We've become fond of you.'

Selena wrapped an arm around her. 'Claire's planning a big art exhibition in the gallery in August. We have loads of paintings to show. Many have "sold" tags on them already. I'll certainly be quite a lot better off financially than when I came.' She was thoughtful for a moment, then she said, 'But I will miss all the friends I've made.'

Laura met her eyes, a meaningful stare, and Selena knew that she was thinking of her relationship with Nick but she was being too tactful to mention it.

Selena sighed. 'I have really enjoyed my time here, and the opportunity to paint and to heal. And I've met the most wonderful people.' She was surprised to feel tears blossoming in her eyes. 'But my time at Sloe Cottage ought to come to an end soon. The ghost and I – Grace, or whoever she is – are becoming a bit too well acquainted. At first it was just small signs of a presence, and I was fine with that in the background, but now I think it's becoming a bit much for me to take. I hardly slept last night.'

'Despite the scent of lavender,' Joely pointed out.

'Stay with us at the cottage – we have a spare room and you'd be very welcome.' Laura smiled at the idea and reached for another baked potato.

'I definitely have a lot to think about,' Selena said. Then her thoughts moved back to Nick, who she would be seeing again in two days' time, and she added, 'And there are some things that need resolving sooner rather than later.'

39

Grace waited for Gabriel to fall asleep in his makeshift cradle then, after she heard Will haul himself to his bedroom, she rummaged behind her pallet bed for the knotted rope ladder entwined with feathers. She found the little doll she had made for the baby and took it out of his cot, examining the heart-shaped spot of blood on the fabric that Nathaniel's pricked finger had left behind. She wrapped both items carefully in a small blanket – it was summer now and Gabriel would not need to be covered too heavily – and she placed them all neatly in a wooden box that Will had painstakingly made for Anne to store her needlework in not long after they had married. Then she went downstairs quietly into the garden, finding the old ladder, simple wooden rungs joined together by a pole, which Will kept to access the thatched roof to make repairs. She brought it inside noiselessly, careful not to wake her father, and leaned it against the chimney breast, lifting her skirts and climbing steadily, the box under one arm.

She was looking down from up high, near the top of the thatch. She felt giddy as the ladder shifted beneath her, but she placed her hand against the chimney breast and found a wide gap in the stones, easing the box inside. No one would find it there. She scrambled down the ladder again and checked that the baby was sleeping. Her spirits lifted:

suddenly she felt safer. She had taken her grandmother's wise advice and the thought made her smile as she spoke softly. 'So, it is done. Now everything will be well.'

* * *

May became June, the weather humid and brooding, and over the next few weeks, Grace heeded her grandmother's words: she stayed away from Ashcomb, from the loose tongues of George, Nancy and Kitty, spending her days milking the cows in the barn and her evenings listening to the babbling well and tending the plants in the garden. Gabriel was sitting up now, taking notice of everything around him, keen to pick up and explore every object, which included putting anything he could find in his mouth. By day, Grace kept him close to her while she sat on her milking stool, turning everything she did into a game to keep her child's attention.

Jennet spent most of the time talking to Margaret and Joanna about her new young man, Henry Brewer, whom she said was the love of her life and more of a proper man than Ned Shears. Grace listened but made no comment. At the end of the day, she was glad of Alice's company, when her friend would visit her before she walked home, often with a basket of eggs or cheese or a piece of mutton. Grace would examine Alice's face for any sign of change, but she lacked the glazed stare and the softness of her chin that were the tell-tale signs of being with child. Grace smiled as Alice lifted Gabriel and kissed his cheeks, but she was secretly sad that Alice's many and varied efforts to help her conceive had not yet resulted in pregnancy.

One Saturday evening, Grace was in the garden with Gabriel, showing him the new plants. All the blossom had fallen from the blackthorn, the foliage now green, masking the sharp thorns Grace always told her son to avoid. Herbs were flourishing: parsley, dill, comfrey, sage and lavender smelled sweet and Gabriel held a handful of summer savoury, attempting to push it in his mouth. Grace lifted him high and laughed, gently tugging the long leaves from between his lips. She knew the herb was good for digestion, it prevented nausea and restored loss of appetite, and she explained this to Gabriel as he smiled into her eyes and she sat him back down on the grass.

Then there was a figure at the gate, a young man in his best clothes, leaning on a wooden stick. He waved, and she called back. 'Ned, it is good to see you.'

He limped towards her eagerly, holding out a bunch of flowers. 'I picked these for you, sweet Grace. I hope you will enjoy them.'

She held them to her nose. 'Thank you. Columbine, thrift, foxgloves and daisies. They are wonderful.'

He stood in front of her; Grace could tell that he was thinking of what to say, then he murmured, 'How fares young Gabriel?'

Grace swept the child up from the ground in her arms. 'He thrives.'

She watched as Ned held out a finger and Gabriel grasped it in his pudgy fist and chuckled. Then Ned's eyes met hers and his voice was low. 'How fare you, dear Grace?'

'I am well.'

'And have you thought again about my words, when we last spoke at the May dance?'

'I have.'

'Do you have an answer for me then?' Ned's words came in a rush. 'I think of nothing else but you and I hope that you will spare me the anguish that is in my heart for fear that you will say no.'

'You are a kind, gentle man, Ned, above all others.'

Grace saw the colour drain from his face as he exhaled. 'Does this mean you will say nay, when all I want in the world is to wed you?'

'No, Ned, I am not refusing you.' She noticed his expression, both fearful and hopeful, and she was filled with soft feelings of sympathy. 'I will marry you, if my father gives his blessing, but I want us to wait until the spring.'

'Oh Grace, my heart is full of you.' Ned grasped her hand. 'But why should we wait?'

'Because it will give Gabriel time to get to know you and...' Grace lowered her eyelids. 'It will give us time to grow together. It will give me time to care deeply for you, which I know I will.'

'You do not love me as I love you.'

'I know that I will learn to, in time.' Grace smiled, believing that her words were true. He was the kindest of men, and she resolved to try her hardest to love him as he deserved. 'You are the best man I have met, Ned Shears, and I will be proud to be made a wife in the coming spring.'

'Not sooner?' Ned put an arm around her and the baby, drawing them both close. 'Not at Michaelmas, or Yuletide?'

'Perhaps,' Grace said. 'Let us spend this summer together, here in the garden or walking in the lanes and the fields, you and Gabriel and me. I give you my promise now that we will wed, once you have spoken to my father and he has given his blessing. But when the summer becomes the autumn, then we will set a date for it.'

Ned kissed her cheek tentatively. 'My Grace, I want nothing more than to be yours.'

'Then it shall be.' Grace closed her eyes happily. Her grandmother had been right: she felt safe, supported, cared for; Ned loved her and he loved her child. Their future would be good, better than good. It would be a blessed one. There would be brothers and sisters for Gabriel; Will could work less in the fields; Grace would wrap the growing family in her arms and give each and every one of them so much care and devotion. And she would learn to love Ned for the honest, good man that he was. All would be well.

She opened her eyes and saw Ned's face, flushed with pride. He took her in his arms and kissed her lips. 'Believe me, Grace, we will be the happiest family on God's earth. I will not let you down. Now let us go and speak with your father.'

* * *

The following Monday, the twenty-first, Midsummer's Day, was a humid day, too hot for milking cows. The beasts were uncomfortable in the strawed-down barn, their usual placid temperament less compliant, bothered by the heat and buzzing flies. Jennet was in a foul temper too; she had argued with Henry Brewer, who had told her that he would not marry until he was twenty-five, and Jennet had refused to court him again. The air was sticky and still, and Gabriel cried often, his face flushed on one side. Grace had noticed that day that his gums were red, and she had rubbed them with her finger and a little valerian and chamomile flower to soothe the new tooth that was coming. He was fractious, waking from sleep and crying, holding out his arms for his mother.

Jennet was irritable. 'Peace, Grace, for the sake of God. I do wish that baby would stint. His crying is making the cows grow stubborn. This one will not let down her milk and Alice will be here soon to check the pails and she will be angry with me again.'

Grace rocked Gabriel in her arms, placing a finger in his mouth to soothe him, and his crying stopped. She continued to milk the cow with one hand, listening to the squirting liquid in the pail, and her expression grew thoughtful. Soon she would have a husband, the kindest of men, and one day she would have a large family to care for. She imagined the garden at Slaugh Cottage crammed with flowers and plants, the blackthorn tapping its branches against the shutters in a light wind, water chattering at the bottom of the well, children playing on the grass. In her imagination, they were surrounded by animals: hares, foxes, rabbits, small hedgehogs and songbirds. She gazed down at the baby; he was sleeping softly now and she placed him in his crib and resumed milking.

By early evening, the sky grew leaden and overcast. Margaret frowned, 'I hope a storm will not come. It is a long walk back to Ashcomb with puddles across the field. I fear my dress will become wet.'

'There will be a storm,' Joanna said. 'We need a good storm to clear the air – it is murky and too hot.'

'There will be no storm.' Jennet pointed towards the sky. 'Look yonder – the sky is lighter. We may have a little rain, then it will be sunny again.'

Grace's pail was full. She patted the cow's hindquarters and whispered thanks, then she was about to untie the cow when Alice appeared, carrying a basket covered with a linen cloth.

Alice looked sharply around the barn, her eyes falling on Jennet. 'Why is it that you girls do not fill your pails as quickly as Grace?' Her voice was irate. 'Is it because you spend all day gossiping? You have the tongues of bawds.'

Jennet made a face, implying that Alice had become exactly like her mother-in-law. 'It is too hot, Alice, and the cows will not let down at all – I swear their udders are dried...'

'Cease your prattle,' Alice snapped. She turned to Grace and held out the basket. 'Would you mind taking this down to the fallow field to Nathaniel? I fear he will be late to supper and I have prepared bread and meat for him.'

Gabriel made a snuffling noise and Grace plucked him from the barrel crib, holding him against her. 'Gabriel is pained by his new tooth coming, Alice.'

'I will go to take Master Nathaniel's basket in her place,' Jennet offered. 'It would be pleasant to wander across the field rather than to sit in this stinking hot barn.'

'Grace will go. I have said it.' Alice folded her arms stubbornly. 'I have an aching back and I must lie down in my bed soon.' She placed the basket on the ground and held out her arms. 'But I will hold Gabriel while you take the basket, Grace. Give him to me.'

Jennet leaned towards Margaret and whispered loudly, 'My sister is no better than Mistress Harriet now. And I believe Alice has her monthly bleeding again. I am not surprised she is in a bad humour. Her husband will be angry too when he discovers her condition...'

Alice shot Jennet a mean look; her cruel words had hit a tender place. She hugged Gabriel closer to her and Grace said, 'I will take the basket. But if he cries, please take heed – the end of a finger on his gum will ease his pain. I will not be long.'

Alice smiled and rocked the baby in her arms, kissing his cheeks over and over. She had not heard Grace; her eyes were only for Gabriel as she made soft soothing noises.

Grace picked up the basket and headed across the fields along the narrow path. To one side, the fields were full of growing wheat, pale stalks waving in the light breeze. She hoped Gabriel would be all right with Alice; she trusted her friend, but Grace was anxious that she wouldn't know how to soothe him. She hurried forwards; Nathaniel was two fields away: she could see him on horseback, circling two men who were standing by a stone wall, waving an arm in instruction. Grace increased her pace: she was not looking forward to meeting Nathaniel, but she would simply offer the basket and rush back to the barn, to her son.

Grace could hear Nathaniel's voice as she approached, giving orders. She recognised the two men in the field. One was George Shears, Nancy's husband, and the other was an older man, the same age as her father, Francis Barnes. They were rebuilding a stone wall while Nathaniel rode on his horse, Squire, a dark beast whose supple coat was glossy in the sunlight.

She opened the gate and approached quietly. Above, a cloud hung low, heavy and ragged. A warm drop of water fell on Grace's face, followed by a second.

Nathaniel thundered over towards her on the horse; his eyes were coal-dark as he saw Grace. He brought the stallion to a halt as she held out the basket and set it down. 'Alice asked me to bring this to you for supper.'

'Grace.' He surveyed her in the cap and plain dress. 'How are you? How is the child?'

'We are both well.'

'And my wife, when you saw her at the barn, how was she?'

'She was tired, a little.'

The dark horse snorted through wide nostrils and Nathaniel made a similar sound. His voice was bitter. 'How can it be, Grace, that you can get with child and yet my wife cannot, after all this time? Tell me – you know these things.'

'It takes time... Be kind to her.'

'No, it takes a proper wife, a woman, and she is a but a dried husk.' Nathaniel sneered. 'Did I choose the wrong woman to wive? Tell me, Grace – did I?'

'I know not.' Grace looked down at her feet for fear that Nathaniel would read her expression: she wondered how differently her life might have been had he chosen her. But he had chosen Alice, and Grace would not speak ill of her. She said quietly, 'You are wed to Alice and she is my good friend.'

Nathaniel frowned. 'Or did you curse me? The day I was in your house, and you had made a poppet and I was pricked by the blackthorn?'

'It was not blackthorn, simply a needle in my sewing.'

'Pass me the basket,' Nathaniel said angrily.

Grace lifted it and he took the handle. He turned the horse round fully, so that he could speak to her again.

'I hear your son is a fine boy.'

'He is.'

'And I believe that he favours me, his dark hair...'

'Gabriel is mine.' Grace stood as tall as she could, her eyes hard as she met his gaze. It had started to rain now, large drops cooling the air.

'It is a pity.' Nathaniel laughed bitterly. 'You have no husband and I have no son and heir.'

'But that may change soon, for both of us.' Grace's thoughts flew to Ned. She felt loyal to him, grateful for his kindness, but she recalled the way Nathaniel had kissed her once and she was filled with new sadness.

Nathaniel's dark blue eyes flashed. 'Are you to wed?'

'I hope to.'

'Then you may have more sons.' He shook his head, his face flushed with anger. 'And I am bound to barren Alice for the rest of my days.'

'I wish you good fortune,' Grace said. 'I wish you happiness.'

Nathaniel was suspicious. 'I do not think you wish me good things at all, Grace. I rather believe you hate me and wish me ill.'

'I do not.'

'I fear that you have blighted my wife's womb with your charms, that you have spoken dark words while you stand in your garden by the blackthorn, and that I am cursed for all my days.'

'No, do not say that, Nathaniel. I loved you once. How could I wish you harm?'

'Then why am I thus cursed with my wife? It can only be at your hand, Grace. My mother has said so, others believe so. I think there is only Alice who trusts you, and look how it serves her to be your friend.' He spat on the ground. 'And I have heard many stories. My men say that you brought a sheep to life and that you blasted Ned Shears' leg.'

'I would not harm him. Ned and I are to wed.'

'Perhaps that is how you enchanted him, by cursing him? No other woman will have him now.' Nathaniel's face was fierce. 'I know you cursed me when I stood in your garden by the chattering well. You put a charm on me so that I couldn't resist you. I thought you beautiful then, soft and kind. But now I know what you are, I will not utter the word aloud.' His voice was low with menace. 'Stay away from me, Grace, and stay away from Alice.'

'Nathaniel, that is not true...'

Nathaniel lifted an arm as if he might strike her. Then he breathed deeply; rage filled his body, and he yelled an order in the direction of George and Francis who stood watching as he turned Squire with a jerk of the reins. Nathaniel dug his heels hard into the stallion's sides, demanding instant speed as the black horse galloped towards the two men. Then, all of a sudden, Squire stumbled on the rough ground and fell, sending Nathaniel crashing down hard and the horse rolled on top of him. Grace stared in shock: the two men's voices rose in alarm as they ran over to Nathaniel, who lay on the baked earth not moving as his horse staggered to its feet and bolted away.

40

Selena was looking through the stack of paintings in the conservatory, pleased with what she had achieved: there were so many landscapes and vistas, each one bringing back memories of her time in Somerset. Her favourite was the stark painting of the blackthorn tree glimpsed through the window. She recalled the time she was painting it by the fireside, the writing that had appeared in the condensation on the window, the crude letters spelling the name Grace. Selena wondered what Grace's story was, why she was so restless.

She glanced at her most recent picture of the Exmoor landscape, finished now, still on the easel; she was satisfied with it and she was keen to start another project. Outside, the back garden was in shadow; it was past ten o'clock and she thought that she ought to go to bed, but she felt edgy and wide awake. Selena was strangely claustrophobic indoors; the air was sticky. It was a humid night and she wanted to be outside. Then it came to her; she could paint the blackthorn tree again, in detail under the moonlight; she'd take her digital camera and snap some pictures close-up to inspire her. It would be cool and calm in the front garden, and she longed to breathe the fresh night air.

Selena took off her shoes by the front door and wandered outside in bare feet, enjoying the sensation of damp grass between her toes. The garden was bathed in pale light, smelling sweet and fresh; the circle of the moon hung overhead, the colour of wax. Selena gazed up at little stars like pinholes in the sky, clustered in groups, and she inhaled, enjoying the cool air against her skin. She could hear the chattering well, a soft bubbling from deep below the earth's surface. Selena recalled Ian or Lesley having said something about it being Welsh water, flowing all the way down from the Brecons. Then her mind wandered to the Cotters, the people who lived in the cottage years ago, when it had been Slaugh Cottage. Grace Cotter must have walked in the garden, touched the same walls with her hands, warmed them in front of the same hearth. Selena wondered again what became of her, and she shuddered. She moved her thoughts to Nick. Tomorrow was Saturday and they would meet in the morning and share the outcome of the latest research, the artefacts they had discovered in the loft, before going to Laura's for lunch. Her pulse quickened at the thought.

The garden was quiet, no sound except the low screech of an owl. Somewhere in a hedgerow, an animal scuttled, the rushing of a hare. Selena looked through the lens of her camera: despite the darkness, the images were clear. She photographed the well, the outline captured in a shaft of moonlight, then she whirled round and took some pictures of the blackthorn tree, the branches stretched upwards, leaves spread like a garland. She took more, close up. Black shadowy bark against silver light, the greys of foliage, the hint of deep red against the spiky thorns.

Her feet were wet now and she was feeling cold. Selena decided she'd go back to the house, make a cup of soothing chamomile tea, review her pictures and then go to bed. She was determined that there would be no ghosts in her room tonight; she would sleep well.

Back in the kitchen, she sipped tea and looked through the large number of photos she had taken outside. They had come out just as she'd hoped; there was a starkness about them, matt black against silver. The well was particularly stunning, bathed in moonlight, and the blackthorn tree had an eerie beauty.

Then Selena stopped, holding her breath. She went back to the previous picture, the blackthorn tree at a distance, staring at it, frowning. The tree was curled over, as if bowed in prayer. She augmented the picture, looking at the details. Coiled in the blackthorn tree was what looked like a trailing mist, but on closer inspection Selena could make out the shape of a slender woman with long pale hair, wearing a white shift. Selena enlarged the picture again and stared at the transparent spectre, her arms stretched upwards in supplication and her mouth open.

Selena put the camera down and gasped. The intense scent of lavender surrounded her and, without knowing why, tears tumbled down her cheeks as she was gripped by an overwhelming sadness.

* * *

Selena woke on Saturday morning, feeling refreshed after a shower, more settled after the troubling events of the previous evening. As she sat at the breakfast table with a cup of tea, staring at the pictures on her phone, she was more convinced than ever. It was definitely not an optical illusion; hidden in the shadows of the tree was the misty shape of a woman with a sad face. Selena sighed; last night, as she'd gazed at the photo, she had been filled with an incredible feeling of regret and loss, as if something tragic had taken place. She wondered what could have happened all those years ago to leave such a strong imprint of the past in Sloe Cottage.

She spent the next two hours in the conservatory; her intention was to paint the blackthorn at night, but the image of the ghostly woman in the tree was scorched on her mind and she found herself painting the shape, trying her hardest to communicate the sadness of the scene. It was coming together well: the sharp outline of the tree, the yellow moon, the woman trapped within criss-crossed branches. Then she noticed that a voice message had come in from Laura: she had been too engrossed in her painting to take the call. She listened to excited garbled words about her father's new discoveries as he researched the parish register. She was just about to listen to the message again when she heard a knock at the front door. Selena ran through the hall eagerly and threw it open.

'Nick.'

'So nice to see you.' He handed her a bunch of sweet peas, the stems wrapped in foil. 'My mother sent you these – I called in to see her and she insisted that I shouldn't arrive here empty-handed.'

Selena took the flowers. 'Thank you – and do thank Lesley. I'll put them in a vase later – there's a lovely cream one somewhere. The flowers will be perfect in the window.' She ushered him into the kitchen. 'Would you like a cup of Earl Grey?'

'Yes please. Can I see your latest paintings?'

'Help yourself.' Selena bustled in the kitchen as Nick wandered through into the conservatory.

She heard him exclaim. 'Is this a new one, the blackthorn tree again?'

'It is...' she called.

'And – is that the shape of our ghost sitting in the branches?'

Selena put two cups on the table. 'Come and see.' He was by her side and she passed her camera to him, the photo of the blackthorn tree ready. 'I took this last night when I was outside. What do you think?'

Nick inhaled. 'That's quite incredible.'

'And I felt an overpowering sadness, as if that was how she felt too.' Selena's words came out in a rush. 'Do you think she's trapped there? What if her body is buried beneath the tree? Do you think she's trying to escape?'

'Or perhaps it's a place of refuge for her,' Nick said. 'I'm not sure what to think, especially after the report that Colleen sent me about the things we found in the attic.'

Selena couldn't stop herself from reaching out and grasping his hand. 'What did she say?'

'Well, first of all the blanket. The fabric is very fragile now, but

Colleen is sure that the date is 1683 and the letter looks more like a G than a C.'

'Grace?'

'It could be. But Colleen was certain about the date, so it would almost certainly have been one of the Cotters who put the old wooden box in the attic. I wonder why they hid it – or if it was a storage place?'

'But why hide those particular things?'

'The other two items are huge clues.' Nick squeezed her hand. 'The little rag thing is some sort of primitive doll. Colleen said it might have been a child's plaything, but it also might have been a poppet.'

Selena stared. 'Poppet meaning sweet and cute, as in "Hello, my poppet", or poppet as in a doll made to represent a person, for casting spells on?'

Nick shrugged. 'I'm not sure we'll ever know, except for what Colleen said about the third item. She's done quite a bit of research on it and she's come up with some incredible findings.'

'Do you mean the piece of rope?'

'She says it was a piece of knotted rope or string, one and a half metres long, with cockerel's feathers woven into it. They were basically shredded dust, but Colleen managed to identify them and she has some interesting facts about the significance of it too.' Nick raised an eyebrow. 'It was a witch's ladder.'

'A witch's ladder? What was that?' Selena asked.

'Colleen has several theories, based on her research of the seventeen hundreds. One is that a witch would make a ladder to stop cows being able to give milk – a sort of curse on a neighbour's farm, so that the cows' udders dry up.'

'Why would someone do that?' Selena was alarmed at the thought.

'A charm or spell of some kind, I suppose.'

Selena leaned forward, her hand still in Nick's. 'And what else did Colleen say?'

'The witch's ladder isn't about someone flying or climbing up it – it was coiled in a roof space and left there deliberately to cause some one's death.'

'My goodness.' Selena caught her breath. 'So, are you saying our Grace was actually a witch?'

'The truth is, no one really knows the answer,' Nick said. 'She may not necessarily have been a witch at all, but the evidence does point that way. Hiding those objects in the chimney could have been a spell to cause harm to someone she had a grudge against. It certainly looks like one of the inhabitants in the cottage was quite handy with some sort of magical powers.'

'There's something else I ought to mention...' Selena was thoughtful. 'I've smelled lavender around the house a few times, from the moment I first arrived. It was really strong last night.'

'What's the significance of lavender in terms of natural healing?' Nick asked.

'It's a calming plant – relaxing, a remedy for pain.'

Nick spoke softly:

'Here's flowers for you;
Hot lavender, mints, savoury, marjoram;
The marigold, that goes to bed wi' the sun
And with him rises weeping.'

'What is that from?' Selena asked.

'*The Winter's Tale.*' Nick smiled. 'The Cotters would have lived some seventy years after Shakespeare was writing his plays, but it goes to show how important herbs and flowers were to people in those days, and how significant a part they played in their lives.'

'There's still evidence of their importance now,' Selena replied. 'Just ask Joely.'

'Definitely. So – what do we now know about our Grace Cotter?'

'Two things,' Selena counted on her fingers. 'One, the supernatural stuff that is difficult to believe is real: doors opening, her name written on the glass, the scent of lavender, the woman I saw outside and in the photo of the blackthorn tree. It all points to some sort of spirit presence.'

'And the other?'

'Hard facts. The stuff we found in your mother's box file – names, dates – and the evidence from your colleague, the archaeologist – the witch's ladder, the little doll.'

'It doesn't look good for Grace – evidence of witchcraft, grudges and ladders, the misty photo of a spirit that lives in the witch's tree.'

'Rob called it that too – he told me the thorns were used to prick wax images of those that they cursed.'

'Or, quite simply, the whole thing is just superstition. Grace may have been simply a victim of prejudice,' Nick said. 'If we're being logical, we know that witches don't exist.'

'Or ghosts?' Selena raised an eyebrow.

'What you saw last night seems real enough. I worry about you living here...' Nick began.

'I'm calmer this morning.' Selena said. 'Things are becoming clear. When I saw her in the tree, I felt an overwhelming sadness. I'm not afraid now, not really. I just want to find out, to help if I can. It's as if she's asking me...'

'I know what you mean. We're getting close to knowing who she is,' Nick agreed. 'So, we're off to Laura's for lunch – and Rob may have some answers for us about the Cotters.'

Selena was suddenly excited. 'I had a message from her this morning, just before you came. Apparently, he's spent hours already on the internet, looking at the parish registers and records.'

'Did she say anything specific?'

'Rob wants to tell us all about it himself. Laura says he's become a little bit obsessed with it – he's found out the Cotters' dates, and who they are related to and what happened to them all. He says we're in for some exciting reading.'

'Then shall we go?' Nick took her hand. 'I'm really looking forward to lunch at Laura's.'

Selena met his eyes, her own shining. 'And we're going out to dinner again tonight?'

'We are,' Nick replied. 'And I'm looking forward to that even more.'

Selena returned his smile. With his hand in hers, she was starting to feel like they were on the brink of being a couple, that something wonderful was about to happen between them. As she walked through the living room, she sighed and the heady scent of lavender stayed in her nostrils.

41

Grace ran towards Nathaniel as the horse bolted away, up the hill towards the farm. The rain was falling steadily. She heard George Shears shout to Francis, 'Go to Hill Top. Fetch Master Joseph. And any of the other men you can find.'

She and George arrived at the same time; Nathaniel was sprawled on the ground on his back, his hands over the left-hand side of his abdomen, groaning. Grace knelt next to him, her heart thumping. He was in pain, broken, and she wasn't sure how to help. 'What ails you, Nathaniel? What must I do?'

His hands moved to his shoulder and then back to his left side. His breathing was ragged and he seemed confused.

George snarled, 'Don't touch him, Grace Cotter. You've done enough damage already.'

'I only want to help...'

Nathaniel's eyes fluttered open. 'I think Squire saw something running in the grass and he shied... or he stumbled. I can't move...

'Where are you hurt?' Grace reached for his hand. Her cap and face were wet in the rain.

'Here – on the left. I can't breathe. I...' He seemed to notice her for the first time and his face became terrified. 'Grace – you made a poppet, and pricked me with a blackthorn... and now the horse has fallen on me...'

'What did he say?' George's voice was loud. 'What did you do to him?'

Nathaniel's eyes closed slightly and he groaned, his breath shallow, wheezing. Voices came from behind, people running down the hill, their heads bent against the rain, and Francis arrived with three other men. One of them was Joseph Harper, Nathaniel's father, a calm-natured man with a slow drawling voice. He crouched down next to his son. 'What happened? Nathaniel, can you hear me speak?'

Nathaniel struggled to breathe, then he gasped, a slow strained sound.

Harriet Harper approached, screaming and hysterical. Alice followed her, clutching Gabriel.

George shouted, 'I saw it all. The horse reared and rolled on top of him.'

Alice rushed to Nathaniel's side, passing Gabriel to Grace, taking her husband's hand. Harriet grasped Nathaniel's other hand, weeping.

Alice pressed his fingers in hers. 'Nathaniel... Nathaniel?'

He gave a low moan, then he exhaled, one long breath. No inhalation followed.

Joseph took off his wide-brimmed hat and leaned forward, listening, then put a hand to his son's chest. He turned to Harriet, his eyes wide with disbelief, his face wet with rain and tears.

'He's gone. Nathaniel – he's gone.'

Harriet's keening cries split the air.

Joseph stood, shaken. Alice hung onto Nathaniel's hand, her cheeks streaked with tears. Joseph asked, 'How did this all come to happen?'

George stepped forward. 'I saw it all, Master Joseph. It was Grace Cotter. She turned herself into a hare and frighted the horse and he fell on Master Nathaniel and rolled right on top of him.'

Grace said, 'That's not true.'

All faces turned to her, mouths gaping, as George added, 'And his last words were that she made a poppet of him and pricked him with a blackthorn. She's cursed him, that's what she's done.'

'I did not.' Grace held Gabriel close, looking from one angry face to another; she saw Harriet's pale fury, Joseph's disbelief, George's triumphant smile.

'She blasted him with her spells. Same as she did with my brother, Ned, and crippled his leg for him, and my daughter, Agnes, with her cursed lip.'

Grace shook her head. 'No...'

'And she turned herself into a hare another time before, when she brought the dead sheep back to life.' George's leer made Grace tremble. 'You know what she is, don't you? You know the word for her.'

Harriet's sobbing stopped; her voice was shrill as she shouted. 'You dried up Alice's womb. I know what you gave her to eat; she cooked the caul you gave her from her sister's birthing, and you know right well the use of the caul is against the Church. And now she is barren. You did it to spite us all.' Her face was crumpled and crimson as she shrieked again. 'And you have murdered my son. Why? What did he ever do to harm you? I cannot forgive you for it... not ever.' She collapsed into her husband's arms, a fallen heap of rags.

'I did not do these things that you say.' Grace's heart was thumping too hard. She whirled around, surrounded by menacing faces, clutching Gabriel tightly.

'We should stop Grace Cotter now before she turns on the rest of us and curses us all. Look at her. She'll blast us all like she did with Master Nathaniel.' George made to move towards Grace. 'We should lock her up.'

She heard Joseph's low mutter. 'Someone, go and fetch the rector. She's acted against the Church.'

'She's been wishting[1] Master Nathaniel for weeks now.' George's voice was loudest. 'I seen her at it – giving him the evil eye.'

Grace twisted round, the startled baby in her arms, and started to run, her feet stumbling on the hard rubble of the fallow field. The skies were dark with rain now. She could hear more accusing voices behind her; Jennet was there, saying something about how Grace cursed the cows so they would not let down milk for anyone else. Harriet screeched that Grace had murdered her son. Grace's feet pounded across the earth, hugging Gabriel tightly, muttering softly to him as she hurried along, desperate to take him as far away from the howling mob as she could.

She arrived at Slaugh Cottage and immediately began collecting things in a basket: Gabriel's clothes, linen, some food. Her mind was racing: she could go to her grandmother's house, but Bett would not be able to hide her for long inside the small cob cottage. Everyone in Ashcomb would hear of Nathaniel's death and Grace feared that the villagers would soon come searching for her. She would walk as far as she could, perhaps to Taunton – she had heard it was a large town, but she would not arrive before nightfall and the thought of walking through the lanes in the dark with her child in her arms frightened her. But Taunton was miles from Ashcomb: perhaps no one would find her there. Her heart was thumping: it was Gabriel's safety she feared for most.

The front door opened and her heart leaped. She heard her father call her name. 'Grace?' His face was haggard as he rushed over to her. 'Is it true? People are saying that Master Nathaniel died because you caused his horse to fall and tumble on him.'

'No – I was there, but I did no such thing.'

He wrapped his arms around her and the baby. 'You are not safe here. You must go.'

Grace nodded, indicating the basket. 'I am ready. Oh, Father, it is so unjust.'

He stroked her hair. 'I fear for you if you stay longer. Quick, go, take your child and Godspeed. I cannot protect you if they find you here.'

'I know.' She pressed her face against his sinewy shoulder. 'What shall I do? How will I live?'

Will's face was a mask of anguish. 'I know not. But you must go, Grace, and quickly.'

'I must.' She adjusted Gabriel in her arms and gave her father one last look, then she rushed towards the door and flung it open.

It had stopped raining. The sun was beating down again, a sticky heat, the air heavy. Then she saw the mob waiting for her outside, in the garden. Grace froze. Reverend Walters, his expression grave, was standing next to a man she had never seen before. Behind them stood Joseph Harper, Harriet, Alice, George Shears and, further back, Jennet, Margaret. Francis Barnes and several more of the farmhands.

Grace searched the faces frantically for someone who might be an ally: she saw Alice, and met her eyes pleadingly, but Alice shook her head slightly, her eyes wide and troubled.

Then the rector, Reverend Walters, a thin man with a long face, said, 'Grace Cotter. That is your name?'

'You know that it is.' Grace trembled, holding Gabriel to her thumping heart.

'This is Barnaby Younger from Hockholler. He wishes to speak with you.'

Barnaby Younger was a burly man with a wide face and a turned-down mouth. He looked Grace over and said, 'We have had a case of typhus in Hockholler. It is convenient that I was visiting Reverend Walters to discuss how we might stop its spread. And he and I both know that it starts with the cursing from a certain type of vile woman.'

Grace stared at him blankly; his words made no sense. She shook her head. 'I know not of what you speak.'

'Have you heard of Mr Robert Hunt of Taunton?'

'I have not.' Grace kissed Gabriel's cheek. He had started to make soft noises of hunger and she feared he would soon cry to be fed.

'He died three years ago; he was buried at Compton Pauncefoot, but he did great work in Taunton throughout his life to rid the world of vile pestilence. I am an admirer of his work and I seek to continue in his name.'

'I do not understand you.' Grace hugged her baby close.' My child grows hungry – I need to nurse him.'

Younger ignored her, and continued to speak. 'Have you heard the name Elizabeth Stile? She was a crone who died in Taunton gaol in 1664 after Mr Hunt got a confession from her. Have you heard of Edmund Bull and Julian Cox? They were hanged in Taunton by Mr Hunt for their crimes.' He shook his head, ignoring Gabriel's snuffling, raising his voice, addressing the crowd gathered around him. 'Catherina Axford of Mere, Elizabeth Castle of Glastonbury, Anne Green of Wincanton who was stabbed so that her spell could be broken, Elizabeth Busher of Hinton, that was buried near the Bull Pit. Our county is rife with such cunning women, and men too, who consort with the Devil to do ill to good folk such as us.'

Gabriel wriggled uncomfortably; Grace rocked him in her arms, her face twisted in anguish. 'He needs to be fed...'

'Who is your child's father?' Barnaby Younger demanded.

Grace's voice was quiet. 'I cannot say his name.'

The crowd exchanged glances and muttered to each other as Younger raised his voice. 'Who is the father?'

Grace opened her mouth, but no sound came.

Then George shouted from the middle of the mob. 'I know who it is. I saw Grace Cotter with him on May Day after the dance.' He looked pleased with himself: all attention was focused on him as he continued. 'My brother, Ned, and I were walking back after the dancing. We'd been in The Royal Oak, had a cup of ale or two, and we were sleeping in the barn at the time – it was afore I was wed—'

'Speak more quickly,' Younger snapped.

'Grace Cotter was in the garden with a man. I seen his face. I remember it as if it was yesterday.'

The crowd held one breath. Grace felt her heart knock harder as Gabriel writhed in her grasp.

George finished with a flourish. 'It was a man all in dark clothes, and he and Grace were on the ground together, making the beast with two backs.' He looked around him, hearing Harriet Harper gasp. 'It was the Devil she was with that night. I seen them both together.'

Barnaby Younger faced Grace, pushing out his chest. 'Grace Cotter, do you admit to consorting with the Devil?'

'I do not.' Grace pressed her lips against Gabriel's hot face. He had started to whimper.

'Do you admit to being a witch?'

'No...' Gabriel was crying now.

'I accuse you of being one of a hellish knot of witches, and I will do the work of Mr Hunt of Taunton now he is no longer with us.' Younger spoke loudly over the cries, making sure the crowd heard every word. 'Do you admit to blasting Nathaniel Harper to death? Do you admit to turning yourself into a hare, and to consorting with the Devil?'

'No, I do not,' Grace replied.

'And there are other accusations,' Younger continued. 'You and your grandmother assisted at the birth of Agnes Shears and you touched a baby's mouth and cursed it, and so the child had the lip of a hare.'

'No.'

'You blighted Ned Shears' leg and you dried Alice Harper's womb so that she could not conceive.'

'I did not.'

Grace felt her father's hand on her shoulder; Will was behind her, whispering in her ear, 'I am here with you.'

Younger frowned. 'It will go easier with you if you admit it now. If you do not, I will have you taken to Taunton, where we will persuade you to say the truth, using whatever means it takes.'

'I will not lie just to please you.' Grace's voice was soft. 'I am no witch.'

The rector spoke, his voice thin and reedy. 'Then perhaps we need to look for other witches who help her to malign the community. She may not work alone. Bett White, her grandmother, for instance. Her father, perhaps...?'

Grace said, 'No.'

'Then tell the truth, Grace.' Younger turned from her to the crowd. 'I can prove she is a witch. Look here.' He produced a long needle from his pocket. 'This bodkin will prove what she truly is. A witch cannot feel pain when pricked.'

George Shears shouted, 'Go on... prove it in front of us all.'

Younger stepped towards Grace, tearing off her kerchief, exposing the flesh of her shoulder and thrusting the needle into her arm. Grace did not flinch. Younger was gleeful. 'Proof, for everyone to witness. She feels no pain from the piercing bodkin. Therefore, I say, she is proven to be a witch.'

Will Cotter pressed his mouth against Grace's ear. 'I saw it disappear inside itself – the bodkin did not break your skin.'

Younger grasped Grace's arm. 'We need no further evidence. So – Grace Cotter, admit you are a witch, or I will take you to Taunton jail and, with you, your father and grandmother, where you will be tried, found guilty of vile deeds and punished, all three.'

Grace exhaled slowly, gazing from one angry face to another. Gabriel was silent now; she felt him sob once and tremble against her. She slumped back against her father, who held her up as she whispered, 'Then it is just as you say. I cannot deny – I am what you say I am.'

A cry went up from the crowd. 'Seize the witch.'

'She has admitted the truth. There is no need for the courts to hear her. We will not delay further.' Younger ordered, 'We will take her to the top of Long Lane and deal with her there.'

Grace twisted round to her father. 'Please... keep Gabriel safe...'

Alice rushed forward. 'I will take him for you.' She plucked the baby from Grace's arms. 'I will care for him, Grace, trust me. We have always been friends and I will make sure he will always have everything he needs...'

Grace held Gabriel a second longer, pressing him to her heart for the last time, then she let go, allowing him to nestle in Alice's arms. Her eyes were filled with tears as she mumbled, 'Thank you, Alice. May God watch over him. Gabriel is the best of me.'

Alice smiled, her eyes hard, glinting in a way that Grace had never noticed before. Grace looked on, numb, her face wet; she watched her friend hold Gabriel close as if he were her own child, nuzzling the baby softness of his skin, inhaling the sweet scent of his hair. Then Alice put her lips against Grace's ear, kissing her cheek lightly. Her voice was low as she whispered, 'And he is the best of Nathaniel too. I have always known it. But he is mine to keep now, as I have always intended.'

42

Selena and Nick held hands as they walked down the lane from Chitterwell to Ashcombe in the sunshine. Selena was thinking about the photograph she had taken of the blackthorn tree. 'I'm going to finish the painting properly next week,' she said as they strolled along in step. 'It will be really powerful, with the misty shape of a woman hiding in the branches, as if she belongs there.'

'I'm looking forward to seeing it,' Nick replied with a smile.

'My journey here as an artist has been incredible – from the first picture of the back garden in springtime, bluebells, tulips and daffodils, and the field behind it, to the ghostly pictures I'm doing now. Grace Cotter has become so much part of my stay at Sloe Cottage.'

Nick was quiet for a moment, then he said, 'I hope you've enjoyed your time here.'

'Oh, I have,' Selena said, wondering how to convey to Nick that he was important to her too: she was not ready to leave him.

She was about to say that she might ask Lesley if she could extend her stay, when Nick said, 'I had an interesting chat with my mother at Hilltop this morning. She's thinking of putting Sloe Cottage on the market.'

'Oh?' Selena felt strangely disappointed: she imagined the cottage belonging to new people, being repainted, extended again and changed, the character altered. Thoughts of the ghost troubled her: she was almost accustomed to Grace's presence and she wondered what would happen to her if new tenants arrived. Selena couldn't afford to buy the house herself. She offered a sad face. 'Why does she want to sell?'

'It's never really been a source of much income and I suppose, now my parents are retired, the money would come in useful and they don't want the bother of renting it. Besides,' he squeezed Selena's hand, 'Mum's been in denial about the ghost for so long and you've convinced her that there is some sort of presence there, so I expect she'd be glad to let someone else take it on.'

'So she's going to sell it, ghost and all?' Selena joked, then she became serious. 'I often think of Grace now – I imagine her walking along this road before the place was called Chitterwell, going into Ashcombe, just as we are now. I wonder what she used to do, where she used to go?'

'It was a farm labourer's cottage all those years ago. She or her parents would have worked at Hilltop Farm.'

'I think about her living there – her hands would have touched the same walls that I touch, the same door; her feet would have trod the same paths.' Selena thought about her words: she was learning to understand Grace. It was as if there was a connection between them.

'Without the tarmac,' Nick grinned. 'I expect it was a dirt track in the seventeenth century.'

'And they'd have had no bathroom or toilet in the cottage – I wonder how they washed clothes?' Selena's eyes widened. 'And no kitchen. They must have lived and cooked in one room, just using the fireplace.'

'It's hard to imagine the poverty,' Nick said. 'It will be good to find out more about the Cotters. I bet they have some stories to tell.'

'Do you think she married, had children?'

'Most women did...' Nick met her eyes. 'It was a hard time then to be a woman, or to be poor.'

'And what if she was really a witch? What then?'

'Accusations of witchcraft were the go-to forms of misogyny and prejudice in those days. Women were persecuted for being too young, too old, too attractive, too lonely, a little bit different – one whisper of a problem in a community and people were calling some poor unfortunate woman a witch.'

'People can be unkind, full of hatred.' Selena felt concerned, desperate to know what had become of Grace. 'Things haven't changed all that much, have they?'

'Not enough,' Nick said.

They had arrived at the cottage. Laura answered the door in shorts and a stripy top, her lilac hair pinned up.

'Come in, come in. My dad's on his way back now.' She ushered Nick and Selena into the garden, where a jug of sparkling water and four glasses had been set on the table. 'He popped into Taunton – he'd ordered a specialist book from the library on Roman Britain and it's just come in.' Laura turned to Nick and held out her hand. 'Long time, no see – I don't think we've met since New Year's Eve in The Royal Oak.'

He grinned. 'I remember that being a night of singing and Badger Spit...'

'It certainly was – I had a terrible hangover the next day,' Laura trilled. 'So, my dad will turn up at any moment, then we'll eat out here, if that's okay. He's so excited to tell you all about the parish register and what he's learned. He's spent ages writing all the notes down for you – I don't know why he did. We have a printer.' She laughed.

Nick accepted a glass of water. 'I'm looking forward to hearing about it. Selena and I found some artefacts in the roof and they seem to have given us some more clues.'

'Oh,' Selena jumped as her phone rang in her pocket. She tugged it out. 'It's Claire. Sorry – I'd better take this.'

Claire's voice was clear in her ear. 'Selena. I'm in the gallery. Is this a good time?'

'It's fine. How can I help?'

'I've just had a visitor – someone who's looking for you, who wants to talk to you. I think you should hear what she has to say.'

'Oh, all right, if you think so.'

There was a pause while Claire passed her phone over. Then a crisp voice said, 'Hello, Selena. It's Veronica Marsh.'

Selena froze. She had no idea why David's wife – his estranged wife – would ring her or why Claire would agree to her using her phone. She took a breath. 'How can I help you, Veronica?'

'I understand David came to see you recently?'

'Yes.' Selena listened hard to Veronica's tone, trying to gauge her mood. She seemed matter-of-fact, determined, although her voice wobbled slightly.

'I threw him out. I suppose he came to you to ask you to take him back? I expect he said he'd left me.'

'He did.'

Veronica exhaled sadly. 'He's not a good man, Selena. I wanted to apologise to you. I came to see you in Ariel Art, but your colleague said you were away on holiday. I hope you're all right.'

'Yes, I am, thanks.' Selena's voice was hushed.

'I'm glad. David and I were together for seven years. He had an affair with another woman before he met you, and he lied to me about that too. He told me you were stalking him and I was a fool to believe him. He has form. I had it out with him and he told me the truth, or his skewed version of it.'

'Ah, I'm sorry...' Selena said. Her heart went out to Veronica: she too had suffered at his hands.

'I feel terrible about phoning you before. I was desperate to find out what happened between you when he told me you'd been chasing him. Of course, my instincts told me there was more to it than just you being fixated. I so badly needed to talk to you, to convince myself that David was telling the truth and that my marriage would be all right, to find some real answers. I suppose I wanted to blame you and believe him. But in my heart, I think I really knew...'

Selena was filled with regret: she and Veronica had so much in common and their pain might have been lessened if they had talked to each other earlier. 'I should have spoken to you – but I was just too hurt...'

'And I know why now – he told me about the miscarriage. He had to rub it in, just to prove his virility and to hurt me again. Of course, I'd already told him to leave – he just threw that one into the mix as a final blow. But I am well rid of him now.' There was a pause, then Veronica's voice was a whisper. 'I'm so sorry about the baby...'

Selena nodded, feeling the familiar ache return once more. She took a breath, wondering what to say, how to articulate the new connection she felt with David's ex, how she profoundly hoped that Veronica would heal and move on. 'I'm glad you're all right now...'

Veronica's voice increased in volume. 'I'm a survivor. I'm having some counselling, but I'll move on in time. It's just annoying that I've wasted seven years of my life on him...'

'And I'm so sorry about what I did,' Selena said. 'I really didn't intend to hurt you. I was so wrong...'

'Thanks, that means a lot,' Veronica replied, her voice quiet now. 'Although I know how persuasive David can be. And, do you know, he took pride in telling me that you didn't even know that I existed for the first few months – he thinks women are putty in his hands. But I don't intend to let that become an issue. I have my own life now.'

Selena could tell that Veronica was swallowing tears, so she said, 'I hope you can move forward soon.'

There was a crack in Veronica's voice. 'I will do, especially now I've spoken to you. And perhaps, you know, when you're back in Manchester, I can come into the gallery and buy one of your paintings, by way of an apology and to find some closure.' She gulped, steeling herself. 'He hurt me.'

'He hurt me too,' Selena replied. 'But that's all in the past.'

'I won't see him again. I have a solicitor taking care of everything.' Veronica sounded bitter. 'I can't even look at him now, after all his lies and deceit. But I wanted to speak to you, and Claire very kindly let me use her phone.'

Selena closed her eyes; a feeling of relief had swept over her. 'Thanks for phoning me – I'm so glad to know that you and I can put all the negativity behind us.'

'David wasn't worth it. We're better off, both of us.'

'We are.' Selena smiled. 'Good luck with everything, Veronica.'

'The same to you.' Veronica sounded like she was smiling too, her voice was more cheerful. 'And I meant what I said about the painting. I'll pop into the gallery sometime...'

'That would be nice. Thank you.'

'Goodbye.'

Selena heard the phone click at the other end, and she turned to Nick and Laura, a smile on her lips. She suddenly felt lighter, as if a weight had been taken from her shoulders. 'That was Veronica, David's ex-wife. I think we've made peace.'

'Perfect timing,' Laura said. 'Dad's here – and the gluten-free tortellini is ready – if I haven't burned the pesto sauce...'

* * *

After lunch, Rob led the way to the small room he used as his study, and Selena, Nick and Laura crowded around his desk. Rob's expression was serious. 'I think I've got to the bottom of the Cotter family. I've written it all down so that you can take the notes away with you.'

'Thank you.' Selena's heartbeat had started to quicken with excitement.

'So, tell us everything,' Laura enthused.

Rob took a deep breath. 'Well, it seems that Ashcombe was a small place in the sixteen hundreds – the same family names keep cropping up – Stokes, Bryant, Shears, Barnes, White, Harper. Your parents' farm, Nick, belonged to the Harpers. Look at this – when the Cotter family lived in Slaugh Cottage, that's William, Anne, and their daughter, Grace, who was born in 1660, a Joseph Harper owned the farm with his wife, Harriet. They had five children, all boys, four of whom died at birth or in infancy and another, Nathaniel, who died in 1683 and left only one child. His wife was Alice Bryant and, if you look at the notes, you'll find there are a lot of families called Bryant. Nancy Bryant married a George Shears – he must be the ancestor of Jonathan Shears, our local chimney sweep.'

'Oh, how interesting,' Laura clapped her hands. 'What happened to George Shears?'

'He moved into Slaugh Cottage in 1684 and died in 1692 of typhus. But not before he'd fathered six children with Nancy, all but one of them dying at birth or in infancy. Look – the first one, Agnes, born 1683, died 1684, typhus. And the others... Mabel, Thomasin, Peter, Stephen. Only George junior survived to have a family of his own. Poor Mrs Shears.'

'That's horrible,' Selena whispered, reaching for Nick's hand.

'His brother was somewhat luckier,' Rob traced the page with his finger. 'Edward Shears, known as Ned, born 1658, died 1736. He lived until a ripe old age – but he never married.'

'I wonder why?' Laura said. 'There must be so many stories behind these names...'

'And this is interesting – Anne Cotter's mother, Grace's grand-mother, Elizabeth White. She had three children, but only the last one, Anne, survived. And she lived a long time, old Mrs White – she was born in 1621 and died in 1702. She lived to be eighty-one.'

'That's impressive for those days,' Nick said. 'She must have been a tough old lady.'

'And the Harpers – they seemed to have a great deal of bad luck. Joseph and Harriet Harper both died in 1684 of typhoid fever; Alice Harper, Nathaniel's wife, was a widow, she lived on until 1703. Her son must have been twenty when he took over the farm.' Rob turned a page. 'Gabriel Harper did very well for himself though. He married a Catherine Stokes, born 1683, and from 1706 they went on to have six children. Remarkably, they all survived, which is rare for those days. They must have been blessed...'

Nick leaned forward. 'And what of the Cotters?'

'William Cotter died in 1684. He suffered a heart attack while he was working in the fields.'

'And Grace?' Selena asked. 'I'm desperate to find out what you know of her. I'm sure it's Grace who is the presence in Sloe Cottage. And given the artefacts that Nick and I discovered in the roof space, it's going to be so interesting to uncover her story.'

'Grace Anne Cotter,' Rob said, reading his notes. 'Daughter of William and Anne. It seems she was a farm worker, first a weeding woman and then a milkmaid. She lived in the cottage after her mother died, so I suppose she must have looked after her father as well.'

'Imagine,' Laura shuddered. 'Working all day and then cooking and cleaning and tending house, and at such a young age.'

'Her story gets more interesting, though.' Rob turned to look at Selena. 'She died in 1683. She was just twenty-three years old.'

'Poor thing.' Selena squeezed Nick's hand. 'Was she ill?'

'No.' Rob paused. 'There's quite a bit about her here in an old document, the things she was accused of doing. It seems that she could change shape, assume the form of a hare, and she could curse people, too.'

'Grace?' Selena felt suddenly cold. 'Surely not.'

'That ties in with the things in the box that we found in the loft,' Nick exchanged glances with Selena.

'I just feel a deep sadness from her,' Selena protested. 'She's not evil.'

'Well, I can see why there might be a restless spirit at Sloe Cottage.' Rob was quiet for a moment. 'It appears that our Grace Cotter was, allegedly, a witch.'

43

Grace was paraded up the lane towards Ashcomb, Reverend Walters and Barnaby Younger at the head, followed by a jeering mob led by George Shears. Some villagers joined the throng, pushing to the front, braying and shouting, some throwing stones, the milkmaids and farmhands following, Alice holding the baby. Joseph Harper put an arm around his wife and they turned away, walking back towards the farm, their heads bent. Will Cotter sank to his knees in the garden of Slaugh Cottage, his hands covering his face as his legs gave way. Then he stared up at the sky and muttered a quiet prayer that his wife in heaven would receive his daughter in her arms.

The air crackled with dry heat as the crowd disappeared up the hill, but their voices could be heard, the ragged excited shouting. Then a lone man with a walking stick hurried down from the farm; Ned Shears had been clearing out a barn and he had not heard the news of Nathaniel's death until much later. His face knotted in anxiety, he limped forward a distance from the crowd, doing his utmost to catch up.

In Ashcomb, the troupe paused while Grace was put into a horse-drawn cart. Her hands were tied in front of her. Her dress was unkempt, smeared with mud and her face was dirty, streaked with tears, but she made no sound. The crowd gathered, more shouting, then Nancy Shears, baby Agnes in her arms, hurled an apple that hit Grace hard on the shoulder, but she did not flinch. Her eyes were on Gabriel, clutched tightly in Alice's arms. She wanted only to see her son, to keep her eyes on his face right up to the end.

Then a shrill cry split the crowd's roar and Bett White elbowed her way to the front. She gripped Reverend Walters' wrist with an iron grasp. 'What is going on here, Reverend? What befalls my Gracie?'

He looked at her scornfully, then turned away. 'She has admitted to being a witch. She has been tried and is guilty.'

'What rubbish and what offal!' Bett screeched. 'Let her go – she is my granddaughter and she is gentle as the rain from heaven.'

'We have work to do,' Younger said. 'Get out of the way, crone, or I will return for you afterwards and you will be tried for a witch too.'

An apple was flung through the air and it hit Bett on the back of her head. She turned and another caught her in the stomach. She keeled forward and George Shears barked a laugh. He could be heard saying, 'Waste of good cider apples,' before he sniggered again.

Bett scrambled to her feet, rushing back to her cottage, sweeping up several stalks of fresh lavender in her fists, then she scuttled back to Grace. She pushed the flowers beneath her granddaughter's nose for a moment, wafting the blooms so that Grace could smell them, then she pressed the stalks in her hands, folding her fingers around them. She leaned towards Grace's ear and hissed, 'Let the scent of the flowers be the last thing you smell before your eyes close. May the lavender calm you and send you to sweet rest, my Gracie.'

Then Bett was elbowed backwards as the crowd began to move again; two of the men urged the horse-drawn cart forward and the mob moved as one. Barnaby Younger called, 'Let us take the witch to the top of Long Lane. There is an elm tree where the crossroads stand as a boundary between the two counties. Let us deal with her there.'

Bett was left behind, gaping as the horde paraded through Ashcomb. Minutes later, she stood alone in the street, a flat hand on her heart, and she cried out a long yell of anguish. Then she saw a man limping towards her, waving his hand, calling out. It was Ned Shears.

Grace felt the cart bump and rattle beneath her on the dusty lane, but still she kept her eyes on Gabriel. He stretched a hand towards her; he wanted her, and she watched him struggle in Alice's arms, reaching out. Grace prayed from her soul for a long life for him, for children, love, blessings. The lavender was still in her hands; she inhaled the scent and hoped it would calm her heart. It was beating like the wings of a bird. She ignored Alice's smile, the satisfied curve of her lips; Grace had eyes only for her son. Around her, the air had become cool on her skin; her dress was ripped, she had lost her cap and kerchief, and her pale hair blew about her face. She knew there were people all around staring and watching, sullen and angry faces, loud voices that pounded in her ears and yelled insults, unpleasant words, but she kept her gaze on Gabriel.

The sun was setting now; beyond a stone wall, the hills and fields were immersed in a deep pink light, the sky shot with vermillion and azure like the bright colours of an artist's palette. Grace muttered to herself, 'It is the end of the day. There will be no more days now.' She thought about her son, his birth, the few months spent with him in the cottage, how every moment she had breathed since then had been for him and he had filled her waking hours with joy. She wished it could be enough. But it was not: she had hoped for a future; she had believed in a time where she would see him grow into a fine man, marry, have children of his own. She had wanted to see his face on each new day, share something special, a moment, a smile, a word. There were so many future memories that would slip through her fingers now and she could not hold onto them. She crushed the lavender stems in her fingers and the scent of the flowers drifted upwards.

Then the cart stopped. The journey had been a quick one – time had seemed to move more rapidly than the wheels of the cart. A rough hand dragged her to her feet and she found herself standing upright in the wagon. Below her, faces stared; Grace did not know who they were, but she sought out Gabriel again, who was at the back, in Alice's arms. His eyes were still on hers.

Then Reverend Walters and Barnaby Younger were standing in front of her; she could smell the rank odour of their breath and sweat on their clothes. The rector produced a Bible from beneath his robes and held it out. 'Do you confess to your sins, Grace? Do you wish to be forgiven for the evils you have committed?'

Grace turned her face away, leaning to one side, straining to see her baby.

The rector began to speak, his voice a low drone. 'And if a man borrow ought of his neighbour, and it be hurt, or die, the owner thereof being not with it, he shall surely make it good. But if the owner thereof be with it, he shall not make it good: if it be an hired thing, it came for his hire. And if a man entice a maid that is not betrothed, and lie with her, he shall surely endow her to be his wife. If her father utterly refuse to give her unto him, he shall pay money according to the dowry of virgins. Thou shalt not suffer a witch to live.' The rector closed his book with a thud and addressed the crowd. 'So spake the Lord. Exodus, Chapter 22, verse 18.'

Grace felt something rough being coiled around her neck; it was the coarse end of a rope, tied in a noose. Her legs became weak and buckled beneath her; the strong arms of Barnaby Younger held her upright.

Reverend Walters spoke to her again. 'Are you sorry, Grace, for the evil you have done, for the death of Nathaniel Harper, for all the other transgressions you have heaped upon the community in Ashcomb due to the vile deeds you have committed in the name of witchcraft. And do you renounce the Devil, with whom you have lain to conceive a child...'

Grace's mouth was dry, her tongue was stuck, but she raised her voice to cry out, 'The father of my child is no devil – it is Nathaniel Harper. Ask George Shears. Ask Ned. They passed by the garden...' Then her words were lost beneath the hollering of the crowd.

Someone threw an apple and it hit her in the chest. She slumped backwards and was hauled immediately upright. She felt the rough rope of the noose pulling against her throat and she thought she would faint.

The rector began to speak, but she didn't hear his words for the blood thudding in her ears. Her eyes closed by themselves and opened again.

Reverend Walters put his mouth next to her ear. 'Did you understand what I just spoke to you, Grace?'

Grace shook her head, her eyes glazed.

'You will be hanged from a branch of the elm tree until you are dead. Your body will be taken to the most distant corner of the churchyard and you will be buried with no obsequies or prayers. No one will visit your grave there, nor will they be allowed to place flowers...'

Grace shook herself from her daze and met the rector's eyes. 'No flowers? No prayers? Then how will I enter Heaven and meet my God?'

She heard a hollow laugh from Younger, who stood next to her, his fingers circling her arm. 'Heaven is not for the likes of you. You belong in the other place to suffer eternal torment.'

Grace's brow puckered, confused. 'Then shall I never be at rest?'

'This is what you merit, given your sins and transgressions,' Younger replied quickly.

Grace sought Reverend Walters, her eyes desperate and filled with tears. 'How then will I meet my mother and, in time, be reunited with my son in the kingdom of Heaven, as you have oft spoken?'

The reverend turned away from her, showing her the back of his cloak as he descended from the cart without another word.

Grace shrieked after him. 'How will my spirit fare?'

Reverend Walters ignored her, his shoulders raised.

Grace called out again. 'Have mercy on my soul, or how will I rest in peace?'

Younger's eyes closed. 'I fear it is too late for mercy. Grace Cotter, you are a witch and, because of the evil you have committed in this life, you will now...'

Grace did not hear the rest of his words. She inhaled frantically, desperate to breathe the calming scent of lavender. Above her, several crows hovered and she glanced up. One settled in the branch of the elm tree above her head; a loud croak rasped from its beak, then another crow came to rest close by, watching. Grace leaned to one side in an attempt to see Gabriel once more, but she couldn't find him in the crowd. She saw George Shears grinning at her; Jennet Bryant was staring, her mouth open. Francis Barnes bowed his head and made the sign of the cross. Then she noticed Alice walking away, Gabriel folded tightly in her arms, passing a man with a stick who limped as fast as he could up the hill. Then Grace was pushed hard, her body falling sideways through the air, the rope tightening around her neck, stopping her breath. She closed her eyes, thinking of Gabriel, wishing she could hold him once more in her arms, kiss the softness of his cheek, breathe the damp sweetness of his hair. Grace desired with all her heart to be back home in Slaugh Cottage, just one more time.

She heard Younger's voice shout, 'From this day forth, Long Lane will be known as Wychanger Lane, as it is here that we have hanged a witch.'

Then all was gone.

44

Selena and Nick sat opposite each other at a candlelit table in the village inn at Holcombe Fitzpaine, their fingers linked as they lingered over coffee. Most diners had already left. They spoke in low voices, still discussing Rob's research of the parish register.

'I just think it's so sad, what Rob said they did to her,' Selena said. 'She was only twenty-three years old.'

'Who knows what really happened?' Nick asked. 'A few scraps of material, a length of string and a few feathers. Perhaps those things were just a young woman's superstitious customs to ward off evil. I wonder what made them believe she was a witch? It's tragic.'

Selena could hardly bring herself to mention Grace's name. 'She would have been an ordinary girl, living a tough life. In some ways, she hardly had a life at all. So many of the villagers died young, but not like she did, in that awful way. How must it have been for her?'

'It's unthinkable.'

'Just imagine what it must have been like, to be accused of witch-craft?' Selena whispered the final word.

'And suggesting that she could turn herself into a hare – that list of accusations was horrifying. It stems from superstition and ignorance.'

Selena sighed. 'Well, I'd better go back to her now. I feel I understand her a little more than I used to. No wonder she's still prowling.'

Nick stood up, waiting for Selena to rise, then he wrapped an arm around her.

They stepped outside into the cold night air, their feet crunching on gravel as they walked across the car park. The sky was cloudless.

His arm tightened around her. 'It's been a lovely evening... thank you.'

Selena took a breath and turned to him. 'I don't want to be by myself tonight.'

Nick touched her hair. 'Is it because of Grace...?'

'No,' she replied, hardly believing her words as she spoke them. 'It's because I want you to stay.'

They were in each other's arms; Selena closed her eyes and lost herself in their first real kiss. She was enveloped in the warmth and the passion of an embrace, in the powerful belief that she trusted him and wanted him wholly for herself, for no other reason than she had chosen it.

When she opened her eyes, Nick was smiling. He kissed her forehead gently, took her hand and said, 'Let's go home.'

* * *

She woke in his arms, rolling over in the bed, feeling the warmth of another body, being pulled into an embrace, enjoying the softness of lips against hers.

Nick murmured, 'Good morning.'

Selena smiled. 'This is the best Sunday breakfast I've had in a long time.'

'Followed by croissants and Earl Grey?'

'In our dressing gowns – in the garden.'

Nick laughed. 'What's the chance of my mother coming round to borrow a cup of sugar? She'll have spotted that my car was here all night...'

Selena stretched her arms luxuriously. 'She'll be delighted.'

'So am I,' Nick murmured and kissed her again.

* * *

They sat in the back garden on a rug, food on a tray, the conservatory doors open, bright sunlight reflecting on the glass. Selena sipped tea and said, 'Grace was quiet last night.'

Nick grinned. 'I think I forgot about her for a while.'

She snuggled closer to him. 'There's the smell of lavender still, on the landing.'

'I noticed it.' Nick kissed her. 'She's still with us.'

Selena nodded. 'It's hard to believe I only have eleven days left in Slaugh Cottage.'

'Eleven wonderful days,' Nick sighed.

'Nick,' Selena sat upright, a thought had come to her. 'I don't suppose you could get up really early on Tuesday morning and come over?'

'Of course I could.' Nick thought for a moment. 'What time is early?'

'Joely and Matty are having a summer solstice breakfast. We're going to stand at the top of their hill at 4.45 and watch the sun rise, then we'll go back to their field and eat.' She leaned forward. 'Laura and Rob will be there. Can you come?'

'I'd love to. I can move things around on Tuesday and start after lunch, work later in the evening. Yes, that should be fine.'

Selena said, 'I've never watched the sun rise before – ever. It will be lovely.'

'It will...' Nick took her hand. 'Shall we go out somewhere today? It's a beautiful day for a walk.'

'Let's – where do you suggest?'

'The beacon? Further afield? Exmoor? The beach.'

'Oh, let's have a beach day.' Selena grabbed his hand. 'It's midsummer and a beach would be great.'

'Agreed.'

'Right.' Selena scrambled to her feet and met Nick's eyes with a smile. 'No time like the present. Let's get dressed and get organised.'

She clutched the tray and Nick folded the blanket. As they stood in the doorway to the conservatory, they heard a crashing sound from another room.

Selena frowned. 'Did you hear that?'

She placed the tray on the table and they rushed into the sitting room. The cream vase of sweet peas had fallen from the window ledge where Selena had placed it yesterday; it was shattered on the floor, flowers strewn around fragments of glass.

'These old windows can be quite draughty,' Nick said. 'Perhaps a breeze blew the vase over?'

Selena met his gaze, frowning. 'It's quite solid...'

Behind the windowpane, the blackthorn branch shook. Selena inhaled: the sweet smell of the flowers was strong, but there was another scent, softer, calming. She frowned as they knelt down together, collecting the flowers and the shards of broken vase. Selena and Nick both looked up at the same time, the same thought in their minds and Nick said, 'It's time to go to the beach and leave Grace behind us for a while. Today is our day.'

* * *

Selena set her alarm for three thirty on Tuesday morning, but she opened her eyes at quarter past, waking with a jolt, staring into the darkness, listening. Something had woken her; she felt instinctively that someone was in the room. She watched every corner for movement, her eyes lingering on every shadow, waiting for it to shift. There was a creak outside the door, on the landing, and Selena held her breath, listening, but no sound followed.

The alarm buzzed, jolting her heart. It was time to get up.

Selena switched on the lamp, showered in the en suite and dressed herself quickly in jeans and a sweatshirt. Nick would arrive at four

o'clock, and the plan was to pick up Laura and Rob and drive to the top
of Wychanger Lane, where the sun was due to rise at 4.52 a.m. and visi-
bility would be good.

She pulled on training shoes and opened her bedroom door,
flicking on the landing light. The door to the second bedroom was ajar.
Selena stood still. A muffled sound came from inside.

Selena held her breath: she had heard a stifled sob; she was sure of
it. Treading softly, she approached the room, steeling herself to peer in.
She hesitated, unsure what she might see, feeling like an intruder. Her
pulse quickened as she imagined who stood beyond the open door,
and the thought came to her that she should rush past the room and
down the stairs to the safety of the kitchen below.

She paused by the door, uncertain, peeping tentatively into the
intense darkness. Her breathing was rapid as she blinked at a slender
shape that shifted position. Selena glimpsed the sheen of pale hair, the
movement of an extended arm as the figure turned to her; she saw the
outline of a dress, and she heard the sob again. Then Selena jerked
backwards: she was moving away from the room, her feet padding
downstairs, blood pounding in her ears. She switched on the kitchen
light, flooding the room with intense brightness, just as she heard a
knock at the front door.

Selena fell into Nick's arms, relief seeping through her body.

He grinned. 'I'm glad you're so pleased to see me.'

Her head against his chest, she breathed, 'I've just seen her, in the
other bedroom. I'm sure it was her.'

Nick stepped inside, his expression serious. 'Do you want to go
back upstairs? Shall we go together?'

'No, not right now.' Selena shook her head vigorously. 'I think I
want to go out...'

'Okay.' Nick was smiling. 'It will be daylight when we come back.'

They drove in darkness, pausing to pick up Laura and Rob, who
both were too tired to join in any conversation, other than Laura
groaning that she wished she'd stayed in bed.

Selena thought about mentioning the stifled sob she'd heard

coming from the bedroom, the outline of a moving figure, but she'd leave it until later, until after the sun had risen.

Nick drove along the narrow lane, rabbits scuttling in the headlights, a badger disappearing into the hedge, then they reached the top where a post and a large rock marked the boundary of the two counties. Joely and Matty were there already, shining the beams of a torch, waving hands.

Six figures stood in darkness gazing across the horizon, waiting.

Nick reached for Selena's hand; it was cold and she felt it become warm in his fingers.

Joely whispered, 'I have the mirror ready... we can take turns?'

'Mirror?' Laura yawned. 'There's no way I'm looking at myself in this state. I must look horrible.'

'You look lovely, my dear,' Rob said affectionately. 'You always remind me so much of your mother.'

'You hold the mirror up, towards the sunlight, and as you reflect the glare, you wish for something your heart desires for the next year,' Joely explained.

'It seems a strange place to make wishes,' Rob said. 'This place has such a history. It's creepy.'

'Why is it creepy?' Selena asked.

'It's where they hanged witches...' Rob replied simply. 'This is where they would have brought your Grace Cotter.'

'Here?' A shiver shook Selena's body. Nick wrapped an arm around her.

'From the elm tree, I suppose...' Matty muttered. 'Long gone, like the poor women they killed.'

'Were there others?' Selena asked.

'I'm not sure if there were any more hangings here – I'll have to check the records for that.' Rob stared towards the horizon. There was no sign of light.

'There were witches killed all over Somerset and beyond though – Europe, the USA,' Nick observed. 'The craze lasted for centuries.'

'I went to see *The Crucible* once, Arthur Miller's play.' Laura winced.

'It was so sad. All those poor women, Goody this and Goody that, blamed for all sorts of things and what surprised me is that their husbands didn't get off scot-free either.'

'It was disgusting,' Joely said. 'I'd have stood no chance in those days...'

Laura touched her lilac hair. 'Nor me.'

'Poor Grace – imagine what happened here, all those years ago,' Selena sighed. 'I feel for her.'

Rob made a soft tutting sound. 'It's heartbreaking.'

Then Nick pointed. 'Is that it, over there?'

Beyond the hill, a streak of pink, a hint of lustre was visible.

'The sun...' Joely breathed.

The six friends wrapped their arms around each other and watched as the darkness became sapphire blue, then blotched with crimson and burnt orange as the first light of the sun emerged.

Joely held up her small mirror towards the light, reflecting the rays, closed her eyes for a few moments and called, 'I've made my wish.' She thrust the mirror into Matty's hand. 'Now it's your turn.'

Matty held the small glass high, squeezing his eyes shut, then he passed it to Selena.

She caught Nick's gaze and smiled, holding the mirror up, avoiding the bright dance of sunlight as it bounced off the glass and she wished hard, the thoughts as strong as a voice in her head. She knew exactly what she wanted, who she wanted to be with from now onwards and what she hoped would come from their union. Then she handed the mirror to Nick, watching his serious expression as he concentrated on his thoughts.

Laura took her turn, smiling as she made her wish, before persuading her reluctant father to follow her lead.

Finally, Joely took her mirror again, held it high and intoned, 'Blessed be.'

Selena closed her eyes, thinking of Grace beneath the elm tree, imagining her alone and frightened amongst an angry mob. The images were startlingly clear; Grace being held by a burly man, her tear-stained face, her chin held high, the crowd around her yelling insults. She suddenly felt very cold.

Then she opened her eyes and the sun was a red circle in a blood-shot sky. Selena gazed at the colours with an artist's eye and promised herself that she would paint the scene, adding an elm tree to the picture instead of the post and the large stone. She took out her phone, focusing on the deep red of the sky bleeding into pleated clouds, before Rob said, 'Is it time for breakfast?'

45

The sun was already sucking the dew from the damp grass as Joely piled pancakes onto plates outside the caravan and Matty poured coffee. Rob was gazing around at the view; Laura was halfway though her first pancake.

'These are amazing, Joely – the berries are gorgeous. Did you forage them in the forest?'

'They came from the supermarket,' Joely grinned. 'Raspberries, blueberries, and I have strawberries in the fridge if you want some.'

'Yes, please,' Laura licked her lips.

Nick leaned towards Selena and took her hand, his voice a whisper. 'Are you okay? You're a bit quiet.'

'Oh, am I? Sorry.' Selena brightened immediately. She gazed at the faces around the table and reached for her coffee. 'I think I saw the ghost this morning – well, I saw something, definitely.'

'My goodness.' Laura frowned. 'What happened?'

'I told Nick – I heard something in my bedroom – it woke me. But there was nothing there. Then I looked into the spare room and I saw a figure, I was sure something moved and I heard a sound like a sob.'

Laura's eyes were wide behind her glasses. 'I'd have been terrified.'

'Then, later on, a vase fell over in the sitting room...' Nick said. 'It might have been the wind...'

Selena shook her head. 'I don't think it was.'

'How can you live in that place, Selena?' Laura asked.

'It was easy at first because I was focused on work, but I have to admit, I've been a bit rattled a couple of times more recently...' She squeezed Nick's fingers. 'I think I understand our ghost a little better now, but it's nicer when I'm not on my own.'

Matty frowned. 'What do your parents think of it all, Nick? It's their cottage.'

'My father is quite amused by the stories. My mum has always turned a blind eye to anything supernatural – she's quite a down-to-earth person and she doesn't believe in ghosts.' Nick shrugged. 'But she's considering selling Sloe Cottage now.'

'Really?' Joely's eyes sparkled. 'It's a shame we can't buy it, Matty – I'd love to live there. The garden and the herbs – the view across to the farm. It's lovely.'

'There's no way I'd live there,' Matty laughed, then he was serious. 'I'm not too bothered about ghosts, but I like the independence of our caravan and the field. I couldn't stand being stuck inside four walls.'

'I've considered making her an offer, buying it myself.' Nick was thoughtful.

'It would be a shame if it became someone's holiday cottage,' Selena sighed. 'Although that's what it is at the moment. But it's so warm and cosy, especially the newer part. It could be a wonderful family home. It's the old part that the ghost tends to visit mostly.' She thought for a moment. 'When I saw the figure in the spare room this morning, I think that's the most afraid I've ever felt in the house. And up on the hill this morning – I couldn't get her out of my mind.'

'Well, it does make sense, after all,' Rob said. 'It was today that it happened.'

'Today that what happened, Dad?' Laura squeezed his arm.

'I read it yesterday in the records. Grace Cotter died on June the twenty-first, 1683.'

No one spoke for a moment, then Laura breathed, 'Oh, my goodness.'

Nick took Selena's hand. 'Perhaps that explains what you heard in the bedroom earlier, the sobs...'

'Where is Grace now, Rob?' Selena sat forward, tears in her eyes. 'Where is she buried? I want to visit her grave. Today of all days.'

Rob shook his head. 'There won't be a trace of her. Corpses in those days were interred without coffins, wrapped in linen, and their graves seldom had headstones. I can research the records if you like. I've kept a file and I can access it from my phone.'

'Please...' Selena wiped a tear away. 'Poor Grace.'

'I think it's awful, how she was treated,' Joely said. 'No wonder her spirit can't rest. It just isn't fair, is it, the way society has always blamed innocent women...'

'Wait...' Rob raised his phone. 'Here's something.'

They all leaned towards Rob as he began to read, 'Grace Cotter's body was buried in the farthest corner of the churchyard. No prayers or obsequies were given. A stone was positioned on top of the grave for fear the witch would rise and return...'

'What does that mean?' Matty asked.

Rob pressed his lips together. 'It means that we should be able to find the spot if it's marked by an old stone. If it hasn't been moved, we'll see the exact place where she would have been laid to rest.'

'Or not resting...' Selena said. 'Can we go there as soon as we've finished breakfast? I want to put some flowers on her grave.'

* * *

Joely and Laura had helped Selena gather some wild flowers from the fields and some from the garden just beyond the caravan. As she stood outside the churchyard of St Bartholomew's, she clutched a bouquet of daisies, buttercups, sweet peas, echinacea, roses, poppies and some lavender.

Selena inhaled the heady fragrance as Nick pressed her arm. 'I'm sure she'll love them.'

'Right,' Rob waved an arm. 'I think I know the place we're going to – it's at the far side of the cemetery.'

He led the way as Selena followed in silence, Laura and Nick at her shoulder, Matty and Joely just behind. They were a silent procession as they trooped through the long graveyard; despite the intense sunlight, the air was sharp and cool. They passed rows of graves, some bent over at odd angles, many discoloured by lichen. A crow sat on top of an arched stone, wings stretched, cleaning oily feathers with a dark beak. Rob led them beyond a leaning willow, its leaves sweeping the ground, then they passed beneath an arch over a gate.

'This is the farthest part of the graveyard, and certainly the oldest,' he murmured.

Selena shivered.

Rob pointed to the far corner, a dark shadowy place beneath a crumbling wall where the grass grew tall and unkempt. 'That's where I think she is.'

Selena followed Rob, hugging the flowers; the others trailed behind. The ground was rocky and unforgiving, full of sharp stones and weeds. The path ended; they stepped over broken gravestones and grassy mounds, stopping in the cold corner beneath the broken stone wall.

Rob knelt down next to a large rock. 'This will be the place.'

'How can you be sure?'

Rob sighed. 'She was allowed no prayers, Selena, no proper funeral because she was a…' He paused, not wishing to say the word in a churchyard. 'This rock is heavy. It was placed on top of where her body would have been. Superstitious people were afraid that she might come back.'

'Perhaps she did come back, in her own way.' Selena felt tears gather in her eyes again; one brimmed over, trickling down her cheek. Nick's hand was on her shoulder and she knew that Joely, Matty and Laura were not far behind her. She lifted the flowers, about to place them on the stone, then she changed her mind; she would not put them on top of the heavy weight that had held her down. Instead, she arranged them around the stone, bright colours against the faded dry grass and hard-packed soil. She whispered, 'I hope you find some peace, Grace.' She gazed up and Rob nodded encouragement, so she added, 'I hope you can rest now.'

Rob's voice was hushed. 'She was denied the Christian burial that would probably have meant so much to her, poor thing. Perhaps we should say something now, Laura? You're used to these things, doing school assemblies and such.'

'All right.' Laura pressed her hands together and took a deep breath. 'Let us pray,'

Selena clasped her hands and closed her eyes. An image of how Grace might have been in her last moments slipped into her mind: a terrified girl, a troubled spirit.

Laura spoke softly.

> *May Grace Cotter know peace.*
> *For as long as the moon shall rise,*
> *For as long as the rivers shall flow,*
> *For as long as the sun shall shine,*
> *For as long as the grass shall grow,*
> *Let her know peace.*

Selena whispered 'Amen' under her breath, stood up and sighed. Nick's arm was around her and she was grateful for it; her legs were suddenly shaking.

Joely's eyes shone. 'That was so beautiful, Laura.'

'It's a Cheyenne prayer for peace,' Laura whispered. 'I just adapted it a bit...'

Rob's voice was low. 'I think we should do this every year, on Midsummer's Day, put flowers on her grave and say a few words.'

'We will.' Laura hugged Selena, whispering in her ear, 'I wish you weren't leaving though...'

Selena nodded. There was a silence. Nick and Selena glanced at each other, then Matty said, 'Well, I can't stand around here all day. I have logs to chop.'

'And I have some comfrey salve to make,' Joely said.

Nick held out his hand, linking his fingers through Selena's. 'I have to be back at work later. We should go.'

'Let's all catch up in the pub on Friday night?' Laura suggested, full of enthusiasm.

'Definitely,' Selena agreed and the group turned to walk back through the cemetery. Selena's head was full of rushing thoughts; she was perturbed by the isolated, lonely location of Grace's grave; the sense of sadness was still with her: Grace had been shunned, cast out for centuries. Nick's hand in hers, Selena counted her blessings; she had so many friends, a wonderful career, a burgeoning relationship that promised so much; he had told her the depth of his feelings last night as they lay, limbs entwined, in her bed. And she realised, a sharp pang to her heart, that she did not want to leave.

* * *

Twenty minutes later, Selena and Nick stood outside Sloe Cottage gazing at the house. The garden was bright, colourful blooms nodding in the breeze, the house nestled against the backdrop of rising hills and farmland.

'I love living here,' Selena said.

'I won't let my mother sell it,' Nick replied quietly.

'It's beautiful – and so full of memories. But it has a future too.' She imagined the house as it could be, the sound of so much laughter, children playing in the garden, family outings, quiet bedtime stories and hugs. Selena sighed.

'I have time for a cup of tea before I head off back to Exeter,' Nick said hopefully.

'Oh, that's good.' Selena did not want him to leave. 'Shall we go in?'

The cottage was warm inside; the hall surprisingly so, with its hard stone walls that held the cold. In the sitting room, Selena paused and gazed at the wood-burning stove, the embers glowing. 'I need to put a few more logs on.'

Nick kissed her. 'I'll make tea then.'

She watched him go towards the kitchen and again she was filled with the thought that she had just over a week left on her tenancy. She would have to rethink her plans, talk to Claire. Manchester was only five hours away: she wouldn't have to be there all the time in order to sell her paintings and, if she was needed for an exhibition, she could drive from Somerset before breakfast and arrive at the gallery at lunchtime. Besides, Claire and Gulliver were becoming inseparable: Selena felt sure it wouldn't be long until he would move in to the flat. And Lesley had said that she would extend the tenancy. Most importantly, she needed to talk to Nick now. She couldn't imagine leaving him easily.

Selena knelt in front of the wood-burning stove, opening the iron doors, placing three small logs on the griddle and closing the handles. She watched through the glass panels as the logs caught, sparks flying up the chimney; flames leaped, licked and slackened. Then she exhaled slowly.

Nick was standing behind her, his hands on her shoulders. She sensed the light pressure, tender as love. He rested his cheek against her head gently, barely a touch, and Selena felt protected. She stayed where she was for a moment, not moving, relishing the sensation as her skin tingled, then she turned round to hold him in her arms.

He was not there.

A shadow, thin as mist, slipped away through the door, a slender shape so transparent that it was hardly visible. Selena was about to follow whatever she had seen into the hall when she heard the front door being flung wide, crashing as it hit the wall. The scent of lavender was all around.

Selena rushed towards the noise, standing in the doorway, looking out at the garden at the vibrant colours, the stone well and the oak tree at the end of the drive, branches outstretched. She gazed around for a moment, then she saw a small pale creature with elongated ears, a hare, sitting on the gravel not far away, staring at her, not moving. Selena met the intense eyes and they held for a moment, an exchange, then the hare hopped away on agile legs into a bush and it was gone.

'Are you okay?' Nick was behind her, whispering in her ear. 'I've put the tea tray in front of the fire.'

'Good.' Selena took his hand and they walked back to the sitting room, curling up on the sofa, sitting quietly. She raised her nose to the air, and whispered, 'Can you smell lavender?'

'Yes,' Nick said.

'She was here with me – she was here and then she left.'

Nick met her gaze. 'And something else – what is it? Something's changed – something has shifted.'

'The air feels lighter, warmer.' Selena was quiet for a moment, then she murmured, 'I think she's gone.'

Nick nodded. 'You may be right.'

'Someone stood behind me, their arms around me – I thought it was you.' Selena saw Nick's expression, his eyes widening. 'It must have been her – I just felt a wonderful peace, not sadness any more, just a sense of pure love. It was as if the house has been holding its breath for an age, and now it's finally breathed out. I followed her out into the garden and there was no one there. Then I saw a hare – of course, it was only a hare – and it bounded away.'

'Let's go outside for a moment, shall we, while the tea brews?' Nick suggested.

'Yes, let's.' Selena walked into the garden, Nick at her shoulder, blinking in the sunlight, the spots of light against dark, the dappled grass. They walked towards the chattering well where Selena stopped, listening; there was the faint murmur of water bubbling from the depths.

'I'm glad we placed flowers on her grave, and that Laura said the prayer,' Selena murmured. 'They buried her beneath a stone; she was trapped, shunned, despised. And what they did to her on the hill was unimaginable...'

'She's found peace...' Nick said. 'I hope she can rest. It's time for new beginnings...'

'New beginnings,' Selena repeated. 'Yes, it is.'

'I want you to stay...'

'I've already decided. I'm not going back to Manchester.' Selena turned to face Nick, the trace of a smile on her lips. 'I want to be here, with you.'

'I'm so glad,' Nick murmured. 'This is home now.'

Selena rested her head against his shoulder. 'It is.'

Nick wrapped an arm around her waist and they stood together, staring across the fields towards Hilltop Farm. Selena closed her eyes, her fingers touching the smooth stone pendant around her neck. She recalled the words of the woman on the market who sold it to her: malachite opens the heart to unconditional love. Selena smiled. 'The sloes will come out in late autumn...'

But her thoughts were moving far beyond berries and seasons. She was thinking of the cottage that had stood for so many years, each inhabitant leaving their own delicate imprint, so many hands that had touched the walls, been warmed by the fire, held others in an embrace. Now it was her turn: Selena and Nick would make their own memories. She imagined the future, one year becoming another, the celebrations, the joy, the love. Their cottage would be filled with laughter and happiness. She smiled at the thought that she would name their first child Grace.

A light breeze, silent and sure as an outbreath, buffeted the blackthorn. The spiny branches touched the window three times, then the tree was still.

EPILOGUE

Two women lived in the house, embraced in its protective hold, watching, waiting. Two women, one then, one now.

Grace stood silently behind the door as the woman called Selena came into the cold from the sunshine, bringing her belongings in the house and filling each room with her sadness. Grace followed. She understood the woman's broken heart; she knew what had brought her to Slaugh Cottage, what she had lost. She felt the same emptiness.

Grace had been holding her breath for three hundred years. She stayed unseen amid shadows as Ned and Francis carried Will Cotter in from the fields, cold and dead. She placed a finger on her father's lips, whispered love in his ear. No one noticed as she touched Ned's cheek tenderly with the palm of her hand. He had grown old so quickly.

She watched from the garden as Gabriel Harper grew from a gentle child into a strong man. He was exactly as she knew he would be, handsome, inquisitive, kind, and Grace loved him with all her being. She stood at the window as he returned from church with Catherine Stokes on his arm. He paused at the gate for a moment, a smile on his lips. She wondered if he remembered her then.

Grace remained after they were all gone from her: Bett, Ned, Gabriel, his children, all taken too soon, one by one. She roamed alone within the walls and the garden, peering through the window each day, her breath leaving no mist on the glass. The sound of the owl came to her in the moonlight as she hid in the branches of the blackthorn. The tree had been in the ground for many times its natural lifespan, unbending in the dawns and dusks of each year. Dark roots delved beneath the earth, deep as unspoken truths: its flowers blossomed each May and it sprouted bitter fruits in October.

Over many years, people came to the cottage but they did not stay long. By day, Grace could not rest: she thought of her son and cried out to be with him. Each night snatches of lullabies were kisses on her lips and the scent of lavender filled the house. It was the last kindness she remembered.

The woman, Selena, had lost a child too. Grace knew it – she comforted her as she sobbed. Grace stood close to her as she shivered by the hearth and held out her palms, warming the span of her hands until they were too hot. They both watched the smoke curl upwards, silent as a spell.

Then it was Midsummer Day again, the same day they had named Grace a witch and dragged her to the elm tree. It was the day they stole her child, her life and her peace. The woman, Selena, had found happiness, but she knew Grace's perpetual pain. That day, soft words were whispered in the cold hard place where they had buried her and weighed down her soul with a stone. It was the only prayer anyone had said for her and it filled the cottage with light.

Then the moment came as sweet as spring rain. As she stood in Slaugh Cottage for the final time, Grace closed her eyes and thought of her father's kind face, her Grandmother Bett's toothless smile, her mother's joyous expression of love. She saw Gabriel's eyes once more and she thought of how good it would feel to run into his strong arms and breathe the softness of his skin. She didn't hesitate – she rushed towards it as a hare would rush towards freedom.

Then all was gone.

AUTHOR'S NOTE

From the fifteenth century until the eighteenth century, witch trials were conducted across England. They resulted in the death of between 500 and 1000 people, 90 per cent of whom were women. Suspicion and accusations of witchcraft were at the most intense stage during the Civil War and the Puritan era of the mid-seventeenth century.

Between 1484 and 1750, women were tortured, burned or hanged, often condemned by the most fragile thread of evidence, baseless allegations that led to them being harassed, accused, tortured and put to death.

Older women from poor backgrounds were often suspected, especially if they had a sign or feature that set them apart: if they were snaggle-toothed, if they had a hairy lip, a pointed chin, warts. Even more so if they were seen to possess a familiar – a cat or a dog being most common.

Younger women were also at risk. People were suspicious if a married woman had too many children, or too few: this set her apart from the others. A woman with skills in healing, or one who was deemed to exhibit 'strange' behaviour, was immediately under suspicion, as was a woman having a birthmark or a mole.

In Somerset, during the period of 1573–1600, 1 per cent of people had their deaths recorded as 'death by blasting' or bewitchment. In the mid-seventeenth century, Edmund Bull and Julian Cox were hanged as witches. Elizabeth Stile was also accused; she died in Taunton jail in 1664. Jane Brooks and Alice Coward from Shepton Mallet were accused of casting spells on a twelve-year-old boy.

In 1887, as workers pulled down an old house of thick cob walls in Wellington, Somerset, they found in a space which separated the roof from the upper room six brooms, an old armchair and a rope with feathers. The workmen believed that these articles were the belongings of a witch, and that the rope was a witch's ladder.

There are some fascinating, evocative place names across Somerset, from Witches Walk in Bridgwater to Stonegallows in Taunton.

The last execution for witchcraft in England was in 1684, when Alice Molland was hanged in Exeter, Devon, although no documentary evidence of her actual execution has been found. Witchcraft was punishable by death during the times of the Tudors and Stuarts. After 1736, 'witches' could no longer be hanged, but it was by no means the end of their persecution. They were perceived to have close associations with the Devil, believed to be his helpers on earth. Ignorance and fear led people to believe that any bad occurrence was the work of the Devil or witches. King James I wrote a book on witchcraft, suggesting various ways of identifying and catching witches.

Against this background, I created the story of Grace Cotter. The village in which she lives, Ashcomb, later Ashcombe, is a composite of Somerset villages around the Blackdown Hills, near Taunton. While Grace is a character of my imagination, she and the people she interacted with in 1682/83 represent the rural farmworkers of Somerset whose lives were deeply affected by superstition and a strong belief in the supernatural. Grace's story begins in the early spring of 1682, ten years before the infamous Salem witch trials in Massachusetts.

During my research for this novel, having seen examples of 'witch's marks' online, I discovered similar markings, a hexafoil, on a wall of my own cottage in the oldest part of the house.

NOTES

Chapter 12

1. Scarecrow

Chapter 41

1. Sometimes called overlooking, bewitching with a glance

ACKNOWLEDGMENTS

I've been writing for several years now under my own name, Judy Leigh, spinning uplifting stories about second chances for older protagonists, about fun and love and optimism. But I am so thrilled to be offered the chance to write books in this exciting genre under another name. My thanks go to so many people who have trusted me and given me this opportunity:

My agent, Kiran Kataria, who is so wise, efficient, professional and lovely.

My publisher, Boldwood Books: Amanda Ridout, CEO, and editor, Sarah Ritherdon, two brilliant, insightful and incredible women.

The Boldwood team, who are like a family. Special mentions for the talented Nia Beynon, Claire Fenby, Megan Townsend and Rachel Gilbey at Rach's Random Resources.

So much credit goes to the team of wonderful people who do incredible work before a novel is born: designers, editors, technicians, magicians, voice actors, reviewers and bloggers. Huge thanks to you all. You are the heartbeat of our books.

I'd like to thank the amazing line-up of Boldwood writers who are unbelievable in their encouragement and support. I often feel like I'm playing for the best football team in the world...

There are so many people who encourage me in my work, whom I keep in my heart: friends I meet all the time, friends I don't meet often enough, friends I haven't met yet but we talk so often on social media, reviewers, bloggers, so many people in so many countries whom I silently thank each day.

Love to our Tony and Kim.

Special love to my mum, who showed me the joy of reading, and to my dad, who proudly never read anything in his life.

Love always to my family, Liam, Maddie, Cait, and to Big G, who is my forever soul mate.

And finally, I want to mention my grandmother, Nell Collins, whose name I've borrowed. She was very much like this novel's Bett White, a healer, a teller of fortunes, and she had the most incredible laugh, a soft 'tee-hee-hee,' like a gang of naughty mice.

And finally, warmest thanks to my readers, whoever and wherever you are. You have helped to make this journey incredible. X

MORE FROM ELENA COLLINS

We hope you enjoyed reading *The Witch's Tree*. If you did, please leave a review.

If you'd like to gift a copy, this book is also available as an ebook, digital audio download and audiobook CD.

Sign up to Elena Collins' mailing list for news, competitions and updates on future books.

https://bit.ly/ElenaCollinsnewsletter

ABOUT THE AUTHOR

Elena Collins is the pen name of Judy Leigh. Judy Leigh is the bestselling author of *Five French Hens*, *A Grand Old Time* and *The Age of Misadventure* and the doyenne of the 'it's never too late' genre of women's fiction. She has lived all over the UK from Liverpool to Cornwall, but currently resides in Somerset.

Visit Judy's website: https://judyleigh.com

Follow Judy on social media:

twitter.com/judyleighwriter
facebook.com/judyleighuk
instagram.com/judyrleigh

Boldwood

Boldwood Books is an award-winning fiction publishing company seeking out the best stories from around the world.

Find out more at www.boldwoodbooks.com

Join our reader community for brilliant books, competitions and offers!

Follow us
@BoldwoodBooks
@BookandTonic

Sign up to our weekly deals newsletter

https://bit.ly/BoldwoodBNewsletter

Made in United States
Orlando, FL
20 August 2023

36261507R00200